DEAN KOONTZ

midnight

BERKLEY

New York

BERKLEY
An imprint of Penguin Random House LLC
penguinrandomhouse.com

Copyright © 1989 by Nkui, Inc.
"Afterword" copyright © 2004 by Dean Koontz
Penguin Random House supports copyright. Copyright fuels creativity,
encourages diverse voices, promotes free speech, and creates a vibrant culture.
Thank you for buying an authorized edition of this book and for complying with
copyright laws by not reproducing, scanning, or distributing any part of it in any
form without permission. You are supporting writers and allowing Penguin
Random House to continue to publish books for every reader.

BERKLEY and the BERKLEY & B colophon are registered trademarks of
Penguin Random House LLC.

Second Berkley trade paperback ISBN: 9780593441367

The Library of Congress has catalogued the G. P. Putnam's Sons hardcover
edition of this book as follows:

Koontz, Dean, date.
Midnight / by Dean Koontz. — 1st American ed.
p. cm.
ISBN 0-399-13390-9
I. Title
PS3561.O55M5 1989 88-22830CIP
813'.54—dc19

G. P. Putnam's Sons hardcover edition / January 1989
First Berkley mass-market edition / November 1989
Berkley afterword edition / February 2004
First Berkley trade paperback edition / November 2011
Second Berkley trade paperback edition / December 2022

Printed in the United States of America
1st Printing

*To Ed and Pat Thomas
of the Book Carnival,
who are such nice people
that sometimes I suspect
they're not really human
but aliens from
another, better world*

part one

ALONG THE NIGHT COAST

Where eerie figures caper
to some midnight music
that only they can hear.

—*The Book of Counted Sorrows*

chapter one

Janice Capshaw liked to run at night.

Nearly every evening between ten and eleven o'clock, Janice put on her gray sweats with the reflective blue stripes across the back and chest, tucked her hair under a headband, laced up her New Balance shoes, and ran six miles. She was thirty-five but could have passed for twenty-five, and she attributed her glow of youth to her twenty-year-long commitment to running.

Sunday night, September 21, she left her house at ten o'clock and ran four blocks north to Ocean Avenue, the main street through Moon-light Cove, where she turned left and headed downhill toward the public beach. The shops were closed and dark. Aside from the faded-brass glow of the sodium-vapor streetlamps, the only lights were in some apartments above the stores, at Knight's Bridge Tavern, and at Our Lady of Mercy Catholic Church, which was open twenty-four hours a day. No cars were on the street, and not another person was in sight. Moonlight Cove always had been a quiet little town, shunning the tour-ist trade that other coastal communities so avidly pursued. Janice liked the slow, measured pace of life there, though sometimes lately the town seemed not merely sleepy but dead.

As she ran down the sloping main street, through pools of amber light, through layered night shadows cast by wind-sculpted cypresses and pines, she saw no movement other than her own—and the sluggish, serpentine advance of the thin fog through the windless air. The only sounds were the soft *slap-slap* of her rubber-soled running shoes on the sidewalk and her labored breathing. From all available evidence, she might have been the last person on earth, engaged upon a solitary post-Armageddon marathon.

She disliked getting up at dawn to run before work, and in the sum-mer it was more pleasant to put in her six miles when the heat of the day had passed, though neither an abhorrence of early hours nor the heat was the real reason for her nocturnal preference; she ran on the same schedule in the winter. She exercised at that hour simply because she liked the night.

Even as a child, she had preferred night to day, had enjoyed sitting out in the yard after sunset, under the star-speckled sky, listening to frogs and crickets. Darkness soothed. It softened the sharp edges of the world, toned down the too-harsh colors. With the coming of twilight, the sky seemed to recede; the universe expanded. The night was *bigger* than the day, and in its realm, life seemed to have more possibilities.

Now she reached the Ocean Avenue loop at the foot of the hill, sprinted across the parking area and onto the beach. Above the thin fog, the sky held only scattered clouds, and the full moon's silver-yellow radiance penetrated the mist, providing sufficient illumination for her to see where she was going. Some nights the fog was too thick and the sky too overcast to permit running on the shore. But now the white foam of the incoming breakers surged out of the black sea in ghostly phosphorescent ranks, and the wide crescent of sand gleamed palely between the lapping tide and the coastal hills, and the mist itself was softly aglow with reflections of the autumn moonlight.

As she ran across the beach to the firmer, damp sand at the water's edge and turned south, intending to run a mile out to the point of the cove, Janice felt wonderfully alive.

Richard—her late husband, who had succumbed to cancer three years ago—had said that her circadian rhythms were so post-midnight focused that she was more than just a night person. "You'd probably love being a vampire, living between sunset and dawn," he'd said, and she'd said, "I vant to suck your blood." God, she had loved him. Initially she worried that the life of a Lutheran minister's wife would be boring, but it never was, not for a moment. Three years after his death, she still missed him every day—and even more at night. He had been—

Suddenly, as she was passing a pair of forty-foot twisted cypresses that had grown in the middle of the beach, halfway between the hills and the waterline, Janice was sure that she was not alone in the night and fog. She saw no movement, and she was unaware of any sound other than her own footsteps, raspy breathing, and thudding heartbeat; only instinct told her that she had company.

She was not alarmed at first, for she thought another runner was sharing the beach. A few local fitness fanatics occasionally ran at night, not by choice, as was the case with her, but of necessity. Two or three times a month she encountered them along her route.

But when she stopped and turned and looked back the way she had come, she saw only a deserted expanse of moonlit sand, a curved ribbon of luminously foaming surf, and the dim but familiar shapes of rock formations and scattered trees that thrust up here and there along the strand. The only sound was the low rumble of the breakers.

Figuring that her instinct was unreliable and that she was alone, she headed south again, along the beach, quickly finding her rhythm. She went only fifty yards, however, before she saw movement from the corner of her eye, thirty feet to her left: a swift shape, cloaked by night and mist, darting from behind a sandbound cypress to a weather-polished rock formation, where it slipped out of sight again.

Janice halted and, squinting toward the rock, wondered what she had glimpsed. It had seemed larger than a dog, perhaps as big as a man, but having seen it only peripherally, she had absorbed no details. The formation—twenty feet long, as low as four feet in some places and as high as ten feet in others—had been shaped by wind and rain until it resembled a mound of half-melted wax, more than large enough to conceal whatever she had seen.

"Someone there?" she asked.

She expected no answer and got none.

She was uneasy but not afraid. If she had seen something more than a trick of fog and moonlight, it surely had been an animal—and not a dog because a dog would have come straight to her and would not have been so secretive. As there were no natural predators along the coast worthy of her fear, she was curious rather than frightened.

Standing still, sheathed in a film of sweat, she began to feel the chill in the air. To maintain high body heat, she ran in place, watching the rocks, expecting to see an animal break from that cover and sprint either north or south along the beach.

Some people in the area kept horses, and the Fosters even ran a breeding and boarding facility near the sea about two and a half miles from there, beyond the northern flank of the cove. Perhaps one of their charges had gotten loose. The thing she'd seen from the corner of her eye had not been as big as a horse, though it might have been a pony. On the other hand, wouldn't she have heard a pony's thudding hoofbeats even in the soft sand? Of course, if it was one of the Fosters' horses—or someone else's—she ought to attempt to recover it or at least let them know where it could be found.

At last, when nothing moved, she ran to the rocks and circled them. Against the base of the formation and within the clefts in the stone were a few velvet-smooth shadows, but for the most part all was revealed in the milky, shimmering lunar glow, and no animal was concealed there.

She never gave serious thought to the possibility that she had seen someone other than another runner or an animal, that she was in real danger. Aside from an occasional act of vandalism or burglary—which was always the work of one of a handful of disaffected teenagers—and traffic accidents, local police had little to occupy them. Crimes against a person—rape, assault, murder—were rare in a town as small and tightly knit as Moonlight Cove; it was almost as if, in this pocket of the coast, they were living in a different and more benign age from that in which the rest of California dwelt.

Rounding the formation and returning to the firmer sand near the roiling surf, Janice decided that she had been snookered by moonlight and mist, two adept deceivers. The movement had been imaginary; she was alone on the shore.

She noted that the fog was rapidly thickening, but she continued along the crescent beach toward the cove's southern point. She was certain that she would get there and be able to return to the foot of Ocean Avenue before visibility declined too drastically.

A breeze sprang up from the sea and churned the incoming fog, which seemed to solidify from a gauzy vapor into a white sludge, as if it were milk being transformed into butter. By the time Janice reached the southern end of the dwindling strand, the breeze was stiffening and the surf was more agitated as well, casting up sheets of spray as each wave hit the piled rocks of the man-made breakwater that had been added to the natural point of the cove.

Someone stood on that twenty-foot-high wall of boulders, looking down at her. Janice glanced up just as a cloak of mist shifted and as moonlight silhouetted him.

Now fear seized her.

Though the stranger was directly in front of her, she could not see his face in the gloom. He seemed tall, well over six feet, though that could have been a trick of perspective.

Other than his outline, only his eyes were visible, and they were what ignited her fear. They were a softly radiant amber like the eyes of an animal revealed in headlight beams.

For a moment, peering directly up at him, she was transfixed by his gaze. Backlit by the moon, looming above her, standing tall and motionless upon ramparts of rock, with sea spray exploding to the right of him, he might have been a carved stone idol with luminous jewel eyes, erected by some demon-worshiping cult in a dark age long passed. Janice wanted to turn and run, but she could not move, was rooted to the sand, in the grip of that paralytic terror she had previously felt only in nightmares.

She wondered if she were awake. Perhaps her late-night run was indeed part of a nightmare, and perhaps she was actually asleep in bed, safe beneath warm blankets.

Then the man made a queer low growl, partly a snarl of anger but also a hiss, partly a hot and urgent cry of need but also cold, cold.

And he moved.

He dropped to all fours and began to descend the high breakwater, not as an ordinary man would climb down those jumbled rocks but with catlike swiftness and grace. In seconds he would be upon her.

Janice broke her paralysis, turned back on her own tracks, and ran toward the entrance to the public beach—a full mile away. Houses with lighted windows stood atop the steep-walled bluff that overlooked the cove, and some of them had steps leading down to the beach, but she was not confident of finding those stairs in the darkness. She did not waste any energy on a scream, for she doubted anyone would hear her. Besides, if screaming slowed her down, even only slightly, she might be overtaken and silenced before anyone from town could respond to her cries.

Her twenty-year commitment to running had never been more important than it was now; the issue was no longer good health but, she sensed, her very survival. She tucked her arms close to her sides, lowered her head, and sprinted, going for speed rather than endurance, because she felt that she only needed to get to the lower block of Ocean Avenue to be safe. She did not believe the man—or whatever the hell he was— would continue to pursue her into that lamplit and populated street.

High-altitude, striated clouds rushed across a portion of the lunar face. The moonlight dimmed, brightened, dimmed, and brightened in an irregular rhythm, pulsing through the rapidly clotting fog in such a way as to create a host of phantoms that repeatedly startled her and appeared to be keeping pace with her on all sides. The eerie, palpitant light contributed to the dreamlike quality of the chase, and she was half convinced that she was really in bed, fast asleep, but she did not halt or look over her shoulder because, dream or not, the man with the amber eyes was still behind her.

She had covered half the strand between the point of the cove and Ocean Avenue, her confidence growing with each step, when she realized that two of the phantoms in the fog were not phantoms after all. One was about twenty feet to her right and ran erect like a man; the other was on her left, less than fifteen feet away, splashing through the edge of the foam-laced sea, loping on all fours, the size of a man but certainly not a man, for no man could be so fleet and graceful in the posture of a dog. She had only a general impression of their shape and size, and she could not see their faces or any details of them other than their oddly luminous eyes.

Somehow she knew that neither of these pursuers was the man

whom she had seen on the breakwater. He was behind her, either running erect or loping on all fours. She was nearly encircled.

Janice made no attempt to imagine who or what they might be. Analysis of this weird experience would have to wait for later; now she simply accepted the existence of the impossible, for as the widow of a preacher and a deeply spiritual woman, she had the flexibility to bend with the unknown and unearthly when confronted by it.

Powered by the fear that had formerly paralyzed her, she picked up her pace. But so did her pursuers.

She heard a peculiar whimpering and only slowly realized that she was listening to her own tortured voice.

Evidently excited by her terror, the phantom forms around her began to keen. Their voices rose and fell, fluctuating between a shrill, protracted bleat and a guttural gnarl. Worst of all, punctuating those ululant cries were bursts of words, too, spoken raspily, urgently: *"Get the bitch, get the bitch, get the bitch . . ."*

What in God's name *were* they? Not men, surely, yet they could stand like men and speak like men, so what else could they *be* but men?

Janice felt her heart swelling in her breast, pounding hard.

"Get the bitch . . ."

The mysterious figures flanking her began to draw closer, and she tried to put on more speed to pull ahead of them, but they could not be shaken. They continued to narrow the gap. She could see them peripherally but did not dare look at them directly because she was afraid that the sight of them would be so shocking that she would be paralyzed again and, frozen by horror, would be brought down.

She was brought down anyway. Something leaped upon her from behind. She fell, a great weight pinning her, and all three creatures swarmed over her, touching her, plucking and tugging at her clothes.

Clouds slipped across most of the moon this time, and shadows fell in as if they were swatches of a black cloth sky.

Janice's face was pressed hard into the damp sand, but her head was turned to one side, so her mouth was free, and she screamed at last, though it was not much of a scream because she was breathless. She thrashed, kicked, flailed with her hands, desperately trying to strike them, but hitting mostly air and sand.

She could see nothing now, for the moon was completely lost.

She heard fabric tearing. The man astride her tore off her Nike jacket, ripped it to pieces, gouging her flesh in the process. She felt the hot touch of a hand, which seemed rough but human.

His weight briefly lifted from her, and she wriggled forward, trying to get away, but they pounced and crushed her into the sand. This time she was at the surf line, her face in the water.

Alternately keening, panting like dogs, hissing and snarling, her attackers loosed frantic bursts of words as they grabbed at her:

". . . *get her, get her, get, get, get* . . ."

". . . *want, want, want it, want it* . . ."

". . . *now, now, quick, now, quick, quick, quick* . . ."

They were pulling at her sweat pants, trying to strip her, but she wasn't sure if they wanted to rape or devour her; perhaps neither; what they wanted was, in fact, beyond her comprehension. She just knew they were overcome by some tremendously powerful urge, for the chilly air was as thick with their *need* as with fog and darkness.

One of them pushed her face deeper into the wet sand, and the water was all around her now, only inches deep but enough to drown her, and they wouldn't let her breathe. She knew she was going to die, she was pinned now and helpless, going to die, and all because she liked to run at night.

chapter two

On Monday, October 13, twenty-two days after the death of Janice Capshaw, Sam Booker drove his rental car from the San Francisco International Airport to Moonlight Cove. During the trip, he played a grim yet darkly amusing game with himself, making a mental list of reasons to go on living. Although he was on the road for more than an hour and a half, he could think of only four things: Guinness Stout, really good Mexican food, Goldie Hawn, and fear of death.

That thick, dark Irish brew never failed to please him and to provide a brief surcease from the sorrows of the world. Restaurants consistently serving first-rate Mexican food were more difficult to locate than Guinness; its solace was therefore more elusive. Sam had long been in love with Goldie Hawn—or the screen image she projected—because she was beautiful *and* cute, earthy and intelligent, and seemed to find life so much damn fun. His chances of meeting Goldie Hawn were about a million times worse than finding a great Mexican restaurant in a northern California coastal town like Moonlight Cove, so he was glad that she was not the *only* reason he had for living.

As he drew near his destination, tall pines and cypresses crowded Highway 1, forming a gray-green tunnel, casting long shadows in the late-afternoon light. The day was cloudless yet strangely forbidding; the sky was pale blue, bleak in spite of its crystalline clarity, unlike the tropical blue to which he was accustomed in Los Angeles. Though the temperature was in the fifties, hard sunshine, like glare bouncing off a field of ice, seemed to freeze the colors of the landscape and dull them with a haze of imitation frost.

Fear of death. That was the best reason on his list. Though he was just forty-two years old—five feet eleven, a hundred and seventy pounds, and currently healthy—Sam Booker had skated along the edge of death six times, had peered into the waters below, and had not found the plunge inviting.

A road sign appeared on the right side of the highway: OCEAN AV-ENUE, MOONLIGHT COVE, 2 MILES.

Sam was not afraid of the pain of dying, for that would pass in a flicker. Neither was he afraid of leaving his life unfinished; for several years he had harbored no goals or hopes or dreams, so there was nothing to finish, no purpose or meaning. But he *was* afraid of what lay beyond life.

Five years ago, more dead than alive on an operating-room table, he had undergone a near-death experience. While surgeons worked frantically to save him, he had risen out of his body and, from the ceiling, looked down on his carcass and the medical team surrounding it. Then suddenly he'd found himself rushing through a tunnel, toward dazzling light, toward the Other Side: the entire near-death cliché that was a staple of sensationalistic supermarket tabloids. At the penultimate moment, the skillful physicians had pulled him back into the land of the living, but not before he had been afforded a glimpse of what lay beyond the mouth of that tunnel. What he'd seen had scared the crap out of him. Life, though often cruel, was preferable to confronting what he now suspected lay beyond it.

He reached the Ocean Avenue exit. At the bottom of the ramp, as Ocean Avenue turned west, under Pacific Coast Highway, another sign read MOONLIGHT COVE 1/2 MILE.

A few houses were tucked in the purple gloom among the trees on both sides of the two-lane blacktop; their windows glowed with soft yellow light even an hour before nightfall. Some were of that half-timbered, deep-eaved Bavarian architecture that a few builders, in the

1940s and '50s, had mistakenly believed was in harmony with the northern California coast. Others were Monterey-style bungalows with white clapboard or shingle-covered walls, cedar-shingled roofs, and rich—if fairy-tale rococo—architectural details. Since Moonlight Cove had enjoyed much of its growth in the past ten years, a large number of houses were sleek, modern, many-windowed structures that looked like ships tossed up on some unimaginably high tide, stranded now on these hillsides above the sea.

When Sam followed Ocean Avenue into the six-block-long commercial district, a peculiar sense of *wrongness* immediately overcame him. Shops, restaurants, taverns, a market, two churches, the town library, a movie theater, and other unremarkable establishments lined the main drag, which sloped down toward the ocean, but to Sam's eyes there was an indefinable though powerful strangeness about the community that gave him a chill.

He could not identify the reasons for his instant negative reaction to the place, though perhaps it was related to the somber interplay of light and shadow. At this dying end of the autumn day, in the cheerless sunlight, the gray stone Catholic church looked like an alien edifice of steel, erected for no human purpose. A white stucco liquor store gleamed as if built from time-bleached bones. Many shop windows were cataracted with ice-white reflections of the sun as it sought the horizon, as if painted to conceal the activities of those who worked beyond them. The shadows cast by the buildings, by the pines and cypress, were stark, spiky, razor-edged.

Sam braked at a stoplight at the third intersection, halfway through the commercial district. With no traffic behind him, he paused to study the people on the sidewalks. Not many were in sight, eight or ten, and they also struck him as wrong, though his reasons for thinking ill of them were less definable than those that formed his impression of the town itself. They walked briskly, purposefully, heads up, with a peculiar air of urgency that seemed unsuited to a lazy, seaside community of only three thousand souls.

He sighed and continued down Ocean Avenue, telling himself that his imagination was running wild. Moonlight Cove and the people in it probably would not have seemed the least unusual if he had just been passing by on a long trip and turned off the coast highway only to have dinner at a local restaurant. Instead, he had arrived with the knowledge that something was rotten there, so of course he saw ominous signs in a perfectly innocent scene.

At least that was what he told himself. But he knew better.

He had come to Moonlight Cove because people had died there, because the official explanations for their deaths were suspicious, and he had a hunch that the truth, once uncovered, would be unusually disturbing. Over the years, he had learned to trust his hunches; that trust had kept him alive.

He parked the rented Ford in front of a gift shop.

To the west, at the far end of a slate-gray sea, the anemic sun sank through a sky that was slowly turning muddy red. Serpentine tendrils of fog began to rise off the choppy water.

chapter three

In the pantry off the kitchen, sitting on the floor with her back against a shelf of canned goods, Chrissie Foster looked at her watch. In the harsh light of the single bare bulb in the ceiling socket, she saw that she had been locked in that small, windowless chamber for nearly nine hours. She had received the wristwatch on her eleventh birthday, more than four months ago, and she had been thrilled by it because it was not a kid's watch with cartoon characters on the face; it was delicate, ladylike, gold-plated, with roman numerals instead of digits, a real Timex like her mother wore. Studying it, Chrissie was overcome by sadness. The watch represented a time of happiness and family togetherness that was lost forever.

Besides feeling sad, lonely, and a little restless from hours of captivity, she was scared. Of course, she was not as scared as she had been that morning, when her father had carried her through the house and thrown her into the pantry. Then, kicking and screaming, she had been *terrified* because of what she had seen. Because of what her parents had become. But that white-hot terror could not be sustained; gradually it subsided to a low-grade fever of fear that made her feel flushed and chilled at the same time, queasy, headachy, almost as if she were in the early stages of flu.

She wondered what they were going to do to her when they finally let her out of the pantry. Well, no, she didn't worry about what they were going to do, for she was pretty sure she already knew the answer to that one: They were going to change her into one of them. What she wondered about, actually, was how the change would be effected—and what, exactly, she would become. She knew that her mother and father were no longer ordinary people, that they were something else, but she had no words to describe what they had become.

Her fear was sharpened by the fact that she lacked the words to explain to herself what was happening in her own home, for she had always been in love with words and had faith in their power. She liked to read just about anything: poetry, short stories, novels, the daily newspaper, magazines, the backs of cereal boxes if nothing else was at hand. She was in sixth grade at school, but her teacher, Mrs. Tokawa, said she read at a tenth-grade level. When she was not reading, she was often writing stories of her own. Within the past year she had decided she was going to grow up to write novels like those of Mr. Paul Zindel or the sublimely silly Mr. Daniel Pinkwater or, best of all, those of Ms. Andre Norton.

But now words failed; her life was going to be far different from what she had imagined. She was frightened as much by the loss of the comfortable, bookish future she had foreseen as she was by the changes that had taken place in her parents. Eight months shy of her twelfth birthday, Chrissie had become acutely aware of life's uncertainty, grim knowledge for which she was ill prepared.

Not that she had already given up. She intended to fight. She was not going to let them change her without resistance. Soon after she had been thrown into the pantry, once her tears had dried, she had looked over the contents of the shelves, searching for a weapon. The pantry contained mostly canned, bottled, and packaged food, but there were also laundry and first-aid and handyman supplies. She had found the perfect thing: a small aerosol-spray can of WD-40, an oil-based lubricant. It was a third the size of an ordinary spray can, easily concealed. If she could surprise them, spray it in their eyes and temporarily blind them, she could make a break for freedom.

As though reading a newspaper headline, she said, "Ingenious Young Girl Saves Self with Ordinary Household Lubricant."

She held the WD-40 in both hands, taking comfort from it.

Now and then a vivid and unsettling memory recurred: her father's face as it had looked when he had thrown her into the pantry—red and swollen with anger, his eyes darkly ringed, nostrils flared, lips drawn back from his teeth in a feral snarl, every feature contorted with rage. "I'll be back for you," he had said, spraying spittle as he spoke. "I'll be back."

He slammed the door and braced it shut with a straight-backed kitchen chair that he wedged under the knob. Later, when the house fell silent and her parents seemed to have gone away, Chrissie had tried the door, pushing on it with all her might, but the tilted chair was an immovable barricade.

I'll be back for you. I'll be back.

His twisted face and bloodshot eyes had made her think of Mr. Robert Louis Stevenson's description of the murderous Hyde in the story of Dr. Jekyll, which she had read a few months ago. There was madness in her father; he was not the same man that he once had been.

More unsettling was the memory of what she had seen in the upstairs hall when she had returned home after missing the school bus and had surprised her parents. No. They were not really her parents any more. They were . . . something else.

She shuddered.

She clutched the can of WD-40.

Suddenly, for the first time in hours, she heard noise in the kitchen. The back door of the house opened. Footsteps. At least two, maybe three or four people.

"She's in there," her father said.

Chrissie's heart stuttered, then found a new and faster beat.

"This isn't going to be quick," said another man. Chrissie did not recognize his deep, slightly raspy voice. "You see, it's more complicated with a child. Shaddack's not sure we're even ready for the children yet. It's risky."

"She's got to be converted, Tucker." That was Chrissie's mother, Sharon, though she did not sound like herself. It was her voice, all right, but without its usual softness, without the natural, musical quality that had made it such a perfect voice for reading fairy tales.

"Of course, yes, she's got to be done," said the stranger, whose name was evidently Tucker. "I know that. Shaddack knows it too. He sent me here, didn't he? I'm just saying it might take more time than usual. We need a place where we can restrain her and watch over her during the conversion."

"Right here. Her bedroom upstairs."

Conversion?

Trembling, Chrissie got to her feet and stood facing the door.

With a scrape and clatter, the tilted chair was removed from under the knob.

She held the spray can in her right hand, down at her side and half behind her, with her forefinger on top of the nozzle.

The door opened, and her father looked in at her.

Alex Foster. Chrissie tried to think of him as Alex Foster, not as her father, just Alex Foster, but it was difficult to deny that in some ways he was still her dad. Besides, "Alex Foster" was no more accurate than "father" because he was someone altogether new.

His face was no longer warped with rage. He appeared more like himself: thick blond hair; a broad, pleasant face with bold features; a smattering of freckles across his cheeks and nose. Nevertheless, she could see a terrible difference in his eyes. He seemed to be filled with a strange urgency, an edgy tension. Hungry. Yes, that was it: Daddy seemed hungry . . . consumed by hunger, frantic with hunger, *starving* . . . but for something other than food. She did not understand his hunger but she sensed it, a fierce *need* that engendered a constant tension in his muscles, a need of such tremendous power, so hot, that waves of it seemed to rise from him like steam from boiling water.

He said, "Come out of there, Christine."

Chrissie let her shoulders sag, blinked as if repressing tears, exaggerated the shivers that swept through her, and tried to look small, frightened, defeated. Reluctantly she edged forward.

"Come on, come on," he said impatiently, motioning her out of the pantry.

Chrissie stepped through the doorway and saw her mother, who was beside and slightly behind Alex. Sharon was pretty—auburn hair, green eyes—but there was no softness or motherliness about her any more. She was hard looking and changed and full of the same barely contained nervous energy that filled her husband.

By the kitchen table stood a stranger in jeans and plaid hunting jacket. He was evidently the Tucker to whom her mother had spoken: tall, lean, all sharp edges and angles. His close-cropped black hair bristled. His dark eyes were set under a deep, bony brow; his sharply ridged nose was like a stone wedge driven into the center of his face; his mouth was a thin slash, and his jaws were as prominent as those of a predator that preyed on small animals and snapped them in half with one bite. He was holding a physician's black leather bag.

Her father reached for Chrissie as she came out of the pantry, and she whipped up the can of WD-40, spraying him in the eyes from a distance of less than two feet. Even as her father howled in pain and surprise, Chrissie turned and sprayed her mother, too, straight in the face. Half-blinded, they fumbled for her, but she slipped away from them and dashed across the kitchen.

Tucker was startled but managed to grab her by the arm.

She spun toward him and kicked him in the crotch.

He did not let go of her, but the strength went out of his big hands. She tore herself away from him and sprinted into the downstairs hallway.

chapter four

From the east, twilight drifted down on Moonlight Cove, as if it were a mist not of water but of smoky purple light. When Sam Booker got out of his car, the air was chilly; he was glad that he was wearing a wool sweater under his corduroy sport-coat. As a photocell activated all the streetlamps simultaneously, he strolled along Ocean Avenue, looking in shop windows, getting a feel for the town.

He knew that Moonlight Cove was prosperous, that unemployment was virtually nonexistent—thanks to New Wave Microtechnology, which had headquartered there ten years ago—yet he saw signs of a faltering economy. Taylor's Fine Gifts and Saenger's Jewelry had vacated their shops; through their dusty, plate-glass windows, he saw bare shelves and empty display cases and deep, still shadows. New Attitudes, a trendy clothing store, was having a going-out-of-business sale, and judging by the dearth of shoppers, their merchandise was moving sluggishly even at fifty to seventy percent off the original prices.

By the time he had walked two blocks west, to the beach end of town, crossed the street, and returned three blocks along the other side of Ocean Avenue to Knight's Bridge Tavern, twilight was swiftly waning. A nacreous fog was moving in from the sea, and the air itself seemed iridescent, shimmering delicately; a plum-colored haze lay over everything, except where the streetlamps cast showers of mist-softened yellow light, and above it all was a heavy darkness coming down.

A single moving car was in sight, three blocks away, and at the moment Sam was the only pedestrian. The solitude combined with the queer light of the dying day to give him the feeling that this was a ghost town, inhabited only by the dead. As the gradually thickening fog seeped up the hill from the Pacific, it contributed to the illusion that *all* of the surrounding shops were vacant, that they offered no wares other than spider webs, silence, and dust.

You're a dour bastard, he told himself. Too grim by half.

Experience had made a pessimist of him. The traumatic course of his life to date precluded grinning optimism.

Tendrils of fog slipped around his legs. At the far edge of the darkening sea, the pallid sun was half extinguished. Sam shivered and went into the tavern to get a drink.

Of the three other customers, none was in a noticeably upbeat mood. In one of the black vinyl booths off to the left, a middle-aged man and woman were leaning toward each other, speaking in low voices. A gray-faced guy at the bar was hunched over his glass of draft beer, holding it in both hands, scowling as if he had just seen a bug swimming in the brew.

In keeping with its name, Knight's Bridge reeked ersatz British atmosphere. A different coat of arms, each no doubt copied from some official heraldic reference book, had been carved from wood and hand-painted and inset in the back of every barstool. A suit of armor stood in one corner. Fox-hunting scenes hung on the walls.

Sam slid onto a stool eight down from the gray-faced man. The bartender hurried to him, wiping a clean cotton rag over the already immaculate, highly polished oak counter.

"Yes, sir, what'll it be?" He was a round man from every aspect: a small round potbelly; meaty forearms with a thick thatching of black hair; a chubby face; a mouth too small to be in harmony with his other features; a puggish nose that ended in a round little ball; eyes round enough to give him a perpetual look of surprise.

"You have Guinness?" Sam asked.

"It's a fundamental of a *real* pub, I'd say. If we didn't have Guinness . . . why, we might as well convert to a tea shop." His was a mellifluous voice; every word he spoke sounded as smooth and round as he looked. He seemed unusually eager to please. "Would you like it cold or just slightly chilled? I keep it both ways."

"Very slightly chilled."

"Good man!" When he returned with a Guinness and a glass, the bartender said, "Name's Burt Peckham. I own the joint."

Carefully pouring the stout down the side of the glass to ensure the smallest possible head, Sam said, "Sam Booker. Nice place, Burt."

"Thanks. Maybe you could spread the word. I try to keep it cozy and well stocked, and we used to have quite a crowd, but lately it seems like most of the town either joined a temperance movement or started brewing their own in their basements, one or the other."

"Well, it's a Monday night."

"These last couple months, it's not been unusual to be half empty even on a Saturday night, which never used to happen." Burt Peckham's round face dimpled with worry. He slowly polished the bar while he talked. "What it is—I think maybe this health kick Californians have been on for so long has finally just gone too far. They're all staying home, doing aerobics in front of the VCR, eating wheat germ and egg whites or whatever the hell it is they eat, drinking nothing but bottled water and fruit juice and titmouse milk. Listen, a tipple or two a day is *good* for you."

Sam drank some of the Guinness, sighed with satisfaction, and said, "This sure tastes as if it ought to be good for you."

"It is. Helps your circulation. Keeps your bowels in shape. Ministers ought to be touting its virtues each Sunday, not preaching against it. *All* things in moderation—and that includes a couple of brews a day." Perhaps realizing that he was polishing the bar a bit obsessively, he hung the rag on a hook and stood with his arms folded across his chest. "You just passing through, Sam?"

"Actually," Sam lied, "I'm taking a long trip up the coast from L.A. to the Oregon line, loafing along, looking for a quiet place to semi-retire."

"Retire? You kidding?"

"*Semi*-retire."

"But you're only, what, forty, forty-one?"

"Forty-two."

"What are you—a bank robber?"

"Stockbroker. Made some good investments over the years. Now I think I can drop out of the rat race and get by well enough just managing my own portfolio. I want to settle down where it's quiet, no smog, no crime. I've had it with L.A."

"People really make money in stocks?" Peckham asked. "I thought it was about as good an investment as a craps table in Reno. Wasn't everybody wiped out when the market blew up a couple years ago?"

"It's a mug's game for the little guy, but you can do all right if you're a broker and if you don't get swept up in the euphoria of a bull market. No market goes up forever or down forever; you just have to guess right about when to start swimming against the current."

"Retiring at forty-two," Peckham said wonderingly. "And when I got into the bar business, I thought I was set for life. Told my wife—in good times, people drink to celebrate, in bad times they drink to forget, so there's no better business than a tavern. Now look." He indicated the nearly empty room with a sweeping gesture of his right hand. "I'd have done better selling condoms in a monastery."

"Get me another Guinness?" Sam asked.

"Hey, maybe this place will turn around yet!"

When Peckham returned with the second bottle of stout, Sam said,

"Moonlight Cove might be what I've been looking for. I guess I'll stay a few days, get the feel of it. Can you recommend a motel?"

"There's only one left. Never been much of a tourist town. No one here really wanted that, I guess. Up until this summer, we had four motels. Now three are out of business. I don't know . . . even as pretty as it is, maybe this burg is dying. As far as I can see, we aren't losing population but . . . dammit, we're losing *something*." He snatched up the bar rag again and began to polish the oak. "Anyway, try Cove Lodge on Cypress Lane. That's the last cross street on Ocean Avenue; it runs along the bluff, so you'll probably have a room with an ocean view. Clean, quiet place."

chapter five

At the end of the downstairs hall, Chrissie Foster threw open the front door. She raced across the wide porch and down the steps, stumbled, regained her balance, turned right, and fled across the yard, past a blue Honda that evidently belonged to Tucker, heading for the stables. The hard slap of her tennis shoes seemed to boom like cannon fire through the swiftly fading twilight. She wished that she could run silently—and faster. Even if her parents and Tucker didn't reach the front porch until she was swallowed by shadows, they would still be able to hear where she was going.

Most of the sky was a burnt-out black, though a deep red glow marked the western horizon, as if all the light of the October day had been boiled down to that intense crimson essence, which had settled at the bottom of the celestial cauldron. Wispy fog crept in from the nearby sea, and Chrissie hoped it would swiftly thicken, dense as pudding, because she was going to need more cover.

She reached the first of the two long stables and rolled aside the big door. The familiar and not unpleasant aroma—straw, hay, feed grain, horseflesh, liniment, saddle leather, and dry manure—wafted over her.

She snapped the night-light switch, and three low-wattage bulbs winked on, bright enough to dimly illuminate the building without disturbing the occupants. Ten generously proportioned stalls flanked each side of the dirt-floored main aisle, and curious horses peered out at her above several of the half-size doors. A few belonged to Chrissie's parents, but most were being boarded for people who lived in and around Moonlight Cove. The horses snuffled and snorted, and one whinnied softly, as Chrissie ran past them to the last box on the left, where a dapple-gray mare named Godiva was in residence.

Access to the stalls also could be had from outside the building, although in this cool season the exterior Dutch-style doors were kept bolted both top and bottom to prevent heat escaping from the barn. Godiva was a gentle mare and particularly amicable with Chrissie, but she was skittish about being approached in the dark; she might rear or bolt if surprised by the opening of her exterior stall door at this hour. Because Chrissie could not afford to lose even a few seconds in calming her mount, she had to reach the mare from inside the stable.

Godiva was ready for her. The mare shook her head, tossing the thick and lustrous white mane for which she had been named, and blew air through her nostrils in greeting.

Glancing back toward the stable entrance, expecting to see Tucker and her parents storm in at any moment, Chrissie unlatched the half-door. Godiva came out into the aisle between the rows of stalls.

"Be a lady, Godiva. Oh, please be sweet for me."

She could not take time to saddle the mare or slip a bit between her teeth. With a hand against Godiva's flank, she guided her mount past the tack room and feed shed that occupied the last quarter of the barn, startling a mouse that scurried across her path into a shadowy corner. She rolled open the door at that end, and cool air swept in.

Without a stirrup to give her a leg up, Chrissie was too small to mount Godiva.

A blacksmith's shoeing stool stood in the corner by the tack room. Keeping a hand against Godiva to gentle her, Chrissie hooked the stool with one foot and pulled it to the horse's side.

Behind her, from the other end of the barn, Tucker shouted, "Here she is! The stable!" He ran toward her.

The stool did not give her much height and was no substitute for a stirrup.

She could hear Tucker's pounding footsteps, close, closer, but she didn't look at him.

He cried, "I got her!"

Chrissie grabbed Godiva's magnificent white mane, threw herself against the big horse and up, up, swinging her leg high, scrabbling desperately against the mare's side, pulling hard on the mane. It must have hurt Godiva, but the old girl was stoic. She didn't rear or whinny in pain, as if some equine instinct told her that this little girl's life depended on equanimity. Then Chrissie was on Godiva's back, tilting precariously but aboard, holding tight with her knees, one hand full of mane, and she slapped the horse's side.

"Go!"

Tucker reached her as she shouted that single word, grabbed at her leg, snared her jeans. His deep-set eyes were wild with anger; his nostrils flared, and his thin lips pulled back from his teeth. She kicked him under the chin, and he lost his grip on her.

Simultaneously Godiva leaped forward, through the open door, into the night.

"She's got a horse!" Tucker shouted. "She's on a horse!"

The dapple-gray sprinted straight toward the meadowed slope that led to the sea a couple of hundred yards away, where the last muddy-red light of the sunset painted faint, speckled patterns on the black water. But Chrissie didn't want to go down to the shore because she was not sure how high the tide was. At some places along the coast, the beach was not broad even at low tide; if the tide were high now, deep water would meet rocks and bluffs at some points, making passage impossible. She could not risk riding into a dead end with her parents and Tucker in pursuit.

Even without the benefit of a saddle and at a full gallop, Chrissie managed to pull herself into a better position astride the mare, and as soon as she was no longer leaning to one side like a stunt rider, she buried both hands in the thick white mane, gripped fistsful of that coarse hair, and tried to use it as a substitute for reins. She urged Godiva to turn left, away from the sea, away from the house as well, back along the stables, and out toward the half-mile driveway that led to the county road, where they were more likely to find help.

Instead of rebelling at this crude method of guidance, patient Godiva responded immediately, turning to the left as prettily as if she had a bit in her teeth and had felt the tug of a rein. The thunder of her hooves echoed off the barn walls as they raced past that structure.

"You're a great old girl!" Chrissie shouted to the horse. "I love you, girl."

They passed safely wide of the east end of the stable, where she had first entered to get the mare, and she spotted Tucker coming out of the door. He was clearly surprised to see her heading that way instead of down to the ocean. He sprinted toward her, and he was startlingly quick, but he was no match for Godiva.

They came to the driveway, and Chrissie kept Godiva on the soft verge, parallel to that hard-surfaced lane. She leaned forward, as tight against the horse as she could get, terrified of falling off, and every hard thud of hooves jarred through her bones. Her head was turned to the side, so she saw the house off to the left, the windows full of light but not welcoming. It was no longer her home; it was hell between four walls, so the light at the windows seemed, to her, to be demonic fires in the rooms of Hades.

Suddenly she saw something racing across the front lawn toward the driveway, toward her. It was low and fast, the size of a man but running on all fours—or nearly so—loping, about twenty yards away and closing. She saw another equally bizarre figure, almost the size of the first, running behind it. Though both creatures were backlit by the house lights, Chrissie could discern little more than their shapes, yet she knew what they were. No, correct that: She knew *who* they probably were, but she still didn't know *what* they were, though she had seen them in the upstairs hall this morning; she knew what they had been—people like her—but not what they were now.

"Go, Godiva, go!"

Even without the flap of reins to signal the need for greater speed, the mare increased the length of her stride, as if she shared a psychic link with Chrissie.

Then they were past the house, tearing flat-out across a grassy field, paralleling the macadam driveway, whizzing toward the county road less than half a mile to the east. The nimble-footed mare worked her great haunch muscles, and her powerful stride was so lullingly rhythmic and exhilarating that Chrissie soon was hardly aware of the rocking-jolting aspect of the ride; it seemed as if they were skimming across the earth, nearly flying.

She looked over her shoulder and did not see the two loping figures, although they were no doubt still pursuing her through the multilayered shadows. With the muddy-red candescence along the western horizon fading to deep purple, with the lights of the house rapidly dwindling, and with a crescent moon beginning to thrust one silver-bright point above the line of hills in the east, visibility was poor.

Though she could not see those pursuers who were on foot, she had no difficulty spotting the headlights of Tucker's blue Honda. In front of the house, a couple of hundred yards behind her now, Tucker swung the car around in the driveway and joined the chase.

Chrissie was fairly confident that Godiva could outrun any man or beast other than a better horse, but she knew that the mare was no match for a car. Tucker would catch them in seconds. The man's face was clear in her memory: the bony brow, sharp-ridged nose, deeply set eyes like a pair of hard, black marbles. He'd had about him that aura of unnatural vitality that Chrissie sometimes had seen in her parents—abundant nervous energy coupled with a queer look of hunger. She knew he would do anything to stop her, that he might even attempt to ram Godiva with the Honda.

He could not, of course, use the car to follow Godiva overland. Reluctantly Chrissie employed her knees and the mane in her right hand to turn the mare away from the driveway and the county road, where they were most likely to reach help quickly. Godiva responded without hesitation, and they headed toward the woods that lay at the far side of the meadow, five hundred yards to the south.

Chrissie could see the forest only as a black, bristly mass vaguely silhouetted against the marginally less dark sky. The details of the terrain she must cross appeared to her more in memory than in reality. She prayed that the horse's night vision was keener than hers.

"That's my girl, go, go, you good old girl, go!" she shouted encouragingly to the mare.

They made their own wind in the crisp, still air. Chrissie was aware of Godiva's hot breath streaming past her in crystallized plumes, and her own breath smoked from her open mouth. Her heart pounded in time with the frantic thumping of hooves, and she felt almost as if she and Godiva were not rider and horse but one being, sharing the same heart and blood and breath.

Though fleeing for her life, she was as pleasantly thrilled as she was terrified, and that realization startled her. Facing death—or in this case something perhaps worse than death—was peculiarly exciting, darkly attractive in a way and to an extent that she could never have imagined. She was almost as frightened of the unexpected thrill as of the people who were chasing her.

She clung tightly to the dapple-gray, sometimes bouncing on the horse's bare back, lifting dangerously high, but holding fast, flexing and contracting her own muscles in sympathy with those of the horse. With every ground-pummeling stride, Chrissie grew more confident that they would escape. The mare had heart and endurance. When they had traversed three-quarters of the field, with the woods looming, Chrissie decided to turn east again when they reached the trees, not straight toward the county road but in that general direction, and—

Godiva fell.

The mare had put a foot in some depression—a ground squirrel's burrow, the entrance to a rabbit's warren, perhaps a natural drainage ditch—stumbled, and lost her balance. She tried to recover, failed, and fell, bleating in terror.

Chrissie was afraid that her mount would crash down on her, that she would be crushed, or at least break a leg. But there were no stirrups to ensnare her feet, no saddle horn to snag her clothes, and because she instinctively let go of the dapple-gray's mane, she was thrown free at once, straight over the horse's head and high into the air. Though the ground was soft and further cushioned by a thick growth of wild grass, she met it with numbing impact, driving the air from her lungs and banging her teeth together so hard that her tongue would have been bitten off if it had been between them. But she was three yards away from the horse and safe in that regard.

Godiva was the first to rise, scrambling up an instant after crashing down. Eyes wide with fright, she cantered past Chrissie, favoring her right foreleg, which evidently was only sprained; if it had been broken, the horse would not have gotten up.

Chrissie called to the mare, afraid the horse would wander off. But her breath was coming in ragged gasps, and the name issued from her in a whisper: "Godiva!"

The horse kept going west, back toward the sea and the stables.

By the time Chrissie got up on her hands and knees, she realized that a lame horse was of no use to her, so she made no further effort to recall the mare. She was gasping for breath and mildly dizzy, but she knew she had to get moving because she was no doubt still being stalked. She could see the Honda, headlights on, parked along the lane more than three hundred yards to the north. With all the bloody glow of sunset having seeped out of the horizon, the meadow was black. She could not determine if low, swift-moving figures were out there, though she knew they must be approaching and that she would surely fall into their hands within a minute or two.

She got to her feet, turned south toward the woods, staggered ten or fifteen yards until her legs recovered from the shock of her fall, and finally broke into a run.

chapter six

Over the years, Sam Booker had discovered that the length of the California coast was graced by charming inns that featured master-quality stonework, weathered wood, cove ceilings, beveled glass, and lushly planted courtyards with used-brick walkways. In spite of the comfortable images its name evoked and the singularly scenic setting that it enjoyed, Cove Lodge was not one of those California jewels. It was just an ordinary stucco, two-story, forty-room, rectangular box, with a drab coffee shop at one end, no swimming pool. Amenities were limited to ice and soda machines on both floors. The sign above the motel office was neither garish nor in the artistic mode of some modern neon, just small and simple—and cheap.

The evening desk clerk gave him a second-floor room with an ocean view, though location didn't matter to Sam. Judging by the dearth of cars in the lot, however, rooms with a view were not in short supply. Each level of the motel had twenty units in banks of ten, serviced by an interior hall carpeted in short-nap orange nylon that seared his eyes. Rooms on the east overlooked Cypress Lane; those on the west faced the Pacific. His quarters were at the northwest corner: a queen-size bed with a sagging mattress and worn blue-green spread, cigarette-scarred nightstands, a television bolted to a stand, table, two straight-back chairs, cigarette-scarred bureau, phone, bathroom, and one big window framing the night-blanketed sea.

When disheartened salesmen, down on their luck and teetering on the edge of economic ruin, committed suicide on the road, they did the deed in rooms like this.

He unpacked his two suitcases, putting his clothes in the closet and bureau drawers. Then he sat on the edge of the bed and stared at the telephone on the nightstand.

He should call Scott, his son, who was back home in Los Angeles, but he couldn't do it from this phone. Later, if the local police became interested in him, they would visit Cove Lodge, examine his long-distance charges, investigate the numbers he had dialed, and try to piece together his real identity from the identities of those with whom he had spoken. To maintain his cover, he must use his room phone only to call his contact number at the Bureau office in L.A., a secure line that would be answered with "Birchfield Securities, may I help you?" Furthermore, in phone-company records that line *was* registered to Birchfield, the nonexistent firm with which Sam was supposedly a stockbroker; it could not be traced ultimately to the FBI. He had nothing to report yet, so he did not lift the receiver. When he went out to dinner, he could call Scott from a pay phone.

He did not want to talk to the boy. It would be purely a duty call. Sam dreaded it. Conversation with his son had ceased to be pleasurable at least three years ago, when Scott had been thirteen and, at that time, already motherless for a year. Sam wondered if the boy would have gone wrong quite as rapidly or so completely if Karen had lived. That avenue of thought led him, of course, to the contemplation of his own role in Scott's decline: Would the boy have turned bad regardless of the quality of the parental guidance that he received; was his fall inevitable, the weakness in him or in his stars? Or was Scott's descent a direct result of his father's failure to find a way to steer him to a better, brighter path?

If he kept brooding about it, he was going to pull a Willy Loman right there in Cove Lodge, even though he was not a salesman.

Guinness stout.

Good Mexican food.

Goldie Hawn.

Fear of death.

As a list of reasons for living, it was damned short and too pathetic to contemplate, but perhaps it was just long enough.

After he used the bathroom, he washed his hands and face in cold water. He still felt tired, not the least refreshed.

He took off his corduroy jacket and put on a thin, supple leather shoulder holster that he retrieved from a suitcase. He'd also packed a Smith & Wesson .38 Chief's Special, which he now loaded. He tucked it into the holster before slipping into his jacket again. His coats were tailored to conceal the weapon; it made no bulge, and the holster fit so far back against his side that the gun could not be seen easily even if he left the jacket unbuttoned.

For undercover assignments, Sam's body and face were as well tailored as his jackets. He was five eleven, neither tall nor short. He weighed one hundred and seventy pounds, mostly bone and muscle, little fat, yet he was not a thick-necked weightlifter type in such superb condition that he would draw attention. His face was nothing special: neither ugly nor handsome, neither too broad nor too narrow, marked neither by unusually sharp nor blunt features, unblemished and unscarred. His sandy-brown hair was barbered in a timelessly moderate length and style that would be unremarkable in an age of brush cuts or in an era of shoulder-length locks.

Of all the aspects of his appearance, only his eyes were truly arresting. They were gray-blue with darker blue striations. Women had often told him that his were the most beautiful eyes they had ever seen. At one time he had cared what women said of him.

He shrugged, making sure the holster was hanging properly.

He did not expect to need the gun that evening. He had not begun to nose around and draw attention to himself; and since he had not yet pushed anyone, no one was ready to push back.

Nevertheless, from now on he would carry the revolver. He could not leave it in the motel room or lock it in his rental car; if someone conducted a determined search, the gun would be found, and his cover would be blown. No middle-aged stockbroker, searching for a coastal haven in which to take early retirement, would go armed with a snub-nosed .38 of that make and model. It was a cop's piece.

Pocketing his room key, he went out to dinner.

chapter seven

After she checked in, Tessa Jane Lockland stood for a long time at the big window in her room at the Cove Lodge, with no lights on. She stared out at the vast, dark Pacific and down at the beach from which her sister, Janice, supposedly had ventured forth on a grimly determined mission of self-destruction.

The official story was that Janice had gone to the shore alone at night, in a state of acute depression. She had taken a massive overdose of Valium, swallowing the capsules with several swigs from a can of Diet Coke. Then she had stripped off her clothes and had swum out toward far Japan. Losing consciousness because of the drugs, she soon slipped into the cold embrace of the sea, and drowned.

"Bullshit," Tessa said softly, as if speaking to her own vague reflection in the cool glass.

Janice Lockland Capshaw had been a hopeful person, unfailingly optimistic—a trait so common in members of the Lockland clan as to be genetic. Not once in her life had Janice sat in a corner feeling sorry for herself; if she had tried it, within seconds she would have begun laughing at the foolishness of self-pity and would have gotten up and gone to a movie, or for a psychologically therapeutic run. Even when Richard died, Janice had not allowed grief to metastasize into depression, though she loved him greatly.

So what would have sent her into such a steep emotional spiral? Contemplating the story the police wanted her to believe, Tessa was driven to sarcasm. Maybe Janice had gone out to a restaurant, been served a bad dinner, and been so crushed by the experience that suicide had been her only possible response. Yeah. Or maybe her television went on the blink, and she missed her favorite soap opera, which plunged her into irreversible despair. Sure. Those scenarios were about as plausible as the nonsense that the Moonlight Cove police and coroner had put in their reports.

Suicide.

"Bullshit," Tessa repeated.

From the window of her motel room, she could see only a narrow band of the beach below, where it met the churning surf. The sand was dimly revealed in the wintry light of a newly risen quarter moon, a pale ribbon curving southwest and northwest around the cove.

Tessa was overcome by the desire to stand on the beach from which her sister had supposedly set out on that midnight swim to the graveyard, the same beach to which the tide had returned her bloated, ravaged corpse days later. She turned from the window and switched on a bedside lamp. She removed a brown leather jacket from a hanger in the closet, pulled it on, slung her purse over her shoulder, and left the room, locking the door behind her. She was certain—irrationally so—that merely by going to the beach and standing where Janice supposedly had stood, she would uncover a clue to the true story, through an amazing insight or flicker of intuition.

chapter eight

As the hammered-silver moon rose above the dark eastern hills, Chrissie raced along the tree line, looking for a way into the woods before her strange pursuers found her. She quickly arrived at Pyramid Rock, thus named because the formation, twice as tall as she was, had three sides and came to a weather-rounded point; when younger, she had fantasized that it had been constructed ages ago by a geographically displaced tribe of inch-high Egyptians. Having played in this meadow and forest for years, she was as familiar with the terrain as with the rooms of her own house, certainly more at home there than her parents or Tucker would be, which gave her an advantage. She slipped past Pyramid Rock, into the gloom beneath the trees, onto a narrow deer trail that led south.

She heard no one behind her and did not waste time squinting back into the darkness. But she suspected that, as predators, her parents and Tucker would be silent stalkers, revealing themselves only when they pounced.

The coastal woodlands were composed mostly of a wide variety of pines, although a few sweet gums flourished, too, their leaves a scarlet blaze of autumn color in daylight but now as black as bits of funeral shrouds. Chrissie followed the winding trail as the land began to slope into a canyon. In more than half the forest, the trees grew far enough apart to allow the cold glow of the partial moon to penetrate to the underbrush and lay an icy crust of light upon the trail. The incoming fog was still too thin to filter out much of that wan radiance, but at other places the interlacing branches blocked the lunar light.

Even where moonlight revealed the way, Chrissie dared not run, for she would surely be tripped by the surface roots of the trees, which spread across the deer-beaten path. Here and there low-hanging branches presented another danger to a runner, but she hurried along.

As if reading from a book of her own adventures, a book like one of those she so much liked, she thought, *Young Chrissie was as sure-*

footed as she was resourceful and quick-thinking, no more intimidated by the darkness than by the thought of her monstrous pursuers. What a girl she was!

Soon she would reach the bottom of the slope, where she could turn west toward the sea or east toward the county route, which bridged the canyon. Few people lived in that area, more than two miles from the outskirts of Moonlight Cove; fewer still lived by the sea, since portions of the coastline were protected by state law and were closed to construction. Though she had little chance of finding help toward the Pacific, her prospects to the east were not noticeably better, because the county road was lightly traveled and few houses were built along it; besides, Tucker might be patrolling that route in his Honda, expecting her to head that way and flag down the first passing car she saw.

Frantically wondering where to go, she descended the last hundred feet. The trees flanking the trail gave way to low, impenetrable tangles of bristly scrub oaks called chaparral. A few immense ferns, ideally suited to the frequent coastal fogs, overgrew the path, and Chrissie shivered as she pushed through them, for she felt as if scores of small hands were grabbing at her.

A broad but shallow stream cut a course through the bottom of the canyon, and she paused by its bank to catch her breath. Most of the streambed was dry. At this time of year, only a couple of inches of water moved lazily through the center of the channel, glimmering darkly in the moonlight.

The night was windless.

Soundless.

Hugging herself, she realized how cold it was. In jeans and a blue-plaid flannel shirt, she was adequately dressed for a crisp October day, but not for the cold, damp air of an autumn night.

She was chilled, breathless, scared, and unsure of what her next move ought to be, but most of all she was angry with herself for those weaknesses of mind and body. Ms. Andre Norton's wonderful adventure stories were filled with dauntless young heroines who could endure far longer chases—and far greater cold and other hardships—than this, and always with wits intact, able to make quick decisions and, usually, right ones.

Spurred by comparing herself to a Norton girl, Chrissie stepped off the bank of the stream. She crossed ten feet of loamy soil eroded from the hills by last season's heavy rains and tried to jump across the shallow, purling band of water. She splashed down a few inches short of the other side, soaking her tennis shoes. Nevertheless, she went on through more loam, which clumped to her wet shoes, ascended the far bank, and headed neither east nor west but south, up the other canyon wall toward the next arm of the forest.

Though she was entering new territory now, at the extremity of the section of the woods that had been her playground for years, she was not afraid of getting lost. She could tell east from west by the movement of the thin, incoming fog and by the position of the moon, and from those signs she could stay on a reliably southward course. She believed that within a mile she would come to a score of houses and to the sprawling grounds of New Wave Microtechnology, which lay between Foster Stables and the town of Moonlight Cove. There she would be able to find help.

Then, of course, her *real* problems would begin. She would have to convince someone that her parents were no longer her parents, that they had changed or been possessed or been somehow taken over by some spirit or . . . force. And that they wanted to turn her into one of them.

Yeah, she thought, good luck.

She was bright, articulate, responsible, but she was also just an eleven-year-old kid. She would have a hard time making anyone believe her. She had no illusions about that. They would listen and nod their heads and smile, and then they would call her parents, and her parents would sound more plausible than she did. . . .

But I've got to try, she told herself, as she began to ascend the sloped southern wall of the canyon. If I don't try to convince someone, what else can I do? Just surrender? No chance.

Behind her, a couple of hundred yards away, from high on the far canyon wall down which she had recently descended, something shrieked. It was not an entirely human cry—not that of any animal, either. The first shrill call was answered by a second, a third, and each shriek was clearly that of a different creature, for each was in a noticeably variant voice.

Chrissie halted on the steep trail, one hand against the deeply fissured bark of a pine, under a canopy of sweet-scented boughs. She looked back and listened as her pursuers simultaneously began to wail, an ululant cry reminiscent of the baying of a pack of coyotes . . . but stranger, more frightening. The sound was so cold, it penetrated her flesh and pierced like a needle to her marrow.

Their baying was probably a sign of their confidence: They were certain they would catch her, so they no longer needed to be quiet.

"What *are* you?" she whispered.

She suspected they could see as well as cats in the dark.

Could they smell her, as if they were dogs?

Her heart began to slam almost painfully within her breast.

Feeling vulnerable and alone, she turned from the puling hunters and scrambled up the trail toward the southern rim of the canyon.

chapter nine

At the foot of Ocean Avenue, Tessa Lockland walked through the empty parking lot and onto the public beach. The night breeze off the Pacific was just cranking up, faint but chilly enough that she was glad to be wearing slacks, a wool sweater, and her leather jacket.

She crossed the soft sand, toward the seaside shadows that lay beyond the radius of the glow from the last streetlamp, past a tall cypress growing on the beach and so radically shaped by ocean winds that it reminded her of an Erté sculpture, all curved lines and molten form. On the damp sand at the surf's edge, with the tide lapping at the strand inches from her shoes, Tessa stared westward. The partial moon was insufficient to light the vast, rolling main; all she could see were the nearest three lines of low, foam-crested breakers surging toward her from out of the gloom.

She tried to picture her sister standing on this deserted beach, washing down thirty or forty Valium capsules with a Diet Coke, then stripping naked and plunging into the cold sea. No. Not Janice.

With growing conviction that the authorities in Moonlight Cove were incompetent fools or liars, Tessa walked slowly south along the curving shoreline. In the pearly luminescence of the immature moon, she studied the sand, the widely separated cypresses farther back on the beach, and the time-worn formations of rock. She was not looking for physical clues that might tell her what had happened to Janice; those had been erased by wind and tide during the past three weeks. Instead, she was hoping that the very landscape itself and the elements of night—darkness, cool wind, and arabesques of pale but slowly thickening fog—would inspire her to develop a theory about what had *really* happened to Janice and an approach she might use to prove that theory.

She was a filmmaker specializing in industrials and documentaries of various kinds. When in doubt about the meaning and purpose of a project, she often found that immersion in a particular geographical locale could inspire narrative and thematic approaches to making a film about it. In the developmental stages of a new travel film, for instance, she often spent a couple of days casually strolling around a city like Singapore or Hong Kong or Rio, just absorbing details, which was more productive than thousands of hours of background reading and brainstorming, though of course the reading and brainstorming had to be a part of it too.

She had walked less than two hundred feet south along the beach, when she heard a shrill, haunting cry that halted her. The sound was distant, rising and falling, rising and falling, then fading.

Chilled more by that strange call than by the brisk October air, she wondered what she had heard. Although it had been partly a canine howl, she was certain it was not the voice of a dog. Though it was also marked by a feline whine and wail, she was equally certain it had not issued from a cat; no domestic cat could produce such volume, and to the best of her knowledge, no cougars roamed the coastal hills, certainly not in or near a town the size of Moonlight Cove.

Just as she was about to move on, the same uncanny cry cut the night again, and she was fairly sure it was coming from atop the bluff that overlooked the beach, farther south, where the lights of sea-facing houses were fewer than along the middle of the cove. This time the howl ended on a protracted and more guttural note, which might have been produced by a large dog, though she still felt it had to have come from some other creature. Someone living along the bluff must be keeping an exotic pet in a cage: a wolf, perhaps, or some big mountain cat not indigenous to the northern coast.

That explanation did not satisfy her, either, for there was some peculiarly familiar quality to the cry that she could not place, a quality not related to a wolf or mountain cat. She waited for another shriek, but it did not come.

Around her the darkness had deepened. The fog was clotting, and a lumpish cloud slid across half of the two-pointed moon.

She decided she could better absorb the details of the scene in the morning, and she turned back toward the mist-shrouded streetlamps at the bottom of Ocean Avenue. She didn't realize she was walking so fast—almost running—until she had left the shore, crossed the beach parking lot, and climbed half the first steep block of Ocean Avenue, at which point she became aware of her pace only because she suddenly heard her own labored breathing.

chapter ten

Thomas Shaddack drifted in a perfect blackness that was neither warm nor cool, where he seemed weightless, where he had ceased to feel any sensation against his skin, where he seemed limbless and without musculature or bones, where he seemed to have no physical substance whatsoever. A tenuous thread of thought linked him to his corporeal self, and in the dimmest reaches of his mind, he was still aware that he was a man—an Ichabod Crane of a man, six feet two, one hundred and sixty-five pounds, lean and bony, with a too-narrow face, a high brow, and brown eyes so light they were almost yellow.

He was also vaguely aware that he was nude and afloat in a state-of-the-art sensory-deprivation chamber, which looked somewhat like an old-fashioned iron lung but was four times larger. The single low-wattage bulb was not lit, and no light penetrated the shell of the tank. The pool in which Shaddack floated was a few feet deep, a ten-percent solution of magnesium sulfate in water for maximum buoyancy. Monitored by a computer—as was every element of that environment—the water cycled between ninety-three degrees Fahrenheit, the temperature at which a floating body was least affected by gravity, and ninety-eight degrees, at which the heat differential between human body temperature and surrounding fluid was marginal.

He suffered from no claustrophobia. A minute or two after he stepped into the tank and closed the hatch behind him, his sense of confinement entirely faded.

Deprived of sensory input—no sight, no sound, little or no taste, no olfactory stimulation, no sense of touch or weight or place or time—Shaddack let his mind break free of the dreary restraints of the flesh, soaring to previously unattainable heights of insight and exploring ideas of a complexity otherwise beyond his reach.

Even without the assistance of sensory deprivation, he was a genius. *Time* magazine had said he was, so it must be true. He had built New Wave Microtechnology from a struggling firm with initial capital of twenty thousand dollars to a three-hundred-million-a-year operation that conceived, researched, and developed cutting-edge microtechnology.

At the moment, however, Shaddack was making no effort to focus his mind on current research problems. He was using the tank strictly for recreational purposes, for the inducement of a specific vision that never failed to enthrall and excite him.

His vision:

Except for that thin thread of thought that tethered him to reality, he believed himself to be within a great, laboring machine, so immense that its dimensions could be ascertained no more easily than could those of the universe itself. It was the landscape of a dream but infinitely more textured and intense than a dream. Like an airborne mote within the eerily lit bowels of that colossal imaginary mechanism, he drifted past massive walls and interconnected columns of whirling drive shafts, rattling drive chains, myriad thrusting piston rods joined by sliding blocks to connecting rods that were in turn joined by crank wrists to well-greased cranks that turned flywheels of all dimensions. Servomotors hummed, compressors huffed, distributors sparked as electrical current flashed through millions of tangled wires to far reaches of the construct.

For Shaddack, the most exciting thing about this visionary world was the manner in which steel drive shafts and alloy pistons and hard rubber gaskets and aluminum cowlings were joined with organic parts to form a revolutionary entity possessed of two types of life: efficient mechanical animation and the throb of organic tissue. For pumps, the designer had employed glistening human hearts that pulsated tirelessly in that ancient lub-dub rhythm, joined by thick arteries to rubber tubing that snaked into the walls; some of them pumped blood to parts of the system that required organic lubrication, while others pumped high-viscosity oil. Incorporated into other sections of the infinite machine were tens of thousands of lung sacs functioning as bellows and filters; tendons and tumorlike excrescences of flesh were employed to join lengths of pipe and rubber hoses with more flexibility and surety of seal than could have been attained with ordinary nonorganic couplings.

Here was the best of organic and machine systems wedded in one perfect structure. As Thomas Shaddack imagined his way through the endless avenues of this dream place, he was enraptured even though he did not understand—or care—what ultimate function any of it had, what product or service it labored to bring forth. He was excited by the entity because it was clearly efficient at whatever it was doing, because its organic and inorganic parts were brilliantly integrated.

All of his life, for as many of his forty-one years as he could recall,

Shaddack had struggled against the limitations of the human condition, striving with all his will and heart to rise above the destiny of his species. He wanted to be more than merely a man. He wanted to have the power of a god and to shape not only his own future but that of all mankind. In his private sensory-deprivation chamber, transported by this vision of a cybernetic organism, he was closer to that longed-for metamorphosis than he could be in the real world, and that was what invigorated him.

For him the vision was not simply intellectually stimulating and emotionally moving, but powerfully erotic too. As he floated through that imaginary semiorganic machine, watching it throb and pulsate, he surrendered to an orgasm that he felt not merely in his genitals but in every fiber; indeed he was unaware of his fierce erection, unaware of the forceful ejaculations around which his entire body contracted, for he perceived the pleasure to be diffused throughout him rather than focused in his penis. Milky threads of semen spread through the dark pool of magnesium-sulfate solution.

A few minutes later the sensory-deprivation chamber's automatic timer activated the interior light and sounded a soft alarm. Shaddack was called back from his dream to the real world of Moonlight Cove.

chapter eleven

Chrissie Foster's eyes adjusted to the darkness, and she was able to find her way swiftly through even unfamiliar territory.

When she reached the rim of the canyon, she passed between a pair of Monterey cypresses and onto another mule-deer trail leading south through the forest. Protected from the wind by the surrounding trees, those enormous cypresses were lush and full, neither badly twisted nor marked by antlerlike branches as they were along the windswept shore. For a moment she considered climbing high into those leafy reaches, with the hope that her pursuers would pass beneath, unaware of her. But she dared not take that chance; if they smelled her or divined her presence by some other means, they would ascend, and she would be unable to retreat.

She hurried on and quickly reached a break in the trees. Beyond lay

a meadow that sloped from east to west, as did most of the land there-
about. The breeze picked up and was strong enough to ruffle her blond
hair continuously. The fog was not as thin as it had been when she'd left
Foster Stables on horseback, but the moonlight was still unfiltered
enough to frost the knee-high, dry grass that rippled when the wind blew.

As she ran across the field toward the next stand of woods, she saw
a large truck, strung with lights as if it were a Christmas tree, heading
south on the interstate, nearly a mile east of her, along the crest of the
second tier of coastal hills. She ruled out seeking help from anyone on
the distant freeway, for they were all strangers headed to faraway
places, therefore even less likely than locals to believe her. Besides, she
read newspapers and watched TV, so she had heard all about the serial
killers that roamed the interstates, and she had no trouble imagining
tabloid headlines summing up her fate: YOUNG GIRL KILLED AND EATEN
BY ROVING CANNIBALS IN DODGE VAN; SERVED WITH A SIDE OF BROC-
COLI AND PARSLEY FOR GARNISH; BONES USED FOR SOUP.

The county road lay half a mile closer, along the tops of the first
hills, but no traffic moved on it. In any case she already had rejected the
idea of seeking help there, for fear of encountering Tucker in his Honda.

Of course she believed that she had heard three distinct voices
among the eerie pulings of those who stalked her, which had to mean
that Tucker had abandoned his car and was with her parents now.
Maybe she could safely head toward the county highway, after all.

She thought about that as she sprinted across the meadow. But before she had made up her mind to change course, those dreadful cries
rose behind her again, still in the woods but closer than before. Two or
three voices yowled simultaneously, as if a pack of baying hounds was
at her heels, though stranger and more savage than ordinary dogs.

Abruptly Chrissie stepped into thin air and found herself falling into
what, for an instant, seemed to be a terrible chasm. But it was only an
eight-foot-wide, six-foot-deep drainage channel that cleaved the meadow,
and she rolled to the bottom of it unharmed.

The angry shrieking of her pursuers grew louder, nearer, and now
their voices had a more frenetic quality . . . a note of need, of hunger.

She scrambled to her feet and started to clamber up the six-foot
wall of the channel, when she realized that to her left, upslope, the ditch
terminated in a large culvert that bored away into the earth. She froze
halfway up the arroyo and considered this new option.

The pale concrete pipe offered the lambent moonlight just enough
of a reflective surface to be visible. When she saw it, she knew immediately that it was the main drainage line that carried rainwater off the
interstate and county road far above and east of her. Judging by the

shrill cries of the hunters, her lead was dwindling. She was increasingly afraid that she would not make the trees at the far side of the meadow before being brought down. Perhaps the culvert was a dead end and would provide her with a haven no more secure than the cypress that she had considered climbing, but she decided to risk it.

She slid to the floor of the arroyo again and scurried to the conduit. The pipe was four feet in diameter. By stooping slightly she was able to walk into it. She went only a few steps, however, before she was halted by a stench so foul that she gagged.

Something was dead and rotting in that lightless passage. She could not see what it was. But maybe she was better off not seeing; the carcass might look worse than it smelled. A wild animal, sick and dying, must have crawled into the pipe for shelter, where it perished from its disease.

She backed hastily out of the drain, drawing deep breaths of the fresh night air.

From the north came intermingled, ululant wails that literally put the hair up on the back of her neck.

They were closing fast, almost on top of her.

She had no choice but to hide deep in the culvert and hope they could not catch her scent. She suddenly realized that the decaying animal might be to her benefit, for if those stalking her *were* able to smell her as though they were hounds, the stench of decomposition might mask her own odor.

Entering the pitch-black culvert again, she followed the convex floor, which sloped gradually upward beneath the meadow. Within ten yards she put her foot in something soft and slippery. The horrid odor of decay burst upon her with even greater strength, and she knew she had stepped in the dead thing.

"Oh, yuck."

She gagged and felt her gorge rise, but she gritted her teeth and *refused* to throw up. When she was past the putrid mass, she paused to scrape her shoes on the concrete floor of the pipe.

Then she hurried farther into the drain. Scurrying with her knees bent, shoulders hunched, and head tucked down, she realized she must have looked like a troll scuttling into its secret burrow.

Fifty or sixty feet past the unidentified dead thing, Chrissie stopped, crouched, and turned to look back toward the mouth of the culvert. Through that circular aperture she had a view of the ditch in moonlight, and she could see more than she had expected because, by contrast with the darkness of the drain, the night beyond seemed brighter than when she had been out there.

All was silent.

A gentle breeze flowed down the pipe from drainage grilles in the highways above and to the east, pushing the odor of the decomposing animal away from her, so she could not detect even a trace of it. The air was tainted only by a mild dankness, a whiff of mildew.

Silence gripped the night.

She held her breath for a moment and listened intently.

Nothing.

Still crouching, she shifted her weight from foot to foot.

Silence.

She wondered if she should head deeper into the culvert. Then she wondered whether snakes were in the pipe. Wouldn't that be a perfect place for snakes to nest when the oncoming night's cool air drove them to shelter?

Silence.

Where were her parents? Tucker? A minute ago they had been close behind her, within striking distance.

Silence.

Rattlesnakes were common in the coastal hills, though not active at this time of year. If a nest of rattlers—

She was so unnerved by the continuing, unnatural silence that she had the urge to scream, just to break that eerie spell.

A shrill cry shattered the quietude outside. It echoed through the concrete tunnel, past Chrissie, and bounced from wall to wall along the passage behind her, as if the hunters were approaching her not only from outside but from the depths of the earth behind her.

Shadowy figures leaped into the arroyo beyond the culvert.

chapter twelve

Sam found a Mexican restaurant on Serra Street, two blocks from his motel. One sniff of the air inside the place was enough to assure him the food would be good. That mélange was the odiferous equivalent of a José Feliciano album: chili powder, bubbling hot *chorizo*, the sweet fragrance of tortillas made with *masa harina*, cilantro, bell peppers, the astringent tang of jalapeño chiles, onions. . . .

The Perez Family Restaurant was as unpretentious as its name, a single rectangular room with blue vinyl booths along the side walls, tables in the middle, kitchen at the rear. Unlike Burt Peckham at Knight's Bridge Tavern, the Perez family had as much business as they could handle. Except for a two-chair table at the back, to which Sam was led by the teenage hostess, the restaurant was filled to capacity.

The waiters and waitresses were dressed casually in jeans and sweaters, the only nod to a uniform being white half-aprons tied around their waists. Sam didn't even ask for Guinness, which he had never found in a Mexican restaurant, but they had Corona, which would be fine if the food was good.

The food was *very* good. Not truly, unequivocably great, but better than he had a right to expect in a northern coastal town of just three thousand people. The corn chips were homemade, the salsa thick and chunky, the *albóndigas* soup rich and sufficiently peppery to break him out in a light sweat. By the time he received an order of crab enchiladas in tomatillo sauce, he was half convinced that he *should* move to Moonlight Cove as soon as possible, even if it meant robbing a bank to finance early retirement.

When he got over his surprise at the food's quality, he began to pay as much attention to his fellow diners as to the contents of his plate. Gradually he noted several odd things about them.

The room was unusually quiet, considering that it was occupied by eighty or ninety people. High-quality Mexican restaurants—with fine food, good beer, and potent margaritas—were festive places. At Perez's, however, diners were talking animatedly at only about a third of the tables. The other two-thirds of the customers ate in silence.

After he tilted his glass and poured from the fresh bottle of Corona that had just been served to him, Sam studied some of the silent eaters. Three middle-aged men sat in a booth on the right side of the room, scarfing up tacos and enchiladas and chimichangas, staring at their food or at the air in front of them, occasionally looking at each other but exchanging not a word. On the other side of the room, in another booth, two teenage couples industriously devoured a double platter of mixed appetizers, never punctuating the meal with the chatter and laughter one expected of kids their age. Their concentration was so intense that the longer Sam watched them, the odder they seemed.

Throughout the room, people of all ages, in groups of all kinds, were fixated on their food. Hearty eaters, they had appetizers, soup, salads, and side dishes as well as entrees; on finishing, some ordered "a couple more tacos" or "another burrito," before also asking for ice cream or flan. Their jaw muscles bulged as they chewed, and as soon as they swallowed, they quickly shoveled more into their mouths. A few ate with their mouths open. Some swallowed with such force that Sam could actually hear them. They were red-faced and perspiring, no doubt from jalapeño-spiced sauces, but not one offered a comment like, "Boy, this is hot," or "Pretty good grub," or even the most elementary conversational gambit to his companions.

To the third of the customers who were happily jabbering away at one another and progressing through their meals at an ordinary pace, the almost fevered eating of the majority apparently went unnoticed. Bad table manners were not rare, of course; at least a quarter of the diners in any town would give Miss Manners a stroke if she dared to eat with them. Nevertheless, the gluttony of many of the customers in the Perez Family Restaurant seemed astonishing to Sam. He supposed that the polite diners were inured to the behavior of the other patrons because they had witnessed it so many times before.

Could the cool sea air of the northern coast be *that* appetite-enhancing? Did some peculiar ethnic background or fractured social history in Moonlight Cove mitigate against the universal development of commonly accepted Western table manners?

What he saw in the Perez Family Restaurant seemed a puzzle for which any sociologist, desperately seeking a doctoral thesis subject, would be eager to find a solution. After a while, however, Sam had to turn his attention away from the more ravenous patrons because their behavior was killing his own appetite.

Later, when he was figuring the tip and putting money on the table to cover his bill, he surveyed the crowd again, and this time realized that none of the heavy eaters was drinking beer, margaritas, or anything alcoholic. They had ice water or Cokes, and some were drinking milk, glass after glass, but every last man and woman of these gourmands seemed to be a teetotaler. He might not have noticed their temperance if he had not been a cop—and a good one—trained not only to observe but to think about what he observed.

He remembered the scarcity of drinkers at Knight's Bridge Tavern.

What ethnic culture or religious group inculcated a disdain for alcohol while encouraging mannerlessness and gluttony?

He could think of none.

By the time Sam finished his beer and got up to leave, he was telling himself that he'd overreacted to a few crude people, that this queer fixation on food was limited to a handful of patrons and not as widespread as it seemed. After all, from his table in the back, he had not been able to see the entire room and every last one of the customers. But on his way out, he passed a table where three attractive and well-dressed young women were eating hungrily, none of them speaking, their eyes glazed; two of them had flecks of food on their chins, of which they seemed oblivious, and the third had so many corn-chip crumbs sprinkled across the front of her royal-blue sweater that she appeared to be breading herself with the intention of going into the kitchen, climbing into an oven, and *becoming* food.

He was glad to get out in the clean night air.

Sweating both from the chili-spiced dishes and the heat in the restaurant, he had wanted to take his jacket off, but he had not been able to do so because of the gun he was packing in a shoulder holster. Now he relished the chilling fog that was being harried eastward by a gentle but steady breeze.

chapter thirteen

Chrissie saw them enter the drainage channel, and for a moment she thought they were all going to clamber up the far side of it and off across the meadow in the direction she had been heading. Then one of them turned toward the mouth of the culvert. The figure approached the drain on all fours, in a few stealthy and sinuous strides. Though Chrissie could see nothing more of it than a shadowy shape, she had trouble believing that this thing was either one of her parents or the man called Tucker. But who else could it be?

Entering the concrete tunnel, the predator peered forward into the gloom. Its eyes shone softly amber-green, not as bright here as in moonlight, dimmer than glow-in-the-dark paint, but vaguely radiant.

Chrissie wondered how well it could see in absolute darkness. Surely its gaze could not penetrate eighty or a hundred feet of lightless pipe to the place where she crouched. Vision of that caliber would be supernatural.

It stared straight at her.

Then again, who was to say that what she was dealing with here was not supernatural? Perhaps her parents had become . . . werewolves.

She was soaked in sour sweat. She hoped the stench of the dead animal would screen her body odor.

Rising from all fours into a crouch, blocking most of the silvery moonlight at the drain entrance, the stalker slowly came forward.

Its heavy breathing was amplified by the curved concrete walls of the culvert. Chrissie breathed shallowly through her open mouth lest she reveal her presence.

Suddenly, only ten feet into the tunnel, the stalker spoke in a raspy, whispery voice and with such urgency that the words were almost run together in a single long string of syllables: *"Chrissie, you there, you, you? Come me, Chrissie, come me, come, want you, want, want, need, my Chrissie, my Chrissie."*

That bizarre, frantic voice gave rise in Chrissie's mind to a terrifying image of a creature that was part lizard, part wolf, part human, part something unidentifiable. Yet she suspected that its actual appearance was even worse than anything she could imagine.

"Help you, want help you, help, now, come me, come, come. You there, there, you there?"

The worst thing about the voice was that, in spite of its cold hoarse note and whispery tone, in spite of its alienness, it was familiar. Chrissie recognized it as her mother's. Changed, yes, but her mother's voice just the same.

Chrissie's stomach was cramped with fear, but she was filled with another pain, too, that for a moment she could not identify. Then she realized that she ached with loss; she missed her mother, wanted her mother back, her *real* mother. If she'd had one of those ornate silver crucifixes like they always used in the fright films, she probably would have revealed herself, advanced on this hateful thing, and demanded that it surrender possession of her mother. A crucifix probably would not work because nothing in real life was as easy as in the movies; besides, whatever had happened to her parents was far stranger than vampires and werewolves and demons jumped up from hell. But if she'd had a crucifix, she would have tried it anyway.

"Death, death, smell death, stink, death . . ."

The mother-thing quickly advanced into the tunnel until it came to the place where Chrissie had stepped in a slippery, putrefying mass. The brightness of the shining eyes was directly related to the nearness of moonlight, for now they dimmed. Then the creature lowered its gaze to the dead animal on the culvert floor.

From beyond the mouth of the drain came the sound of something descending into the ditch. Footfalls and the clatter of stones were followed by another voice, equally as fearsome as that of the stalker now hunched over the dead animal. Calling into the pipe, it said, *"She there, there, she? What found, what, what?"*

"*. . . raccoon . . .*"

"*What, what it, what?*"

"*Dead raccoon, rotten, maggots, maggots,*" the first one said.

Chrissie was stricken by the macabre fear that she had left a tennis-shoe imprint in the rotting muck of the dead raccoon.

"*Chrissie?*" the second asked as it ventured into the culvert.

Tucker's voice. Evidently her father was searching for her across the meadow or in the next section of the forest.

Both stalkers were fidgeting constantly. Chrissie could hear them scraping—claws?—against the concrete floor of the pipe. Both sounded panicky too. No, not panicky, really, because no fear was audible in their voices. Frantic. Frenzied. It was as if an engine in each of them was racing faster, faster, almost out of control.

"*Chrissie there, she there, she?*" Tucker asked.

The mother-thing raised its gaze from the dead raccoon and peered straight at Chrissie through the lightless tunnel.

You can't see me, Chrissie thought-prayed. I'm invisible.

The radiance of the stalker's eyes had faded to twin spots of tarnished silver.

Chrissie held her breath.

Tucker said, "*Got to eat, eat, want eat.*"

The creature that had been her mother said, "*Find girl, girl, find her first, then eat, then.*"

They sounded as if they were wild animals magically gifted with crude speech.

"*Now, now, burning it up, eat now, now, burning,*" Tucker said urgently, insistently.

Chrissie was shaking so badly that she was half afraid they would hear the shudders that rattled her.

Tucker said, "*Burning it up, little animals in meadow, hear them, smell them, track, eat, eat, now.*"

Chrissie held her breath.

"*Nothing here,*" the mother-thing said. "*Only maggots, stink, go, eat, then find her, eat, eat, then find her, go.*"

Both stalkers retreated from the culvert and vanished.

Chrissie dared to breathe.

After waiting a minute to be sure they were really gone, she turned and troll-walked deeper into the upsloping culvert, blindly feeling the walls as she went, hunting a side passage. She must have gone two hundred yards before she found what she wanted: a tributary drain, half the size of the main line. She slid into it, feetfirst and on her back, then squirmed onto her belly and faced out toward the bigger tunnel. That was where she would spend the night. If they returned to the culvert to see if they could detect her scent in the cleaner air beyond the decomposing raccoon, she would be out of the downdraught that swept the main line, and they might not smell her.

She was heartened because their failure to probe deeper into the culvert was proof that they were not possessed of supernatural powers, neither all-seeing nor all-knowing. They were abnormally strong and quick, strange and terrifying, but they could make mistakes too. She began to think that when daylight came she had a fifty-fifty chance of getting out of the woods and finding help before she was caught.

chapter fourteen

In the lights outside of the Perez Family Restaurant, Sam Booker checked his watch. Only 7:10.

He went for a walk along Ocean Avenue, building up the courage to call Scott in Los Angeles. The prospect of that conversation with his son soon preoccupied him and drove all thoughts of the mannerless, gluttonous diners out of his mind.

At 7:30, he stopped at a telephone booth near a Shell service station at the corner of Juniper Lane and Ocean Avenue. He used his credit card to make a long-distance call to his house in Sherman Oaks.

At sixteen Scott thought he was mature enough to be home alone when his father was away on an assignment. Sam did not entirely agree and preferred that the boy stay with his Aunt Edna. But Scott won his way by making life pure hell for Edna, so Sam was reluctant to put her through that ordeal.

He had repeatedly drilled the boy in safety procedures—keep all doors and windows locked; know where the fire extinguishers are; know how to get out of the house from any room in an earthquake or other emergency—and had taught him how to use a handgun. In Sam's judgment Scott was still too immature to be home alone for days at a time; but at least the boy was well prepared for every contingency.

The number rang nine times. Sam was about to hang up, guiltily relieved that he'd failed to get through, when Scott finally answered.

"Hello."

"It's me, Scott. Dad."

"Yeah?"

Heavy-metal rock was playing at high volume in the background. He was probably in his room, his stereo cranked up so loud that the windows shook.

Sam said, "Could you turn the music down?"

"I can hear you," Scott mumbled.

"Maybe so, but I'm having trouble hearing you."

"I don't have anything to say, anyway."

"Please turn it down," Sam said, with emphasis on the "please."

Scott dropped the receiver, which clattered on his nightstand. The sharp sound hurt Sam's ear. The boy lowered the volume on the stereo but only slightly. He picked up the phone and said, "Yeah?"

"How're you doing?"

"Okay."

"Everything all right there?"

"Why shouldn't it be?"

"I just asked."

Sullenly: "If you called to see if I'm having a party, don't worry. I'm not."

Sam counted to three, giving himself time to keep his voice under control. Thickening fog swirled past the glass-walled phone booth. "How was school today?"

"You think I didn't go?"

"I know you went."

"You don't trust me."

"I trust you," Sam lied.

"You think I didn't go."

"Did you?"

"Yeah."

"So how was it?"

"Ridiculous. The same old shit."

"Scott, please, you know I've asked you not to use that kind of language when you're talking to me," Sam said, realizing that he was being forced into a confrontation against his will.

"So sorry. Same old *poop*," Scott said in such a way that he might have been referring either to the day at school or to Sam.

"It's pretty country up here," Sam said.

The boy did not reply.

"Wooded hillsides slope right down to the ocean."

"So?"

Following the advice of the family counselor whom he and Scott had been seeing both together and separately, Sam clenched his teeth, counted to three again, and tried another approach. "Did you have dinner yet?"

"Yeah."

"Do your homework?"

"Don't have any."

Sam hesitated, then decided to let it pass. The counselor, Dr. Adamski, would have been proud of such tolerance and cool self-control.

Beyond the phone booth, the Shell station's lights acquired multiple halos, and the town faded into the slowly congealing mist.

At last Sam said, "What're you doing this evening?"

"I *was* listening to music."

Sometimes it seemed to Sam that the music was part of what had turned the boy sour. That pounding, frenetic, unmelodic heavy-metal rock was a collection of monotonous chords and even more monotonous atonal riffs, so soul-less and mind-numbing that it might have been the music produced by a civilization of intelligent machines long after man had passed from the face of the earth. After a while Scott had lost interest in most heavy-metal bands and switched allegiance to U2, but their simplistic social consciousness was no match for nihilism. Soon he grew interested in heavy-metal again, but the second time around he focused on black metal, those bands espousing—or using dramatic trappings of—satanism; he became increasingly self-involved, antisocial, and somber. On more than one occasion, Sam had considered confiscating the kid's record collection, smashing it to bits, and disposing of it, but that seemed an absurd overreaction. After all, Sam himself had been sixteen when the Beatles and Rolling Stones were coming on the scene, and his parents had railed against *that* music and predicted it would lead Sam and his entire generation into perdition. He'd turned out all right in spite of John, Paul, George, Ringo, and the Stones. He was the product of an unparalleled age of tolerance, and he did not want his mind to close up as tight as his parents' minds had been.

"Well, I guess I better go," Sam said.

The boy was silent.

"If any unexpected problems come up, you call your Aunt Edna."

"There's nothing *she* could do for me that I couldn't do myself."

"She loves you, Scott."

"Yeah, sure."

"She's your mother's sister; she'd like to love you as if you were her own. All you have to do is give her the chance." After more silence, Sam took a deep breath and said, "I love you, too, Scott."

"Yeah? What's that supposed to do—turn me all gooey inside?"

"No."

"'Cause it doesn't."

"I was just stating a fact."

Apparently quoting from one of his favorite songs, the boy said:

> *"Nothing lasts forever;*
> *even love's a lie,*
> *a tool for manipulation;*
> *there's no God beyond the sky."*

Click.

Sam stood for a moment, listening to the dial tone. "Perfect." He returned the receiver to its cradle.

His frustration was exceeded only by his fury. He wanted to kick the shit out of something, anything, and pretend that he was savaging whoever or whatever had stolen his son from him.

He also had an empty, achy feeling in the pit of his stomach, because he *did* love Scott. The boy's alienation was devastating.

He knew he could not go back to the motel yet. He was not ready to sleep, and the prospect of spending a couple of hours in front of the idiot box, watching mindless sitcoms and dramas, was intolerable.

When he opened the phone-booth door, tendrils of fog slipped inside and seemed to pull him out into the night. For an hour he walked the streets of Moonlight Cove, deep into the residential neighborhoods, where there were no streetlamps and where trees and houses seemed to float within the mist, as if they were not rooted to the earth but tenuously tethered and in danger of breaking loose.

Four blocks north of Ocean Avenue, on Iceberry Way, as Sam walked briskly, letting the exertion and the chilly night air leech the anger from him, he heard hurried footsteps. Someone running. Three people, maybe four. It was an unmistakable sound, though curiously stealthy, not the straightforward slap-slap-slap of joggers' approach.

He turned and looked back along the gloom-enfolded street.

The footsteps ceased.

Because the partial moon had been engulfed by clouds, the scene was brightened mostly by light fanning from the windows of Bavarian-, Monterey-, English-, and Spanish-style houses nestled among pines and junipers on both sides of the street. The neighborhood was long-established, with great character, but the lack of big-windowed modern homes contributed to the murkiness. Two properties in that block had hooded, downcast Malibu landscape lighting, and a few had carriage lamps at the ends of front walks, but the fog damped those pockets of illumination. As far as Sam could see, he was alone on Iceberry Way.

He began to walk again but went less than half a block before he heard the hurried footfalls. He swung around, but as before saw no one. This time the sound faded, as though the runners had moved off a paved surface onto soft earth, then between two of the houses.

Perhaps they were on another street. Cold air and fog could play tricks with sound.

He was cautious and intrigued, however, and he quietly stepped off the cracked and root-canted sidewalk, onto someone's front lawn, into the smooth blackness beneath an immense cypress. He studied the neighborhood, and within half a minute he saw furtive movement on the west side of the street. Four shadowy figures appeared at the corner of a house, running low, in a crouch. When they crossed a lawn that was patchily illuminated by a pair of hurricane lamps on iron poles, their freakishly distorted shadows leaped wildly over the front of a white stucco house. They went to ground again in dense shrubbery before he could ascertain their size or anything else about them.

Kids, Sam thought, and they're up to no good.

He didn't know why he was so sure they were kids, perhaps because neither their quickness nor behavior was that of adults. They were either engaged on some prank against a disliked neighbor—or they were after Sam. Instinct told him that he was being stalked.

Were juvenile delinquents a problem in a community as small and closely knit as Moonlight Cove?

Every town had a few bad kids. But in the semirural atmosphere of a place like this, juvenile crime rarely included gang activities like assault and battery, armed robbery, mugging, or thrill killing. In the country, kids got into trouble with fast cars, booze, girls, and a little unsophisticated theft, but they did not prowl the streets in packs the way their counterparts did in the inner cities.

Nevertheless, Sam was suspicious of the quartet that crouched, invisible, among shadow-draped ferns and azaleas, across the street and three houses west of him. After all, something was wrong in Moonlight Cove, and conceivably the trouble was related to juvenile delinquents. The police were concealing the truth about several deaths in the past couple of months, and perhaps they were protecting someone; as unlikely as it seemed, maybe they were covering for a few kids from prominent families, kids who had taken the privileges of class too far and had gone beyond permissible, civilized behavior.

Sam was not afraid of them. He knew how to handle himself, and he was carrying a .38. Actually he would have enjoyed teaching the brats a lesson. But a confrontation with a group of teenage hoods would mean a subsequent scene with the local police, and he preferred not to bring himself to the attention of the authorities, for fear of jeopardizing his investigation.

He thought it peculiar that they would consider assaulting him in a residential neighborhood like this. One shout of alarm from him would bring people to their front porches to see what was happening. Of course, because he wanted to avoid calling even that much notice to himself, he would not cry out.

The old adage about discretion being the better part of valor was in no circumstance more applicable than in his. He moved back from the cypress under which he had taken shelter, away from the street and toward the lightless house behind him. Confident that those kids were not sure where he had gone, he planned to slip out of the neighborhood and lose them altogether.

He reached the house, hurried alongside it, and entered a rear yard, where a looming swing set was so distorted by shadows and mist that it looked like a giant spider stilting toward him through the gloom. At the end of the yard he vaulted a rail fence, beyond which was a narrow alley that serviced the block's detached garages. He intended to go south, back toward Ocean Avenue and the heart of town, but a shiver of prescience shook him toward another route. Stepping straight across the narrow back street, past a row of metal garbage cans, he vaulted another low fence, landing on the back lawn of another house that faced out on the street parallel to Iceberry Way.

No sooner had he left the alley than he heard soft, running footsteps on that hard surface. The juvies—if that's what they were—sounded as swift but not quite as stealthy as they had been.

They were coming in Sam's direction from the end of the block. He had the odd feeling that with some sixth sense they would be able to determine which yard he had gone into and that they would be on him before he could reach the next street. Instinct told him to stop running and go to ground. He was in good shape, yes, but he was forty-two, and they were no doubt seventeen or younger, and any middle-aged man who believed he could outrun kids was a fool.

Instead of sprinting across the new yard, he moved swiftly to a side door on the nearby clapboard garage, hoping it would be unlocked. It was. He stepped into total darkness and pulled the door shut, just as he heard four pursuers halt in the alleyway in front of the big roll-up door at the other end of the building. They had stopped there not because they knew where he was, but probably because they were trying to decide which way he might have gone.

In tomblike blackness Sam fumbled for a lock button or dead-bolt latch to secure the door by which he had entered. He found nothing.

He heard the four kids murmuring to one another, but he could not make out what they were saying. Their voices sounded strange: whispery and urgent.

Sam remained at the smaller door. He gripped the knob with both hands to keep it from turning, in case the kids searched around the garage and gave it a try.

They fell silent.

He listened intently.

Nothing.

The cold air smelled of grease and dust. He could see nothing, but he assumed a car or two occupied that space.

Although he was not afraid, he was beginning to feel foolish. How had he gotten himself into this predicament? He was a grown man, an FBI agent trained in a variety of self-defense techniques, carrying a revolver with which he possessed considerable expertise, yet he was hiding in a garage from four kids. He had gotten there because he had acted instinctively, and he usually trusted instinct implicitly but this was—

He heard furtive movement along the outer wall of the garage. He tensed. Scraping footsteps. Approaching the small door at which he stood. As far as Sam could tell, he was hearing only one of the kids.

Leaning back, holding the knob in both hands, Sam pulled the door tight against the jamb.

The footsteps stopped in front of him.

He held his breath.

A second ticked by, two seconds, three.

Try the damn lock and move on, Sam thought irritably.

He was feeling more foolish by the second and was on the verge of confronting the kid. He could pop out of the garage as if he were a jack-in-the-box, probably scare the hell out of the punk, and send him screaming into the night.

Then he heard a voice on the other side of the door, inches from him, and although he did not know what in God's name he was hearing, he knew at once that he had been wise to trust to instinct, wise to go to ground and hide. The voice was thin, raspy, utterly chilling, and the urgent cadences of the speech were those of a frenzied psychotic or a junkie long overdue for a fix:

"Burning, need, need . . ."

He seemed to be talking to himself and was perhaps unconscious of speaking, as a man in a fever might babble deliriously.

A hard object scraped down the outside of the wooden door. Sam tried to imagine what it was.

"*Feed the fire, fire, feed it, feed,*" the kid said in a thin, frantic voice that was partly a whisper and partly a whine and partly a low and menacing growl. It was not much like the voice of any teenager Sam had ever heard—or any adult, for that matter.

In spite of the cold air, his brow was covered with sweat.

The unknown object scraped down the door again.

Was the kid armed? Was it a gun barrel being drawn along the wood? The blade of a knife? Just a stick?

"*. . . burning, burning . . .*"

A claw?

That was a crazy idea. Yet he could not shake it. In his mind was the clear image of a sharp and hornlike claw—a talon—gouging splinters from the door as it carved a line in the wood.

Sam held tightly to the knob. Sweat trickled down his temples.

At last the kid tried the door. The knob twisted in Sam's grip, but he would not let it move much.

"*. . . oh, God, it burns, hurts, oh God . . .*"

Sam was finally afraid. The kid sounded so damned weird. Like a PCP junkie flying out past the orbit of Mars somewhere, only worse than that, far stranger and more dangerous than any angel-dust freak. Sam was scared because he didn't know what the hell he was up against.

The kid tried to pull the door open.

Sam held it tight against the jamb.

Quick, frenetic words: "*. . . feed the fire, feed the fire . . .*"

I wonder if he can smell me in here? Sam thought, and under the circumstances that bizarre idea seemed no crazier than the image of the kid with claws.

Sam's heart was hammering. Stinging perspiration seeped into the corners of his eyes. The muscles in his neck, shoulders, and arms ached fiercely; he was straining much harder than necessary to keep the door shut.

After a moment, apparently deciding that his quarry was not in the garage after all, the kid gave up. He ran along the side of the building, back toward the alley. As he hurried away, a barely audible keening issued from him; it was a sound of pain, need . . . and animal excitement. He was struggling to contain that low cry, but it escaped him anyway.

Sam heard cat-soft footsteps approaching from several directions. The other three would-be muggers rejoined the kid in the alley, and their whispery voices were filled with the same frenzy that had marked his, though they were too far away now for Sam to hear what they were saying. Abruptly, they fell silent and, a moment later, as if they were members of a wolfpack responding instinctively to the scent of game or danger, they ran as one along the alleyway, heading north. Soon their sly footsteps faded, and again the night was grave-still.

For several minutes after the pack left, Sam stood in the dark garage, holding fast to the doorknob.

chapter fifteen

The dead boy was sprawled in an open drainage ditch along the county road on the southeast side of Moonlight Cove. His frost-white face was spotted with blood. In the glare of the two tripod-mounted police lamps flanking the ditch, his wide eyes stared unblinkingly at a shore immeasurably more distant than the nearby Pacific.

Standing by one of the hooded lamps, Loman Watkins looked down at the small corpse, forcing himself to bear witness to the death of Eddie Valdoski because Eddie, only eight years old, was his godson. Loman had gone to high school with Eddie's father, George, and in a strictly platonic sense he had been in love with Eddie's mother, Nella, for almost twenty years. Eddie had been a great kid, bright and inquisitive and well behaved. Had been. But now . . . Hideously bruised, savagely bitten, scratched and torn, neck broken, the boy was little more than a pile of decomposing trash, his promising potential destroyed, his flame snuffed, deprived of life—and life of him.

Of the innumerable terrible things Loman had encountered in twenty-one years of police work, this was perhaps the worst. And because of his personal relationship with the victim, he should have been deeply shaken if not devastated. Yet he was barely affected by the sight of the small, battered body. Sadness, regret, anger, and a flurry of other emotions touched him, but only lightly and briefly, the way unseen fish might brush past a swimmer in a dark sea. Of grief, which should have pierced him like nails, he felt nothing.

Barry Sholnick, one of the new officers on the recently expanded

Moonlight Cove police force, straddled the ditch, one foot on each bank, and took a photograph of Eddie Valdoski. For an instant the boy's glazed eyes were silvery with a reflection of the flash.

Loman's growing inability to *feel* was, strangely, the one thing that evoked strong feelings: It scared the shit out of him. Lately he was increasingly frightened by his emotional detachment, an unwanted but apparently irreversible hardening of the heart that would soon leave him with auricles of marble and ventricles of common stone.

He was one of the New People now, different in many ways from the man he had once been. He still looked the same—five-ten, squarely built, with a broad and remarkably innocent face for a man in his line of work—but he wasn't only what he appeared to be. Perhaps a greater control of emotions, a more stable and analytical outlook, was an unanticipated benefit of the Change. But was that really beneficial? Not to feel? Not to grieve?

Though the night was chilly, sour sweat broke out on his face, the back of his neck, and under his arms.

Dr. Ian Fitzgerald, the coroner, was busy elsewhere, but Victor Callan, owner of Callan's Funeral Home and the assistant coroner, was helping another officer, Jules Timmerman, scour the ground between the ditch and the nearby woods. They were looking for clues that the killer might have left behind.

Actually they were just putting on a show for the benefit of the score of area residents who had gathered on the far side of the road. Even if clues were found, no one would be arrested for the crime. No trial would ever take place. If they found Eddie's killer, they would cover for him and deal with him in their own way, in order to conceal the existence of the New People from those who had not yet undergone the Change. Because without doubt the killer was what Thomas Shaddack called a "regressive," one of the New People gone bad. Very bad.

Loman turned away from the dead boy. He walked back along the county road, toward the Valdoski house, which was a few hundred yards north and veiled in mist.

He ignored the onlookers, although one of them called to him: "Chief? What the hell's going on, Chief?"

This was a semirural area barely within the town limits. The houses were widely separated, and their scattered lights did little to hold back the night. Before he was halfway to the Valdoski place, though he was within hailing distance of the men at the crime scene, he felt isolated. Trees, tortured by ages of sea wind on nights far less calm than this one, bent toward the two-lane road, their scraggly branches overhanging the gravel shoulder on which he walked. He kept imagining movement in the dark boughs above him, and in the blackness and fog between the twisted trunks of the trees.

He put his hand on the butt of the revolver that was holstered at his side.

Loman Watkins had been the chief of police in Moonlight Cove for nine years, and in the past month more blood had been spilled in his jurisdiction than in the entire preceding eight years and eleven months. He was convinced that worse was coming. He had a hunch that the regressives were more numerous and more of a problem than Shaddack realized—or was willing to admit.

He feared the regressives almost as much as he feared his own new, cool, dispassionate perspective.

Unlike happiness and grief and joy and sorrow, stark fear was a survival mechanism, so perhaps he would not lose touch with it as thoroughly as he was losing touch with other emotions. That thought made him as uneasy as did the phantom movement in the trees.

Is fear, he wondered, the only emotion that will thrive in this brave new world we're making?

chapter sixteen

After a greasy cheeseburger, soggy fries, and an icy bottle of Dos Equis in the deserted coffee shop at Cove Lodge, Tessa Lockland returned to her room, propped herself up in bed with pillows, and called her mother in San Diego. Marion answered the phone on the first ring, and Tessa said, "Hi, Mom."

"Where are you, Teejay?" As a kid, Tessa could never decide whether she wanted to be called by her first name or her middle, Jane, so her mother always called her by her initials, as if that were a name in itself.

"Cove Lodge," Tessa said.

"Is it nice?"

"It's the best I could find. This isn't a town that worries about having first-rate tourist facilities. If it didn't have such a spectacular view, Cove Lodge is one of those places that would be able to survive only by showing closed-circuit porn movies on the TV and renting rooms by the hour."

"Is it clean?"

"Reasonably."

"If it wasn't clean, I'd insist you move out right now."

"Mom, when I'm on location, shooting a film, I don't always have luxury accommodations, you know. When I did that documentary on the Miskito Indians in Central America, I went on hunts with them and slept in the mud."

"Teejay, dear, you must never tell people that you slept in the mud. Pigs sleep in the mud. You must say you roughed it or camped out, but never that you slept in the mud. Even unpleasant experiences can be worthwhile if one keeps one's sense of dignity and style."

"Yes, Mom, I know. My point was that Cove Lodge isn't great, but it's better than sleeping in the mud."

"Camping out."

"Better than camping out," Tessa said.

Both were silent a moment. Then Marion said, "Dammit, I should be there with you."

"Mom, you've got a broken leg."

"I should have gone to Moonlight Cove as soon as I heard they'd found poor Janice. If I'd been there, they wouldn't have cremated the body. By God, they wouldn't! I'd have stopped that, and I'd have arranged another autopsy by *trustworthy* authorities, and now there'd be no need for you to get involved. I'm so angry with myself."

Tessa slumped back in the pillows and sighed. "Mom, don't do this to yourself. You broke your leg three days before Janice's body was even found. You can't travel easily now, and you couldn't travel easily then, either. It's not your fault."

"There was a time when a broken leg couldn't have stopped me."

"You're not twenty any more, Mom."

"Yes, I know, I'm old," Marion said miserably. "Sometimes I think about how old I am, and it's scary."

"You're only sixty-four, you look not a day past fifty, and you broke your leg skydiving, for God's sake, so you're not going to get any pity from me."

"Comfort and pity is what an elderly parent expects from a good daughter."

"If you caught me calling you elderly or treating you with pity, you'd kick my ass halfway to China."

"The chance to kick a daughter's ass now and then is one of the pleasures of a mother's later life, Teejay. Damn, where did that tree come from, anyway? I've been skydiving for thirty years, and I've never landed in a tree before, and I swear it wasn't there when I looked down on the final approach to pick my drop spot."

Though a certain amount of the Lockland family's unshakable optimism and spirited approach to life came from Tessa's late father, Bernard, a large measure of it—with a full measure of indomitability as well—flowed from Marion's gene pool.

Tessa said, "Tonight, just after I got here, I went down to the beach where they found her."

"This must be awful for you, Teejay."

"I can handle it."

When Janice died, Tessa had been traveling in rural regions of Afghanistan, researching the effects of genocidal war on the Afghan people and culture, intending to script a documentary on that subject. Her mother had been unable to get word of Janice's death to Tessa until two weeks after the body washed up on the shore of Moonlight Cove. Five days ago, on October 8, she had flown out of Afghanistan with a sense of having failed her sister somehow. Her load of guilt was at least as heavy as her mother's, but what she said was true: She *could* handle it.

"You were right, Mom. The official version stinks."

"What've you learned?"

"Nothing yet. But I stood right there on the sand, where she was supposed to have taken the Valium, where she set out on her last swim, where they found her two days later, and I knew their whole story was garbage. I feel it in my guts, Mom. And one way or another, I'm going to find out what really happened."

"You've got to be careful, dear."

"I will."

"If Janice was . . . murdered . . ."

"I'll be okay."

"And if, as we suspect, the police up there can't be trusted . . ."

"Mom, I'm five feet four, blond, blue-eyed, perky, and about as dangerous-looking as a Disney chipmunk. All my life I've had to work against my looks to be taken seriously. Women all want to mother me or be my big sister, and men either want to be my father or get me in the sack, but darned few can see immediately through the exterior and realize I've got a brain that is, I strongly believe, bigger than that of a gnat; usually they have to know me a while. So I'll just use my appearance instead of struggling against it. No one here will see me as a threat."

"You'll stay in touch?"

"Of course."

"If you feel you're in danger, just leave, get out."

"I'll be all right."

"Promise you won't stay if it's dangerous," Marion persisted.

"I promise. But you have to promise *me* that you won't jump out of any more airplanes for a while."

"I'm too old for that, dear. I'm elderly now. Ancient. I'm going to have to pursue interests suitable to my age. I've always wanted to learn to water-ski, for instance, and that documentary you did on dirt-bike racing made those little motorcycles look like so much fun."

"I love you to pieces, Mom."

"I love you, Teejay. More than life itself."

"I'll make them pay for Janice."

"If there's anyone who deserves to pay. Just remember, Teejay, that our Janice is gone, but you're still here, and your *first* allegiance should never be to the dead."

chapter seventeen

George Valdoski sat at the Formica-topped kitchen table. Though his work-scarred hands were clasped tightly around a glass of whiskey, he could not prevent them from trembling; the surface of the amber bourbon shivered constantly.

When Loman Watkins entered and closed the door behind him, George didn't even look up. Eddie had been his only child.

George was tall, solid in the chest and shoulders. Thanks to deeply and closely set eyes, a thin-lipped mouth, and sharp features, he had a hard, mean look in spite of his general handsomeness. His forbidding appearance was deceptive, however, for he was a sensitive man, soft-spoken and kind.

"How you doin'?" Loman asked.

George bit his lower lip and nodded as if to say that he would get through this nightmare, but he did not meet Loman's eyes.

"I'll look in on Nella," Loman said.

This time George didn't even nod.

As Loman crossed the too-bright kitchen, his hard-soled shoes squeaked on the linoleum floor. He paused at the doorway to the small dining room and looked back at his friend. "We'll find the bastard, George. I swear we will."

At last George looked up from the whiskey. Tears shimmered in his eyes, but he would not let them flow. He was a proud, hardheaded Pole, determined to be strong. He said, "Eddie was playin' in the backyard toward dusk, just right out there in the backyard, where you could see him if you looked out any window, right in his *own* yard. When Nella called him for supper just after dark, when he didn't come or answer, we thought he'd gone to one of the neighbors' to play with some other kids, without asking like he should've." He had related all of this before, more than once, but he seemed to need to go over it again and again, as if repetition would wear down the ugly reality and thereby change it as surely as ten thousand playings of a tape cassette would eventually scrape away the music and leave a hiss of white noise. "We started lookin' for him, couldn't find him, wasn't scared at first; in fact we were a little angry with him; but then we got worried and then scared, and I was just about to call you for help when we found him there in the ditch, sweet Jesus, all torn up in the ditch." He took a deep breath and another, and the pent-up tears glistened brightly in his eyes. "What kind of monster would do that to a child, take him away somewhere and do that, and *then* be cruel enough to bring him back here and drop him where we'd find him? Had to've been that way, 'cause we'd have heard . . . heard the screaming if the bastard had done all that to Eddie right here somewheres. *Had* to've taken him away, done all that, then brought him back so we'd find him. What kind of man, Loman? For God's sake, what kind of man?"

"Psychotic," Loman said, as he had said before, and that much was true. The regressives were psychotic. Shaddack had coined a term for their condition: metamorphic-related psychosis. "Probably on drugs," he added, and he was lying now. Drugs—at least the conventional illegal pharmacopoeia—had nothing to do with Eddie's death. Loman was still surprised at how easy it was for him to lie to a close friend, something that he had once been unable to do. The immorality of lying was a concept more suited to the Old People and their turbulently emotional world. Old-fashioned concepts of what was immoral might ultimately have no meaning to the New People, for if they changed as Shaddack believed they would, efficiency and expediency and maximum performance would be the only moral absolutes. "The country's rotten with drug freaks these days. Burnt-out brains. No morals, no goals but cheap thrills. They're our inheritance from the recent Age of Do Your Own Thing. This guy was a drug-disoriented freak, George, and I swear we'll get him."

George looked down at his whiskey again. He drank some.

Then to himself more than to Loman, he said, "Eddie was playin' in the backyard toward dusk, just right out there in the backyard, where you could see him if you looked out any window. . . ." His voice trailed away.

Reluctantly Loman went upstairs to the master bedroom to see how Nella was coping.

She was lying on the bed, propped up a bit with pillows, and Dr. Jim Worthy was sitting in a chair that he had moved to her side. He was the youngest of Moonlight Cove's three doctors, thirty-eight, an earnest man with a neatly trimmed mustache, wire-rimmed glasses, and a proclivity for bow ties.

The physician's bag was on the floor at his feet. A stethoscope hung around his neck. He was filling an unusually large syringe from a six-ounce bottle of golden fluid.

Worthy turned to look at Loman, and their eyes met, and they did not need to say anything.

Either having heard Loman's soft footsteps or having sensed him by some subtler means, Nella Valdoski opened her eyes, which were red and swollen from crying. She was still a lovely woman with flaxen hair and features that seemed too delicate to be the work of nature, more like the finely honed art of a master sculptor. Her mouth softened and trembled when she spoke his name: "Oh, Loman."

He went around the bed, to the side opposite Dr. Worthy, and took hold of the hand that Nella held out to him. It was clammy, cold, and trembling.

"I'm giving her a tranquilizer," Worthy said. "She needs to relax, even sleep if she can."

"I don't want to sleep," Nella said. "I *can't* sleep. Not after . . . not after this . . . not ever again after this."

"Easy," Loman said, gently rubbing her hand. He sat on the edge of the bed. "Just let Dr. Worthy take care of you. This is for the best, Nella."

For half his life, Loman had loved this woman, his best friend's wife, though he had never acted upon his feelings. He had always told himself that it was a strictly platonic attraction. Looking at her now, however, he knew passion had been a part of it.

The disturbing thing was . . . well, though he *knew* what he had felt for her all these years, though he remembered it, he could not feel it any longer. His love, his passion, his pleasant yet melancholy longing had faded as had most of his other emotional responses; he was still aware of his previous feelings for her, but they were like another aspect of him that had split off and drifted away like a ghost departing a corpse.

Worthy set the filled syringe on the nightstand. He unbuttoned and pushed up the loose sleeve on Nella's blouse, then tied a length of rubber tubing around her arm, tight enough to make a vein more evident.

As the physician swabbed Nella's arm with an alcohol-soaked cottonball, she said, "Loman, what are we going to do?"

"Everything will be fine," he said, stroking her hand.

"No. How can you say that? Eddie's dead. He was so sweet, so small and sweet, and now he's gone. Nothing will be fine again."

"Very soon you'll feel better," Loman assured her. "Before you know it the hurt will be gone. It won't matter as much as it does now. I promise it won't."

She blinked and stared at him as if he were talking nonsense, but then she did not know what was about to happen to her.

Worthy slipped the needle into her arm.

She twitched.

The golden fluid flowed out of the syringe, into her bloodstream.

She closed her eyes and began to cry softly again, not at the pain of the needle but at the loss of her son.

Maybe it *is* better not to care so much, not to love so much, Loman thought.

The syringe was empty.

Worthy withdrew the needle from her vein.

Again Loman met the doctor's gaze.

Nella shuddered.

The Change would require two more injections, and someone would have to stay with Nella for the next four or five hours, not only to administer the drugs but to make sure that she did not hurt herself during the conversion. Becoming a New Person was not a painless process.

Nella shuddered again.

Worthy tilted his head, and the lamplight struck his wire-rimmed glasses at a new angle, transforming the lenses into mirrors that for a moment hid his eyes, giving him an uncharacteristically menacing appearance.

Shudders, more violent and protracted this time, swept through Nella.

From the doorway George Valdoski said, "What's going on here?"

Loman had been so focused on Nella that he had not heard George coming. He got up at once and let go of Nella's hand. "The doctor thought she needed—"

"What's that horse needle for?" George said, referring to the huge syringe. The needle itself was no larger than an ordinary hypodermic.

"Tranquilizer," Dr. Worthy said. "She needs to—"

"Tranquilizer?" George interrupted. "Looks like you gave her enough to knock down a bull."

Loman said, "Now, George, the doctor knows what he's—"

On the bed Nella fell under the thrall of the injection. Her body suddenly stiffened, her hands curled into tight fists, her teeth clenched, and her jaw muscles bulged. In her throat and temples, the arteries swelled and throbbed visibly as her heartbeat drastically accelerated. Her eyes glazed over, and she passed into the peculiar twilight that was the Change, neither conscious nor unconscious.

"What's wrong with her?" George demanded.

Between clenched teeth, lips peeled back in a grimace of pain, Nella let out a strange, low groan. She arched her back until only her shoulders and heels were in contact with the bed. She appeared to be full of violent energy, as if she were a boiler straining with excess steam pressure, and for a moment she seemed about to explode. Then she collapsed back onto the mattress, shuddered more violently than ever, and broke out in a copious sweat.

George looked at Worthy, at Loman. He clearly realized that something was very wrong, though he could not begin to understand the nature of that wrongness.

"Stop." Loman drew his revolver as George stepped backward toward the second-floor hall. "Come all the way in here, George, and lie down on the bed beside Nella."

In the doorway George Valdoski froze, staring in disbelief and dismay at the revolver.

"If you try to leave," Loman said, "I'll have to shoot you, and I don't really want to do that."

"You wouldn't," George said, counting on decades of friendship to protect him.

"Yes, I would," Loman said coldly. "I'd kill you if I had to, and we'd cover it with a story you wouldn't like. We'd say that we caught you in a contradiction, that we found some evidence that *you* were the one who killed Eddie, killed your own boy, some twisted sex thing, and that when we confronted you with proof, you grabbed my revolver out of my holster. There was a struggle. You were shot. Case closed."

Coming from someone who was supposed to be a close and treasured friend, Loman's threat was so monstrous that at first George was speechless. Then, as he stepped back into the room, he said, "You'd let everyone think . . . think I did those terrible things to Eddie? Why? What're you doing, Loman? What the hell are you doing? Who . . . who are you protecting?"

"Lie down on the bed," Loman said.

Dr. Worthy was preparing another syringe for George.

On the bed Nella was shivering ceaselessly, twitching, writhing. Sweat trickled down her face; her hair was damp and tangled. Her eyes were open, but she seemed unaware that others were in the room. Maybe she was not even conscious of her whereabouts. She was seeing a place beyond this room or looking within herself; Loman didn't know which and could remember nothing of his own conversion except that the pain had been excruciating.

Reluctantly approaching the bed, George Valdoski said, "What's happening, Loman? Christ, what is this? What's wrong?"

"Everything'll be fine," Loman assured him. "It's for the best, George. It's really for the best."

"What's for the best? What in God's name—"

"Lie down, George. Everything'll be fine."

"What's happening to Nella?"

"Lie down, George. It's for the best," Loman said.

"It's for the best," Dr. Worthy agreed as he finished filling the syringe from a new bottle of the golden fluid.

"It's really for the best," Loman said. "Trust me." With the revolver he waved George toward the bed and smiled reassuringly.

chapter eighteen

Harry Talbot's house was Bauhaus-inspired redwood, with a wealth of big windows. It was three blocks south of the heart of Moonlight Cove, on the east side of Conquistador Avenue, a street named for the fact that Spanish conquerors had bivouacked in that area centuries earlier, when accompanying the Catholic clergy along the California coast to establish missions. On rare occasions Harry dreamed of being one of those ancient soldiers, marching northward into unexplored territory, and it was always a nice dream because, in that adventure fantasy, he was never wheelchair-bound.

Most of Moonlight Cove was built on wooded hillsides facing the sea, and Harry's lot sloped down to Conquistador, providing a perfect perch for a man whose main activity in life was spying on his fellow townsmen. From his third-floor bedroom at the northwest corner of the house, he could see at least portions of all the streets between Conquistador and the cove—Juniper Lane, Serra Street, Roshmore Way, and Cypress Lane—as well as the intersecting streets that ran east to west. To the north, he could glimpse pieces of Ocean Avenue and even beyond. Of course the breadth and depth of his field of vision would have been drastically limited if his house hadn't been one story higher than most of those around it and if he hadn't been equipped with a 60mm f/8 refractor telescope and a good pair of binoculars.

At 9:30 Monday night, October 13, Harry was in his custom-made stool, between the enormous west and north windows, bent to the eyepiece of the telescope. The high stool had arms and a backrest like a chair, four wide-spread sturdy legs for maximum balance, and a weighted base to prevent it from tipping over easily when he was levering himself into it from the wheelchair. It also had a harness, something like that in an automobile, allowing him to lean forward to the telescope without slipping off the stool and falling to the floor.

Because he had no use whatsoever of his left leg and left arm, because his right leg was too weak to support him, because he could rely only on his right arm—which, thank God, the Viet Cong had spared—even transferring from the battery-powered wheelchair to a custom-made stool was a torturous undertaking. But the effort was worthwhile because every year Harry Talbot lived more through his binoculars and telescope than he had the year before. Perched on his special stool, he sometimes almost forgot his handicaps, for in his own way he was participating in life.

His favorite movie was *Rear Window* with Jimmy Stewart. He had watched it probably a hundred times.

At the moment the telescope was focused on the back of Callan's Funeral Home, the only mortuary in Moonlight Cove, on the east side of Juniper Lane, which ran parallel to Conquistador but was one block closer to the sea. He was able to see the place by focusing between two houses on the opposite side of his own street, past the thick trunk of a Big Cone pine, and across the service alley that ran between Juniper and Conquistador. The funeral home backed up to that alley, and Harry had a view that included a corner of the garage in which the hearse was parked, the rear entrance to the house itself, and the entrance to the new wing in which the corpses were embalmed and prepared for viewing, or cremated.

During the past two months he had seen some strange things at Callan's. Tonight, however, no unusual activity enlivened Harry's patient watch over the place.

"Moose?"

The dog rose from his resting place in the corner and padded across the unlighted bedroom to Harry's side. He was a full-grown black Labrador, virtually invisible in the darkness. He nuzzled Harry's leg: the right one, in which Harry still had some feeling.

Reaching down, Harry petted Moose. "Get me a beer, old fella."

Moose was a service dog raised and trained by Canine Companions for Independence, and he was always happy to be needed. He hurried to the small refrigerator in the corner, which was designed for under-the-counter use in restaurants and could be opened with a foot pedal.

"None there," Harry said. "I forgot to bring a six-pack up from the kitchen this afternoon."

The dog had already discovered that the bedroom fridge contained no Coors. He padded into the hallway, his claws clicking softly on the polished wood floor. No room had carpets, for the wheelchair rolled more efficiently on hard surfaces. In the hall the dog leaped and hit the elevator button with one paw, and immediately the purr and whine of the lift machinery filled the house.

Harry returned his attention to the telescope and to the rear of Callan's Funeral Home. Fog drifted through town in waves, some thick and blinding, some wispy. But lights brightened the rear of the mortuary, giving him a clear view; through the telescope, he seemed to be standing between the twin brick pilasters flanking the driveway that served the back of the property. If the night had been fogless, he would have been able to count the rivets in the metal door of the embalmery-crematorium.

Behind him the elevator doors rolled open. He heard Moose enter the lift. Then it started down to the first floor.

Bored with Callan's, Harry slowly swiveled the scope to the left, moving the field of vision southward to the large vacant lot adjacent to the funeral home. Adjusting the focus, he looked across that empty property and across the street to the Gosdale house on the west side of Juniper, drawing in on the dining-room window.

With his good hand, he unscrewed the eyepiece and put it on a high metal table beside his stool, quickly and deftly replacing it with one of several other eyepieces, thus allowing a clearer focus on the Gosdales. Because the fog was at that moment in a thinning phase, he could see into the Gosdale dining room almost as well as if he had been crouched on their porch with his face to the window. Herman and Louise Gosdale were playing pinochle with their neighbors, Dan and Vera Kaiser, as they did every Monday night and on some Fridays.

The elevator reached the ground floor; the motor stopped whining, and silence returned to the house. Moose was now two floors below, hurrying along the hallway to the kitchen.

On an unusually clear night, when Dan Kaiser was sitting with his back to the window and at the correct angle, Harry occasionally could see the man's pinochle hand. A few times he had been tempted to call Herman Gosdale and describe his adversary's cards to him, with some advice on how to play out the trick.

But he dared not let people know he spent much of his day in his bedroom—darkened at night to avoid being silhouetted at the window—vicariously participating in their lives. They would not understand. Those whole of limb were uneasy about a handicapped person from the start, for they found it too easy to believe that the crippling twist of legs and arms extended to the mind. They would think he was nosy; worse, they might mark him as a Peeping Tom, a degenerate voyeur.

That was not the case. Harry Talbot had set down strict rules governing his use of the telescope and binoculars, and he faithfully abided by them. For one thing, he would never try to get a glimpse of a woman undressed.

Arnella Scarlatti lived across the street from him and three doors north, and he once discovered, by accident, that she spent some evenings in her bedroom, listening to music or reading in the nude. She turned on only a small bedside lamp, and gauzy sheers hung between the drapes, and she always stayed away from the windows, so she saw no need to draw the drapes on every occasion. In fact she could not be seen by anyone less prepared to see her than Harry was. Arnella was lovely. Even through the sheers and in the dim lamplight, her exquisite body had been revealed to Harry in detail. Astonished by her nakedness, riveted by surprise and by the sensuous concavities and convexities of her full-breasted, long-legged body, he had stared for perhaps a minute. Then, as hot with embarrassment as with desire, he had turned the scope from her. Though Harry had not been with a woman in more than twenty years, he never invaded Arnella's bedroom again. On many mornings he looked at an angle into the side window of her tidy first-floor kitchen and watched her at breakfast, studying her perfect face as she had her juice and muffin or toast and eggs. She was beautiful beyond his abilities of description, and from what he knew of her life, she seemed to be a nice person, as well. In a way he supposed he was in love with her, as a boy could love a teacher who was forever beyond his reach, but he never used unrequited love as an excuse to caress her unclothed body with his gaze.

Likewise, if he caught one of his neighbors in another kind of embarrassing situation, he looked away. He watched them fight with one another, yes, and he watched them laugh together, eat, play cards, cheat on their diets, wash dishes, and perform the countless other acts of daily life, but not because he wanted to get any dirt on them or find reason to feel superior to them. He got no cheap thrill from his observations of them. What he wanted was to be a part of their lives, to reach out to them—even if one-sidedly—and make of them an extended family; he wanted to have reason to *care* about them and, through that caring, to experience a fuller emotional life.

The elevator motor hummed again. Moose evidently had gone into the kitchen, opened one of the four doors of the under-the-counter refrigerator, and fetched a cold can of Coors. Now he was returning with the brew.

Harry Talbot was a gregarious man, and on coming home from the war with only one useful limb, he was advised to move into a group home for the disabled, where he might have a social life in a caring atmosphere. The counselors warned him that he would not be accepted if he tried to live in the world of the whole and healthy; they said he would encounter unconscious yet hurtful cruelty from most people he met, especially the cruelty of thoughtless exclusion, and would finally fall into the grip of a deep and terrible loneliness. But Harry was as stubbornly independent as he was gregarious, and the prospect of living in a group home, with only the companionship of disabled people and caretakers, seemed worse than no companionship at all. Now he lived alone, but for Moose, with few visitors other than his once-a-week housekeeper, Mrs. Hunsbok (from whom he hid the telescope and binoculars in a bedroom closet). Much of what the counselors warned him about was proved true daily; however, they had not imagined Harry's ability to find solace and a sufficient sense of family through surreptitious but benign observation of his neighbors.

The elevator reached the third floor. The door slid open, and Moose padded into the bedroom, straight to Harry's high stool.

The telescope was on a wheeled platform, and Harry pushed it aside. He reached down and patted the dog's head. He took the cold can from the Labrador's mouth. Moose had held it by the bottom for maximum cleanliness. Harry put the can between his limp legs, plucked a penlight off the table on the other side of his stool, and directed the beam on the can to be sure it was Coors and not Diet Coke.

Those were the two beverages that the dog had been taught to fetch, and for the most part the good pooch recognized the difference between the words "beer" and "Coke," and was able to keep the command in mind all the way to the kitchen. On rare occasions he forgot along the way and returned with the wrong drink. Rarer still, he brought odd items that had nothing to do with the command he'd been given: a slipper; a newspaper; twice, an unopened bag of dog biscuits; once, a hardboiled egg, carried so gently that the shell was not cracked between his teeth; strangest of all, a toilet-bowl brush from the housekeeper's supplies. When he brought the wrong item, Moose always proved successful on the second try.

Long ago Harry had decided that the pooch often was not mistaken but only having fun with him. His close association with Moose had convinced him that dogs were gifted with a sense of humor.

This time, neither mistaken nor joking, Moose had brought what he'd been asked to bring. Harry grew thirstier at the sight of the can of Coors.

Switching off the penlight, he said, "Good boy. Good, good, *gooood* dog."

Moose whined happily. He sat at attention in the darkness at the foot of the stool, waiting to be sent on another errand.

"Go, Moose. Lie down. That's a good dog."

Disappointed, the Lab moseyed into the corner and curled up on the floor, while his master popped the tab on the beer and took a long swallow.

Harry set the Coors aside and pulled the telescope in front of him. He returned to his scrutiny of the night, the neighborhood, and his extended family.

The Gosdales and Kaisers were still playing cards.

Nothing but eddying fog moved at Callan's Funeral Home.

One block south on Conquistador, at the moment illuminated by the walkway lamps at the Sternback house, Ray Chang, the owner of the town's only television and electronics store, was coming this way. He was walking his dog, Jack, a golden retriever. They moved at a leisurely pace, as Jack sniffed each tree along the sidewalk, searching for just the right one on which to relieve himself.

The tranquillity and familiarity of those scenes pleased Harry, but the mood was shattered abruptly when he shifted his attention through his north window to the Simpson place. Ella and Denver Simpson lived in a cream-colored, tile-roofed Spanish house on the other side of Conquistador and two blocks north, just beyond the old Catholic cemetery and one block this side of Ocean Avenue. Because nothing in the graveyard—except part of one tree—obstructed Harry's view of the Simpsons' property, he was able to get an angled but tight focus on all the windows on two sides of the house. He drew in on the lighted kitchen. Just as the image in the eyepiece resolved from a blur to a sharp-lined picture, he saw Ella Simpson struggling with her husband, who was pressing her against the refrigerator; she was twisting in his grasp, clawing at his face, screaming.

A shiver sputtered the length of Harry's shrapnel-damaged spine.

He knew at once that what was happening at the Simpsons' house was connected with other disturbing things he had seen lately. Denver was Moonlight Cove's postmaster, and Ella operated a successful beauty parlor. They were in their mid-thirties, one of the few local black couples, and as far as Harry knew, they were happily married. Their physical conflict was so out of character that it had to be related to the recent inexplicable and ominous events that Harry had witnessed.

Ella wrenched free of Denver. She took only one twisting step away from him before he swung a fist at her. The blow caught her on the side of the neck. She went down. Hard.

In the corner of Harry's bedroom, Moose detected the new tension in his master. The dog raised his head and chuffed once, twice.

Bent forward on his stool, riveted to the eyepiece, Harry saw two men step forward from a part of the Simpson kitchen that was out of line with the window. Though they were not in uniform, he recognized them as Moonlight Cove police officers: Paul Hawthorne and Reese Dorn. Their presence confirmed Harry's intuitive sense that this incident was part of the bizarre pattern of violence and conspiracy of which he had become increasingly aware during the past several weeks. Not for the first time, he wished to God he could figure out what was going on in his once serene little town. Hawthorne and Dorn plucked Ella off the floor and held her firmly between them. She appeared to be only half conscious, dazed by the punch her husband had thrown.

Denver was speaking to Hawthorne, Dorn, or his wife. Impossible to tell which. His face was contorted with rage of such intensity that Harry was chilled by it.

A third man stepped into sight, moving straight to the windows to close the Levolor blinds. A thicker vein of fog flowed eastward from the sea, clouding the view, but Harry recognized this man too: Dr. Ian Fitzgerald, the oldest of Moonlight Cove's three physicians. He had maintained a family practice in town for almost thirty years and had long been known affectionately as Doc Fitz. He was Harry's own doctor, an unfailingly warm and concerned man, but at the moment he looked colder than an iceberg. As the slats of the Levolor blind came together, Harry stared into Doc Fitz's face and saw a hardness of features and a fierceness in the eyes that weren't characteristic of the man; thanks to the telescope, Harry seemed to be only a foot from the old physician, and what he saw was a familiar face but, simultaneously, that of a total stranger.

Unable to peer into the kitchen any longer, he pulled back for a wider view of the house. He was pressing too hard against the eyepiece; dull pain radiated outward from the socket, across his face. He cursed the curdling fog but tried to relax.

Moose whined inquisitively.

After a minute, a light came on in the room at the southeast corner of the second floor of the Simpson house. Harry immediately zoomed in on a window. The master bedroom. In spite of the occluding fog, he saw Hawthorne and Dorn bring Ella in from the upstairs hall. They threw her onto the quilted blue spread on the queen-size bed.

Denver and Doc Fitz entered the room behind them. The doctor put his black leather bag on a nightstand. Denver drew the drapes at the front window that looked out on Conquistador Avenue, then came to the graveyard-side window on which Harry was focused. For a moment Denver stared out into the night, and Harry had the eerie feeling that the man saw him, though they were two blocks away, as if Denver had the vision of Superman, a built-in biological telescope of his own. The same sensation had gripped Harry on other occasions, when he was "eye-to-eye" with people this way, long before odd things had begun to happen in Moonlight Cove, so he knew that Denver was not actually aware of him. He was spooked nonetheless. Then the postmaster pulled those curtains shut, as well, though not as tightly as he should have done, leaving a two-inch gap between the panels.

Trembling now, damp with cold perspiration, Harry worked with a series of eyepieces, adjusting the power on the scope and trying to sharpen the focus, until he had pulled in so close to the window that the lens was filled by the narrow slot between the drapes. He seemed to be not merely *at* the window but beyond it, standing in that master bedroom, behind the drapes.

The denser scarves of fog slipped eastward, and a thinner veil floated in from the sea, further improving Harry's view. Hawthorne and Dorn were holding Ella Simpson on the bed. She was thrashing, but they had her by the legs and arms, and she was no match for them.

Denver held his wife's face by the chin and stuffed a wadded handkerchief or piece of white clothing into her mouth, gagging her.

Harry had a brief glimpse of the woman's face as she struggled with her assailants. Her eyes were wide with terror.

"Oh, shit."

Moose got up and came to him.

In the Simpsons' house, Ella's valiant struggle had caused her skirt to ride up. Her pale yellow panties were exposed. Buttons had popped open on her green blouse. In spite of that, the scene conveyed no feeling that rape was imminent, not even a hint of sexual tension. Whatever they were doing to her was perhaps even more menacing and cruel—and certainly stranger—than rape.

Doc Fitz stepped to the foot of the bed, blocking Harry's view of Ella and her oppressors. The physician held a bottle of amber fluid, from which he was filling a hypodermic syringe.

They were giving Ella an injection.

But of what?

And why?

chapter nineteen

After talking with her mother in San Diego, Tessa Lockland sat on her motel bed and watched a nature documentary on PBS. Aloud, she critiqued the camerawork, the composition of shots, lighting, editing techniques, scripted narration, and other aspects of the production, until she abruptly realized she sounded foolish talking to herself. Then she mocked herself by imitating various television movie critics, commenting on the documentary in each of their styles, which turned out to be fun because most TV critics were pompous in one way or another, with the exception of Roger Ebert. Nevertheless, although having fun, Tessa *was* talking to herself, which was too eccentric even for a nonconformist who had reached the age of thirty-three without ever having to take a nine-to-five job. Visiting the scene of her sister's "suicide" had made her edgy. She was seeking comic relief from that grim pilgrimage. But at certain times, in certain places, even the irrepressible Lockland buoyancy was inappropriate.

She clicked off the television and retrieved the empty plastic ice bucket from the bureau. Leaving the door to her room ajar, taking only some coins, she headed toward the south end of the second floor to the ice-maker and soda-vending machine.

Tessa had always prided herself on avoiding the nine-to-five grind. Absurdly proud, actually, considering that she often put in twelve and fourteen hours a day instead of eight, and was a tougher boss than any she could have worked for in a routine job. Her income was nothing to preen about, either. She had enjoyed a few flush years, when she could not have stopped making money if she'd tried, but they were far outnumbered by the years in which she had earned little more than a subsistence living. Averaging her income for the twelve years since she had finished film school, she'd recently calculated that her annual earnings were around twenty-one thousand, though that figure would be drastically readjusted downward if she did not have another boom year soon.

Though she was not rich, though free-lance documentary filmmaking offered no security to speak of, she *felt* like a success, and not just because her work generally had been well received by the critics and not only because she was blessed with the Lockland disposition toward optimism. She felt successful because she had always been resistant to authority and had found, in her work, a way to be the master of her own destiny.

At the end of the long corridor, she pushed through a heavy fire door and stepped onto a landing, where the ice-maker and soda cooler stood to the left of the head of the stairs. Well stocked with cola, root beer, Orange Crush, and 7-Up, the tall vending machine was humming softly, but the ice-maker was broken and empty. She would have to fill up her bucket at the machine on the ground floor. She descended the stairs, her footsteps echoing off the concrete-block walls. The sound was so hollow and cold that she might have been in a vast pyramid or some other ancient structure, alone but for the companionship of unseen spirits.

At the foot of the stairs, she found no soda or ice machines, but a sign on the wall indicated that the ground-floor refreshment center was at the north end of the motel. By the time she got her ice and Coke, she would have walked off enough calories to deserve a regular, sugar-packed cola instead of a diet drink.

As she reached for the handle of the fire door that led to the ground-floor corridor, she thought she heard the upper door open at the head of the stairs. If so, it was the first indication she'd had, since checking in, that she was not the only guest in the motel. The place had an abandoned air.

She went through the fire door and found that the lower corridor was carpeted in the same hideous orange nylon as was the upper hall. The decorator had a clown's taste for bright colors. It made her squint.

She would have preferred to be a more successful filmmaker, if only because she could have afforded lodgings that did not assault the senses. Of course, this was the only motel in Moonlight Cove, so even wealth could not have saved her from that eye-blistering orange glare. By the time she walked to the end of the hall, pushed through another fire door, and stepped into the bottom of the north stairwell, the sight of gray concrete-block walls and concrete steps was positively restful and appealing.

There, the ice-maker was working. She slid open the top of the chest and dipped the plastic bucket into the deep bin, filling it with half-moon pieces of ice. She set the full bucket atop the machine. As she closed the chest, she heard the door at the head of the stairs open with a faint but protracted squeak of hinges.

She stepped to the soda vendor to get her Coke, expecting someone to descend from the second floor. Only as she dropped a third quarter into the slot did she realize something was *sneaky* about the way the overhead door opened: the long, slow squeak . . . as if someone knew the hinges were unoiled, and was trying to minimize the noise.

With one finger poised over the Diet Coke selection button, Tessa hesitated, listening.

Nothing.

Cool concrete silence.

She felt exactly as she had felt on the beach earlier in the evening, when she had heard that strange and distant cry. Now, as then, her flesh prickled.

She had the crazy notion that someone was on the landing above, holding the fire door open now that he had come through it. He was waiting for her to push the button, so the squeak of the upper door's hinges would be covered by the clatter-thump of the can rolling into the dispensing trough.

Many modern women, conscious of the need to be tough in a tough world, would have been embarrassed by such apprehension and would have shrugged off the intuitive chill. But Tessa knew herself well. She was not given to hysteria or paranoia, so she did not wonder for a moment if Janice's death had left her overly sensitive, did not doubt her mental image of a hostile presence at the upper landing, out of sight around the turn.

Three doors led from the bottom of that concrete shaft. The first was in the south wall, through which she had come and through which she could return to the ground-floor corridor. The second was in the west wall, which opened to the back of the motel, where a narrow walk or service passage evidently lay between the building and the edge of the sea-facing bluff, and the third was in the east wall, through which she probably could reach the parking lot in front of the motel. Instead of pushing the vendor button to get her Coke, leaving her full ice bucket as well, she stepped quickly and quietly to the south door and pulled it open.

She glimpsed movement at the distant end of the ground-floor hall. Someone ducked back through that other fire door into the south stairwell. She didn't see much of him, only his shadowy form, for he had not been on the orange carpet in the corridor itself but at the far threshold, and therefore able to slip out of sight in a second. The door eased shut in his wake.

At least two men—she presumed they were men, not women—were stalking her.

Overhead, in her own stairwell, the unoiled hinges of that door produced a barely audible, protracted rasp and squeal. The other man evidently had tired of waiting for her to make a covering noise.

She could not go into the hallway. They'd trap her between them.

Though she could scream in the hope of calling forth other guests and frightening these men away, she hesitated because she was afraid the motel might be as deserted as it seemed. Her scream might elicit no help, while letting the stalkers know that she was aware of them and that they no longer had to be cautious.

Someone was stealthily descending the stairs above her.

Tessa turned away from the corridor, stepped to the east door, and ran out into the foggy night, along the side of the building, into the parking lot beyond which lay Cypress Lane. Gasping, she sprinted past the front of Cove Lodge to the motel office, which was adjacent to the now closed coffee shop.

The office was open, the doorstep was bathed in a mist-diffused glow of pink and yellow neon, and the man behind the counter was the same one who had registered her hours ago. He was tall and slightly plump, in his fifties, clean-shaven and neatly barbered if a little rumpled looking in brown corduroy slacks and a green and red flannel shirt. He put down a magazine, lowered the volume of the country music on the radio, got up from his spring-backed desk chair, and stood at the counter, frowning at her while she told him, a bit too breathlessly, what had happened.

"Well, this isn't the big city, ma'am," he said when she had finished. "It's a peaceful place, Moonlight Cove. You don't have to worry about that sort of thing here."

"But it happened," she insisted, nervously glancing out at the neon-painted mist that drifted through the darkness beyond the office door and window.

"Oh, I'm sure you saw and heard someone, but you put the wrong spin on it. We *do* have a couple other guests. That's who you saw and heard, and they were probably just getting a Coke or some ice, like you."

He had a warm, grandfatherly demeanor when he smiled. "This place can seem a little spooky when there aren't many guests."

"Listen, mister . . ."

"Quinn. Gordon Quinn."

"Listen, Mr. Quinn, it wasn't that way at all." She felt like a skittish and foolish female, though she knew she was no such thing. "I didn't mistake innocent guests for muggers and rapists. I'm not a hysterical woman. These guys were up to no damn good."

"Well . . . all right. I think you're wrong, but let's have a look." Quinn came through the gate in the counter, to her side of the office.

"Are you just going like that?" she asked.

"Like what?"

"Unarmed?"

He smiled again. As before, she felt foolish.

"Ma'am," he said, "in twenty-five years of motel management, I haven't yet met a guest I couldn't handle."

Though Quinn's smug, patronizing tone angered Tessa, she did not argue with him but followed him out of the office and through the eddying fog to the far end of the building. He was big, and she was petite, so she felt somewhat like a little kid being escorted back to her room by a father determined to show her that no monster was hiding either under the bed or in the closet.

He opened the metal door through which she had fled the north service stairs, and they went inside. No one waited there.

The soda-vending machine purred, and a faint clinking arose from the ice-maker's laboring mechanism. Her plastic bucket still stood atop the chest, filled with half-moon chips.

Quinn crossed the small space to the door that led to the ground-floor hall, pulled it open. "Nobody there," he said, nodding toward the silent corridor. He opened the door in the west wall, as well, and looked outside, left and right. He motioned her to the threshold and insisted that she look too.

She saw a narrow, railing-flanked serviceway that paralleled the back of the lodge, between the building and the edge of the bluff, illuminated by a yellowish night-light at each end. Deserted.

"You said you'd already put your money in the vendor but hadn't got your soda?" Quinn asked, as he let the door swing shut.

"That's right."

"What did you want?"

"Well . . . Diet Coke."

At the vending machine, he pushed the correct button, and a can rolled into the trough. He handed it to her, pointed at the plastic container that she had brought from her room, and said, "Don't forget your ice."

Carrying the ice bucket and Coke, a hot blush on her cheeks and cold anger in her heart, Tessa followed him up the north stairs. No one lurked there. The unoiled hinges of the upper door squeaked as they went into the second-floor hallway, which was also deserted.

The door to her room was ajar, which was how she left it. She was hesitant to enter.

"Let's check it out," Quinn said.

The small room, closet, and adjoining bath were untenanted.

"Feel better?" he asked.

"I wasn't imagining things."

"I'm sure you weren't," he said, still patronizing her.

As Quinn returned to the hallway, Tessa said, "They were there, and they were real, but I guess they've gone now. Probably ran away when they realized I was aware of them and that I went for help."

"Well, all's well then," he said. "You're safe. If they're gone, that's almost as good as if they'd never existed in the first place."

Tessa required all of her restraint to avoid saying more than, "Thank you," then she closed the door. On the knob was a lock button, which she depressed. Above the knob was a dead-bolt lock, which she engaged. A brass security chain was also provided; she used it.

She went to the window and examined it to satisfy herself that it couldn't be opened easily by a would-be assailant. Half of it slid to the left when she applied pressure to a latch and pulled, but it could not be opened from outside unless someone broke it and reached through to disengage the lock. Besides, as she was on the second floor, an intruder would need a ladder.

For a while she sat in bed, listening to distant noises in the motel. Now every sound seemed strange and menacing. She wondered what, if any, connection her unsettling experience had with Janice's death more than three weeks ago.

chapter twenty

After a couple of hours in the storm drain under the sloping meadow, Chrissie Foster was troubled by claustrophobia. She had been locked in the kitchen pantry a great deal longer than she had been in the drain, and the pantry had been smaller, yet the grave-black concrete culvert was by far the worse of the two. Maybe she began to feel caged and smothered because of the cumulative effect of spending all day and most of the evening in cramped places.

From the superhighway far above, where the drainage system began, the heavy roar of trucks echoed down through the tunnels, giving rise in her mind to images of growling dragons. She put her hands over her ears to block out the noise. Sometimes the trucks were widely spaced, but on occasion they came in trains of six or eight or a dozen, and the continuous rumble became oppressive, maddening.

Or maybe her desire to get out of the culvert had something to do with the fact that she was underground. Lying in the dark, listening to the trucks, searching the intervening silences for the return of her parents and Tucker, Chrissie began to feel she was in a concrete coffin, a victim of premature burial.

Reading aloud from the imaginary book of her own adventures, she said, "Little did young Chrissie know that the culvert was about to collapse and fill with earth, squishing her as if she were a bug and trapping her forever."

She knew she should stay where she was. They might still be prowling the meadow and woods in search of her. She was safer in the culvert than out of it.

But she was cursed with a vivid imagination. Although she was no doubt the only occupant of the lightless passageway in which she sprawled, she envisioned unwanted company in countless grisly forms: slithering snakes; spiders by the hundreds; cockroaches; rats; colonies of blood-drinking bats. Eventually she began to wonder if, over the years, a child might have crawled into the tunnels to play and, getting lost in the branching culverts, might have died there, undiscovered. His soul, of course, would have remained restless and earthbound, for his death had been unjustly premature and there had been no proper burial service to free his spirit. Now perhaps that ghost, sensing her presence, was animating those hideous skeletal remains, dragging the decomposed and age-dried corpse toward her, scraping off pieces of leathery and half-petrified flesh as it came. Chrissie was eleven years old and levelheaded for her age, and she repeatedly told herself that there were no such things as ghosts, but then she thought of her parents and Tucker, who seemed to be some kind of *werewolves*, for God's sake, and when the big trucks passed on the interstate, she was afraid to cover her ears with her hands for fear that the dead child was using the cover of that noise to creep closer, closer.

She had to get out.

chapter twenty-one

When he left the dark garage where he had taken refuge from the pack of drugged-out delinquents (which is what he had to believe they were; he knew no other way to explain them), Sam Booker went straight to Ocean Avenue and stopped in Knight's Bridge Tavern just long enough to buy a six-pack of Guinness Stout to go.

Later, in his room at Cove Lodge, he sat at the small table and drank beer while he pored over the facts of the case. On September 5, three National Farmworkers Union organizers—Julio Bustamante, his sister Maria Bustamante, and Maria's fiancé, Ramon Sanchez—were driving south from the wine country, where they had been conducting discussions with vineyard owners about the upcoming harvest. They were in a four-year-old, tan Chevy van. They stopped for dinner in Moonlight Cove. They'd eaten at the Perez Family Restaurant and had drunk too many margaritas (according to witnesses among the waiters and customers at Perez's that night), and on their way back to the interstate, they'd taken a dangerous curve too fast; their van had rolled and caught fire. None of the three had survived.

That story might have held up and the FBI might never have been drawn into the case, but for a few inconsistencies. For one thing, according to the Moonlight Cove police department's official report, Julio Bustamante had been driving. But Julio had never driven a car in his life; furthermore, he was unlikely to do so after dark, for he suffered from a form of night blindness. Furthermore, according to witnesses quoted in the police report, Julio and Maria and Ramon were *all* intoxicated, but no one who knew Julio or Ramon had ever seen them drunk before; Maria was a lifelong teetotaler.

The Sanchez and Bustamante families, of San Francisco, also were made suspicious by the behavior of the Moonlight Cove authorities. None of them were told of the three deaths until September 10, five days after the accident. Police chief Loman Watkins had explained that Julio's, Maria's, and Ramon's paper IDs had been destroyed in the intense fire and that their bodies had been too completely burned to allow swift identification by fingerprints. What of the van's license plates? Curiously, Loman had not found any on the vehicle or torn loose and lying in the vicinity of the crash. Therefore, with three badly mangled and burned bodies to deal with and no way to locate next of kin on a timely basis, he had authorized the coroner, Dr. Ian Fitzgerald, to fill out death certificates and thereafter dispose of the bodies by cremation. "We don't have the facilities of a big-city morgue, you understand," Watkins had explained. "We just can't keep cadavers long term, and we had no way of knowing how much time we'd need to identify these people. We thought they might be itinerants or even illegals, in which case we might never be able to ID them."

Neat, Sam thought grimly, as he leaned back in his chair and took a long swallow of Guinness.

Three people had died violent deaths, been certified victims of an accident, and cremated before their relatives were notified, before any other authorities could step in to verify, through the application of modern forensic medicine, whether the death certificates and police report in fact contained the whole story.

The Bustamantes and Sanchezes were suspicious of foul play, but the National Farmworkers Union was convinced of it. On September 12, the union's president sought the intervention of the Federal Bureau of Investigation on the grounds that antiunion forces were responsible for the deaths of Bustamante, Bustamante, and Sanchez. Generally, the crime of murder fell into the FBI's jurisdiction only if the suspected killer had crossed state borders either to commit the act, or during its commission, or to escape retribution subsequent to the act; or, as in this case, if federal authorities had reason to believe that murder had been committed as a consequence of the willful violation of the victims' civil rights.

On September 26, after the absurd if standard delays associated with government bureaucracy and the federal judiciary, a team of six FBI agents—including three men from the Scientific Investigation Division—

moved into picturesque Moonlight Cove for ten days. They interviewed police officers, examined police and coroner files, took statements from witnesses who were at the Perez Family Restaurant on the night of September 5, sifted through the wreckage of the Chevy van at the junkyard, and sought whatever meager clues might remain at the accident site itself. Because Moonlight Cove had no agricultural industry, they could find no one interested in the farm-union issue let alone angered by it, which left them short of people motivated to kill union organizers.

Throughout their investigation, they received the full and cordial cooperation of the local police and coroner. Loman Watkins and his men went so far as to volunteer to submit to lie-detector tests, which subsequently were administered, and all of them passed without a hint of deception. The coroner also took the tests and proved to be a man of unfailing honesty.

Nevertheless, something about it reeked.

The local officials were almost too eager to cooperate. And all six of the FBI agents came to feel that they were objects of scorn and derision when their backs were turned—though they never saw any of the police so much as raise an eyebrow or smirk or share a knowing look with another local. Call it Bureau Instinct, which Sam knew was at least as reliable as that of any creature in the wild.

Then the *other* deaths had to be considered.

While investigating the Sanchez-Bustamante case, the agents had reviewed police and coroner records for the past couple of years to ascertain the usual routine with which sudden deaths—accidental and otherwise—were handled in Moonlight Cove, in order to determine if local authorities had dealt with this recent case differently from previous ones, which would be an indication of police complicity in a cover-up. What they discovered was puzzling and disturbing—but not like anything they had *expected* to find. Except for one spectacular car crash involving a teenage boy in an extensively souped-up Dodge, Moonlight Cove had been a singularly safe place to live. During that time, its residents were untroubled by violent death—until August 28, eight days before the deaths of Sanchez and the Bustamantes, when an unusual series of mortalities began to show up on the public records.

In the pre-dawn hours of August 28, the four members of the Mayser family were the first victims: Melinda, John, and their two children, Carrie and Billy. They had perished in a house fire, which the authorities later attributed to Billy playing with matches. The four bodies were so badly burned that identification could be made only from dental records.

Having finished his first bottle of Guinness, Sam reached for a second but hesitated. He had work to do yet tonight. Sometimes, when he was in a particularly dour mood and started drinking stout, he had trouble stopping short of unconsciousness.

Holding the empty bottle for comfort, Sam wondered why a boy, having started a fire, would not cry out for help and wake his parents when he saw the blaze was beyond control. Why would the boy not run before being overcome with smoke? And just what kind of fire, except one fueled by gasoline or another volatile fluid (of which there was no indication in official reports), would spread so fast that none of the family could escape and would reduce the house—and the bodies therein—to heaps of ashes before firemen could arrive and quench it?

Neat again. The bodies were so consumed by flames that autopsies would be of little use in determining if the blaze had been started not by Billy but by someone who wanted to conceal the true causes of death. At the suggestion of the funeral director—who was the owner of Callan's Funeral Home and also the assistant coroner, therefore a suspect in any official cover-up—the Maysers' next of kin, Melinda Mayser's mother, authorized cremation of the remains. Potential evidence not destroyed by the original fire was thus obliterated.

"How tidy," Sam said aloud, putting his feet up on the other straight-backed chair. "How splendidly clean and tidy."

Body count: four.

Then the Bustamantes and Sanchez on September 5. Another fire. Followed by more speedy cremations.

Body count: seven.

On September 7, while trace vapors of the Bustamante and Sanchez remains might still have lingered in the air above Moonlight Cove, a twenty-year resident of the town, Jim Armes, put to sea in his thirty-foot boat, the *Mary Leandra,* for an early-morning sail—and was never seen again. Though he was an experienced seaman, though the day was clear and the ocean calm, he'd apparently gone down in an outbound tide, for no identifiable wreckage had washed up on local beaches.

Body count: eight.

On September 9, while fish presumably were nibbling on Armes's drowned body, Paula Parkins was torn apart by five Dobermans. She was a twenty-nine-year-old woman living alone, raising and training guard dogs, on a two-acre property near the edge of town. Evidently one of her Dobermans turned against her, and the others flew into a frenzy at the scent of her blood. Paula's savaged remains, unfit for viewing, had been sent in a sealed casket to her family in Denver. The dogs were shot, tested for rabies, and cremated.

Body count: nine.

Six days after entering the Bustamante-Sanchez case, on October 2, the FBI had exhumed Paula Parkins's body from a grave in Denver. An autopsy revealed that the woman indeed had been bitten and clawed to death by multiple animal assailants.

Sam remembered the most interesting part of that autopsy report word for word: . . . *however, bite marks, lacerations, tears in the body cavity, and specific damage to breasts and sex organs are not entirely consistent with canine attack. The teeth pattern and size of bite do not fit the dental profile of the average Doberman or other animals known to be aggressive and capable of successfully attacking an adult.* And later in the same report, when referring to the specific nature of Parkins's assailants: *Species unknown.*

How had Paula Parkins really died?

What terror and agony had she known?

Who was trying to blame it on the Dobermans?

And in fact what evidence might the Dobermans' bodies have provided about the nature of their own deaths and, therefore, the truthfulness of the police story?

Sam thought of the strange, distant cry he had heard tonight—like that of a coyote but not a coyote, like that of a cat but not a cat. And he thought also of the eerie, frantic voices of the kids who had pursued him. Somehow it all fit. Bureau Instinct.

Species unknown.

Unsettled, Sam tried to soothe his nerves with Guinness. The bottle was still empty. He clinked it thoughtfully against his teeth.

Six days after Parkins's death and long before the exhumation of her body in Denver, two more people met untimely ends in Moonlight Cove. Steve Heinz and Laura Dalcoe, unmarried but living together, were found dead in their house on Iceberry Way. Heinz left a typed, incoherent, unsigned suicide note, then killed Laura with a shotgun while she slept, and took his own life. Dr. Ian Fitzgerald's report was murder-suicide, case closed. At the coroner's suggestion, the Dalcoe and Heinz families authorized cremation of the grisly remains.

Body count: eleven.

"There's an ungodly amount of cremation going on in this town," Sam said aloud, and turned the empty beer bottle around in his hands.

Most people still preferred to have themselves and their loved ones embalmed and buried in a casket, regardless of the condition of the body. In most towns cremations accounted for perhaps one in four or one in five dispositions of cadavers.

Finally, while investigating the Bustamante-Sanchez case, the FBI team from San Francisco found that Janice Capshaw was listed as a Valium suicide. Her sea-ravaged body had washed up on the beach two days after she disappeared, three days before the agents arrived to launch their investigation into the deaths of the union organizers.

Julio Bustamante, Maria Bustamante, Ramon Sanchez, the four Maysers, Jim Armes, Paula Parkins, Steven Heinz, Laura Dalcoe, Janice Capshaw: a body count of twelve in less than a month—exactly twelve times the number of violent deaths that had occurred in Moonlight Cove during the previous *twenty-three months*. Out of a population of just three thousand, twelve violent deaths in little more than three weeks was one hell of a mortality rate.

Queried about his reaction to this astonishing chain of deadly events, Chief Loman Watkins had said, "It's horrible, yes. And it's sort of frightening. Things were so calm for so long that I guess, statistically, we were just overdue."

But in a town that size, even spread over two years, twelve such violent deaths went off the top of the statisticians' charts.

The six-man Bureau team was unable to find one shred of evidence of any local authorities' complicity in those cases. And although a polygraph was not an entirely dependable determiner of truth, the technology was not so unreliable that Loman Watkins, his officers, the coroner, and the coroner's assistant could all pass the examination without a single indication of deception if in fact they were guilty.

Yet . . .

Twelve deaths. Four cremated in a house fire. Three cremated in a demolished Chevy van. Three suicides, two by shotgun and one by Valium, all subsequently cremated at Callan's Funeral Home. One lost at sea—no body at all. And the only victim available for autopsy appeared not to have been killed by dogs, as the coroner's report claimed, though she had been bitten and clawed by something, dammit.

It was enough to keep the Bureau's file open. By the ninth of October, four days after the San Francisco team departed Moonlight Cove, a decision was made to send in an undercover operative to have a look at certain aspects of the case that might be more fruitfully explored by a man who was not being watched.

One day after that decision, on October 10, a letter arrived in the San Francisco office that clinched the Bureau's determination to maintain involvement. Sam had that note committed to memory as well:

Gentlemen:

I have information pertinent to a recent series of deaths in the town of Moonlight Cove. I have reason to believe local authorities are involved in a conspiracy to conceal murder.

I would prefer you contact me in person, as I do not trust the privacy of our telephone here. I must insist on absolute discretion because I am a disabled Vietnam veteran with severe physical limitations, and I am naturally concerned about my ability to protect myself.

It was signed, *Harold G. Talbot.*

United States Army records confirmed that Talbot was indeed a disabled Vietnam vet. He had been repeatedly cited for bravery in combat. Tomorrow, Sam would discreetly visit him.

Meanwhile, considering the work he had to do tonight, he wondered if he could risk a second bottle of stout on top of what he'd drunk at dinner. The six-pack was on the table in front of him. He stared at it for a long time. Guinness, good Mexican food, Goldie Hawn, and fear of death. The Mexican food was in his belly, but the taste of it was forgotten. Goldie Hawn was living on a ranch somewhere with Kurt Russell, whom she had the bad sense to prefer to one ordinary-looking, scarred, and hope-deserted federal agent. He thought of twelve dead men and women, of bodies roasting in a crematorium until they were reduced to bone splinters and ashes, and he thought of shotgun murder and shotgun suicide and fish-gnawed corpses and a badly bitten woman, and all those thoughts led him to morbid philosophizing about the way of all flesh. He thought of his wife, lost to cancer, and he thought of Scott and their long-distance telephone conversation, too, and that was when he finally opened a second beer.

chapter twenty-two

Chased by imaginary spiders, snakes, beetles, rats, bats, and by the *possibly* imaginary reanimated body of a dead child, and by the real if dragonlike roar of distant trucks, Chrissie crawled out of the tributary drain in which she had taken refuge, troll-walked down the main culvert, stepped again in the slippery remains of the decomposing raccoon, and plunged out into the silt-floored drainage channel. The air was clean and sweet. In spite of the eight-foot-high walls of the ditch, fog-filtered moonlight, and fog-hidden stars, Chrissie's claustrophobia abated. She drew deep lungsful of cool, moist air, but tried to breathe with as little noise as possible.

She listened to the night, and before long she was rewarded by those alien cries, echoing faintly across the meadow from the woods to the south. As before, she was sure that she heard three distinct voices. If her mother, father, and Tucker were off to the south, looking for her in the forest that eventually led to the edge of New Wave Microtech's property, she might be able to head back the way she had come, through the northern woods, into the meadow where Godiva had thrown her, then east toward the county road and into Moonlight Cove by that route, leaving them searching fruitlessly in the wrong place.

For sure, she could not stay where she was.

And she could not head south, straight toward *them*.

She clambered out of the ditch and ran north across the meadow, retracing the route she had taken earlier in the evening, and as she went she counted her miseries. She was hungry because she'd had no dinner, and she was tired. The muscles in her shoulders and back were cramped from the time she had spent in the tight, cold concrete tributary drain. Her legs ached.

So what's your problem? she asked herself as she reached the trees at the edge of the meadow. Would you rather have been dragged down by Tucker and "converted" into one of them?

chapter twenty-three

Loman Watkins left the Valdoski house, where Dr. Worthy was overseeing the conversion of Ella and George. Farther down the county road, his officers and the coroner were loading the dead boy into the hearse. The crowd of onlookers was entranced by the scene.

Loman got into his cruiser and switched on the engine. The compact video-display lit at once, a soft green. The computer link was mounted on the console between the front seats. It began to flash, indicating that HQ had a message for him—one that they chose not to broadcast on the more easily intercepted police-band radio.

Though he had been working with microwave-linked mobile computers for a few years, he was still sometimes surprised upon first getting into a cruiser and seeing the VDT light up. In major cities like Los Angeles, for the better part of the past decade, most patrol cars had been equipped with computer links to central police data banks, but such electronic wonders were still rare in smaller cities and unheard of in jurisdictions as comparatively minuscule as Moonlight Cove. His department boasted state-of-the-art technology not because the town's treasury was overflowing but because New Wave—a leader in mobile microwave-linked data systems, among other things—had equipped his office and cars with their in-development hardware and software, updating the system constantly, using the Moonlight Cove police force as something of a proving ground for every advancement that they hoped ultimately to integrate into their line of products.

That was one of the many ways Thomas Shaddack had insinuated himself into the power structure of the community even before he had reached for *total* power through the Moonhawk Project. At the time Loman had been thickheaded enough to think New Wave's largesse was a blessing. Now he knew better.

From his mobile VDT, Loman could access the central computer in the department's headquarters on Jacobi Street, one block south of Ocean Avenue, to obtain any information in the data banks or to "speak" with the on-duty dispatcher who could communicate with him almost as easily by computer as by police-band radio. Furthermore, he could sit comfortably in his car and, through the HQ computer, reach out to the Department of Motor Vehicles computer in Sacramento to get a make on a license plate, or the Department of Prisons data banks in the same city to call up information on a particular felon, or any other computer tied in to the nationwide law-enforcement electronic network.

He adjusted his holster because he was sitting on his revolver.

Using the keyboard under the display terminal, he entered his ID number, accessing the system.

The days when *all* fact-gathering required police legwork had begun to pass in the mid-eighties. Now only TV cops like Hunter were forced to rush hither and yon to turn up the smallest details because that was more dramatic than a depiction of the high-tech reality. In time, Watkins thought, the gumshoe might be in danger of becoming the gumbutt, with his ass parked for hours in front of either a mobile VDT or one on a desk at HQ.

The computer accepted his number.

The VDT stopped flashing.

Of course, if all the people of the world were New People, and if the problem of the regressives were solved, ultimately there would be no more crime and no need of policemen. Some criminals were spawned by social injustice, but all men would be equal in the new world that was coming, as equal as one machine to another, with the same goals and desires, with no competitive or conflicting needs. Most criminals were genetic defectives, their sociopathic behavior virtually encoded in their chromosomes; however, except for the regressive element among them, the New People would be in perfect genetic repair. That was Shaddack's vision, anyway.

Sometimes Loman Watkins wondered where free will fit into the plan. Maybe it didn't. Sometimes he didn't seem to care if it fit in or not. At other times his inability to care . . . well, it scared the hell out of him.

Lines of words began to appear from left to right on the screen, one line at a time, in soft green letters on the dark background:

FOR: LOMAN WATKINS
SOURCE: SHADDACK
JACK TUCKER HAS NOT REPORTED IN FROM THE FOSTER PLACE. NO ONE ANSWERS PHONE THERE. URGENT THAT SITUATION BE CLARIFIED. AWAIT YOUR REPORT.

Shaddack had direct entry to the police-department computer from his own computer in his house out on the north point of the cove. He could leave messages for Watkins or any of the other men, and no one could call them up except the intended recipient.

The screen went blank.

Loman Watkins popped the hand brake, put the patrol car in gear, and set out for Foster Stables, though the place was actually outside the city limits and beyond his bailiwick. He no longer cared about such things as jurisdictional boundaries and legal procedures. He was still a cop only because it was the role he had to play until all of the town had undergone the Change. None of the old rules applied to him any more because he was a New Man. Such disregard for the law would have appalled him only a few months ago, but now his arrogance and his disdain for the rules of the Old People's society did not move him in the least.

Most of the time nothing moved him any more. Day by day, hour by hour, he was less emotional.

Except for fear, which his new elevated state of consciousness still allowed: fear because it was a survival mechanism, useful in a way that love and joy and hope and affection were not. He was afraid right now, in fact. Afraid of the regressives. Afraid that the Moonhawk Project would somehow be revealed to the outside world and crushed—and him with it. Afraid of his only master, Shaddack. Sometimes, in fleeting bleak moments, he was afraid of himself, too, and of the new world coming.

chapter twenty-four

Moose dozed in a corner of the unlighted bedroom. He chuffed in his sleep, perhaps chasing bushy-tailed rabbits in a dream—although, being the good service dog that he was, even in his dreams he probably ran errands for his master.

Belted in his stool at the window, Harry leaned to the eyepiece of the telescope and studied the back of Callan's Funeral Home over on Juniper Lane, where the hearse had just pulled into the service drive. He watched Victor Callan and the mortician's assistant, Ned Ryedock, as they used a wheeled gurney to transfer a body from the black Cadillac hearse into the embalming and cremation wing. Zippered inside a half-collapsed, black plastic body bag, the corpse was so small that it must have been that of a child. Then they closed the door behind them, and Harry could see no more.

Sometimes they left the blinds raised at the two high, narrow windows, and from his elevated position Harry was able to peer down into that room, to the tilted and guttered table on which the dead were embalmed and prepared for viewing. On those occasions he could see much more than he *wanted* to see. Tonight, however, the blinds were lowered all the way to the windowsills.

He gradually shifted his field of vision southward along the fog-swaddled alley that served Callan's and ran between Conquistador and Juniper. He was not looking for anything in particular, just slowly scanning, when he saw a pair of grotesque figures. They were swift and dark, sprinting along the alley and into the large vacant lot adjacent to the funeral home, running neither on all fours nor erect, though closer to the former than the latter.

Boogeymen.

Harry's heart began to race.

He'd seen their like before, three times in the past four weeks, though the first time he had not believed what he had seen. They had been so shadowy and strange, so briefly glimpsed, that they seemed like phantoms of the imagination; therefore he named them Boogeymen.

They were quicker than cats. They slipped through his field of vision and vanished into the dark, vacant lot before he could overcome his surprise and follow them.

Now he searched that property end to end, back to front, seeking them in the three- to four-foot grass. Bushes offered concealment too. Wild holly and a couple of clumps of chaparral snagged and held the fog as if it were cotton.

He found them. Two hunched forms. Man-size. Only slightly less black than the night. Featureless. They crouched together in the dry grass in the middle of the lot, just to the north of the immense fir that spread its branches (all high ones) like a canopy over half the property.

Trembling, Harry pulled in even tighter on that section of the lot and adjusted the focus. The Boogeymen's outlines sharpened. Their bodies grew paler in contrast to the night around them. He still could not see any details of them because of the darkness and eddying mist.

Although it was quite expensive and tricky to obtain, he wished that through his military contacts he had acquired a Tele-Tron, which was a new version of the Star Tron night-vision device that had been used by most armed services for years. A Star Tron took available light—moonlight, starlight, meager electric light if any, the vague natural radiance of certain minerals in soil and rocks—and amplified it eighty-five thousand times. With that single-lens gadget, an impenetrable nightscape was transformed into a dim twilight or even late-afternoon grayness. The Tele-Tron employed the same technology as the Star Tron, but it was designed to be fitted to a telescope. Ordinarily, available light was sufficient to Harry's purposes, and most of the time he was looking through windows into well-lighted rooms; but to study the quick and furtive Boogeymen, he needed some high-tech assistance.

The shadowy figures looked west toward Juniper Lane, then north toward Callan's, then south toward the house that, with the funeral home, flanked that open piece of land. Their heads turned with a quick, fluid movement that made Harry think of cats, although they were definitely not feline.

One of them glanced back to the east. Because the telescope put Harry right in the lot with the Boogeymen, he saw the thing's eyes—soft gold, palely radiant. He had never seen their eyes before. He shivered, but not just because they were so uncanny. Something was familiar about those eyes, something that reached deeper than Harry's conscious or subconscious mind to stir dim recognition, activating primitive racial memories carried in his genes.

He was suddenly cold to the marrow and overcome by fear more intense than anything he had known since Nam.

Dozing, Moose was attuned nonetheless to his master's mood. The Labrador got up, shook himself as if to cast off sleep, and came to the stool. He made a low, mewling, inquisitive sound.

Through the telescope Harry glimpsed the nightmare face of one of the Boogeymen. He had no more than the briefest flash of it, at most two seconds, and the malformed visage was limned only by an ethereal spray of moonlight, so he saw little; in fact the inadequate lunar glow did less to reveal the thing than to deepen the mystery of it.

But he was gripped by it, stunned, frozen.

Moose issued an interrogatory *"Woof?"*

For an instant, unable to look up from the eyepiece if his life had depended on it, Harry stared at an apelike countenance, though it was leaner and uglier and more fierce and infinitely stranger than the face of an ape. He was reminded, as well, of wolves, and in the gloom the thing even seemed to have something of a reptilian aspect. He thought he saw the enameled gleam of wickedly sharp teeth, gaping jaws. But the light was poor, and he could not be certain how much of what he saw was a trick of shadow or a distortion of fog. Part of this hideous vision had to be attributed to his fevered imagination. A man with a pair of useless legs and one dead arm *had* to have a vivid imagination if he was to make the most of life.

As suddenly as the Boogeyman looked toward him, it looked away. At the same time both creatures moved with an animal fluidity and quickness that startled Harry. They were nearly the size of big jungle cats and as fast. He turned the scope to follow them, and they virtually flew through the darkness, south across the vacant lot, disappearing over a split-rail fence into the backyard of the Claymore house, up and gone with such alacrity that he could not hold them in his field of view.

He continued to search for them, as far as the junior-senior high school on Roshmore, but he found only night and fog and the familiar buildings of his neighborhood. The Boogeymen had vanished as abruptly as they always did in a small boy's bedroom the moment the lights were turned on.

At last he lifted his head from the eyepiece and slumped back in his stool.

Moose immediately stood up with his forepaws on the arm of the stool, begging to be petted, as if he had seen what his master had seen and needed to be reassured that malign spirits did not actually run loose in the world.

With his good right hand, which at first trembled violently, Harry stroked the Labrador's head. In a while the petting calmed him almost as much as it calmed the dog.

If the FBI eventually responded to the letter he had sent over a week ago, he did not know if he would tell them about the Boogeymen. He would tell them everything else he had seen, and a lot of it might be useful to them. But this . . . On the one hand, he was sure that the beasts he had glimpsed so fleetingly on three occasions—four now—were somehow related to all the other curious events of recent weeks. They were a different magnitude of strangeness, however, and in speaking of them he might appear addled, even crazed, causing the Bureau agents to discount everything else he said.

Am I addled? he wondered as he petted Moose. Am I crazed?

After twenty years of confinement to a wheelchair, housebound, living vicariously through his telescope and binoculars, perhaps he had become so desperate to be more involved with the world and so starved for excitement that he had evolved an elaborate fantasy of conspiracy and the uncanny, putting himself at the center of it as The One Man Who Knew, convinced that his delusions were real. But that was highly unlikely. The war had left his body pathetically damaged and weak, but his mind was as strong and clear as it had ever been, perhaps even tempered and made stronger by adversity. *That*, not madness, was his curse.

"Boogeymen," he said to Moose.

The dog chuffed.

"What next? Will I look up at the moon some night and see the silhouette of a witch on a broomstick?"

chapter twenty-five

Chrissie came out of the woods by Pyramid Rock, which once had inspired her fantasies of inch-high Egyptians. She looked west toward the house and Foster Stables, where lights now wore rainbow-hued halos in the fog. For a moment she entertained the idea of going back for Godiva or another horse. Maybe she could even slip into the house to grab a jacket. But she decided that she would be less conspicuous and safer on foot. Besides, she was not as dumb as movie heroines who repeatedly returned to the Bad House, knowing the Bad Thing was likely to find them there. She turned east-northeast and headed up through the meadow toward the county road.

Exhibiting her usual cleverness (she thought, as if reading a line from an adventure novel), *Chrissie wisely turned away from the cursed house and set off into the night, wondering if she would ever again see that place of her youth or find solace in the arms of her now alienated family.*

Tall, autumn-dry grass lashed at her legs, as she angled out toward the middle of the field. Instead of staying near the tree line, she wanted to be in the open in case something leaped at her from the forest. She didn't think she could outrun them once they spotted her, not even if she had a minute's head start, but at least she intended to give herself a chance to try.

The night chill had deepened during the time she'd taken refuge in the culvert. Her flannel shirt seemed hardly more warming than a short-sleeved summer blouse. If she were an adventurer-heroine of the breed that Ms. Andre Norton created, she would know how to weave a coat out of available grass and other plants, with a high insulation factor. Or she would know how to trap, painlessly kill, and skin fur-bearing animals, how to tan their hides and stitch them together, clothing herself in garments as astonishingly stylish as they were practical.

She simply had to stop thinking about the heroines of those books. Her comparative ineptitude depressed her.

She already had enough to be depressed about. She'd been driven from her home. She was alone, hungry, cold, confused, afraid—and stalked by weird and dangerous creatures. But more to the point . . . though her mother and father always had been a bit distant, not given to easy displays of affection, Chrissie had loved them, and now they were gone, perhaps gone forever, changed in some way she did not understand, alive but soulless and, therefore, as good as dead.

When she was less than a hundred feet from the two-lane county route, paralleling the long driveway at about the same distance, she heard a car engine. She saw headlights on the road, coming from the south. Then she saw the car itself, for the fog was thinner in that direction than toward the sea, and visibility was reasonably good. Even at that distance she identified it as a police cruiser; though no siren wailed, blue and red lights were revolving on its roof. The patrol car slowed and turned in the driveway by the sign for Foster Stables.

Chrissie almost shouted, almost ran toward the car, because she always had been taught that policemen were her friends. She actually raised one hand and waved, but then realized that in a world where she could not trust her own parents, she certainly could not expect all policemen to have her best interests in mind.

Spooked by the thought that the cops might have been "converted" the way Tucker had intended to convert her, the way her parents had been converted, she dropped down, crouching in the tall grass. The headlights had not come anywhere near her when the car had turned into the driveway. The darkness on the meadow and the fog no doubt made her invisible to the occupants of the cruiser, and she was not exactly so tremendously tall that she stood out on the flat land. But she did not want to take any chances.

She watched the car dwindle down the long driveway. It paused briefly beside Tucker's car, which was abandoned halfway along the lane, then drove on. The thicker fog in the west swallowed it.

She rose from the grass and hurried eastward again, toward the county route. She intended to follow that road south, all the way into Moonlight Cove. If she remained watchful and alert, she could scramble off the pavement into a ditch or behind a patch of weeds each time she heard approaching traffic.

She would not reveal herself to anyone she did not know. Once she reached town, she could go to Our Lady of Mercy and seek help from Father Castelli. (He said he was a modern priest and preferred to be called Father Jim, but Chrissie had *never* been able to address him so casually.) Chrissie had been an indefatigable worker at the church's summer festival and had expressed a desire to be an altar girl next year, much to Father Castelli's delight. She was sure he liked her and would believe her story, no matter how wild it was. If he didn't believe her . . . well, then she would try Mrs. Tokawa, her sixth-grade teacher.

She reached the county road, paused, and looked back toward the distant house, which was only a collection of glowing points in the fog. Shivering, she turned south toward Moonlight Cove.

chapter twenty-six

The front door of the Foster house stood open to the night.

Loman Watkins went through the place from bottom to top and down again. The only odd things he found were an overturned chair in the kitchen and Jack Tucker's abandoned black bag filled with syringes and doses of the drug with which the Change was effected—and a spray-can of WD-40 on the floor of the downstairs hall.

Closing the front door behind him, he went out onto the porch, stood at the steps that led down to the front yard, and listened to the ethereally still night. A sluggish breeze had risen and fallen fitfully during the evening, but now it had abated entirely. The air was uncannily still. The fog seemed to dampen all sounds, leaving a world as silent as if it had been one vast graveyard.

Looking toward the stables, Loman called out: "Tucker! Foster! Is anyone here?"

An echo of his voice rolled back to him. It was a cold and lonely sound.

No one answered him.

"Tucker? Foster?"

Lights were on at one of the long stables, and a door was open at the nearest end. He supposed he should go have a look.

Loman was halfway to that building when an ululant cry, like the wavering note of a distant horn, came from far to the south, faint but unmistakable. It was shrill yet guttural, filled with anger, longing, excitement, and need. The shriek of a regressive in mid-hunt.

He stopped and listened, hoping that he had misheard.

The sound came again. This time he could discern at least two voices, perhaps three. They were a long way off, more than a mile, so their eerie keening could not be in reply to Loman's shouts.

Their cries chilled him.

And filled him with a strange yearning.

No.

He made such tight fists of his hands that his fingernails dug into his palms, and he fought back the darkness that threatened to well up within him. He tried to concentrate on police work, the problem at hand.

If those cries came from Alex Foster, Sharon Foster, and Jack Tucker—as was most likely the case—where was the girl, Christine?

Maybe she escaped as they were preparing her for conversion. The overturned kitchen chair, Tucker's abandoned black bag, and the open front door seemed to support that unsettling explanation. In pursuit of the girl, caught up in the excitement of the chase, the Fosters and Tucker might have surrendered to a latent urge to regress. Perhaps not so latent. They might have regressed on other occasions, so this time they had slipped quickly and eagerly into that altered state. And now they were stalking her in the wildlands to the south—or had long ago run her down, torn her to pieces, and were still regressed because they got a dark thrill from being in that debased condition.

The night was cool, but suddenly Loman was sweating.

He wanted . . . needed. . . .

No!

Earlier in the day, Shaddack had told Loman that the Foster girl had missed her school bus and, returning home from the bus stop at the county road, had walked in on her parents as they were experimenting with their new abilities. So the girl had to be conducted through the Change slightly sooner than planned, the first child to be elevated. But maybe "experimenting" was a lie that the Fosters had used to cover their asses. Maybe they had been in deep regression when the girl had come upon them, which they could not reveal to Shaddack without marking themselves as degenerates among the New People.

The Change was meant to elevate mankind; it was forced evolution.

Willful regression, however, was a sick perversion of the power bestowed by the Change. Those who regressed were outcasts. And those regressives who killed for the primal thrill of blood sport were the worst of all: psychotics who had chosen devolution over evolution.

The distant cries came again.

A shiver crackled the length of Loman's spine. It was a pleasant shiver. He was seized by a powerful longing to shed his clothes, drop closer to the ground, and race nude and unrestrained through the night in long, graceful strides, across the broad meadow and into the woods, where all was wild and beautiful, where prey waited to be found and run down and broken and torn . . .

No.

Control.

Self-control.

The faraway cries pierced him.

He must exhibit self-control.

His heart pounded.

The cries. The sweet, eager, wild cries . . .

Loman began to tremble, then to shake violently, as in his mind's eye he saw himself freed from the rigid posture of *Homo erectus*, freed from the constraints of civilized form and behavior. If the primal man within him could be set loose at long last and allowed to live in a natural state—

No. Unthinkable.

His legs became weak, and he fell to the ground, though not onto all fours, no, because that posture would encourage him to surrender to these unspeakable urges; instead he curled into the fetal position, on his side, knees drawn up to his chest, and struggled against the swelling desire to regress. His flesh grew as hot as if he had been lying for hours in midday summer sun, but he realized that the heat was coming not from any external source but from deep within him; the fire arose not merely from vital organs or the marrow of his bones, but from the material within the walls of his cells, from the billions of nuclei that harbored the genetic material that made him what he was. Alone in the dark and fog in front of the Foster house, seduced by the echoey cry of the regressives, he longed to exercise the control of his physical being that the Change had granted him. But he knew if once he succumbed to that temptation, he would never be Loman Watkins again; he would be a degenerate masquerading as Loman Watkins, Mr. Hyde in a body from which he had banished Dr. Jekyll forever.

With his head tucked down, he was looking at his hands, which were curled against his chest, and in the dim light from the windows of the Foster house, he thought he saw several of his fingers begin to change. Pain flashed through his right hand. He *felt* the bones crunching and re-forming, knuckles swelling, digits lengthening, the pads of his fingers growing broader, sinews and tendons thickening, nails hardening and sharpening into talonlike points.

He screamed in stark terror and denial, and he *willed* himself to hold fast to his born identity, to what remained of his humanity. He resisted the lavalike movement of his living tissue. Through clenched teeth he repeated his name—"Loman Watkins, Loman Watkins, Loman Watkins"—as if that were a spell that would prevent this evil transformation.

Time passed. Perhaps a minute. Perhaps ten. An hour. He didn't know. His struggle to retain his identity had conveyed him into a state of consciousness beyond time.

Slowly, he returned to awareness. With relief he found himself still on the ground in front of the house, unchanged. He was drenched in sweat. But the white-hot fire in his flesh had subsided. His hands were as they'd always been, with no freakish elongation of the fingers.

For a while he listened to the night. He heard no more of the distant cries, and he was grateful for that silence.

Fear, the only emotion that had not daily lost vividness and power since he had become one of the New People, was now as sharp as knives within him, causing him to cry out. For some time he had been afraid that he was one of those with the potential to become a regressive, and now that dark speculation was proven true. But if he had surrendered to the yearning, he would have lost both the old world he had known before he'd been converted *and* the brave new world Shaddack was making; he would belong in neither.

Worse: He was beginning to suspect that he was not unique, that in fact *all* of the New People had within them the seeds of devolution. Night by night, the regressives seemed to be increasing in number.

Shakily, he got to his feet.

The film of sweat was like a crust of ice on his skin now that his inner fires had been banked.

Moving dazedly toward his patrol car, Loman Watkins wondered if Shaddack's research—and the technological application of it—was so fundamentally flawed that there was no benefit whatsoever in the Change. Maybe it was an unalloyed curse. If the regressives were not a statistically insignificant percentage of the New People, if instead they were *all* doomed to drift toward regression sooner or later. . . .

He thought of Thomas Shaddack out there in the big house on the north point of the cove, overlooking the town where beasts of his creation roamed the shadows, and a terrible bleakness overcame him. Because reading for pleasure had been his favorite pastime since he was a boy, he thought of H. G. Wells's Dr. Moreau, and he wondered if that was who Shaddack had become. Moreau reincarnate. Shaddack might be a Moreau for the age of microtechnology, obsessed with an insane vision of transcendence through the forced melding of man and machine. Certainly he suffered from delusions of grandeur, and had the hubris to believe that he could lift mankind to a higher state, just as the original Moreau had believed he could make men from savage animals and beat God at His game. If Shaddack was not *the* genius of his century, if he was an overreacher like Moreau, then they were all damned.

Loman got in the car and pulled the door shut. He started the engine and turned on the heater to warm his sweat-chilled body.

The computer screen lit, awaiting use.

For the sake of protecting the Moonhawk Project—which, flawed or not, represented the only future open to him—he had to assume the girl, Christine, had escaped, and that the Fosters and Tucker hadn't caught her. He must arrange for men to stand watch surreptitiously along the county road and on the streets entering the north end of Moonlight Cove. If the girl came into town seeking help, they could intercept her. More likely than not, she would unknowingly approach one of the New People with her tale of possessed parents, and that would be the end of her. Even if she got to people not yet converted, they weren't likely to believe her wild story. But he could take no chances.

He had to talk to Shaddack about a number of things, and attend to several pieces of police business.

He also had to get something to eat.

He was inhumanly hungry.

chapter twenty-seven

Something was wrong, something was wrong, something, something.

Mike Peyser had slipped through the dark woods to his house on the southeast edge of town, down through the wild hills and trees, stealthy and alert, slinking and quick, naked and quick, returning from a hunt, blood in his mouth, still excited but tired after two hours of playing games with his prey, cautiously by-passing the homes of his neighbors, some of whom were his kind and some of whom were not. The houses in that area were widely separated, so he found it relatively easy to creep from shadow to shadow, tree to tree, through tall grass, low to the ground, cloaked in the night, swift and sleek, silent and swift, naked and silent, powerful and swift, straight to the porch of the single-story house where he lived alone, through the unlocked door, into the kitchen, still tasting the blood in his mouth, blood, the lovely blood, exhilarated by the hunt though also glad to be home, but then—

Something was wrong.

Wrong, wrong, God, he was burning up, full of fire, hot, burning up, in need of food, nourishment, fuel, fuel, and that was normal, that was to be expected—the demands on his metabolism were tremendous when he was in his altered state—but the fire was not wrong, not the inner fire, not the frantic and consuming need for nourishment. What was wrong was that he could not, he could not, he could not—

He could not change back.

Thrilled by the exquisitely fluid movement of his body, by the way his muscles flexed and stretched, flexed and stretched, he came into the darkened house, seeing well enough without lights, not as well as a cat might but better than a man, because he was more than just a man now, and he roamed for a couple of minutes through the rooms, silent and swift, almost hoping he would find an intruder, someone to savage, someone to savage, savage, someone to savage, bite and tear, but the house was deserted. In his bedroom, he settled to the floor, curled on his side, and called his body back to the form that had been his birthright, to the familiar form of Mike Peyser, to the shape of a man who walked erect and looked like a man, and within himself he felt a surge toward normalcy, a *shift* in the tissues, but not *enough* of a shift, and then a sliding away, away, like an outgoing tide pulling back from a beach, away, away from normalcy, so he tried again, but this time there was no shift at all, not even a partial return to what he had been. He was stuck, trapped, locked in, locked, locked in a form that earlier had seemed the essence of freedom and inexpressibly desirable, but now it was not a desirable form at all because he could not forsake it at will, was trapped in it, trapped, and he panicked.

He sprang up and hurried out of the room. Although he could see fairly well in the darkness, he brushed a floor lamp, and it fell with a crash, the brittle sound of shattering glass, but he kept going into the short hall, the living room. A rag rug spun out from under him. He felt that he was in a prison; his body, his own transformed body, had become his prison, prison, metamorphosed bones serving as the bars of a cell, bars holding him captive from within; he was restrained by his own reconfigured flesh. He circled the room, scrambled this way and that, circled, circled, frenzied, frantic. The curtains fluttered in the wind of his passage. He weaved among the furniture. An end table toppled over in his wake. He could run but not escape. He carried his prison with him. No escape. No escape. Never. That realization made his heart thump more wildly. Terrified, frustrated, he knocked over a magazine rack, spilling its contents, swept a heavy glass ashtray and two pieces of decorative pottery off the cocktail table, tore at the sofa cushions until he had shredded both the fabric and the foam padding within, whereupon a terrible pressure filled his skull, pain, such pain, and he wanted to scream but he was afraid to scream, afraid that he would not be able to stop.

Food.

Fuel.

Feed the fire, feed the fire.

He suddenly realized that his inability to return to his natural form might be related to a severe shortage of energy reserves needed to fuel the tremendous acceleration of his metabolism associated with a transformation. To do what he was demanding, his body must produce enormous quantities of enzymes, hormones, and complex biologically active chemicals; in mere minutes the body must undergo a forced degeneration and rebuilding of tissues equal in energy requirements to years of ordinary growth, and for that it needed fuel, material to convert, proteins and minerals, carbohydrates in quantity.

Hungry, starving, starving, Peyser hurried into the lightless kitchen, clutched the handle on the refrigerator door, pulled himself up, tore the door open, hissed as the light stung his eyes, saw two-thirds of a three-pound canned ham, solid ham, good ham, sealed in Saran Wrap on a blue plate, so he seized it, ripped away the plastic, threw the plate aside, where it smashed against a cabinet door, and he dropped back to the floor, bit into the hunk of meat, bit and bit into it, bit deep, ripped, chewed feverishly, bit deep.

He loved to strip out of his clothes and seek another form as soon after nightfall as possible, sprinting into the woods behind his house, up into the hills, where he chased down rabbits and raccoons, foxes and ground squirrels, tore them apart in his hands, with his teeth, fed the fire, the deep inner burning, and he loved it, loved it, not merely because he felt such freedom in that incarnation but because it gave him an overwhelming sense of power, godlike power, more intensely erotic than sex, more satisfying than anything he had experienced before, power, savage power, raw power, the power of a man who had tamed nature, transcended his genetic limits, the power of the wind and the storm, freed of all human limitations, set loose, liberated. He had fed tonight, sweeping through the woods with the confidence of an inescapable predator, as irresistible as the darkness itself, but whatever he had consumed must have been insufficient to empower his return to the form of Michael Peyser, software designer, bachelor, Porsche-owner, ardent collector of movies on video disk, marathon runner, Perrier-drinker.

So now he ate the ham, all two pounds of it, and he snatched other items out of the refrigerator and ate them as well, stuffing them into his mouth with both tine-fingered hands: a bowlful of cold, leftover rigatoni and one meatball; half of an apple pie that he'd bought yesterday at the bakery in town; a stick of butter, an entire quarter of a pound, greasy and cloying but good food, good fuel, just the thing to feed the fire; four raw eggs; and more, more. This was a fire that, when fed, did not burn brighter but cooled, subsided, for it was not a real fire at all but a physical symptom of the desperate need for fuel to keep the metabolic processes running smoothly. Now the fire began to lose some of its heat, shrinking from a roaring blaze to sputtering flames to little more than the glow of hot coals.

Sated, Mike Peyser collapsed to the floor in front of the open refrigerator, in a litter of broken dishes and food and Saran Wrap and eggshells and Tupperware containers. He curled up again and willed himself toward that form in which the world would recognize him, and once more he felt a *shift* taking place in his marrow and bones, in his blood and organs, in sinews and cartilage and muscles and skin, as tides of hormones and enzymes and other biological chemicals were produced by his body and washed through it, but as before the change was arrested with transformation woefully incomplete, and his body eased toward its more savage state, inevitably regressing though he strained with all his will, all his will, strained and struggled to seek the higher form.

The refrigerator door had swung shut. The kitchen was in the grasp of shadows again, and Mike Peyser felt as if that darkness was not merely all around him but also within him.

At last he screamed. As he had feared, once he began to scream, he could not stop.

chapter twenty-eight

Shortly before midnight Sam Booker left Cove Lodge. He wore a brown leather jacket, blue sweater, jeans, and blue running shoes—an outfit that allowed him to blend effectively with the night but that didn't look suspicious, though perhaps slightly too youthful for a man of his relentlessly melancholy demeanor. Ordinary as it looked, the jacket had several unusually deep and capacious inner pockets, in which he was carrying a few basic burglary and auto-theft tools. He descended the south stairs, went out the rear door at the bottom, and stood for a moment on the walkway behind the lodge.

Thick fog poured up the face of the bluff and through the open railing, driven by a sudden sea breeze that finally had disturbed the night's calm. In a few hours the breeze would harry the fog inland and leave the coast in relative clarity. By then Sam would have finished the task ahead of him and, no longer needing the cover that the mist provided, would be at last asleep—or more likely fighting insomnia—in his motel-room bed.

He was uneasy. He had not forgotten the pack of kids from whom he'd run on Iceberry Way, earlier in the evening. Because their true nature remained a mystery, he continued to think of them as punks, but he knew they were more than just juvenile delinquents. Strangely, he had the feeling that he *did* know what they were, but the knowledge stirred in him far below even a subconscious plain, in realms of primitive consciousness.

He rounded the south end of the building, walked past the back of the coffee shop, which was now closed, and ten minutes later, by a roundabout route, he arrived at the Moonlight Cove Municipal Building on Jacobi Street. It was exactly as the Bureau's San Francisco agents had described it: a two-story structure—weathered brick on the lower floor, white siding on the upper—with a slate roof, forest-green storm shutters flanking the windows, and large iron carriage lamps at the main entrance. The municipal building and the property on which it stood occupied half a block on the north side of the street, but its anti-institutional architecture was in harmony with the otherwise residential neighborhood. Exterior and interior ground-floor lights were on even at that hour because in addition to the city-government offices and water authority, the municipal building housed the police department, which of course never closed.

From across the street, pretending to be out for a late-night constitutional, Sam studied the place as he passed it. He saw no unusual activity. The sidewalk in front of the main entrance was deserted. Through the glass doors he saw a brightly lighted foyer.

At the next corner he went north and into the alley in the middle of the block. That unlighted serviceway was bracketed by trees and shrubbery and fences that marked the rear property lines of the houses on Jacobi Street and Pacific Drive, by some garages and outbuildings, by groups of garbage cans, and by the large unfenced parking area behind the municipal building.

Sam stepped into a niche in an eight-foot-tall evergreen hedge at the corner of the yard that adjoined the public property. Though the alley was very dark, two sodium-vapor lamps cast a jaundiced glow over the city lot, revealing twelve vehicles: four late-model Fords of the stripped-down, puke-green variety that was produced for federal, state, and local government purchase; a pickup and van both bearing the seal of the city and the legend WATER AUTHORITY; a hulking street-sweeping machine; a large truck with wooden sides and tailgate; and four police cars, all Chevy sedans.

The quartet of black-and-whites were what interested Sam because they were equipped with VDTs linking them to the police department's central computer. Moonlight Cove owned eight patrol cars, a large number for a sleepy coastal town, five more than other communities of similar size could afford and surely in excess of need.

But everything about this police department was bigger and better than necessary, which was one of the things that had triggered silent alarms in the minds of the Bureau agents who'd come to investigate the deaths of Sanchez and the Bustamantes. Moonlight Cove had twelve full-time and three part-time officers, plus four full-time office support personnel. A lot of manpower. Furthermore, they were all receiving salaries competitive with law-enforcement pay scales in major West Coast cities, therefore excessive for a town as small as this. They had the finest uniforms, the finest office furniture, a small armory of hand-guns and riot guns and tear gas, and—most astonishing of all—they were computerized to an extent that would have been the envy of the boys manning the end-of-the-world bunkers at the Strategic Air Command in Colorado.

From his bristly nook in the fragrant evergreen hedge, Sam studied the lot for a couple of minutes to be sure no one was sitting in any of the vehicles or standing in deep shadows along the back of the building. Levolor blinds were closed at the lighted windows on the ground floor, so no one inside had a view of the parking area.

He took a pair of soft, supple goatskin gloves from a jacket pocket and pulled them on.

He was ready to move when he heard something in the alley behind him. A scraping noise. Back the way he'd come.

Pressing deeper into the hedge, he turned his head to search for the source of the sound. A pale, crumpled cardboard box, twice the size of a shoebox, slid along the blacktop, propelled by the breeze that was increasingly rustling the leaves of the shrubs and trees. The carton met a garbage can, wedged against it, and fell silent.

Streaming across the alley, flowing eastward on the breeze, the fog now looked like smoke, as if the whole town were afire. Squinting back through that churning vapor, he satisfied himself that he was alone, then turned and sprinted to the nearest of the four patrol cars in the unfenced lot.

It was locked.

From an inner jacket pocket, he withdrew a Police Automobile-Lock Release Gun, which could instantly open any lock without dam-aging the mechanism. He cracked the car, slipped in behind the steering wheel, and closed the door as quickly and quietly as possible.

Enough light from the sodium-vapor lamps penetrated the car for him to see what he was doing, though he was experienced enough to work virtually in the dark. He put the lock gun away and took an ignition-socket wrench from another pocket. In seconds he popped the ignition-switch cylinder from the steering column, exposing the wires.

He hated this part. To click on the video-display mounted on the car's console, he had to start the engine; the computer was more power-ful than a lap-top model and communicated with its base data center by energy-intensive microwave transmissions, drawing too much power to run off the battery. The fog would cover the exhaust fumes but not the sound of the engine. The black-and-white was parked eighty feet from the building, so no one inside was likely to hear it. But if someone stepped out of the back door for some fresh air or to take one of the off-duty cruisers out on a call, the idling engine would not escape notice. Then Sam would be in a confrontation that—given the frequency of violent death in this town—he might not survive.

Sighing softly, lightly depressing the accelerator with his right foot, he separated the ignition wires with one gloved hand and twisted the bare contact points together. The engine turned over immediately, without any harsh grinding.

The computer screen blinked on.

The police department's elaborate computerization was provided free by New Wave Microtechnology because they were supposedly using Moonlight Cove as a sort of testing ground for their own systems and software. The source of the excess funds so evident in every other aspect of the department was not easy to pin down, but the suspicion was that it came from New Wave or from New Wave's majority stockholder and chief executive officer, Thomas Shaddack. Any citizen was free to support his local police or other arms of government in excess of his taxes, of course, but if that was what Shaddack was doing, why wasn't it a matter of public record? No innocent man gives large sums of money to a civic cause with *complete* self-effacement. If Shaddack was being secretive about supporting the local authorities with private funds, then the possibility of bought cops and in-the-pocket officials could not be discounted. And if the Moonlight Cove police were virtually soldiers in Thomas Shaddack's private army, it followed that the suspicious number of violent deaths in recent weeks could be related to that unholy alliance.

Now the VDT in the car displayed the New Wave logo in the bottom righthand corner, just as the IBM logo would have been featured if this had been one of their machines.

During the San Francisco office's investigation of the Sanchez-Bustamante case, one of the Bureau's better agents, Morrie Stein, had been in a patrol car with one of Watkins's officers, Reese Dorn, when Dorn accessed the central computer for information in departmental files. By then Morrie had suspected that the computer was even more sophisticated than Watkins or his men had revealed, serving them in some way that exceeded the legal limits of police authority and that they were not willing to discuss, so he had memorized the code number with which Reese had tapped into the system. When he had flown to the Los Angeles office to brief Sam, Morrie had said, "I think every cop in that twisted little town has his own computer-access number, but Dorn's ought to work as well as any. Sam, you've got to get into their computer and let it throw some menus at you, see what it offers, play around with it when Watkins and his men aren't looking over your shoulder. Yeah, I sound paranoid, but there's too much high-tech for their size and needs, unless they're up to something dirty. At first it seems like any town, even more pleasant than most, rather pretty . . . but, dammit, after a while you get the feeling the whole burg is wired, that you're watched everywhere you go, that Big Brother is looking over your shoulder every damn minute. Honest to God, after a few days you're gut-sure you're in a miniature police state, where the control is so subtle you can hardly see it but still complete, iron-fisted. Those cops are bent, Sam; they're deep into something—maybe drug traffic, who knows—and the computer is part of it."

Reese Dorn's number was 262699, and Sam tapped it out on the VDT keyboard. The New Wave logo disappeared. The screen was blank for a second. Then a menu appeared.

```
CHOOSE ONE
A.   DISPATCHER
B.   CENTRAL FILES
C.   BULLETIN BOARD
D.   OUTSYSTEM MODEM
```

To Sam, the first item on the menu indicated that a cruising officer could communicate with the dispatcher at headquarters not only by means of the police-band radio with which the car was equipped but also through the computer link. But why would he want to go to all the trouble of typing in questions to the dispatcher and reading the transmitted replies off the VDT when the information could be gotten so much easier and quicker on the radio? Unless . . . there were some things that these cops did not want to talk about on radio frequencies that could be monitored by anyone with a police-band receiver.

He did not open the link to the dispatcher because then he would have to begin a dialogue, posing as Reese Dorn, and that would be like shouting, *Hey, I'm out here in one of your cruisers, poking my nose in just where you don't want, so why don't you come and chop it off.*

Instead, he tapped B and entered it. Another menu appeared.

```
CHOOSE ONE
A.   STATUS—CURRENT ARRESTEES
B.   STATUS—CURRENT COURT CASES
```

C.   STATUS—PENDING COURT CASES
D.   PAST ARREST RECORDS—COUNTY
E.   PAST ARREST RECORDS—CITY
F.   CONVICTED CRIMINALS LIVING IN COUNTY
G.   CONVICTED CRIMINALS LIVING IN CITY

Just to satisfy himself that the offerings on the menu were what they appeared to be and not code for other information, he punched in selection F, to obtain data on convicted criminals living in the county. Another menu appeared, offering him ten choices: MURDER, MANSLAUGHTER, RAPE, SEX OFFENSES, ASSAULT AND BATTERY, ARMED ROBBERY, BURGLARY, BREAKING AND ENTERING, OTHER THEFT, MISCELLANEOUS LESSER OFFENSES.

He called forth the file on murder and discovered three convicted killers—all guilty of murder in either the first or second degree—were now living as free men in the county after having served anywhere from twelve to forty years for their crimes before being released on parole. Their names, addresses, and telephone numbers appeared on the screen with the names of their victims, economically summarized details of their crimes, and the dates of their imprisonment; none lived in the city limits of Moonlight Cove.

Sam looked up from the screen and scanned the parking lot. It remained deserted. The omnipresent mist was filled with thicker veins of fog that rippled bannerlike as they flowed past the car, and he felt almost as if he were under the sea in a bathyscaphe, peering out at long ribbons of kelp fluttering in marine currents.

He returned to the main menu and asked for item C, BULLETIN BOARD. That proved to be a collection of messages that Watkins and his officers had left for one another regarding matters that seemed sometimes related to police work and sometimes private. Most were in such cryptic shorthand that Sam didn't feel he could puzzle them out or that they would be worth the effort to decipher.

He tried item D on the main menu, OUTSYSTEM MODEM, and was shown a list of computers nationwide with which he could link through the telephone modem in the nearby municipal building. The department's possible connections were astonishing: LOS ANGELES PD (for police department), SAN FRANCISCO PD, SAN DIEGO PD, DENVER PD, HOUSTON PD, DALLAS PD, PHOENIX PD, CHICAGO PD, MIAMI PD, NEW YORK CITY PD, and a score of other major cities; CALIFORNIA DEPARTMENT OF MOTOR VEHICLES, DEPARTMENT OF PRISONS, HIGHWAY PATROL, and many other state agencies with less obvious connections to police work; U.S. ARMY PERSONNEL FILES, NAVY PERSONNEL FILES,

AIR FORCE; FBI CRIMINAL RECORDS, FBI LLEAS (Local Law-Enforcement Assistance System, a relatively new Bureau program); even INTERPOL's New York office, through which the international organization could access its central files in Europe.

What in the hell would a small police force in rural California need with all those sources of information?

And there was more: data to which even fully computerized police agencies in cities like Los Angeles would not have easy access. By law, some of it was stuff that police could not obtain without a court order, such as the files at TRW, the nation's premier credit-reporting firm. The Moonlight Cove Police Department's ability to access TRW's database at will had to be a secret kept from TRW itself, for the company would not have cooperated in a wholesale disgorgement of its files without a subpoena. The system also offered entrance to CIA databases in Virginia, which were supposedly secured against access from any computer beyond the Agency's walls, and to certain FBI files, which were likewise believed to be inviolate.

Shaken, Sam retreated from the OUTSYSTEM MODEM options and returned to the main menu.

He stared out at the parking lot, thinking.

When briefing Sam a few days ago, Morrie Stein had suggested that Moonlight Cove's police might somehow be trafficking in drugs, and that New Wave's generosity with computer systems might indicate complicity on the part of certain unidentified officers of that firm. But the Bureau was also interested in the possibility that New Wave was illegally selling sensitive high technology to the Soviets and that it had bought the Moonlight Cove police because, through these law-enforcement contacts, the company would be alerted at the earliest possible moment to a nascent federal probe into its activities. They had no explanation of how either of those crimes accounted for all the recent deaths, but they had to start with *some* theory.

Now Sam was ready to discount both the idea that New Wave was selling to the Soviets and that some executives of the firm were in the drug trade. The far-reaching web of databases that the police had made available to themselves through their modem—one hundred and twelve were listed on that menu!—was greatly in excess of anything they would require for either drug trafficking or sniffing out federal suspicions of possible Soviet connections at New Wave.

They had created an informational network more suitable to the operational necessities of an entire state government—or, even more accurately, a small nation. A small, *hostile* nation. This data web was designed to provide its owner with enormous power. It was as if this picturesque little town suffered under the governing hand of a megalo-maniac whose central delusion was that he could create a tiny kingdom from which he would eventually conquer vast territory.

Today, Moonlight Cove; tomorrow, the world.

"What the fuck are they doing?" Sam wondered aloud.

chapter twenty-nine

Safely locked in her room at Cove Lodge—dressed for bed in pale yellow panties and a white T-shirt emblazoned with Kermit the Frog's smiling face—Tessa drank Diet Coke and tried to watch a repeat of the *Tonight* show, but she couldn't get interested in the conversations that Johnny Carson conducted with a witless actress, a witless singer, and a witless comedian. Diet thought to accompany Diet Coke.

The more time that passed after her unsettling experience in the motel's halls and stairwells, the more she wondered if indeed she had imagined being stalked. She was distraught about Janice's death, after all, preoccupied by the thought that it was murder rather than suicide. And she was still dyspeptic from the cheeseburger she'd eaten for dinner, which had been so greasy that it might have been deep-fried, bun and all, in impure yak lard. As Scrooge had first believed of Marley's ghost, so Tessa now began to view the phantoms that had frightened her earlier: Perhaps they'd been nothing more than an undigested bit of beef, a blot of mustard, a crumb of cheese, a fragment of an underdone potato.

As Carson's current guest talked about a weekend he'd spent at an arts festival in Havana with Fidel Castro—"a great guy, a funny guy, a compassionate guy"—Tessa got up from the bed and went to the bathroom to wash her face and brush her teeth. As she was squeezing Crest onto the brush, she heard someone try the door to her room.

The small bath was off the smaller foyer. When she stepped to the threshold, she was within a couple of feet of the door to the hall, close enough to see the knob twisting back and forth as someone tested the lock. They weren't even being subtle about it. The knob clicked and rattled, and the door clattered against the frame.

She dropped her toothbrush and hurried to the telephone that stood on the nightstand.

No dial tone.

She jiggled the cutoff buttons, pressed 0 for operator, but nothing worked. The motel switchboard was shut down. The phone was dead.

chapter thirty

Several times Chrissie had to scurry off the road, taking cover in the brush along the verge, until an approaching car or truck went past. One of them was a Moonlight Cove police car, heading toward town, and she was pretty sure it was the one that had come out to the house. She hunkered down in tall grass and milkweed stalks, and remained there until the black-and-white's taillights dwindled to tiny red dots and finally vanished around a turn.

A few houses were built along the first mile and a half of that two-lane blacktop. Chrissie knew some of the people who lived in them: the Thomases, the Stones, the Elswicks. She was tempted to go to one of those places, knock on the door, and ask for help. But she couldn't be sure that those people were still the nice folks they had once been. They might have changed, too, like her parents. Either something supernatural or from outer space was taking possession of people in and around Moonlight Cove, and she had seen enough scary movies and read enough scary books to know that when *those* kinds of forces were at work, you could no longer trust anyone.

She was betting nearly everything on Father Castelli at Our Lady of Mercy because he was a holy man, and no demons from hell would be able to get a grip on him. Of course, if the problem was aliens from another world, Father Castelli would not be protected just because he was a man of God.

In that case, if the priest had been taken over, and if Chrissie managed to get away from him after she discovered he was one of the enemy, she'd go straight to Mrs. Irene Tokawa, her teacher. Mrs. Tokawa was the smartest person Chrissie knew. If aliens were taking over Moonlight Cove, Mrs. Tokawa would have realized something was wrong before it was too late. She would have taken steps to protect herself, and she would be one of the last that the monsters would get their hooks into. Hooks or tentacles or claws or pincers or whatever.

So Chrissie hid from passing traffic, sneaked past the houses scattered along the county road, and proceeded haltingly but steadily toward town. The horned moon, sometimes revealed above the fog, had traversed most of the sky; it would soon be gone. A stiff breeze had swept in from the west, marked by periodic gusts strong enough to whip her hair straight up in the air as if it were a blond flame leaping from her head. Although the temperature had fallen to only about fifty degrees, the night felt much colder during those turbulent moments when the breeze temporarily became a blustering wind. The positive side was that the more miserable the cold and wind made her, the less aware she was of that other discomfort—hunger.

"Waif Found Wandering Hungry and Dazed After Encounter with Space Aliens," she said, reading that imagined headline from an issue of *The National Enquirer* that existed only in her mind.

She was approaching the intersection of the county route and Holliwell Road, feeling good about the progress she was making, when she nearly walked into the arms of those she was trying to avoid.

To the east of the county route, Holliwell was a dirt road leading up into the hills, under the interstate, and all the way to the old, abandoned Icarus Colony—a dilapidated twelve-room house, barn, and collapsing outbuildings—where a group of artists had tried to establish an ideal communal society back in the 1950s. Since then it had been a horse-breeding facility (failed), the site of a weekly flea market and auction (failed), a natural-food restaurant (failed), and had long ago settled into ruin. Kids knew all about it because it was a spooky place and thus the site of many tests of courage. To the west, Holliwell Road was paved and led along the edge of the town limits, past some of the newer homes in the area, past New Wave Microtech, and eventually out to the north point of the cove, where Thomas Shaddack, the computer genius, lived in a huge, weird-looking house. Chrissie didn't intend to go either east or west on Holliwell; it was just a milestone on her trek, and when she crossed it she would be at the northeast corner of the Moonlight Cove city limits.

She was within a hundred feet of Holliwell when she heard the low but swiftly swelling sound of a racing engine. She stepped away from the road, over a narrow ditch at the verge, waded through weeds, and took cover against the thick trunk of an ancient pine. Even as she hunkered down by the tree, she got a fix on the direction from which the vehicle was approaching—west—and then she saw its headlights spearing into the intersection just south of her. A truck pulled into view on Holliwell, ignoring the stop sign, and braked in the middle of the intersection. Fog whirled and plumed around it.

Chrissie could see that heavy-duty, black, extended-bed pickup fairly well because, as the junction of Holliwell and the county road was the site of frequent accidents, a single streetlight had been installed on the northeast corner for better visibility and as a warning to drivers. The truck bore the distinctive New Wave insignia on the door, which she could recognize even at a distance because she had seen it maybe a thousand times before: a white and blue circle the size of a dinner plate, the bottom half of which was a cresting blue wave. The truck had a large bed, and at the moment its cargo was men; six or eight were sitting in the back.

The instant that the pickup halted in the intersection, two men vaulted over the tailgate. One of them went to the wooded point at the northwest corner of the intersection and slipped into the trees, no more than a hundred feet south of the pine from which Chrissie was watching him. The other crossed to the southeast corner of the junction and took up a position in weeds and chaparral.

The pickup turned south on the county road and sped away.

Chrissie suspected that the remaining men in the truck would be let off at other points along the eastern perimeter of Moonlight Cove, where they would take up watch positions. Furthermore, the truck had been big enough to carry at least twenty men, and no doubt others had been dropped off as it had come eastward along Holliwell from the New Wave building in the west. They were surrounding Moonlight Cove with sentries. She was quite sure they were looking for her. She had seen something she had not been meant to see—her parents in the act of a hideous transformation, shucking off their human disguise—and now she had to be found and "converted"—as Tucker had put it—before she had a chance to warn the world.

The sound of the black truck receded.

Silence settled in like a damp blanket.

Fog swirled and churned and eddied in countless currents, but the overriding tidal forces in the air pushed it relentlessly toward the dark and serried hills.

Then the breeze abruptly ratcheted up until it became a real wind again, whispering in the tall weeds, soughing through the evergreens. It produced a soft and strangely forlorn thrumming from a nearby road sign.

Though Chrissie knew where the two men had gone to ground, she could not see them. They were well hidden.

chapter thirty-one

Fog flew past the patrol car and eastward through the night, driven by a breeze that was swiftly becoming a full wind, and ideas flew through Sam's mind with the same fluidity. His thoughts were so disturbing that he would have preferred to have sat in mindless stupefaction.

From considerable prior computer experience, he knew that part of a system's capabilities could be hidden if the program designer simply deleted some choices from the task menus that appeared on the screen. He stared at the primary menu on the car's display—A, DISPATCHER; B, CENTRAL FILES; C, BULLETIN BOARD; D, OUTSYSTEM MODEM—and he pressed E, though no E task was offered.

Words appeared on the terminal: HELLO, OFFICER DORN.

There *was* an E. He'd entered either a secret database requiring ritual responses for access or an interactive information system that would respond to questions he typed on the keyboard. If the former was the case, if passwords or phrases were required, and if he typed the wrong response, he was in trouble; the computer would shut him out and sound an alarm in police headquarters to warn them that an impersonator was using Dorn's number.

Proceeding with caution, he typed: HELLO.

MAY I BE OF ASSISTANCE?

Sam decided to proceed as if this was just what it seemed to be—a straightforward, question-and-answer program. He tapped the keyboard: MENU.

The screen blanked for a moment, then the same words reappeared: MAY I BE OF ASSISTANCE?

He tried again: PRIMARY MENU.

MAY I BE OF ASSISTANCE?

MAIN MENU.

MAY I BE OF ASSISTANCE?

Using a system accessed by question and response, with which one was unfamiliar, meant finding the proper commands more or less by trial and error. Sam tried again: FIRST MENU.

At last he was rewarded.

CHOOSE ONE

A.   NEW WAVE PERSONNEL
B.   PROJECT MOONHAWK
C.   SHADDACK

He had found a secret connection between New Wave, its founder Thomas Shaddack, and the Moonlight Cove police. But he didn't know yet what the connection was or what it meant.

He suspected that choice C might link him to Shaddack's personal computer terminal, allowing him to have a dialogue with Shaddack that would be more private than a conversation conducted on police-band radio. If that was the case, then Shaddack and the local cops were indeed involved in a conspiracy so criminal that it required a very high degree of security. He did not punch C because, if he called up Shaddack's computer and got Mr. Big himself on the other end, there was no way he could successfully pretend to be Reese Dorn.

Choice A probably would provide him with a roster of New Wave's executives and department heads, and maybe with codes that would allow him to link up with their personal terminals as well. He didn't want to talk with any of them, either.

Besides, he felt that he was on borrowed time. He surveyed the parking lot again and peered especially hard at the deeper pools of shadow beyond the reach of the sodium-vapor lamps. He'd been in the patrol car for fifteen minutes, and no one had come or gone from the municipal-building lot in that time. He doubted his luck would hold much longer, and he wanted to learn as much as possible in whatever minutes remained before he was interrupted.

PROJECT MOONHAWK was the most mysterious and interesting of the three choices, so he pushed B, and another menu appeared.

CHOOSE ONE:

A.   CONVERTED
B.   PENDING CONVERSION
C.   SCHEDULE OF CONVERSION—LOCAL
D.   SCHEDULE OF CONVERSION—SECOND STAGE

He punched choice A, and a column of names and addresses appeared on the screen. They were people in Moonlight Cove, and at the head of the column was the notation 1967 NOW CONVERTED.

Converted? From what? To what? Was there something religious about this conspiracy? Some strange cult? Or maybe "converted" was used in some euphemistic sense or as a code.

The word gave him the creeps.

Sam discovered that he could either scroll through the list or access it in alphabetized chunks. He looked up the names of residents whom he either knew of or had met. Loman Watkins was on the converted list. So was Reese Dorn. Burt Peckham, the owner of Knight's Bridge Tavern, was not among the converted, but the entire Perez family, surely the same that operated the restaurant, was on that roster.

He checked Harold Talbot, the disabled vet with whom he intended to make contact in the morning. Talbot was not on the converted list.

Puzzled as to the meaning of it all, Sam closed out that file, returned to the main menu, and punched B, PENDING CONVERSION. This brought another list of names and addresses to the VDT, and the column was headed by the words 1104 PENDING CONVERSION. On this roster he found Burt Peckham and Harold Talbot.

He tried C, SCHEDULE OF CONVERSION—LOCAL, and a submenu of three headings appeared:

A.   MONDAY, OCTOBER 13, 6:00 P.M.
      THROUGH
      TUESDAY, OCTOBER 14, 6:00 A.M.
B.   TUESDAY, OCTOBER 14, 6:00 A.M.
      THROUGH
      TUESDAY, OCTOBER 14, 6:00 P.M.
C.   TUESDAY, OCTOBER 14, 6:00 P.M.
      THROUGH
      MIDNIGHT

It was now 12:39 A.M., Tuesday, about halfway between the times noted in choice A, so he punched that one first. It was another list of names headed by the notation 380 CONVERSIONS SCHEDULED.

The fine hairs were bristling on the back of Sam's neck, and he didn't know why except that the word "conversions" unsettled him. It made him think of that old movie with Kevin McCarthy, *Invasion of the Body Snatchers*.

He also thought of the pack that had pursued him earlier in the night. Had they been . . . converted?

When he looked up Burt Peckham, he found the tavern owner on the schedule for conversion before 6:00 A.M. However, Harry Talbot was not listed.

The car shook.

Sam snapped his head up and reached for the revolver holstered under his jacket.

Wind. It was only wind. A series of hard gusts shredded holes in the fog and lightly rocked the car. After a moment the wind died to a strong breeze again, and the torn fabric of fog mended itself, but Sam's heart was still thudding painfully.

chapter thirty-two

As Tessa put down the useless telephone, the doorknob stopped rattling. She stood by the bed for a while, listening, then ventured warily into the foyer to press her ear against the door.

She heard voices but not immediately beyond that portal. They were farther down the hallway, peculiar voices that spoke in urgent, raspy whispers. She could not make out anything they said.

She was sure they were the same ones who had stalked her, unseen, when she had gone for ice and a Diet Coke. Now they were back. And somehow they had knocked out the phones, so she couldn't call for help. It was crazy, but it was happening.

Such persistence on their part indicated to Tessa that they were not ordinary rapists or muggers, that they had focused on her because she was Janice's sister, because she was there to look into Janice's death. However, she wondered how they had become aware of her arrival in town and why they had chosen to move against her so precipitously, without even waiting to see if she was just going to settle Janice's affairs and leave. Only she and her mother knew that she intended to attempt a murder investigation of her own.

Gooseflesh prickled her bare legs, and she felt vulnerable in just a T-shirt and panties. She went quickly to the closet, pulled on jeans and a sweater.

She wasn't alone in the motel. There were other guests. Mr. Quinn had said so. Maybe not many, perhaps only another two or three. But if worse came to worst, she could scream, and the other guests would hear her, and her would-be assailants would have to flee.

She picked up her Rockports, in which she had stuffed the white athletic socks she'd been wearing, and returned to the door.

Low, hoarse voices hissed and muttered at the far end of the hall—

then a bone-jarring crash slammed through the lodge, making her cry out and twitch in surprise. Another crash followed at once. She heard a door give way at another room.

A woman screamed, and a man shouted, but the *other* voices were what brought a chill of horror to Tessa. There were several of them, three or even four, and they were eerie and shockingly savage. The public corridor beyond her door was filled with harsh wolflike growls, murderous snarls, shrill and excited squeals, an icy keening that was the essence of blood hunger, and other less describable sounds, but worst of all was that those same inhuman voices, clearly belonging to beasts not men, nevertheless also spat out a few recognizable words: "... *need, need ... get her, get ... get, get ... blood, bitch, blood ...*"

Leaning against the door, holding on to it for support, Tessa tried to tell herself that the words she heard were from the man and woman whose room had been broken into, but she knew that was not true, because she also heard both a man and woman screaming. Their screams were horrible, almost unbearable, full of terror and agony, as if they were being beaten to death or worse, much worse, being torn apart, ripped limb from limb and gutted.

A couple of years ago Tessa had been in Northern Ireland, making a documentary about the pointlessness of the needless violence there, and she'd been unfortunate enough to be at a cemetery, at the funeral of one of the endless series of "martyrs"—Catholic or Protestant, it didn't matter any more, both had a surfeit of them—when the crowd of mourners had metamorphosed into a pack of savages. They had streamed from the churchyard into nearby streets, looking for those of a different faith, and soon they'd come across two British plainclothes army officers patrolling the area in an unmarked car. By its sheer size, the mob blocked the car's advance, encircled it, smashed in the windows, and dragged the would-be peacekeepers out onto the pavement. Tessa's two technical assistants had fled, but she had waded into the melee with her shoulder-mounted videotape camera, and through the lens she had seemed to be looking beyond the reality of this world into hell itself. Eyes wild, faces distorted with hatred and rage, grief forgotten and bloodlust embraced, the mourners had tirelessly kicked the fallen Britons, then pulled them to their feet only to pummel and stab them, slammed them repeatedly against the car until their spines broke and their skulls cracked, then dropped them and stomped them and tore at them and stabbed them again, though by that time they were both dead. Howling and shrieking, cursing, chanting slogans that degenerated into meaningless chains of sounds, mindless rhythms, like a flock of carrion-eating birds, they plucked at the shattered bodies, though they weren't like earthly birds, neither buzzards nor vultures, but like demons that had flown up from the pit, tearing at the dead men not only with the intention of consuming their flesh but with the hot desire to rip out and steal their souls. Two of those frenzied men had noticed Tessa, had seized her camera and smashed it, and had thrown her to the ground. For one terrible moment she was sure that they would dismember her in their frenzy. Two of them leaned down, grabbing at her clothes. Their faces were so wrenched with hatred that they no longer looked human, but like gargoyles that had come to life and had climbed down from the roofs of cathedrals. They had surrendered all that was human in themselves and let loose the gene-encoded ghosts of the primitives from whom they were descended. "For God's sake, no!" she had cried. "For God's sake, please!" Perhaps it was the mention of God or just the sound of a human voice that had *not* devolved into the hoarse gnarl of a beast, but for some reason they let go and hesitated. She seized that reprieve to scramble away from them, through the churning, blood-crazed mob to safety.

What she heard now, at the other end of the motel corridor, was just like that. Or worse.

chapter thirty-three

Beginning to sweat even though the patrol car's heater was not on, still spooked by every sudden gust of wind, Sam called up submenu item B, which showed the conversions scheduled from 6:00 this coming morning until 6:00 P.M. that evening. Those names were preceded by the heading 450 CONVERSIONS SCHEDULED. Harry Talbot's name was not on that list, either.

Choice C, six o'clock Tuesday evening through midnight the same day, indicated that 274 conversions were scheduled. Harry Talbot's name and address were on that third and final list.

Sam mentally added the numbers mentioned in each of the three conversion periods—380, 450, and 274—and realized they totaled 1104, which was the same number that headed the list of pending conversions.

Add that number to 1967, the total listed as already converted, and the grand total, 3071, was probably the population of Moonlight Cove. By the next time the clock struck midnight, a little less than twenty-three hours from now, the entire town would be converted—whatever the hell *that* meant.

He keyed out of the submenu and was about to switch off the car's engine and get out of there when the word ALERT appeared on the VDT and began to flash. Fear thrilled through him because he was sure they had discovered an intruder poking around in their system; he must have tripped some subtle alarm in the program.

Instead of opening the door and making a run for it, however, he watched the screen for a few more seconds, held by curiosity.

TELEPHONE SWEEP INDICATES FBI AGENT IN MOONLIGHT COVE.
POINT OF CALL:
PAY PHONE, SHELL STATION, OCEAN AVENUE.

The alert *was* related to him, though not because they knew he was currently sitting in one of their patrol cars and probing the New Wave/ Moonhawk conspiracy. Evidently the bastards were tied into the phone company's data banks and periodically swept those records to see who had made calls from what numbers to what numbers—even from all of the town's pay telephones, which in ordinary circumstances could have been counted on to provide secure communications for a field agent. They were paranoid and security conscious and electronically connected to an extent and degree that proved increasingly astounding with each revelation.

TIME OF CALL:
7:31 P.M., MONDAY,
OCTOBER 13.

At least they didn't keep a minute-by-minute or even hour-by-hour link with the telephone company. Their computer obviously swept those records on a programmed schedule, perhaps every four or six or eight hours. Otherwise they would have been on the lookout for him shortly after he had made the call to Scott earlier in the evening.

After the legend CALL PLACED TO, his home phone number appeared, then his name and his address in Sherman Oaks. Followed by:

CALL PLACED BY:
SAMUEL H. BOOKER.

MEANS OF PAYMENT:
TELEPHONE CREDIT CARD.

TYPE OF CARD:
EMPLOYER-BILLED.

BILLING ADDRESS:
FEDERAL BUREAU OF INVESTIGATION,
WASHINGTON, D.C.

They would start checking motels in the entire county, but as he was staying in Moonlight Cove's only lodgings, the search would be a short one. He wondered if he had time to sprint back to Cove Lodge, get his car, and drive to the next town, Aberdeen Wells, where he could call the Bureau office in San Francisco from an unmonitored phone. He had learned enough to know that something damned strange was going on in this town, enough to justify an imposition of federal authority and a far-reaching investigation.

But the very next words that appeared on the VDT convinced him that if he went back to Cove Lodge to get his car, he would be caught before he could get out of town. And if they got their hands on him, he might be just one more nasty accidental-death statistic.

They knew his home address, so Scott might be in danger too—not right now, not down there in Los Angeles, but maybe by tomorrow.

DIALOGUE INVOKED
WATKINS: SHOLNICK, ARE YOU LINKED IN?
SHOLNICK: HERE.
WATKINS: TRY COVE LODGE.
SHOLNICK: ON MY WAY.

Already an officer, Sholnick, was on his way to see if Sam was a registered guest at Cove Lodge. And the cover story that Sam had established with the desk clerk—that he was a successful stockbroker from Los Angeles, contemplating early retirement in one coastal town or another—was blown.

WATKINS: PETERSON?
PETERSON: HERE.

They probably didn't have to type in their names. Each man's link would identify him to the main computer, and his name would be automatically printed in front of the brief input that he typed. Clean, swift, easy to use.

WATKINS: BACK UP SHOLNICK.
PETERSON: DONE.
WATKINS: DON'T KILL HIM UNTIL WE CAN QUESTION.

All over Moonlight Cove, cops in patrol cars were talking to one another by computer, off the public airwaves, where they could not be easily overheard. Even though Sam was eavesdropping on them without their knowledge, he felt that he was up against a formidable enemy nearly as omniscient as God.

WATKINS: DANBERRY?
DANBERRY: HERE. HQ.
WATKINS: BLOCK OCEAN AVENUE TO INTERSTATE.
DANBERRY: DONE.
SHADDACK: WHAT ABOUT THE FOSTER GIRL?

Sam was startled to see Shaddack's name appear on the screen. The alert apparently had flashed on his computer at home, perhaps also sounding an audible alarm and waking him.

WATKINS: STILL LOOSE.
SHADDACK: CAN'T RISK BOOKER STUMBLING ACROSS HER.
WATKINS: TOWN'S RINGED WITH SENTRIES. THEY'LL CATCH
            HER COMING IN.
SHADDACK: SHE'S SEEN TOO MUCH.

Sam had read about Thomas Shaddack in magazines, newspapers. The guy was a celebrity of sorts, the computer genius of the age, and somewhat geeky looking besides.

Fascinated by this revealing dialogue, which incriminated the famous man and his bought police force, Sam had not immediately picked up on the meaning of the exchanges between Chief Watkins and Danberry: *Danberry . . . Here. HQ . . . Block Ocean Avenue to interstate . . . Done.* He realized that Officer Danberry was at headquarters, HQ, which was the municipal building, and that any moment he was going to come out the back door and rush to one of the four patrol cars in the parking lot.

"Oh, shit." Sam grabbed the ignition wires, tearing them apart.

The engine coughed and died, and the video-display went dark.

A fraction of a second later, Danberry threw open the rear door of the municipal building and ran into the parking lot.

chapter thirty-four

When the screaming stopped, Tessa broke out of a trance of terror and went straight to the phone again. The line was still dead.

Where was Quinn? The motel office was closed at this hour, but didn't the manager have an adjacent apartment? He would respond to the ruckus. Or was he one of the savage pack in the corridor?

They had broken down one door. They could break down hers too.

She grabbed one of the straight-backed chairs from the table by the window, hurried to the door with it, tilted it back, and wedged it under the knob.

She no longer thought they were after her just because she was Janice's sister and bent on uncovering the truth. That explanation didn't account for their attack on the other guests, who had nothing to do with Janice. It was nuts. She didn't understand what was happening, but she clearly understood the implications of what she had heard: a psychotic killer, no, several psychotics, judging by the noise they had made—some bizarre cult like the Manson family maybe, or worse— were loose in the motel. They had already killed two people, and they could kill her, too, evidently for the sheer pleasure of it. She felt as if she were in a bad dream.

She expected the walls to bulge and flow in that amorphous fashion of nightmare places, but they remained solid, fixed, and the colors of things were too sharp and clear for this to be a dreamscape.

Frantically she pulled on her socks and shoes, unnerved by being barefoot, as earlier her near nakedness had made her feel vulnerable— as if death could be foiled by an adequate wardrobe.

She heard those voices again. Not at the end of the hallway any more. Near her own door. Approaching. She wished the door featured one of those one-way, fisheye lenses that allowed a wide-angled view, but there was none.

At the sill was a half-inch crack, however, so Tessa dropped to the floor, pressed one side of her face against the carpet, and squinted out at the corridor. From that limited perspective, she saw something move past her room so quickly that her eyes could not quite track it, though she caught a glimpse of its feet, which was enough to alter dramatically her perception of what was happening. This was not an incidence of human savagery akin to the bloodbath she had witnessed—and to which she nearly had succumbed—in Northern Ireland. This was, instead, an encounter with the unknown, a breach of reality, a sudden sideslip out of the normal world into the uncanny. They were leathery, hairy, dark-skinned feet, broad and flat and surprisingly long, with toes so extrusile and multiple jointed that they almost seemed to have the function of fingers.

Something hit the door. Hard.

Tessa scrambled to her feet and out of the foyer.

Crazed voices filled the hall: that same weird mix of harsh animal sounds punctuated by bursts of breathlessly spoken but for the most part disconnected words.

She went around the bed to the window, disengaged the pressure latch, and slid the movable pane aside.

Again the door shook. The boom was so loud that Tessa felt as if she were inside a drum. It would not collapse as easily as the other guests' door, thanks to the chair, but it would not hold for more than a few additional blows.

She sat on the sill, swung her legs out, looked down. The fog-dampened walk glistened in the dim yellow glow of the serviceway lamps about twelve feet below the window. An easy jump.

They hit the door again, harder. Wood splintered.

Tessa pushed off the windowsill. She landed on the wet walkway and, because of her rubber-soled shoes, skidded but did not fall.

Overhead, in the room she had left, wood splintered more noisily than before, and tortured metal screeched as the lock on the door began to disintegrate.

She was near the north end of the building. She thought she saw something moving in the darkness in that direction. It might have been nothing more than a clotting of fog churning eastward on the wind, but she didn't want to take a chance, so she ran south, with the vast black sea beyond the railing at her right side. By the time she reached the end of the building, a crash echoed through the night—the sound of the door to her room going down—which was followed by the howling of the pack as it entered that place in search of her.

chapter thirty-five

Sam could not have slipped out of the patrol car without drawing Danberry's attention. Four cruisers awaited the cop's use, so there was a seventy-five-percent chance that Sam would be undetected if he stayed in the car. He slid down in the driver's seat as far as he could and leaned to his right, across the computer keyboard on the console.

Danberry went to the next car in line.

With his head on the console, his neck twisted so he could look up through the window on the passenger's side, Sam watched as Danberry unlocked the door of that other cruiser. He prayed that the cop would keep his back turned, because the interior of the car in which Sam slouched was revealed by the sulfurous glow of the parking-lot lights. If Danberry even glanced his way, Sam would be seen.

The cop got into the other black-and-white and slammed the door, and Sam sighed with relief. The engine turned over. Danberry pulled out of the municipal lot. When he hit the alley he gunned the engine, and his tires spun and squealed for a moment before they bit in, and then he was gone.

Though Sam wanted to hot-wire the car and switch on the computer again to find out whether Watkins and Shaddack were still conversing, he knew he dared not stay any longer. As the manhunt escalated, the police department's offices in the municipal building were sure to become busy.

Because he didn't want them to know that he had been probing in their computer or that he had eavesdropped on their VDT conversation—the greater they assumed his ignorance to be, the less effective they would be in their search for him—Sam used his tools to replace the ignition core in the steering column. He got out, pushed the lock button down, and closed the door.

He didn't want to leave the area by the alleyway because a patrol car might turn in from one end or the other, capturing him in its headlights. Instead he dashed straight across that narrow back street from the parking lot and opened a gate in a simple wrought-iron fence. He entered the rear yard of a slightly decrepit Victorian-style house whose owners had let the shrubbery run so wild that it looked as if a macabre cartoon family from the pen of Gahan Wilson might live in the place. He walked quietly past the side of the house, across the front lawn, to Pacific Drive, one block south of Ocean Avenue.

The night calm was not split by sirens. He heard no shouts, no running footsteps, no cries of alarm. But he knew he had awakened a many-headed beast and that this singularly dangerous Hydra was looking for him all over town.

chapter thirty-six

Mike Peyser didn't know what to do, didn't know, he was scared, confused and scared, so he could not think clearly, though he *needed* to think sharp and clear like a man, except the wild part of him kept intruding; his mind worked quickly, and it was sharp, but he could not hold to a single train of thought for more than a couple of minutes. Quick thinking, rapid-fire thinking, was not good enough to solve a problem like this; he had to think quick *and* deep. But his attention span was not what it should have been.

When he finally was able to stop screaming and get up from the kitchen floor, he hurried into the dark dining room, through the unlighted living room, down the short hall to the bedroom, then into the master bath, going on all fours part of the way, rising onto his hind feet as he crossed the bedroom threshold, unable to rise all the way up and stand entirely straight, but flexible enough to get more than halfway erect. In the bathroom, which was lit only by the vague and somewhat scintillant moon-glow that penetrated the small window above the shower stall, he gripped the edge of the sink and stared into the mirrored front of the medicine cabinet, where he could see only a shadowy reflection of himself, without detail.

He wanted to believe that in fact he had returned to his natural form, that his feeling of being trapped in the altered state was pure hallucination, yes, yes, he wanted to believe that, badly needed to believe, believe, even though he could not stand fully erect, even though he could feel the difference in his impossibly long-fingered hands and in the queer set of his head on his shoulders and in the way his back joined his hips. He needed to believe.

Turn on the light, he told himself.

He could not do it.

Turn on the light.

He was afraid.

He had to turn on the light and look at himself.

But he gripped the sink and could not move.

Turn on the light.

Instead he leaned toward the tenebrous mirror, peering intently at the indistinct reflection, seeing little more than the pale amber radiance of strange eyes.

Turn on the light.

He let out a thin mewl of anguish and terror.

Shaddack, he thought suddenly. Shaddack, he must tell Shaddack, Tom Shaddack would know what to do, Shaddack was his best hope, maybe his only hope, Shaddack.

He let go of the sink, dropped to the floor, hurried out of the bathroom, into the bedroom, toward the telephone on the nightstand. As he went, in a voice alternately shrill and guttural, piercing and whispery, he repeated the name as if it were a word with magic power: *"Shaddack, Shaddack, Shaddack, Shaddack . . ."*

chapter thirty-seven

Tessa Lockland took refuge in a twenty-four-hour coin-operated laundry four blocks east of Cove Lodge and half a block off Ocean Avenue. She wanted to be someplace bright, and the banks of overhead fluorescents allowed no shadows. Alone in the laundry, she sat in a badly scarred, yellow plastic chair, staring at rows of clothes-dryer portals, as if understanding would be visited upon her from some cosmic source communicating on those circles of glass.

As a documentarist, she had to have a keen eye for the patterns in life that would give coherence to a film narratively and visually, so she had no trouble seeing patterns of darkness, death, and unknown forces in this deeply troubled town. The fantastic creatures in the motel surely had been the source of the cries she'd heard on the beach earlier that night, and her sister had no doubt been killed by those same beings, whatever the hell they were. Which sort of explained why the authorities had been so insistent that Marion okay the cremation of Janice's body—not because the remains were corroded by seawater and half-devoured by fish, but because cremation would cover wounds that would raise unanswerable questions in an unbiased autopsy. She also saw reflections of the corruption of local authorities in the physical appearance of Ocean Avenue, where too many storefronts were empty and too many businesses were suffering, which was inexplicable for a town in which unemployment was virtually nil. She had noted an air of solemnity about the people she had seen on the streets, as well as a briskness and purposefulness that seemed odd in a laid-back northern coastal town where the hurly-burly of modern life hardly intruded.

However, her awareness of the patterns included no explanation of *why* the police would want to conceal the true nature of Janice's killing. Or why the town seemed in an economic depression in spite of its prosperity. Or what in the name of God those nightmare things in the motel had been. Patterns were clues to underlying truths, but her ability to recognize them did not mean she could find the answers and reveal the truths at which the patterns hinted.

She sat, shivering, in the fluorescent glare and breathed trace fumes of detergents, bleaches, fabric softeners, and the lingering staleness of the cigarette butts in the two free-standing sand-filled ashtrays, while she tried to figure what to do next. She had not lost her determination to probe into Janice's death. But she no longer had the audacity to think she could play detective all by herself. She was going to need help and would probably have to obtain it from county or state authorities.

The first thing she had to do was get out of Moonlight Cove in one piece.

Her car was at Cove Lodge, but she did not want to go back there for it. Those . . . creatures might still be in the motel or watching it from the dense shrubs and trees and omnipresent shadows that were an integral part of the town. Like Carmel, California, elsewhere along the coast, Moonlight Cove was a town virtually built in a seaside forest. Tessa loved Carmel for its splendid integration of the works of man and nature, where geography and architecture often appeared to be the product of the same sculptor's hand. Right now, however, Moonlight Cove did not draw style and grace from its verdant lushness and artful night shadows, as did Carmel; rather, this town seemed to be dressed in the thinnest veneer of civilization, beneath which something savage—even primal—watched and waited. Every grove of trees and every dark street was not the home of beauty but of the uncanny and of death. She would have found Moonlight Cove far more attractive if every street and alley and lawn and park had been lit with the same plenitude of fluorescent bulbs as the Laundromat in which she had taken refuge.

Maybe the police had shown up at Cove Lodge by now in response to the screams and commotion. But she would not feel any safer returning there just because cops were around. Cops were part of the problem. They would want to question her about the murders of the other guests. They would find out that Janice had been her sister, and though she might not tell them she was in town to poke into the circumstances of Janice's death, they would suspect as much. If they *had* participated in a conspiracy to conceal the true nature of Janice's death, they probably wouldn't hesitate to deal with Tessa in a firm and final way.

She had to abandon the car.

But damned if she was going to walk out of town at night. She might be able to hitch a ride on the interstate—perhaps even from an honest trucker instead of a mobile psychopath—but between Moonlight Cove and the freeway, she would have to walk through a dark and semirural landscape, where surely she would be at even greater risk of encountering more of those mysterious beasts that had broken down her motel-room door.

Of course, they had come after her in a relatively public and well-lighted place. She had no real reason to assume that she was safer in this coin-operated laundry than in the middle of the woods. When the membrane of civilization ruptured and the primordial terror burst through, you weren't safe anywhere, not even on the steps of a church, as she had learned in Northern Ireland and elsewhere.

Nevertheless, she would cling to the light and shun the darkness. She had stepped through an invisible wall between the reality she had always known and a different, more hostile world. As long as she remained in that Twilight Zone, it seemed wise to assume that shadows offered even less comfort and security than did bright places.

Which left her with no plan of action. Except to sit in the Laundromat and wait for morning. In daylight she might risk a long walk to the freeway.

The blank glass of the dryer windows returned her stare.

An autumn moth thumped softly against the frosted plastic panels that were suspended under the fluorescent bulbs.

chapter thirty-eight

Unable to walk boldly into Moonlight Cove as she had planned, Chrissie retreated from Holliwell Road, heading back the way she had come. She stayed in the woods, moving slowly and cautiously from tree to tree, trying to avoid making a sound that might carry to the nearer of the sentries who had been posted at the intersection.

In a couple of hundred yards, when she was beyond those men's sight and hearing, she moved more aggressively. Eventually she came to one of the houses that lay along the county route. The single-story ranch home was set behind a large front lawn and sheltered by several pines and firs, barely visible now that the moon was waning. No lights were on inside or out, and all was silent.

She needed time to think, and she wanted to get out of the cold, dampish night. Hoping there were no dogs at the house, she hurried to the garage, staying off the gravel driveway to keep from making a lot of noise. As she expected, in addition to the large front door through which the cars entered and exited, there was a smaller side entrance. It was unlocked. She stepped into the garage and closed the door behind her.

"Chrissie Foster, secret agent, penetrated the enemy facility by the bold and clever use of a side door," she said softly.

The secondhand radiance of the sinking moon penetrated the panes in the door and two high, narrow windows on the west wall, but it was insufficient to reveal anything. She could see only a few darkly gleaming curves of chrome and windshield glass, just enough to suggest the presence of two cars.

She edged toward the first of those vehicles with the caution of a blind girl, hands out in front of her, afraid of knocking something over. The car was unlocked. She slipped inside behind the wheel, leaving the door open for the welcome glow of the interior lamp. She supposed a trace of that light might be visible at the garage windows if anyone in the house woke up and looked out, but she had to risk it.

She searched the glove compartment, the map-storage panels on the doors, and under the seats, hoping to find food, because most people kept candy bars or bags of nuts or crackers or *something* to snack on in their cars. Though she had eaten midafternoon, while locked in the pantry, she'd had nothing for ten hours. Her stomach growled. She wasn't expecting to find a hot fudge sundae or the fixings for a jelly sandwich, but she certainly hoped to do better than a single stick of chewing gum and one green Lifesaver that, retrieved from beneath the seat, was furry with dirt, lint, and carpet fuzz.

As if reading tabloid headlines, she said, "Starvation in the Land of Plenty, A Modern Tragedy, Young Girl Found Dead in Garage, 'I Only Wanted a Few Peanuts' Written in Her Own Blood."

In the other car she found two Hershey's bars with almonds.

"Thank you, God. Your friend, Chrissie."

She hogged down the first bar but savored the second one in small bites, letting it melt on her tongue.

While she ate, she thought about ways to get into Moonlight Cove. By the time she finished the chocolate—

CHOCOHOLIC YOUNG GIRL FOUND DEAD IN GARAGE FROM TERMINAL CASE OF GIANT ZITS

—she had devised a plan.

Her usual bedtime had passed hours ago, and she was exhausted from all the physical activity with which the night had been filled, so she just wanted to stay there in the car, her belly full of milk chocolate and almonds, and sleep for a couple of hours before putting her plan into effect. She yawned and slumped down in the seat. She ached all over, and her eyes were as heavy as if some overanxious mortician had weighted them with coins.

That image of herself as a corpse was so unsettling that she immediately got out of the car and closed the door. If she dozed off in the car, she most likely wouldn't wake until someone found her in the morning. Maybe the people who kept their cars in this garage were converted, like her own parents, in which case she'd be doomed.

Outside, shivering as the wind nipped at her, she headed back to the county road and turned north. She passed two more dark and silent houses, another stretch of woods, and came to a fourth house, another single-story ranch-style place with shake-shingle roof and redwood siding.

She knew the people who lived there, Mr. and Mrs. Eulane. Mrs. Eulane managed the cafeteria at school. Mr. Eulane was a gardener with many accounts in Moonlight Cove. Early every morning, Mr. Eulane drove into town in his white truck, the back of which was loaded with lawnmowers and hedge clippers and rakes and shovels and bags of mulch and fertilizer and everything else a gardener might need; only a few students had arrived by the time he dropped Mrs. Eulane off at school, then went about his own work. Chrissie figured she could find a place to hide in the back of the truck—which had board sides— among Mr. Eulane's gardening supplies and equipment.

The truck was in the Eulanes' garage, which was unlocked, just as the other one had been. But this was the country, after all, where people still trusted one another—which was good except that it gave invading aliens an extra edge.

The only window was small and in the wall that could not be seen from the house, so Chrissie risked turning on the overhead light when she stepped inside. She quietly scaled the side of the truck and made her way in among the gardening equipment, which was stored in the rear two-thirds of the cargo bed, nearest the tailgate. Toward the front, against the back wall of the truck cab, flanked by fifty-pound bags of fertilizer, snail bait, and potting soil, was a three-foot-high stack of folded burlap tarps in which Mr. Eulane bundled grass clippings that had to be hauled to the dump. She could use some tarps as a mattress, others as blankets, and bed down until morning, remaining hidden in the burlap and between the piles of fifty-pound bags all the way to Moonlight Cove.

She climbed out of the truck, switched off the garage lights, then returned in the dark and carefully climbed aboard once more. She made a nest for herself in the tarps. The burlap was a little scratchy. After years of use it was permeated with the scent of new-mown grass, which was nice at first but quickly palled. At least a few layers of tarps trapped her body heat, and in minutes she was warm for the first time all night.

And as the night deepened (she thought), *young Chrissie, masking her telltale human odors in the scent of grass that saturated the burlap, cleverly concealed herself from the pursuing aliens—or maybe werewolves—whose sense of smell was almost as good as that of hounds.*

chapter thirty-nine

Sam took temporary refuge on the unlighted playground of Thomas Jefferson Elementary School on Palomino Street on the south side of town. He sat on one of the swings, holding the suspension chains with both hands, actually swinging a bit, while he considered his options.

He could not leave Moonlight Cove by car. His rental was back at the motel, where he'd be apprehended if he showed his face. He could steal a car, but he remembered the exchange on the computer when Loman Watkins had ordered Danberry to establish a blockade on Ocean Avenue, between town and the interstate. They'd have sealed off every exit.

He could go overland, sneaking from street to street, to the edge of the town limits, then through the woods and fields to the freeway. But Watkins had also said something about having ringed the entire community with sentries, to intercept the "Foster girl." Although Sam was confident of his instincts and survival abilities, he had not had experience in taking evasive action over open territory since his service in the war more than twenty years ago. If men were stationed around the town, waiting to intercept the girl, Sam was likely to walk straight into one or more of them.

Though he was willing to risk getting caught, he must not fall into their hands until he had placed a call to the Bureau to report and to ask for emergency backup. If he became a statistic in this accidental-death capital of the world, the Bureau would send new men in his place, and ultimately the truth could come out—but perhaps too late.

As he swung gently back and forth through the rapidly thinning fog, pushed mostly by the wind, he thought about those schedules he had seen on the VDT. Everyone in town would be "converted" in the next twenty-three hours. Although he had no idea what the hell people were being converted *to*, he didn't like the sound of it. And he sensed that once those schedules had been met, once everyone in town was converted, getting to the truth in Moonlight Cove would be no easier than cracking open an infinite series of laser-welded, titanium boxes nested in Chinese-puzzle fashion.

Okay, so the first thing he had to do was get to a phone and call the Bureau. The phones in Moonlight Cove were compromised, but he did not care if the call was noted in a computer sweep or even recorded word for word. He just needed thirty seconds or a minute on the line with the office, and massive reinforcements would be on the way. Then he'd have to keep moving around, dodging cops for a couple of hours, until other agents arrived.

He couldn't just walk up to a house and ask to use their phone because he didn't know whom he could trust. Morrie Stein had said that after being in town a day or two, you were overcome with the paranoid feeling that eyes were on you wherever you went and that Big Brother was always just an arm's reach away. Sam had attained that stage of paranoia in only a few hours and was rapidly moving beyond it to a state of constant tension and suspicion unlike anything he'd known since those jungle battlegrounds two decades ago.

A pay phone. But not the one at the Shell station that he had used earlier. A wanted man was foolish to return to a place he was known to have frequented before.

From his walks around town, he remembered one or maybe two other pay phones. He got up from the swing, slipped his hands in his jacket pockets, hunched his shoulders against the chilling wind, and started across the schoolyard toward the street beyond.

He wondered about the Foster girl to whom Shaddack and Watkins referred on the computer link. Who was she? What had she seen? He suspected she was a key to understanding this conspiracy. Whatever she had witnessed might explain what they meant by "conversion."

chapter forty

The walls appeared to be bleeding. Red ooze, as if seeping from the Sheetrock, tracked down the pale yellow paint in many rivulets.

Standing in that second-floor room at Cove Lodge, Loman Watkins was repelled by the carnage . . . but also strangely excited.

The male guest's body was sprawled near the disarranged bed, hideously bitten and torn. In worse condition, the dead woman lay outside the room, in the second-floor hall, a scarlet heap on the orange carpet.

The air reeked of blood, bile, feces, urine—a melange of odors with which Loman was becoming increasingly familiar, as the victims of the regressives turned up more frequently week by week and day by day. This time, however, as never before, an alluring sweetness lay under the acrid surface of the stench. He drew deep breaths, unsure why that terrible redolence should have any appeal whatsoever. But he was unable to deny—or resist—its attraction any more than a hound could resist the fox's scent. Though he could not withstand the tempting fragrance, he was frightened by his response to it, and the blood in his veins seemed to grow colder as his pleasure in the biological stink grew more intense.

Barry Sholnick, the officer Loman had dispatched to Cove Lodge via computer link to apprehend Samuel Booker, and who had found this death and destruction instead of the Bureau agent, now stood in the corner by the window, staring intently at the dead man. He had been at the motel longer than anyone, almost half an hour, long enough to have begun to regard the victims with the detachment that police had to cultivate, as if dead and ravaged bodies were no more remarkable a part of the scene than the furniture. Yet Sholnick could not shift his gaze from the eviscerated corpse, the gore-spattered wreckage, and the blood-streaked walls. He was clearly electrified by that horrendous detritus and the violence of which it was a remembrance.

We hate what the regressives have become and what they do, Loman thought, but in some sick way we're also envious of them, of their ultimate freedom.

Something within him—and, he suspected, in all of the New People—cried out to join the regressives. As at the Foster place, Loman felt the urge to employ his newfound bodily control not to elevate himself, as Shaddack had intended, but to devolve into a wild state. He yearned to descend to a level of consciousness in which thoughts of the purpose and meaning of life would not trouble him, in which intellectual challenge would be nonexistent, in which he would be a creature whose existence was defined almost entirely by *sensation*, in which every decision was made solely on the basis of what would give him pleasure, a condition untroubled by complex thought. Oh, God, to be freed from the burdens of civilization and higher intelligence!

Sholnick made a low sound in the back of his throat.

Loman looked up from the dead man.

In Sholnick's brown eyes a wild light burned.

Am I as pale as he? Loman wondered. As sunken-eyed and strange?

For a moment Sholnick met the chief's gaze, then looked away as if he had been caught in a shameful act.

Loman's heart was pounding.

Sholnick went to the window. He stared out at the lightless sea. His hands were fisted at his sides.

Loman was trembling.

The smell, darkly sweet. The smell of the hunt, the kill.

He turned away from the corpse and walked out of the room, into the hallway, where the sight of the dead woman—half naked, gouged, lacerated—was no relief. Bob Trott, one of several recent additions to the force when it expanded to twelve men last week, stood over the battered body. He was a big man, four inches taller and thirty pounds heavier than Loman, with a face of hard planes and chiseled edges. He looked down at the cadaver with a faint, unholy smile.

Flushed, his vision beginning to blur, his eyes smarting in the harsh fluorescent glare, Loman spoke sharply: "Trott, come with me." He set off along the hall to the other room that had been broken into. With evident reluctance, Trott finally followed him.

By the time Loman reached the shattered door of that unit, Paul Amberlay, another of his officers, appeared at the head of the north stairs, returning from the motel office where Loman had sent him to check the register. "The couple in room twenty-four were named Jenks, Sarah and Charles," Amberlay reported. He was twenty-five, lean and sinewy, intelligent. Perhaps because the young officer's face was slightly pointed, with deep-set eyes, he had always reminded Loman of a fox. "They're from Portland."

"And in thirty-six here?"

"Tessa Lockland from San Diego."

Loman blinked. "Lockland?"

Amberlay spelled it.

"When did she check in?"

"Just tonight."

"The minister's widow, Janice Capshaw," Loman said. "Her maiden name was Lockland. I had to deal with her mother by phone, and she was in San Diego. Persistent old broad. A million questions. Had some trouble getting her to consent to cremation. She said her other daughter was out of the country, somewhere really remote, couldn't be reached quickly, but would come around within a month to empty the house and settle Mrs. Capshaw's affairs. So this is her, I guess."

Loman led them into Tessa Lockland's room, two doors down from unit forty, in which Booker was registered. Wind huffed at the open window. The place was littered with broken furniture, torn bedding, and the glass from a shattered TV set, but unmarked by blood. Earlier they had checked the room for a body and found none; the open window indicated that the occupant fled before the regressives had managed to smash through the door.

"So Booker's out there," Loman said, "and we've got to assume he saw the regressives or heard the killing. He knows something's wrong here. He doesn't understand it, but he knows enough . . . too much."

"You can bet he's busting his ass to get a call out to the damn Bureau," Trott said.

Loman agreed. "And now we've also got this Lockland bitch, and she's got to be thinking her sister never committed suicide, that she was killed by the same things that killed the couple from Portland—"

"Most logical thing for her to do," Amberlay said, "is come straight to us—to the police. She'll walk right into our arms."

"Maybe," Loman said, unconvinced. He began to pick through the rubble. "Help me find her purse. With them bashing down the door, she'd have gone out the window without pausing to grab her purse."

Trott found it wedged between the bed and one of the nightstands.

Loman emptied the contents onto the mattress. He snatched up the wallet, flipped through the plastic windows full of credit cards and photographs, until he found her driver's license. According to the license data, she was five-four, one hundred and four pounds, blond, blue-eyed. Loman held up the ID so Trott and Amberlay could see the photograph.

"She's a looker," Amberlay said.

"I'd like to get a bite of that," Trott said.

His officer's choice of words gave Loman a chill. He couldn't help wondering whether Trott meant "bite" as a euphemism for sex or whether he was expressing a very real subconscious desire to savage the woman as the regressives had torn apart the couple from Portland.

"We know what she looks like," Loman said. "That helps."

Trott's hard, sharp features were inadequate for the expression of gentler emotions like affection and delight, but they perfectly conveyed the animal hunger and urge to violence that seethed deep within him. "You want us to bring her in?"

"Yes. She doesn't know anything, really, but on the other hand she knows too much. She knows the couple down the hall were killed, and she probably saw a regressive."

"Maybe the regressives followed her through the window and got her," Amberlay suggested. "We might find her body somewhere outside, on the grounds of the lodge."

"Could be," Loman said. "But if not, we have to find her and bring her in. You called Callan?"

"Yeah," Amberlay said.

"We've got to get this place cleaned up," Loman said. "We've got to keep a lid on until midnight, until everyone in town's been put through the Change. Then, when Moonlight Cove's secure, we can concentrate on finding the regressives and eliminating them."

Trott and Amberlay met Loman's eyes, then looked at each other. In the glances they exchanged, Loman saw the dark knowledge that they all were potential regressives, that they, too, felt the call toward that unburdened, primitive state. It was an awareness of which none of them dared speak, for to give it voice was to admit that Moonhawk was a deeply flawed project and that they might all be damned.

chapter forty-one

Mike Peyser heard the dial tone and fumbled with the buttons, which were too small and closely set for his long, tinelike fingers. Abruptly he realized that he could not call Shaddack, *dared* not call Shaddack, though they had known each other for more than twenty years, since their days together at Stanford, could not call Shaddack even though it was Shaddack who had made him what he was, because Shaddack would consider him an outlaw now, a regressive, and Shaddack would have him restrained in a laboratory and either treat him with all the tenderness that a vivisectionist bestowed upon a white rat or destroy him because of the threat he posed to the ongoing conversion of Moonlight Cove. Peyser shrieked in frustration. He tore the telephone out of the wall and threw it across the bedroom, where it hit the dresser mirror, shattering the glass.

His sudden perception of Shaddack as a powerful enemy rather than a friend and mentor was the last entirely clear and rational thought that Peyser had for a while. His fear was a trapdoor that opened under him, casting him down into the darkness of the primeval mind that he had unleashed for the pleasure of a night hunt. He moved back and forth through the house, sometimes in a frenzy, sometimes in a sullen slouch, not sure why he was alternately excited, depressed, or smoldering with savage needs, driven more by feelings than intellect.

He relieved himself in a corner of the living room, sniffed his own urine, then went into the kitchen in search of more food. Now and then his mind cleared, and he tried to call his body back to its more civilized form, but when his tissues would not respond to his will, he cycled down into the darkness of animal thought again. Several times he was clearheaded enough to appreciate the irony of having been reduced to savagery by a process—the Change—meant to elevate him to superhuman status, but that line of thought was too bleak to be endured, and a new descent into the savage mind was almost welcome.

Repeatedly, both when in the grip of a primitive consciousness and when the clouds lifted from his mind, he thought of the boy, Eddie Valdoski, the boy, the tender boy, and he thrilled to the memory of blood, sweet blood, fresh blood steaming in the cold night air.

chapter forty-two

Physically and mentally exhausted, Chrissie nevertheless was not able to sleep. In the burlap tarps in the back of Mr. Eulane's truck, she hung from the thin line of wakefulness, wanting nothing more than to let go and fall into unconsciousness.

She felt incomplete, as though something had been left undone—and suddenly she was crying. Burying her face in the fragrant and slightly scratchy burlap, she bawled as she'd not done in years, with the abandon of a baby. She wept for her mother and father, perhaps lost forever, not taken cleanly by death but by something foul, dirty, inhuman, satanic. She wept for the adolescence that would have been hers—horses and seaside pastures and books read on the beach—but that had been shattered beyond repair. She wept, as well, over some loss she felt but could not quite identify, though she suspected it was innocence or maybe faith in the triumph of good over evil.

None of the fictional heroines she admired would have indulged in uncontrolled weeping, and Chrissie was embarrassed by her torrent of tears. But to weep was as human as to err, and perhaps she needed to cry, in part, to prove to herself that no monstrous seed had been planted in her of the sort that had germinated and spread tendrils through her parents. Crying, she was still Chrissie. Crying was proof that no one had stolen her soul.

She slept.

chapter forty-three

Sam had seen another pay phone at a Union 76 service station one block north of Ocean. The station was out of business. The windows were filmed with gray dust, and a hastily lettered FOR SALE sign hung in one of them, as if the owner actually didn't care whether the place was sold or not and had made the sign only because it was expected of him. Crisp, dead leaves and dry pine needles from surrounding trees had blown against the gasoline pumps and lay in snowlike drifts.

The phone booth was against the south wall of the building and visible from the street. Sam stepped through the open door but did not pull it shut, for fear of completing a circuit that would turn on the overhead bulb and draw him to the attention of any cops who happened by.

The line was dead. He deposited a coin, hoping that would activate the dial tone. The line was still dead.

He jiggled the hook from which the handset hung. His coin was returned.

He tried again but to no avail.

He believed that pay phones in or adjacent to a service station or privately owned store were sometimes joint operations, the income shared between the telephone company and the businessman who allowed the phone to be installed. Perhaps they had turned off the phone when the Union 76 had closed up.

However, he suspected the police had used their access to the telephone-company's computer to disable all coin-operated phones in Moonlight Cove. The moment they had learned an undercover federal agent was in town, they could have taken extreme measures to prevent him from contacting the world outside.

Of course he might be overestimating their capabilities. He had to try another phone before giving up hope of contacting the Bureau.

On his walk after dinner, he had passed a coin laundry half a block north of Ocean Avenue and two blocks west of this Union 76. He was pretty sure that when glancing through the plate-glass window, he had seen a telephone on the rear wall, at the end of a row of industrial-size dryers with stainless-steel fronts.

He left the Union 76. As much as possible staying away from the streetlamps—which illuminated side streets only in the first block north and south of Ocean—using alleyways where he could, he slipped through the silent town, toward where he remembered having seen the laundry. He wished the wind would die and leave some of the rapidly dissipating fog.

At an intersection one block north of Ocean and half a block from the laundry, he almost walked into plain sight of a cop driving south toward the center of town. The patrolman was half a block from the intersection, coming slowly, surveying both sides of the street. Fortunately he was looking the other way when Sam hurried into the unavoidable fall of lamplight at the corner.

Sam scrambled backward and pressed into a deep entranceway on the side of a three-story brick building that housed some of the town's professionals: A plaque in the recess, to the left of the door, listed a dentist, two lawyers, a doctor, and a chiropractor. If the patrol turned left at the corner and came past him, he'd probably be spotted. But if it either went straight on toward Ocean or turned right and headed west, he would not be seen.

Leaning against the locked door and as far back in the shadows as he could go, waiting for the infuriatingly slow car to reach the intersection, Sam had a moment for reflection and realized that even for one-thirty in the morning, Moonlight Cove was peculiarly quiet and the streets unusually deserted. Small towns had night owls as surely as did cities; there should have been a pedestrian or two, a car now and then, *some* signs of life other than police patrols.

The black-and-white turned right at the corner, heading west and away from him.

Although the danger had passed, Sam remained in the unlighted entranceway, mentally retracing his journey from Cove Lodge to the municipal building, from there to the Union 76, and finally to his current position. He could not recall passing a house where music was playing, where a television blared, or where the laughter of late revelers indicated a party in progress. He had seen no young couples sharing a last kiss in parked cars. The few restaurants and taverns were apparently closed, and the movie theater was out of business, and except for his movements and those of the police, Moonlight Cove might have been a ghost town.

Its living rooms, bedrooms, and kitchens might have been peopled only by moldering corpses—or by robots that posed as people during the day and were turned off at night to save energy when it was not as essential to maintain the illusion of life.

Increasingly worried by the word "conversion" and its mysterious meaning in the context of this thing they called the Moonhawk Project, he left the entranceway, turned the corner, and ran along the brightly lighted street to the laundry. He saw the phone as he was pushing open the glass door.

He hurried halfway through the long room—dryers on the right, a double row of washers back-to-back in the middle, some chairs at the end of the washers, more chairs along the left wall with the candy and detergent machines and the laundry-folding counter—before he realized the place was not deserted. A petite blonde in faded jeans and a blue pullover sweater sat on one of the yellow plastic chairs. None of the washers or dryers was running, and the woman did not seem to have a basket of clothes with her.

He was so startled by her—a live person, a live *civilian*, in this sepulchral night—that he stopped and blinked.

She was perched on the edge of the chair, visibly tense. Her eyes were wide. Her hands were clenched in her lap. She seemed to be holding her breath.

Realizing that he had frightened her, Sam said, "Sorry."

She stared at him as if she were a rabbit facing down a fox.

Aware that he must look wild-eyed, even frantic, he added, "I'm not dangerous."

"They all say that."

"They do?"

"But I *am*."

Confused, he said, "You are what?"

"Dangerous."

"Really?"

She stood up. "I'm a black belt."

For the first time in days, a genuine smile pulled at Sam's face. "Can you kill with your hands?"

She stared at him for a moment, pale and shaking. When she spoke, her defensive anger was excessive. "Hey, don't laugh at me, asshole, or I'll bust you up so bad that when you walk, you'll clink like a bag of broken glass."

At last, astonished by her vehemency, Sam began to assimilate the observations he'd made on entering. No washers or dryers in operation. No clothes basket. No box of detergent or bottle of fabric softener.

"What's wrong?" he asked, suddenly suspicious.

"Nothing, if you keep your distance."

He wondered if she knew somehow that the local cops were eager to get hold of him. But that seemed nuts. How could she know? "What're you doing here if you don't have clothes to wash?"

"What's it your business? You own this dump?" she demanded.

"No. And don't tell me you own it, either."

She glared at him.

He studied her, gradually absorbing how attractive she was. She had eyes as piercingly blue as a June sky and skin as clear as summer air, and she seemed radically out of place along this dark, October coast, let alone in a grungy Laundromat at one-thirty in the morning. When her beauty finally, fully registered with him, so did other things about her, including the intensity of her fear, which was revealed in her eyes and in the lines around them and in the set of her mouth. It was fear far out of proportion to any threat he could pose. If he had been a six-foot-six, three-hundred-pound, tattooed biker with a revolver in one hand and a ten-inch knife in the other, and if he had burst into the laundry chanting paeans to Satan, the utterly bloodless paleness of her face and the hard edge of terror in her eyes would have been understandable. But he was only Sam Booker, whose greatest attribute as an agent was his guy-next-door ordinariness and an aura of harmlessness.

Unsettled by *her* unsettledness, he said, "The phone."

"What?"

He pointed at the pay phone.

"Yes," she said, as if confirming it was indeed a phone.

"Just came in to make a call."

"Oh."

Keeping one eye on her, he went to the phone, fed it his quarter, but got no dial tone. He retrieved his coin, tried again. No luck.

"Damn!" he said.

The blonde had edged toward the door. She halted, as though she thought he might rush at her and drag her down if she attempted to leave the Laundromat.

The Cove engendered in Sam a powerful paranoia. Increasingly over the past few hours he had come to think of everyone in town as a potential enemy. And suddenly he perceived that this woman's peculiar behavior resulted from a state of mind precisely like his. "Yes, of course—you're not *from* here, are you, from Moonlight Cove?"

"So?"

"Neither am I."

"So?"

"And you've seen something."

She stared at him.

He said, "Something's happened, you've seen something, and you're scared, and I'll bet you've got damned good reason to be."

She looked as if she'd sprint for the door.

"Wait," he said quickly. "I'm with the FBI." His voice cracked slightly. "I really am."

chapter forty-four

Because he was a night person who had always preferred to sleep during the day, Thomas Shaddack was in his teak-paneled study, dressed in a gray sweat suit, working on an aspect of Moonhawk at a computer terminal, when Evan, his night servant, rang through to tell him that Loman Watkins was at the front door.

"Send him to the tower," Shaddack said. "I'll join him shortly."

He seldom wore anything but sweat suits these days. He had more than twenty in the closet—ten black, ten gray, and a couple navy blue. They were more comfortable than other clothes, and by limiting his choices, he saved time that otherwise would be wasted coordinating each day's wardrobe, a task at which he was not skilled. Fashion was of no interest to him. Besides, he was gawky—big feet, lanky legs, knobby knees, long arms, bony shoulders—and too thin to look good even in finely tailored suits. Clothes either hung strangely on him or emphasized his thinness to such a degree that he appeared to be Death personified, an unfortunate image reinforced by his flour-white skin, nearly black hair, sharp features, and yellowish eyes.

He even wore sweat suits to New Wave board meetings. If you were a genius in your field, people expected you to be eccentric. And if your personal fortune was in the hundreds of millions, they accepted all eccentricities without comment.

His ultramodern, reinforced-concrete house at cliff's edge near the north point of the cove was another expression of his calculated non-conformity. The three stories were like three layers of a cake, though each layer was of a different size than the others—the largest on top, the smallest in the middle—and they were not concentric but misaligned, creating a profile that in daylight lent the house the appearance of an enormous piece of avant-garde sculpture. At night, its myriad windows aglow, it looked less like sculpture than like the star-traveling mothership of an invading alien force.

The tower was eccentricity piled on eccentricity, rising off-center from the third level, soaring an additional forty feet into the air. It was not round but oval, not anything like a tower in which a princess might pine for a crusade-bound prince or in which a king might have his enemies imprisoned and tortured, but reminiscent of the conning tower of a submarine. The large, glass-walled room at the top could be reached by elevator or by stairs that spiraled around the inside of the tower wall, circling the metal core in which the elevator was housed.

Shaddack kept Watkins waiting for ten minutes, just for the hell of it, then chose to take the lift to meet him. The interior of the cab was paneled with burnished brass, so although the mechanism was slow, he seemed to be ascending inside a rifle cartridge.

He had added the tower to the architect's designs almost as an afterthought, but it had become his favorite part of the huge house. That high place offered endless vistas of calm (or wind-chopped), sun-spangled (or night-shrouded) sea to the west. To the east and south, he looked out and *down* on the whole town of Moonlight Cove; his sense of superiority was comfortably reinforced by that lofty perspective on the only other visible works of man. From that room, only four months ago, he had seen the moonhawk for the third time in his life, a sight that few men were privileged to see even once—which he took to be a sign that he was destined to become the most influential man ever to walk the earth.

The elevator stopped. The doors opened.

When Shaddack entered the dimly lighted room that encircled the elevator, Loman Watkins rose quickly from an armchair and respectfully said, "Good evening, sir."

"Please be seated, Chief," he said graciously, even affably, but with a subtle note in his voice that reinforced their mutual understanding that it was Shaddack, not Watkins, who decided how formal or casual the meeting would be.

Shaddack was the only child of James Randolph Shaddack, a former circuit-court judge in Phoenix, now deceased. The family had not been wealthy, though solidly upper middle-class, and that position on the economic ladder, combined with the prestige of a judgeship, gave James considerable stature in his community. And power. Throughout his childhood and adolescence, Tom had been fascinated by how his father, a political activist as well as a judge, had used that power not only to acquire material benefits but to control others. The control—the exercise of power for power's sake—was what had most appealed to James, and that was what had deeply excited his son, too, from an early age.

Now Tom Shaddack held power over Loman Watkins and Moonlight Cove by reason of his wealth, because he was the primary employer in town, because he gripped the reins of the political system, and because of the Moonhawk Project, named after the thrice-received vision. But his ability to manipulate them was more extensive than anything old James had enjoyed as a judge and canny politico. He possessed the power of life and death over them—literally. If an hour from now he decided they all must die, they would be dead before midnight. Furthermore he could condemn them to the grave with no more chance of being punished than a god risked when raining fire on his creations.

The only lights in the tower room were concealed in a recess under the immense windows, which extended from the ceiling to within ten inches of the floor. The hidden lamps ringed the chamber, subtly illuminating the plush carpet but casting no glare on the huge panes. Nevertheless, if the night had been clear, Shaddack would have flicked the switch next to the elevator button, plunging the room into near darkness, so his ghostly reflection and those of the starkly modern furnishings would not fall on the glass between him and his view of the world over which he held dominion. He left the lights on, however, because some milky fog still churned past glass walls, and little could be seen now that the horned moon had found the horizon.

Barefoot, Shaddack crossed the charcoal-gray carpet. He settled into a second armchair, facing Loman Watkins across a low, white-marble cocktail table.

The policeman was forty-four, less than three years older than Shaddack, but he was Shaddack's complete physical opposite: five-ten, a hundred and eighty pounds, large-boned, broad in the shoulders and chest, thick-necked. His face was broad, too, as open and guileless as Shaddack's was closed and cunning. His blue eyes met Shaddack's yellow-brown gaze, held it only for a moment, then lowered to stare at his strong hands, which were clasped so rigidly in his lap that the sharp knuckles seemed in danger of piercing the taut skin. His darkly tanned scalp showed through brush-cut brown hair.

Watkins's obvious subservience pleased Shaddack, but he was even more gratified by the chief's fear, which was evident in the tremors that the man was struggling—with some success—to repress and in the haunted expression that deepened the color of his eyes. Because of the Moonhawk Project, because of what had been done to him, Loman Watkins was in many ways superior to most men, but he was also now and forever in Shaddack's thrall as surely as a laboratory mouse, clamped down and attached to electrodes, was at the mercy of the scientist who conducted experiments on him. In a manner of speaking, Shaddack was Watkins's maker, and he possessed, in Watkins's eyes, the position and power of a god.

Leaning back in his chair, folding his pale, long-fingered hands on his chest, Shaddack felt his manhood swelling, hardening. He was not aroused by Loman Watkins, because he had no tendency whatsoever toward homosexuality; he was aroused not by anything in Watkins's physical appearance but by the awareness of the tremendous authority he wielded over the man. Power aroused Shaddack more fully and easily than sexual stimuli. Even as an adolescent, when he saw pictures of naked women in erotic magazines, he was turned on not by the sight of bared breasts, not by the curve of a female bottom or the elegant line of long legs, but by the thought of *dominating* such women, totally controlling them, holding their very lives in his hands. If a woman looked at him with undisguised fear, he found her infinitely more appealing than if she regarded him with desire. And since he reacted more strongly to terror than to lust, his arousal was not dependent upon the sex or age or physical attractiveness of the person who trembled in his presence.

Enjoying the policeman's submissiveness, Shaddack said, "You've got Booker?"

"No, sir."

"Why not?"

"He wasn't at Cove Lodge when Sholnick got there."

"He's got to be found."

"We'll find him."

"And converted. Not just to prevent him from telling anyone what he's seen . . . but to give us one of our own *inside* the Bureau. That'd be a coup. His being here could turn out to be an incredible plus for the project."

"Well, whether Booker's a plus or not, there's worse than him. Regressives attacked some of the guests at the lodge. Quinn himself was either carried off, killed, and left where we haven't found him yet . . . or he was one of the regressives himself and is off now . . . doing whatever they do after a kill, maybe baying at the goddamn moon."

With growing dismay and agitation, Shaddack listened to the report.

Perched on the edge of his chair, Watkins finished, blinked, and said, "These regressives scare the hell out of me."

"They're disturbing," Shaddack agreed.

On the night of September fourth, they had cornered a regressive,

Jordan Coombs, in the movie theater on Main Street. Coombs had been a maintenance man at New Wave. That night, however, he had been more ape than man, although actually neither, but something so strange and savage that no single word could describe him. The term "regressive" was only adequate, Shaddack had discovered, if you never came face-to-face with one of the beasts. Because once you'd seen one close up, "regressive" insufficiently conveyed the horror of the thing, and in fact all words failed. Their attempt to take Coombs alive had failed, too, for he had proved too aggressive and powerful to be subdued; to save themselves, they'd had to blow his head off.

Now Watkins said, "They're more than disturbing. Much more than just that. They're . . . psychotic."

"I know they're psychotic," Shaddack said impatiently. "I've named their condition myself: metamorphic-related psychosis."

"They *enjoy* killing."

Thomas Shaddack frowned. He had not foreseen the problem of the regressives, and he refused to believe that they constituted more than a minor anomaly in the otherwise beneficial conversion of the people of Moonlight Cove. "Yes, all right, they enjoy killing, and in their regressed state they're designed for it, but we've only a few of them to identify and eliminate. Statistically, they're an insignificant percentage of those we've put through the Change."

"Maybe not so insignificant," Watkins said hesitantly, unable to meet Shaddack's eyes, a reluctant bearer of bad tidings. "Judging by all the bloody wreckage lately, I'd guess that among those nineteen hundred converted as of this morning, there were fifty or sixty of these regressives out there."

"Ridiculous!"

To admit regressives existed in large numbers, Shaddack would have to consider the possibility that his research was flawed, that he had rushed his discoveries out of the laboratory and into the field with too little consideration of the potential for disaster, and that his enthusiastic application of the Moonhawk Project's revolutionary discoveries to the people of Moonlight Cove was a tragic mistake. He could admit nothing of the sort.

He had yearned all his life for the nth degree of power that was now nearly within his reach, and he was psychologically incapable of retreating from the course he had set. Since puberty he had denied himself certain pleasures because, had he acted upon those needs, he would have been hunted down by the law and made to pay a heavy price. All those years of denial had created a tremendous internal pressure that he desperately needed to relieve. He had sublimated his antisocial desires in his work, focused his energies into socially acceptable endeavors—which had, ironically, resulted in discoveries that would make him immune to authority and therefore free to indulge his long-suppressed urges without fear of censure or punishment.

Besides, not just psychologically but also in practical terms, he had gone too far to turn back. He had brought something revolutionary into the world. Because of him, nineteen hundred New People walked the earth, as different from other men and women as Cro-Magnons had been different from their more primitive Neanderthal ancestors. He did not have the ability to undo what he had done any more than other scientists and technicians could *un*invent the wheel or atomic bomb.

Watkins shook his head. "I'm sorry . . . but I don't think it's ridiculous at all. Fifty or sixty regressives. Or more. Maybe a lot more."

"You'll need proof to convince me of that. You'll have to name them for me. Are you any closer to identifying even *one* of them—other than Quinn?"

"Alex and Sharon Foster, I think. And maybe even your own man, Tucker."

"Impossible."

Watkins described what he had found at the Foster place—and the cries he had heard in the distant woods.

Reluctantly Shaddack considered the possibility that Tucker was one of those degenerates. He was disturbed by the likelihood that his control among his inner circle was not as absolute as he had thought. If he could not be sure of those men closest to him, how could he be certain of his ability to control the masses? "Maybe the Fosters are regressives, though I doubt it's true of Tucker. But even if Tucker's one of them, that means you've found four. Not fifty or sixty. Just *four*. Who're all these others you imagine are out there?"

Loman Watkins stared at the fog, which pressed in ever-changing patterns against the glass walls of the tower room. "Sir, I'm afraid it isn't easy. I mean . . . think about it. If the state or federal authorities learned what you've done, if they could *understand* what you've done and really believe it, and if then they wanted to prevent us from bringing the Change to everyone beyond Moonlight Cove, they'd have one hell of a time stopping us, wouldn't they? After all, those of us who've been converted . . . we walk undetected among ordinary people. We seem like them, no different, unchanged."

"So?"

"Well . . . that's the same problem *we* have with the regressives. They're New People like us, but the thing that makes them different from us, the rottenness in them, is impossible to see; they're as indistinguishable from us as we are from the unchanged population of Old People."

Shaddack's iron erection had softened. Impatient with Watkins's negativism, he rose from his armchair and moved to the nearest of the big windows. Standing with his hands fisted in the pockets of his sweat-suit jacket, he stared at the vague reflection of his own long, lupine face, which was ghostlike in its transparency. He met his own gaze, as well, then quickly looked through the reflection of his eye sockets and past the glass into the darkness beyond, where vagrant sea breezes worked the loom of night to bring forth a fragile fabric of fog. He kept his back to Watkins, for he did not want the man to see that he was concerned, and he avoided the glass-caught image of his own eyes because he did not want to admit to himself that his concern might be marbled with veins of fear.

chapter forty-five

He insisted on moving to the chairs, so they could not be seen as easily from the street. Tessa was leery about sitting beside him. He said that he was operating undercover and therefore carried no Bureau ID, but he showed her everything else in his wallet: driver's license, credit cards, library card, video rental card, photos of his son and his late wife, a coupon for a free chocolate-chip cookie at any Mrs. Fields store, a picture of Goldie Hawn torn from a magazine. Would a homicidal maniac carry a cookie coupon? In a while, as he took her back through her story of the massacre at Cove Lodge and picked relentlessly at the details, making sure that she told him everything and that he understood all of it, she began to trust him. If he was only pretending to be an agent, his pretense would not have been so elaborate or sustained.

"You didn't actually *see* anybody murdered?"

"They were killed," she insisted. "You wouldn't have any doubt if you'd heard their screams. I've stood in a mob of human monsters in Northern Ireland and seen them beat men to death. I was filming an industrial in a steel mill once, when there was a spill of molten metal that splattered all over workers' bodies, their faces. I've been with Miskito Indians in the Central American jungles when they were hit with antipersonnel bombs—millions of little bits of sharp steel, bodies pierced by a thousand needles—and I've heard *their* screams. I know what death sounds like. And this was the worst I've ever heard."

He stared at her for a long time. Then he said, "You look deceptively . . ."

"Cute?"

"Yes."

"Therefore innocent? Therefore naive?"

"Yes."

"My curse."

"And an advantage sometimes?"

"Sometimes," she acknowledged. "Listen, you know something, so tell me: What's going on in this town?"

"Something's happening to the people here."

"What?"

"I don't know. They're not interested in movies, for one thing. The theater closed. And they're not interested in luxury goods, fine gifts, that sort of thing, because those stores have all closed too. They no longer get a kick from champagne . . ." He smiled thinly. "The barrooms are all going out of business. The only thing they seem to be interested in is food. And killing."

chapter forty-six

Still standing at a tower-room window, Tom Shaddack said, "All right, Loman, here's what we'll do. Everyone at New Wave has been converted, so I'll assign a hundred of them to you, to augment the police force. You can use them to help in your investigation in any way you see fit—starting now. With that many at your command, you'll catch one of the regressives in the act, surely . . . and you'll be more likely to find this man Booker too."

The New People did not require sleep. The additional deputies could be brought into the field immediately.

Shaddack said, "They can patrol the streets on foot and in their cars—quietly, without drawing attention. And with that assistance, you'll grab at least one of the regressives, maybe all of them. If we can catch one in a devolved state, if I've a chance to *examine* one of them, I might be able to develop a test—physical or psychological—with which we can screen the New People for degenerates."

"I don't feel adequate to deal with this."

"It's a police matter."

"No, it isn't, really."

"It's no different than if you were tracking down an ordinary killer," Shaddack said irritably. "You'll apply the same techniques."

"But . . ."

"What is it?"

"Regressives could be among the men you assign me."

"There won't be any."

"But . . . how can you be sure?"

"I told you there won't be," Shaddack said sharply, still facing the window, the fog, the night.

They were both silent a moment.

Then Shaddack said, "You've got to put everything into finding these damned deviants. Everything, you hear me? I want at least one of them to examine by the time we've taken all of Moonlight Cove through the Change."

"I thought . . ."

"Yes?"

"Well, I thought . . ."

"Come on, come on. You thought what?"

"Well . . . just that maybe you'd suspend the conversions until we understand what's happening here."

"Hell no!" Shaddack turned from the window and glared at the police chief, who flinched satisfactorily. "These regressives are a minor problem, very minor. What the shit do you know about it? You're not the one who designed a new race, a new world. *I* am. The dream was mine, the vision mine. I had the brains and nerve to make the dream real. And I *know* this is an anomaly indicative of nothing. So the Change will take place according to schedule."

Watkins looked down at his white-knuckled hands.

As he spoke, Shaddack paced barefoot along the curved glass wall, then back again. "We now have more than enough doses to deal with the remaining townspeople. In fact, we've initiated a new round of conversions this evening. Hundreds will be brought into the fold by dawn, the rest by midnight. Until everyone in town is with us, there's a chance we'll be found out, a risk of someone carrying a warning to the outside world. Now that we've overcome the problems with the production of the biochips, we've got to take Moonlight Cove quickly, so we can proceed with the confidence that comes from having a secure home base. Understand?"

Watkins nodded.

"Understand?" Shaddack repeated.

"Yes. Yes, sir."

Shaddack returned to his chair and sat down. "Now what's this other thing you called me about earlier, this Valdoski business?"

"Eddie Valdoski, eight years old," Watkins said, looking at his hands, which he was now virtually wringing, as if trying to squeeze something from them in the way he might have squeezed water from a rag. "He was found dead a few minutes past eight. In a ditch along the country road. He'd been . . . tortured . . . bitten, gutted."

"You think one of the regressives did it?"

"Definitely."

"Who found the body?"

"Eddie's folks. His dad. The boy had been playing in the backyard, and then he . . . disappeared near sunset. They started searching, couldn't find him, got scared, called us, continued to search while we were on our way . . . and found the body just before my men got there."

"Evidently the Valdoskis aren't converted?"

"They weren't. But they are now."

Shaddack sighed. "There won't be any trouble about the boy if they've been brought into the fold."

The police chief raised his head and found the courage to look directly at Shaddack again. "But the boy's still dead." His voice was rough.

Shaddack said, "That's a tragedy, of course. This regressive element among the New People could not have been foreseen. But no great advancement in human history has been without its victims."

"He was a fine boy," the policeman said.

"You knew him?"

Watkins blinked. "I went to high school with his father, George Valdoski. I was Eddie's godfather."

Considering his words carefully, Shaddack said, "It's a terrible thing. And we'll find the regressive who did it. We'll find all of them and eliminate them. Meanwhile, we can take some comfort in the fact that Eddie died in a great cause."

Watkins regarded Shaddack with unconcealed astonishment. "Great cause? What did Eddie know of a great cause? He was eight years old."

"Nevertheless," Shaddack said, hardening his voice, "Eddie was caught up in an unexpected side effect of the conversion of Moonlight Cove, which makes him part of this wonderful, historical event." He knew that Watkins had been a patriot, absurdly proud of his flag and country, and he supposed that some of that sentiment still reposed in the man, even subsequent to conversion, so he said: "Listen to me, Loman. During the Revolutionary War, when the colonists were fighting for independence, some innocent bystanders died, women and children, not just combatants, and those people did not die in vain. They were martyrs every bit as much as the soldiers who perished in the field. It's the same in any revolution. The important thing is that justice prevail and that those who die can be said to have given their lives for a noble purpose."

Watkins looked away from him.

Rising from his armchair again, Shaddack rounded the low cocktail table to stand beside the policeman. Looking down at Watkins's bowed head, he put one hand on the man's shoulder.

Watkins cringed from the touch.

Shaddack did not move his hand, and he spoke with the fervor of an evangelist. He was a cool evangelist, however, whose message did not involve the hot passion of religious conviction but the icy power of logic, reason. "You're one of the New People now, and that does not just mean that you're stronger and quicker than ordinary men, and it doesn't just mean you're virtually invulnerable to disease and have a greater power to mend your injuries than anything any faith healer ever dreamed of. It *also* means you're clearer of mind, more rational than the Old People—so if you consider Eddie's death carefully and in the context of the miracle we're working here, you'll see that the price he paid was not too great. Don't deal with this situation emotionally, Loman; that's definitely not the way of New People. We're making a world that'll be more efficient, more ordered, and infinitely more stable precisely because men and women will have the power to control their emotions, to view every problem and event with the analytical coolness of a computer. Look at Eddie Valdoski's death as but another datum in the great flow of data that is the birth of the New People. You've got the power in you now to transcend human emotional limitations, and when you *do* transcend them, you'll know true peace and happiness for the first time in your life."

After a while Loman Watkins raised his head. He turned to look up at Shaddack. "Will this really lead to peace?"

"Yes."

"When there's no one left unconverted, will there be brotherhood at last?"

"Yes."

"Tranquillity?"

"Eternal."

chapter forty-seven

The Talbot house on Conquistador was a three-story redwood with lots of big windows. The property was sloped, and steep stone steps led up from the sidewalk to a shallow porch. No streetlamps lit that block, and there were no walkway or landscape lights at Talbot's, for which Sam was grateful.

Tessa Lockland stood close to him on the porch as he pressed the buzzer, just as she had stayed close all the way from the laundry. Above the noisy rustle of the wind in the trees, he could hear the doorbell ring inside.

Looking back toward Conquistador, Tessa said, "Sometimes it seems more like a morgue than a town, peopled by the dead, but then . . ."

"Then?"

". . . in spite of the silence and the stillness, you can feel the energy of the place, tremendous pent-up energy, as if there's a huge hidden machine just beneath the streets, beneath the ground . . . and as if the houses are filled with machinery, too, all of it powered up and straining at cogs and gears, just waiting for someone to engage a clutch and set it all in motion."

That was *exactly* Moonlight Cove, but Sam had not been able to put the feeling of the place into words. He rang the bell again and said, "I thought filmmakers were required to be borderline illiterates."

"Most Hollywood filmmakers are, but I'm an outcast documentarian, so I'm permitted to think—as long as I don't do too much of it."

"Who's there?" said a tinny voice, startling Sam. It came from an intercom speaker that he'd not noticed. "Who's there, please?"

Sam leaned close to the intercom. "Mr. Talbot? Harold Talbot?"

"Yes. Who're you?"

"Sam Booker," he said quietly, so his voice would not carry past the perimeter of Talbot's porch. "Sorry to wake you, but I've come in response to your letter of October eighth."

Talbot was silent. Then the intercom clicked, and he said, "I'm on the third floor. I'll need time to get down there. Meanwhile I'll send Moose. Please give him your ID so he can bring it to me."

"I have no Bureau ID," Sam whispered. "I'm undercover here."

"Driver's license?" Talbot asked.

"Yes."

"That's enough." He clicked off.

"Moose?" Tessa asked.

"Damned if I know," Sam said.

They waited almost a minute, feeling vulnerable on the exposed porch, and they were both startled again when a dog pushed out through a pet door they had not seen, brushing between their legs. For an instant Sam didn't realize what it was, and he stumbled backward in surprise, nearly losing his balance.

Stooping to pet the dog, Tessa whispered, "Moose?"

A flicker of light had come through the small swinging door with the dog; but that was gone now that the door was closed. The dog was black and hardly visible in the night.

Squatting beside it, letting it lick his hand, Sam said, "I'm supposed to give my ID to you?"

The dog wuffed softly, as if answering in the affirmative.

"You'll eat it," Sam said.

Tessa said, "He won't."

"How do you know?"

"He's a good dog."

"I don't trust him."

"I guess that's your job."

"Huh?"

"Not to trust anyone."

"And my nature."

"Trust him," she insisted.

He offered his wallet. The dog plucked it from Sam's hand, held it in his teeth, and went back into the house through the pet door.

They stood on the dark porch for another few minutes, while Sam tried to stifle his yawns. It was after two in the morning, and he was considering adding a fifth item to his list of reasons for living: good

Mexican food, Guinness Stout, Goldie Hawn, fear of death, and *sleep*. Blissful sleep. Then he heard the clack and rattle of locks being laboriously disengaged, and the door finally opened inward on a dimly lighted hallway.

Harry Talbot waited in his motorized wheelchair, dressed in blue pajamas and a green robe. His head was tilted slightly to the left in a permanently quizzical angle that was part of his Vietnam legacy. He was a handsome man, though his face was prematurely aged, too deeply lined for that of a forty-year-old. His thick hair was half white, and his eyes were ancient. Sam could see that Talbot had once been a strapping young man, though he was now soft from years of paralysis. One hand lay in his lap, the palm up, fingers half curled, useless. He was a living monument to what might have been, to hopes destroyed, to dreams incinerated, a grim remembrance of war pressed between the pages of time.

As Tessa and Sam entered and closed the door behind them, Harry Talbot extended his good hand and said, "God, am I glad to see you!" His smile transformed him astonishingly. It was the bright, broad, warm, and genuine smile of a man who believed he was perched in the lap of the gods, with too many blessings to count.

Moose returned Sam's wallet, uneaten.

chapter forty-eight

After leaving Shaddack's house on the north point, but before returning to headquarters to coordinate the assignments of the hundred men who were being sent to him from New Wave, Loman Watkins stopped at his home on Iceberry Way, on the north side of town. It was a modest, two-story, three-bedroom, Monterey-style house, white with pale-blue trim, nestled among conifers.

He stood for a moment in the driveway beside his patrol car, studying the place. He had loved it as if it were a castle, but he could not find that love in himself now. He remembered much happiness related to the house, to his family, but he could not *feel* the memory of that happiness. A lot of laughter had graced life in that dwelling, but now the laughter had faded until recollection of it was too faint even to induce a smile in remembrance. Besides, these days, his smiles were all counterfeit, with no humor behind them.

The odd thing was that laughter and joy had been a part of his life as late as this past August. It had all seeped away only within the past couple of months, after the Change. Yet it seemed an ancient memory.

Funny.

Actually, not so funny at all.

When he went inside he found the first floor dark and silent. A vague, stale odor lingered in the deserted rooms.

He climbed the stairs. In the unlighted, second-floor hallway he saw a soft glow along the bottom of the closed door to Denny's bedroom. He went in and found the boy sitting at his desk, in front of the computer. The PC had an oversize screen, and currently that was the only light in the room.

Denny did not look up from the terminal.

The boy was eighteen years old, no longer a child; therefore, he had been converted with his mother, shortly after Loman himself had been put through the Change. He was two inches taller than his dad and better looking. He'd always done well in school, and on IQ tests he'd scored so high it spooked Loman a bit to think his kid was *that* smart. He had always been proud of Denny. Now, at his son's side, staring down at him, Loman tried to resurrect that pride but could not find it. Denny had not fallen from favor; he had done nothing to earn his father's disapproval. But pride, like so many other emotions, seemed an encumbrance to the higher consciousness of the New People and interfered with their more efficient thought patterns.

Even before the Change, Denny had been a computer fanatic, one of those kids who called themselves hackers, to whom computers were not only tools, not only fun and games, but a way of life. After the conversion, his intelligence and high-tech expertise were put to use by New Wave. He was provided with a more powerful home terminal and a modem link to the supercomputer at New Wave headquarters—a behemoth that, according to Denny's description, incorporated four thousand miles of wiring and thirty-three thousand high-speed processing units—which, for reasons Loman didn't understand, they called Sun, though perhaps that was its name because all research at New Wave made heavy use of the machine and therefore revolved around it.

As Loman stood beside his son, voluminous data flickered across the terminal screen. Words, numbers, graphs, and charts appeared and disappeared at such speed that only one of the New People, with somewhat heightened senses and powerfully heightened concentration, could extract meaning from them.

In fact Loman could not read them because he had not undergone the training that Denny had received from New Wave. Besides, he'd had neither the time nor the need to learn to fully focus his new powers of concentration.

But Denny absorbed the rushing waves of data, staring blankly at the screen, no frown lines in his brow, his face completely relaxed. Since being converted, the boy was as much a solid-state electronic entity as he was flesh and blood, and that new part of him related to the computer with an intimacy that exceeded any man-machine relationship any of the Old People had ever known.

Loman knew that his son was learning about the Moonhawk Project. Ultimately he would join the task group at New Wave that was endlessly refining the software and hardware related to the project, working to make each generation of New People superior to—and more efficient than—the one before it.

An endless river of data washed across the screen.

Denny stared unblinkingly for so long that tears would have formed in his eyes if he had been one of the Old People.

The light of the ever-moving data danced on the walls and sent a continuous blur of shadows chasing around the room.

Loman put one hand on the boy's shoulder.

Denny did not look up or in any way respond. His lips began to move, as if he were talking, but he made no sound. He was speaking to himself, oblivious of his father.

In a garrulous, evangelistic moment, Thomas Shaddack had spoken of one day developing a link that would connect a computer directly to a surgically implanted socket in the base of the human spine, thereby merging real and artificial intelligence. Loman had not understood why such a thing was either wise or desirable, and Shaddack had said, "The New People are a bridge between man and machine, Loman. But one day our species will entirely cross that bridge, become *one* with the machines, because only then will mankind be *completely* efficient, *completely* in control."

"Denny," Loman said softly.

The boy did not respond.

At last Loman left the room.

Across the hall and at the end of it was the master bedroom. Grace was lying on the bed, in the dark.

Of course, since the Change, she could never be entirely blinded by a mere insufficiency of light, for her eyesight had improved. Even in this lightless room, she could see—as Loman could—the shapes of the furniture and some textures, though few details. For them, the night world was no longer black but darkish gray.

He sat on the edge of the mattress. "Hello."

She said nothing.

He put one hand on her head and stroked her long auburn hair. He touched her face and found her cheeks wet with tears, a detail that even his improved eyes could not discern.

Crying. She was crying, and that jolted him because he had never seen one of the New People cry.

His heartbeat accelerated, and a brief but wonderful thrill of hope throbbed through him. Perhaps the deadening of emotions was a transient condition.

"What is it?" he asked. "What're you crying about?"

"I'm afraid."

The pulse of hope swiftly faded. Fear had brought her to tears, fear and the desolation associated with it, and he already knew those feelings were a part of this brave new world, those and no other.

"Afraid of what?"

"I can't sleep," Grace said.

"But you don't need to sleep."

"Don't I?"

"None of us needs to sleep any more."

Prior to the Change, men and women had needed to sleep because the human body, being strictly a biological mechanism, was terribly inefficient. Downtime was required to rest and repair the damage of the day, to deal with the toxic substances absorbed from the external world and the toxics created internally. But in the New People, every bodily process and function was superbly regulated. Nature's work had been highly refined. Every organ, every system, every cell operated at a far higher efficiency, producing less waste, casting off waste faster than before, cleansing and rejuvenating itself every hour of the day. Grace knew that as well as he did.

"I long for sleep," she said.

"All you're feeling is the pull of habit."

"Too many hours in the day now."

"We'll fill up the time. The new world will be a busy one."

"What're we going to do in this new world when it comes?"

"Shaddack will tell us."

"Meanwhile . . ."

"Patience," he said.

"I'm afraid."

"Patience."

"I yearn for sleep, hunger for it."

"We don't need to sleep," he said, exhibiting the patience that he had encouraged in her.

"We don't need sleep," she said cryptically, "but we *need* to sleep." They were both silent a while.

Then she took his hand in hers, and moved it to her breasts. She was nude.

He tried to pull away from her, for he was afraid of what might happen, of what had happened before, since the Change, when they had made love. No. Not love. They didn't make love any more. They had sex. There was no feeling beyond physical sensation, no tenderness or affection. They thrust hard and fast at each other, pushed and pulled, flexed and writhed against each other, striving to maximize the excitation of nerve endings. Neither of them cared for or about the other, only about himself, his own satisfaction. Now that their emotional life was no longer rich, they tried to compensate for that loss with pleasures of the senses, primarily food and sex. However, without the emotional factor, every experience was . . . hollow, and they tried to fill that emptiness by overindulgence: A simple meal became a feast; a feast became an unrestrained indulgence in gluttony. And sex degenerated into a frenzied, bestial coupling.

Grace pulled him onto the bed.

He did not want to go. He could not refuse. Literally *could not* refuse.

Breathing hard, shuddering with excitement, she tore at his clothes and mounted him. She was making strange wordless sounds.

Loman's excitement matched hers and swelled, and he thrust at her, into her, into, losing all sense of time and place, existing only to stoke the fire in his loins, stoke it relentlessly until it was an unbearable heat, heat, friction and heat, wet and hot, heat, stoking the heat to a flashpoint at which his entire body would be consumed in the flames. He shifted positions, pinning her down, hammering himself into her, into her, into, into, pulling her against him so roughly that he must be bruising her, but he didn't care. She reached back and clawed at him, her fingernails digging into his arm, drawing blood, and he tore at her, too, because the blood was exciting, the smell of the blood, the sweet smell, so exciting, blood, and it didn't matter that they wounded each other, for these were superficial wounds and would heal within seconds, because they were New People; their bodies were efficient; blood flowed briefly, and then the wounds closed, and they clawed again, again. What he really wanted—what they both wanted—was to let go, indulge the wild spirit within, cast off all the inhibitions of civilization, including the inhibition of higher human form, go wild, go savage, regress, surrender, because then sex would have an even greater thrill, a purer thrill; surrender, and the emptiness would be filled; they would be fulfilled, and when the sex was done they could hunt together, hunt and kill, swift and silent, sleek and swift, bite and tear, bite deep and hard, hunt and kill, sperm and then blood, sweet fragrant blood. . . .

•

For a while Loman was disoriented.

When a sense of time and place returned to him, he first glanced at the door, realizing that it was ajar. Denny could have seen them if he'd come down the hall—surely *had* heard them—but Loman couldn't make himself care whether they had been seen or heard. Shame and modesty were two more casualties of the Change.

As he became fully oriented to the world around him, fear slipped into his heart, and he quickly touched himself—his face, arms, chest, legs—to be sure that he was in no way less than he ought to be. In the midst of sex, the wildness in him grew, and sometimes he thought that approaching orgasm he *did* change, regress, if only slightly. But upon regaining awareness, he never found evidence of backsliding.

He was, however, sticky with blood.

He switched on the bedside lamp.

"Turn it off," Grace said at once.

But he was not satisfied with even his enhanced night vision. He wanted to look at her closely to determine if she was in any way . . . different.

She had not regressed. Or, if she *had* regressed, she had already returned to the higher form. Her body was smeared with blood, and a few welts showed on her flesh, where he had gouged her and where she had not finished healing.

He turned the light off and sat on the edge of the bed.

Because the recuperative powers of their bodies had been vastly improved by the Change, superficial cuts and scrapes healed in only minutes; you could actually watch your flesh knit its wounds. They were impervious to disease now, their immune systems too aggressive for the most infectious virus or bacterium to survive long enough to replicate. Shaddack believed that their life spans would prove to be of great duration, as well, perhaps hundreds of years.

They could be killed, of course, but only by a wound that tore and stopped the heart or shattered the brain or destroyed their lungs and prevented a flow of oxygen to the blood. If a vein or artery was severed, the blood supply was drastically reduced to that vessel for the few minutes required to heal it. If a vital organ other than the heart or lungs or brain was damaged, the body could limp along for hours while accelerated repairs were under way. They were not yet as fully reliable as machines, for machines could not die; with the right spare parts, a machine could be rebuilt even from rubble and could work again; but they were closer to that degree of corporeal endurance than anyone outside Moonlight Cove would have believed.

To live for hundreds of years . . .

Sometimes Loman brooded about that.

To live for hundreds of years, knowing only fear and physical sensation . . .

He rose from the bed, went into the adjacent bathroom, and took a quick shower to sluice off the blood.

He could not meet his eyes in the bathroom mirror.

In the bedroom again, without turning on a light, he pulled on a fresh uniform that he took from his closet.

Grace was still lying on the bed.

She said, "I wish I could sleep."

He sensed that she was still crying silently.

When he left the room, he closed the door behind him.

chapter forty-nine

They gathered in the kitchen, which Tessa liked because some of her happiest memories of childhood and adolescence involved family conferences and impromptu chats in the kitchen of their house in San Diego. The kitchen was the heart of a home and in a way the heart of a family. Somehow the worst problems became insignificant when you discussed them in a warm kitchen redolent of coffee and hot cocoa, nibbling on home-baked cake or pastry. In a kitchen she felt secure.

Harry Talbot's kitchen was large, for it had been remodeled to suit a man in a wheelchair, with lots of clearance around the central cooking island, which was built low—as were the counters along the walls—to be accessible from a sitting position. Otherwise it was a kitchen like many others: cabinets painted a pleasant creamy shade; pale yellow ceramic tile; a quietly purring refrigerator. The Levolor blinds at the windows were electrically operated by a button on one of the counters, and Harry put them down.

After trying the phone and discovering that the line was dead, that not just the pay phones but the town's entire phone system had been interdicted, Sam and Tessa sat at a round table in one corner, at Harry's insistence, while he made a pot of good Colombian in a Mr. Coffee machine. "You look cold," he said. "This'll do you good."

Chilled and tired, in need of the caffeine, Tessa did not decline the offer. Indeed, she was fascinated that Harry, with such severe disabilities, could function well enough to play the gracious host to unexpected visitors.

With his one good hand and some tricky moves, he got a package of apple-cinnamon muffins from the bread box, part of a chocolate cake from the refrigerator, plates and forks, and paper napkins. When Sam and Tessa offered to help, he gently declined their assistance with a smile.

She sensed that he was not trying to prove anything either to them or to himself. He was simply enjoying having company, even at this hour and under these bizarre circumstances. Perhaps it was a rare pleasure.

"No cream," he said. "Just a carton of milk."

"That's fine," Sam said.

"And no elegant porcelain cream pitcher, I'm afraid," said Harry, putting the milk carton on the table.

Tessa began to consider shooting a documentary about Harry, about the courage required to remain independent in his circumstances: She was drawn by the siren call of her art in spite of what had transpired in the past few hours. Long ago, however, she had learned that an artist's creativity could not be turned off; the eye of a filmmaker could not be capped as easily as the lens of her camera. In the midst of grief over her sister's death, ideas for projects had continued to come to her, narrative concepts, interesting shots, angles. Even in the terror of war, running with Afghan rebels as Soviet planes strafed the ground at their heels, she'd been excited by what she was getting on film and by what she would be able to make of it when she got into an editing room—and her three-man crew had reacted much the same. So she no longer felt awkward or guilty about being an artist on the make, even in times of tragedy; for her, that was just natural, a part of being creative and *alive*.

Customized to his needs, Harry's wheelchair included a hydraulic lift that raised the seat a few inches, bringing him nearly to normal chair height, so he could sit at an ordinary table or writing desk. He took a place beside Tessa and across from Sam.

Moose was lying in the corner, watching, occasionally raising his head as if interested in their conversation—though more likely drawn by the smell of chocolate cake. The Labrador did not come sniffing and pawing around, whining for handouts, and Tessa was impressed by his discipline.

As they passed the coffeepot and carved up the cake and muffins, Harry said, "You've told me what brings you here, Sam—not just my letter but all these so-called accidents." He looked at Tessa, and because she was on his right side, the permanent cock of his head to the left made it seem as if he were leaning back from her, regarding her with suspicion or at least skepticism, though his true attitude was belied by his warm smile. "But just where do you fit in, Miss Lockland?"

"Call me Tessa, please. Well . . . my sister was Janice Capshaw—"

"Richard Capshaw's wife, the Lutheran minister's wife?" he said, surprised.

"That's right."

"Why, they used to come to visit me. I wasn't a member of their congregation, but that's how they were. We became friends. And after he died, she still stopped by now and then. Your sister was a dear and wonderful person, Tessa." He put down his coffee cup and reached out to her with his good hand. "She was my friend."

Tessa held his hand. It was leathery and calloused from use, and very strong, as if all the frustrated power of his paralyzed body found expression through that single extremity.

"I watched them take her into the crematorium at Callan's Funeral Home," Harry said. "Through my telescope. I'm a watcher. That's what I do with my life, for the most part. I watch." He blushed slightly. He held Tessa's hand a bit tighter. "It's not just snooping. In fact it isn't snooping at all. It's . . . participating. Oh, I like to read, too, and I've got a lot of books, and I do a heavy load of thinking, for sure, but it's watching, mainly, that gets me through. We'll go upstairs later. I'll show you the telescope, the whole setup. I think maybe you'll understand. I hope you will. Anyway, I saw them take Janice into Callan's that night . . . though I didn't know who it was until two days later, when the story of her death was in the county paper. I couldn't believe she died the way they said she did. Still don't believe it."

"Neither do I," Tessa said. "And that's why I'm here."

Reluctantly, with a final squeeze, Harry let go of Tessa's hand. "So many bodies lately, most of them hauled into Callan's at night, and more than a few times with cops hanging around, overseeing things—it's strange as hell for a quiet little town like this."

From across the table, Sam said, "Twelve accidental deaths or suicides in less than two months."

"Twelve?" Harry said.

"Didn't you realize it was that many?" Sam asked.

"Oh, it's more than that."

Sam blinked.

Harry said, "Twenty, by my count."

chapter fifty

After Watkins left, Shaddack returned to the computer terminal in his study, reopened his link to Sun, the supercomputer at New Wave, and set to work again on a problematic aspect of the current project. Though it was two-thirty in the morning, he would put in a few more hours, for the earliest he went to bed was dawn.

He had been at the terminal a few minutes when his most private phone line rang.

Until Booker was apprehended, the telephone company computer was allowing service only among those who had been converted, *from* one of their numbers *to* one of their numbers. Other lines were cut off, and calls to the outside world were interrupted before being completed. Incoming calls to Moonlight Cove were answered by a recording that pleaded equipment failure, promised a return to full service within twenty-four hours, and expressed regret at the inconvenience.

Therefore, Shaddack knew the caller must be among the converted and, because it was his most private line, must also be one of his closest associates at New Wave. A LED readout on the base of the phone displayed the number from which the call was being placed, which he recognized as that of Mike Peyser. He picked up the receiver and said, "Shaddack here."

The caller breathed heavily, raggedly into the phone but said nothing. Frowning, Shaddack said, "Hello?"

Just the breathing.

Shaddack said, "Mike, is that you?"

The voice that finally responded to him was hoarse, guttural, but with a shrill edge, whispery yet forceful, Peyser's voice yet not his, strange: "... *something wrong, wrong, something wrong, can't change, can't ... wrong ... wrong ...*"

Shaddack was reluctant to admit that he recognized Mike Peyser's voice in those queer inflections and eerie cadences. He said, "Who is this?"

"... *need, need ... need, want, I need ...*"

"Who is this?" Shaddack demanded angrily, but in his mind was another question: *What* is this?

The caller issued a sound that was a groan of pain, a mewl of deepest anguish, a thin cry of frustration, and a snarl, all twisted into one rolling bleat. The receiver dropped from his hand with a hard clatter.

Shaddack put his own phone down, turned back to the VDT, tapped into the police data system, and sent an urgent message to Loman Watkins.

chapter fifty-one

Sitting on the stool in the dark third-floor bedroom, bent to the eyepiece, Sam Booker studied the rear of Callan's Funeral Home. All but scattered scrims of fog had blown away on the wind, which still blustered at the window and shook the trees all along the hillsides on which most of Moonlight Cove was built. The serviceway lamps were extinguished now, and the rear of Callan's lay in darkness but for the thin light radiating from the blind-covered windows of the crematorium wing. No doubt they were busily feeding the flames with the bodies of the couple who had been murdered at Cove Lodge.

Tessa sat on the edge of the bed behind Sam, petting Moose, who was lying with his head in her lap.

Harry was in his wheelchair nearby. He used a penlight to study a spiral-bound notebook in which he had kept a record of the unusual activities at the mortuary.

"First one—at least the first unusual one I noticed—was on the night of August twenty-eighth," Harry said. "Twenty minutes to midnight. They brought four bodies at once, using the hearse and the city ambulance. Police accompanied them. The corpses were in body bags, so I couldn't see anything about them, but the cops and the ambulance attendants and the people at Callan's were visibly . . . well . . . upset. I saw it in their faces. Fear. They kept looking around at the neighboring houses and the alleyway, as if they were afraid someone was going to see what they were up to, which seemed peculiar because they were only doing their jobs. Right? Anyway, later, in the county paper, I read about the Mayser family dying in a fire, and I knew that was who'd been brought to Callan's that night. I supposed they didn't die in a fire any more than your sister killed herself."

"Probably not," Tessa said.

Still watching the back of the funeral home, Sam said, "I have the Maysers on my list. They were turned up in the investigation of the Sanchez-Bustamante case."

Harry cleared his throat and said, "Six days later, September third, two bodies were brought to Callan's shortly after midnight. And this was even weirder because they didn't come in a hearse or an ambulance. Two police cars pulled in at the back of Callan's, and they unloaded a body from the rear seat of each of them, wrapped in blood-streaked sheets."

"September third?" Sam said. "There's no one on my list for that date. Sanchez and the Bustamantes were on the fifth. No death certificates were issued on the third. They kept those two off the official records."

"Nothing in the county paper about anyone dying then, either," Harry said.

Tessa said, "So who were those two people?"

"Maybe they were out-of-towners who were unlucky enough to stop in Moonlight Cove and stumble into something dangerous," Sam said. "People whose deaths could be completely covered up, so no one would know *where* they'd died. As far as anyone knows, they just vanished on the road somewhere."

"Sanchez and the Bustamantes were on the night of the fifth," Harry said, "and then Jim Armes on the night of the seventh."

"Armes disappeared at sea," Sam said, looking up from the telescope and frowning at the man in the wheelchair.

"They brought the body to Callan's at eleven o'clock at night," Harry said, consulting his notebook for details. "The blinds weren't drawn at the crematorium windows, so I could see straight in there, almost as good as if I'd been right there in that room. I saw the body . . . the mess it was in. And the face. Couple of days later, when the paper ran a story about Armes's disappearance, I recognized him as the guy they'd fed to the furnace."

The large bedroom was dressed in cloaks of shadow except for the narrow beam of the penlight, which was half shielded by Harry's hand and confined to the open notebook. Those white pages seemed to glow with light of their own, as if they were the leaves of a magic or holy—or unholy—book.

Harry Talbot's careworn countenance was more dimly illumined by the backsplash from those pages, and the peculiar light emphasized the lines in his face, making him appear older than he was. Each line, Sam knew, had its provenance in tragic experience and pain. Profound sympathy stirred in him. Not pity. He could never pity anyone as determined as Talbot. But Sam appreciated the sorrow and loneliness of Harry's restricted life. Watching the wheelchair-bound man, Sam grew angry with the neighbors. Why hadn't they done more to bring Harry into their lives? Why hadn't they invited him to dinner more often, drawn him into their holiday celebrations? Why had they left him so much on his own that his primary means of participating in the life of his community was through a telescope and binoculars? Sam was cut by a pang of despair at people's reluctance to reach out to one another, at the way they isolated themselves and one another. With a jolt, he thought of his inability to communicate with his own son, which only left him feeling bleaker still.

To Harry, he said, "What do you mean when you say Armes's body was a mess?"

"Cut. Slashed."

"He didn't drown?"

"Didn't look it."

"Slashed . . . Exactly what do you mean?" Tessa asked.

Sam knew that she was thinking about the people whose screams she had heard at the motel—and about her own sister.

Harry hesitated, then said: "Well, I saw him on the table in the crematorium, just before they slipped him into the furnace. He'd been . . . disemboweled. Nearly decapitated. Horribly . . . *torn*. He looked as bad as if he'd been standing on an antipersonnel mine when it went off and been riddled by shrapnel."

They sat in mutual silence, considering that description.

Only Moose seemed unperturbed. He made a soft, contented sound as Tessa gently scratched behind his ears.

Sam thought it might not be so bad to be one of the lower beasts, a creature mostly of feelings, untroubled by a complex intellect. Or at the other extreme . . . a genuinely intelligent computer, all intellect and no feelings whatsoever. The great dual burden of emotion and high intelligence was singular to humankind, and it was what made life so hard; you were always thinking about what you were feeling instead of just going with the moment, or you were always trying to feel what you thought you *should* feel in a given situation. Thoughts and judgment were inevitably colored by emotions—some of them on a subconscious level, so you didn't even entirely understand *why* you made certain decisions, acted in certain ways. Emotions clouded your thinking; but thinking too hard about your feelings took the edge off them. Trying to feel deeply and think perfectly clearly at the same time was like simultaneously juggling six Indian clubs while riding a unicycle backward along a high wire.

"After the story in the paper about Armes disappearing," Harry said, "I kept waiting for a correction, but none was printed, and that's when I began to realize that the odd goings-on at Callan's weren't *just* odd but probably criminal, as well—and that the cops were part of it."

"Paula Parkins was torn apart too," Sam said.

Harry nodded. "Supposedly by her Dobermans."

"Dobermans?" Tessa asked.

At the laundry Sam had told her that her sister was one of many curious suicides and accidental deaths, but he had not gone into any details about the others. Now he quickly told her about Parkins.

"Not her own dogs," Tessa agreed. "She was savaged by whatever killed Armes. And the people tonight at Cove Lodge."

This was the first that Harry Talbot had heard about the murders at Cove Lodge. Sam had to explain about that and about how he and Tessa had met at the laundry.

A strange expression settled on Harry's prematurely aged face. To Tessa, he said, "Uh . . . you didn't see these things at the motel? Not even a glimpse?"

"Only the foot of one of them, through the crack under the door."

Harry started to speak, stopped, and sat in thoughtful silence.

He knows something, Sam thought. More than we do.

For some reason Harry was not ready to share what he knew, for he returned his scrutiny to the notebook on his lap and said, "Two days after Paula Parkins died, there was one body taken to Callan's, around nine-thirty at night."

"That would be September eleventh?" Sam asked.

"Yes."

"There's no record of a death certificate issued that day."

"Nothing about it in the paper, either."

"Go on."

Harry said, "September fifteenth—"

"Steve Heinz, Laura Dalcoe. He supposedly killed her, then took his own life," Sam said. "Lovers' quarrel, we're to believe."

"Another quick cremation," Harry noted. "And three nights later, on the eighteenth, two more bodies delivered to Callan's shortly after one in the morning, just as I was about to go to bed."

"No public record of those, either," Sam said.

"Two more out-of-towners who drove off the interstate for a visit or just dinner?" Tessa wondered. "Or maybe someone from another part of the county, passing on the county road along the edge of town?"

"Could even have been locals," Harry said. "I mean, there're always a few people around who haven't lived here a long time, newcomers who rent instead of own their houses, don't have many ties to the community, so if you wanted to cover their murders, you could maybe concoct an acceptable story about them moving away suddenly, for a new job, whatever, and their neighbors might buy it."

If their neighbors weren't already "converted" and participating in the cover-up, Sam thought.

"Then September twenty-third," Harry said. "That would have been your sister's body, Tessa."

"Yes."

"By then I knew I had to tell someone what I'd seen. Someone in authority. But who? I didn't trust anyone local because I'd watched the cops bring in some of those bodies that were never reported in the newspaper. County Sheriff? He'd believe Watkins before he'd believe me, wouldn't he? Hell, everyone thinks a cripple is a little strange anyway—strange in the head, I mean—they equate physical disabilities with mental disabilities at least a little, at least subconsciously. So they'd be predisposed not to believe me. And admittedly it *is* a wild story, all these bodies, secret cremations. . . ." He paused. His face clouded. "The fact that I'm a decorated veteran wouldn't have made me any more believable. That was a long time ago, ancient history for some of them. In fact . . . no doubt they'd hold the war against me in a way. Post-Vietnam stress syndrome, they'd call it. Poor old Harry finally went crackers—don't you see?—from the war."

Thus far Harry had been speaking matter-of-factly, without much emotion. But the words he had just spoken were like a piece of glass held against the surface of a rippled pool, revealing realms below—in his case, realms of pain, loneliness, and alienation.

Now emotion not only entered his voice but, a few times, made it crack: "And I've got to say, part of the reason I didn't try to tell anyone what I'd seen was because . . . I was afraid. I didn't know what the hell was going on. I couldn't be sure how big the stakes were. I didn't know if they'd silence me, feed *me* to the furnace at Callan's one night. You'd think that having lost so much I'd be reckless now, unconcerned about losing more, about dying, but that's not the way it is, not at all. Life's probably more precious to me than to men who're whole and healthy. This broken body slowed me down so much that I've spent the last twenty years out of the whirl of activity in which most of you exist, and I've had time to really *see* the world, the beauty and intricacy of it. In the end my disabilities have led me to appreciate and love life more. So I was afraid they'd come for me, kill me, and I hesitated to tell anyone what I'd seen. God help me, if I'd spoken out, if I'd gotten in touch with the Bureau sooner, maybe some people might have been saved. Maybe . . . your sister would've been saved."

"Don't even think of that," Tessa said at once. "If you'd done anything differently, no doubt you'd be ashes now, scraped out of the bottom of Callan's furnace and thrown in the sea. My sister's fate was sealed. You couldn't unseal it."

Harry nodded, then switched off the penlight, plunging the room into deeper darkness, though he had not yet finished going through the information in his notebook. Sam suspected that Tessa's unhesitating generosity of spirit had brought tears to Harry's eyes and that he did not want them to see.

"On the twenty-fifth," he continued, not needing to consult the notebook for details, "one body was brought to Callan's at ten-fifteen at night. Weird, too, because it didn't come in either an ambulance or hearse or police car. It was brought by Loman Watkins—"

"Chief of police," Sam said for Tessa's benefit.

"—but he was in his private car, out of uniform," Harry said. "They took the body out of his trunk. It was wrapped in a blanket. The blinds weren't shut at their windows that night, either, and I was able to get in tight with the scope. I didn't recognize the body, but I did recognize the condition of it—the same as Armes."

"Torn?" Sam asked.

"Yes. Then the Bureau *did* come to town on the Sanchez-Bustamante thing, and when I read about it in the newspaper, I was so relieved because I thought it was all going to come out in the open at last, that we'd have revelations, explanations. But then there were two more bodies disposed of at Callan's on the night of October fourth—"

"Our team was in town then," Sam said, "in the middle of their investigation. They didn't realize any death certificates were filed during that time. You're saying this happened under their noses?"

"Yeah. I don't have to look in the notebook; I remember it clearly. The bodies were brought around in Reese Dorn's camper truck. He's a local cop, but he was out of uniform that night. They hauled the stiffs into Callan's, and the blind at one window was open, so I saw them shove both bodies into the crematorium together, as if they were in a real sweat to dispose of them. And there was more activity at Callan's late on the night of the seventh, but the fog was so thick, I can't swear that it was more bodies being taken in. And finally . . . earlier tonight. A child's body. A small child."

"Plus the two who were killed at Cove Lodge," Tessa said. "That makes twenty-two victims, not the twelve that brought Sam here. This town's become a slaughterhouse."

"Could be even more than we think," Harry said.

"How so?"

"Well, after all, I don't watch the place every evening, all evening long. And I go to bed by one-thirty, no later than two. Who's to say there weren't visits I missed, that more bodies weren't brought in during the dead hours of the night?"

Brooding about that, Sam looked through the eyepiece again. The rear of Callan's remained dark and still. He slowly moved the scope to the right, shifting the field of vision northward through the neighborhood.

Tessa said, "But *why* were they killed?"

No one had an answer.

"And by what?" she asked.

Sam studied a cemetery farther north on Conquistador, then sighed and looked up and told them about his experience earlier in the night, on Iceberry Way. "I thought they were kids, delinquents, but now what I think is that they were the same things that killed the people at Cove Lodge, the same as the one whose foot you saw through the crack under the door."

He could almost feel Tessa frowning with frustration in the darkness when she said, "But what *are* they?"

Harry Talbot hesitated. Then: "Boogeymen."

chapter fifty-two

Not daring to use sirens, dousing headlights on the last quarter mile of the approach, Loman came down on Mike Peyser's place at three-ten in the morning, with two cars, five deputies, and shotguns. Loman hoped they did not have to use the guns for more than intimidation. In their only previous encounter with a regressive—Jordan Coombs on the fourth of September—they had not been prepared for its ferocity and had been forced to blow its head off to save their own lives. Shaddack had been left with only a carcass to examine. He'd been furious at the lost chance to delve into the psychology—and the functioning physiology—of one of these metamorphic psychopaths. A tranquilizer gun would be of little use, unfortunately, because regressives were New People gone bad, and all New People, regressive or not, had radically altered metabolisms that not only allowed for magically fast healing but for the rapid absorption, breakdown, and rejection of toxic substances like poison or tranquilizers. The only way to sedate a regressive would be to get him to agree to be put on a continuous IV drip, which wasn't very damn likely.

Mike Peyser's house was a one-story bungalow with front and rear porches on the west and east sides respectively, nicely maintained, on an acre and a half, sheltered by a few huge sweet gums that had not yet lost their leaves. No lights shone at the windows.

Loman sent one man to watch the north side, another the south, to prevent Peyser from escaping through a window. He stationed a third man at the foot of the front porch to cover that door. With the other two men—Sholnick and Penniworth—he circled to the rear of the place and quietly climbed the steps to the back porch.

Now that the fog had been blown away, visibility was good. But the huffing and skirling wind was a white noise that blocked out other sounds they might need to hear while stalking Peyser.

Penniworth stood against the wall of the house to the left of the door, and Sholnick stood to the right. Both carried semiautomatic 20-gauge shotguns.

Loman tried the door. It was unlocked. He pushed it open and stepped back.

His deputies entered the dark kitchen, one after the other, their shotguns lowered and ready to fire, though they were aware that the objective was to take Peyser alive if at all possible. But they were not going to sacrifice themselves just to bring the living beast to Shaddack. A moment later one of them found a light switch.

Carrying a 12-gauge of his own, Loman went into the house after them. Empty bowls, broken dishes, and dirty Tupperware containers were scattered on the floor, as were a few rigatoni red with tomato sauce, half of a meatball, eggshells, a chunk of pie crust, and other bits of food. One of the four wooden chairs from the breakfast set was lying on its side; another had been hammered to pieces against a counter top, cracking some of the ceramic tiles.

Straight ahead, an archway led into a dining room. Some of the spill-through light from the kitchen vaguely illuminated the table and chairs in there.

To the left, beside the refrigerator, was a door. Barry Sholnick opened it defensively. Shelves of canned goods flanked a landing. Stairs led down to the basement.

"We'll check that later," Loman said softly. "After we've gone through the house."

Sholnick soundlessly snatched a chair from the breakfast set and braced the door shut so nothing could come up from the cellar and creep in behind them after they went into other rooms.

They stood for a moment, listening.

Gusting wind slammed against the house. A window rattled. From the attic above came the creaking of rafters, and from higher still the muffled clatter of a loose cedar shingle on the roof.

His deputies looked at Loman for guidance. Penniworth was only twenty-five, could pass for eighteen, and had a face so fresh and guile-less that he looked more like a door-to-door peddler of religious tracts than a cop. Sholnick was ten years older and had a harder edge to him.

Loman motioned them toward the dining room.

They entered, turning the lights on as they went. The dining room was deserted, so they moved cautiously into the living room.

Penniworth clicked a wall switch that turned on a chrome and brass lamp, which was one of the few items not broken or torn apart. The cushions on the sofa and chairs had been slashed; wads of foam padding, like clumps of a poisonous fungus, lay everywhere. Books had been pulled from shelves and ripped to pieces. A ceramic lamp, a couple of vases, and the glass top of a coffee table were shattered. The doors had been torn off the cabinet-style television set, and the screen had been smashed. Blind rage and savage strength had been at work here.

The room smelled strongly of urine . . . and of something else less pungent and less familiar. It was, perhaps, the scent of the creature responsible for the wreckage. Part of that subtler stink was the sour odor of perspiration, but something stranger was in it, too, something that simultaneously turned Loman's stomach and tightened it with fear.

To the left, a hallway led back to the bedrooms and baths. Loman kept it covered with his shotgun.

The deputies went into the foyer, which was connected to the living room by a wide archway. A closet was on the right, just inside the front door. Sholnick stood in front of it, his 20-gauge lowered. From the side Penniworth jerked open the door. The closet contained only coats.

The easy part of the search was behind them. Ahead lay the narrow hall with three doors off it, one half open and two ajar, dark rooms beyond. There was less space in which to maneuver, more places from which an assailant might attack.

Night wind soughed in the eaves. It fluted across a rain gutter, producing a low, mournful note.

Loman had never been the kind of leader who sent his men ahead into danger while he stayed back in a position of safety. Although he had shed pride and self-respect and a sense of duty along with most other Old People attitudes and emotions, duty was still a habit with him—in fact, less conscious than a habit, more like a reflex—and he operated as he would have done before the Change. He entered the hall first, where two doors waited on the left and one on the right. He moved swiftly to the end, to the second door on the left, which was half open; he kicked it inward, and in the light from the hall he saw a small, deserted bathroom before the door bounced off the wall and swung shut again.

Penniworth took the first room on the left. He went in and found the light switch by the time Loman reached that threshold. It was a study with a desk, worktable, two chairs, cabinets, tall bookshelves crammed full of volumes with brightly colored spines, two computers. Loman moved in and covered the closet, where Penniworth warily rolled aside first one and then the other of two mirrored doors.

Nothing.

Barry Sholnick remained in the hallway, his 20-gauge leveled at the room they hadn't investigated. When Loman and Penniworth rejoined him, Sholnick shoved that door all the way open with the barrel of his shotgun. As it swung wide, he jerked back, certain that something would fly at him from the darkness, though nothing did. He hesitated, then stepped into the doorway, fumbled with one hand for the light switch, found it, said, "Oh, my God," and stepped quickly back into the hall.

Looking past his deputy into a large bedroom, Loman saw a hellish thing crouched on the floor and huddled against the far wall. It was a regressive, no doubt Peyser, but it did not look as much like the regressed Jordan Coombs as Loman expected. There were similarities, yes, but not many.

Easing by Sholnick, Loman crossed the threshold. "Peyser?"

The thing at the other end of the room blinked at him, moved its twisted mouth. In a voice that was whispery yet guttural, savage yet tortured as only the voice of an at least halfway intelligent creature could be, it said, ". . . *Peyser, Peyser, Peyser, me, Peyser, me, me . . .*"

The odor of urine was here, too, but that other scent was now the dominant one—sharp, musky.

Loman moved farther into the room. Penniworth followed. Sholnick stayed at the doorway. Loman stopped twelve feet from Peyser, and Penniworth moved off to one side, his 20-gauge held ready.

When they'd cornered Jordan Coombs in the shuttered movie theater back on September fourth, he had been in an altered state somewhat resembling a gorilla with a squat and powerful body. Mike Peyser, however, had a far leaner appearance, and as he crouched against the bedroom wall, his body looked more lupine than apelike. His hips were set at an angle to his spine, preventing him from standing or sitting completely erect, and his legs seemed too short in the thighs, too long in the calves. He was covered in thick hair but not so thick that it could be called a pelt.

"*Peyser, me, me, me . . .*"

Coombs's face had been partly human, though mostly that of a higher primate, with a bony brow, flattened nose, and thrusting jaw to accommodate large, wickedly sharp teeth like those of a baboon. Mike Peyser's hideously transformed countenance had, instead, a hint of the wolf in it, or dog; his mouth and nose were drawn forward into a deformed snout. His massive brow *was* like that of an ape, though exaggerated, and in his bloodshot eyes, set in shadowy sockets deep beneath that bony ridge, was a look of anguish and terror that was entirely human.

Raising one hand and pointing at Loman, Peyser said, ". . . *help me, me, help, something wrong, wrong, wrong, help . . .*"

Loman stared at that mutated hand with both fear and amazement, remembering how his own hand had begun to change when he had felt the call of regression at the Fosters' place earlier in the night. Elongated fingers. Large, rough knuckles. Fierce claws instead of fingernails. Human hands in shape and degree of dexterity, they were otherwise utterly alien.

Shit, Loman thought, those hands, those *hands*. I've seen them in the movies, or at least on the TV, when we rented the cassette of *The Howling*. Rob Bottin. That was the name of the special-effects artist who created the werewolf. He remembered it because Denny had been a nut about special effects before the Change. More than anything else these looked like the goddamn hands of the werewolf in *The Howling*!

Which was too crazy to contemplate. Life imitating fantasy. The fantastic made flesh. As the twentieth century rushed into its last decade, scientific and technological progress had reached some divide, where mankind's dream of a better life often could be fulfilled but also where nightmares could be made real. Peyser was a bad, bad dream that had crawled out of the subconscious and become flesh, and now there was no escaping him by waking up; he would not disappear as did the monsters that haunted sleep.

"How can I help you?" Loman asked warily.

"Shoot him," Penniworth said.

Loman responded sharply: "No!"

Peyser raised both of his tine-fingered hands and looked at them for a moment, as if seeing them for the first time. A groan issued from him, then a thin and miserable wail. *". . . change, can't change, can't, tried, want, need, want, want, can't, tried, can't . . ."*

From the doorway Sholnick said, "My God, he's stuck like that—he's trapped. I thought the regressives could change back at will."

"They can," Loman said.

"*He* can't," Sholnick said.

"That's what he said," Penniworth agreed, his voice quick and nervous. "He said he can't change."

Loman said, "Maybe, maybe not. But the other regressives can change, because if they *couldn't*, then we'd have found all of them by now. They retreat from their altered state and then walk among us."

Peyser seemed oblivious of them. He was staring at his hands, mewling in the back of his throat as if what he saw terrified him.

Then the hands began to change.

"You see," Loman said.

Loman had never witnessed such a transformation; he was gripped by curiosity, wonder, and terror. The claws receded. The flesh was suddenly as malleable as soft wax: It bulged, blistered, pulsed not with the rhythmic flow of blood in arteries but strangely, obscenely; it assumed new form, as if an invisible sculptor were at work on it. Loman heard bones crunching, splintering, as they were broken down and remade; the flesh melted and resolidified with a sickening, wet sound. The hands became nearly human. Then the wrists and forearms began to lose some of their rawboned lupine quality. In Peyser's face were indications that the human spirit was struggling to banish the savage that was now in control; the features of a predator began to give way to a gentler and more civilized mien. It was as if the monstrous Peyser was only a beast's reflection in a pool of water out of which the real and human Peyser was now rising.

Though he was no scientist, no genius of microtechnology, only a policeman with a high-school education, Loman knew that this profound and rapid transformation could not be attributed solely to the New People's drastically improved metabolic processes and ability to heal themselves. No matter what great tides of hormones, enzymes, and other biological chemicals Peyser's body could now produce at will, there was no way that bone and flesh could be re-formed so dramatically in such a brief period of time. Over days or weeks, yes, but not in *seconds*. Surely it was physically impossible. Yet it was happening. Which meant that another force was at work in Mike Peyser, something more than biological processes, something mysterious and frightening.

Suddenly the transformation halted. Loman could see that Peyser was straining toward full humanity, clenching his half-human yet still wolflike jaws together and grinding his teeth, a look of desperation and iron determination in his strange eyes, but to no avail. For a moment he trembled on the edge of human form. It seemed that if he could just push the transformation one step further, just one small step, then he would cross a watershed after which the rest of the metamorphosis would take place almost automatically, without the strenuous exertion of will, as easily as a stream flowing downhill. But he could not reach that divide.

Penniworth made a low, strangled sound, as if he were sharing Peyser's anguish.

Loman glanced at his deputy. Penniworth's face glistened with a thin film of perspiration.

Loman realized he was perspiring too; he felt a bead trickle down his left temple. The bungalow was warm—an oil furnace kept clicking on and off—but not warm enough to wring moisture from them. This was a cold sweat of fear, but more than that. He also felt a tightness in his chest, a thickening in his throat that made it hard to swallow, and he was breathing fast, as if he'd sprinted up a hundred steps—

Letting out a thin, agonized cry, Peyser began to regress again. With the brittle splintering noise of bones being remade, the oily-wet sound of flesh being rent and re-knit, the savage creature reasserted itself, and in moments Peyser was as he had been when they had first seen him: a hellish beast.

Hellish, yes, and a beast, but enviably powerful and with an odd, terrible beauty of its own. The forward carriage of the large head was awkward by comparison to the set of the human head, and the thing lacked the sinuous inward curve of the human spine, yet it had a dark grace of its own.

They stood in silence for a moment.

Peyser huddled on the floor, head bowed.

From the doorway, Sholnick finally said, "My God, he *is* trapped."

Although Mike Peyser's problem could have been related to some glitch in the technology on which conversion from Old to New Person was based, Loman suspected that Peyser still possessed the power to reshape himself, that he could become a man if he wanted to badly enough, but that he lacked the desire to be fully human again. He had become a regressive because he found that altered state appealing, so maybe he found it so much more exciting and satisfying than the human condition that now he did not truly *want* to return to a higher state.

Peyser raised his head and looked at Loman, then at Penniworth, then at Sholnick, and finally at Loman again. His horror at his condition was no longer apparent. The anguish and terror were gone from his eyes. With his twisted muzzle he seemed to smile at them, and a new wildness—both disturbing and appealing—appeared in his eyes. He raised his hands before his face again and flexed the long fingers, clicked the claws together, studying himself with what might have been wonder.

"... *hunt, hunt, chase, hunt, kill, blood, blood, need, need* ..."

"How the hell can we take him alive if he doesn't want to be taken?" Penniworth's voice was peculiar, thick and slightly slurred.

Peyser dropped one hand to his genitals and scratched lightly, absentmindedly. He looked at Loman again, then at the night pressing against the windows.

"I feel ..." Sholnick left the sentence unfinished.

Penniworth was no more articulate: "If we ... well, we could ..."

The pressure in Loman's chest had grown greater. His throat was tighter, too, and he was still sweating.

Peyser let out a soft, ululant cry as eerie as any sound Loman had ever heard, an expression of longing, yet also an animal challenge to the night, a statement of his power and his confidence in his own strength and cunning. The wail should have been harsh and unpleasant in the confines of that bedroom, but instead it stirred in Loman the same un-speakable yearning that had gripped him outside of the Fosters' house when he had heard the trio of regressives calling to one another far away in the darkness.

Clenching his teeth so hard that his jaws ached, Loman strove to resist that unholy urge.

Peyser loosed another cry, then said, "*Run, hunt, free, free, need, free, need, come with me, come, come, need, need . . .*"

Loman realized that he was relaxing his grip on the 12- gauge. The barrel was tilting down. The muzzle was pointing at the floor instead of at Peyser.

"*. . . run, free, free, need . . .*"

From behind Loman came an unnerving, orgasmic cry of release.

He glanced back at the bedroom doorway in time to see Sholnick drop his shotgun. Subtle transformations had occurred in the deputy's hands and face. He pulled off his quilted, black uniform jacket, cast it aside, and tore open his shirt. His cheekbones and jaws dissolved and flowed forward, and his brow retreated as he sought an altered state.

chapter fifty-three

When Harry Talbot finished telling them about the Boogeymen, Sam leaned forward on the high stool to the telescope eyepiece. He swung the instrument to the left, until he focused on the vacant lot beside Callan's, where the creatures had most recently put in an appearance.

He was not sure what he was looking for. He didn't believe that the Boogeymen would have returned to that same place at precisely this time to give him a convenient look at them. And there were no clues in the shadows and trampled grass and shrubs, where they had crouched only a few hours ago, to tell him what they might have been or on what mission they had been embarked. Maybe he was just trying to anchor the fantastic image of ape-dog-reptilian Boogeymen in the real world, tie them in his mind to that vacant lot, and thereby make them more concrete, so he could deal with them.

In any event Harry had another story besides that one. As they sat in the darkened room, as if listening to ghost stories around a burnt-out campfire, he told them how he'd seen Denver Simpson, Doc Fitz, Reese Dorn, and Paul Hawthorne overpower Ella Simpson, take her upstairs to the bedroom, and prepare to inject her with an enormous syringeful of some golden fluid.

Operating the telescope at Harry's direction, Sam was able to find and draw in tight on the Simpsons' house, on the other side of Conquistador and just north of the Catholic cemetery. All was dark and motionless.

From the bed where she still had the dog's head in her lap, Tessa said, "All of it's got to be connected somehow: these 'accidental' deaths, whatever those men were doing to Ella Simpson, and these . . . Boogeymen."

"Yes, it's tied together," Sam agreed. "And the knot is New Wave Microtechnology."

He told them what he had uncovered while working with the VDT in the patrol car behind the municipal building.

"Moonhawk?" Tessa wondered. "Conversions? What on earth are they converting people into?"

"I don't know."

"Surely not into . . . these Boogeymen?"

"No, I don't see the purpose of *that*, and besides, from what I turned up, I gather almost two thousand people in town have been . . . given this treatment, put through this change, whatever the hell it is. If there were that many of Harry's Boogeymen running loose, they'd be everywhere; the town would be crawling with them, like a zoo in the Twilight Zone."

"Two thousand," Harry said. "That's two-thirds of the town."

"And the rest by midnight," Sam said. "Just under twenty-one hours from now."

"Me, too, I guess?" Harry asked.

"Yeah. I looked you up on their lists. You're scheduled for conversion in the final stage, between six o'clock this coming evening and midnight. So we've got about fourteen and a half hours before they come looking for you."

"This is nuts," Tessa said.

"Yeah," Sam agreed. "Totally nuts."

"It can't be happening," Harry said. "But if it isn't happening, then why's the hair standing up on the back of my neck?"

chapter fifty-four

"Sholnick!"

Throwing aside his uniform shirt, kicking off his shoes, frantic to strip out of all his clothes and complete his regression, Barry Sholnick ignored Loman.

"Barry, stop, for God's sake, don't let this happen," Penniworth said urgently. He was pale and shaking. He glanced from Sholnick to Peyser and back again, and Loman suspected that Penniworth felt the same degenerate urge to which Sholnick had surrendered himself.

"... run free, hunt, blood, blood, need ..."

Peyser's insidious chant was like a spike through Loman's head, and he wanted it to stop. No, truthfully, it wasn't like a spike splitting his skull, because it wasn't at all painful and was, in fact, thrilling and strangely melodic, reaching deep into him, piercing him not like a shaft of steel but like music. *That* was why he wanted it to stop: because it appealed to him, enticed him; it made him want to shed his responsibilities and concerns, retreat from the too-complex life of the intellect to an existence based strictly on feelings, on physical pleasures, a world whose boundaries were defined by sex and food and the thrill of the hunt, a world where disputes were settled and needs were met strictly by the application of muscle, where he'd never have to think again or worry or care.

"... need, need, need, need, need, kill ..."

Sholnick's body bent forward as his spine re-formed. His back lost the concave curvature distinctive of the human form. His skin appeared to be giving way to scales—

"come, quick, quick, the hunt, blood, blood ..."

—and as Sholnick's face was reshaped, his mouth split impossibly wide, opening nearly to each ear, like the mouth of some ever-grinning reptile.

The pressure in Loman's chest was growing greater by the second. He was hot, sweltering, but the heat came from within him, as if his metabolism was racing at a thousand times ordinary speed, readying him for transformation. "No." Sweat streamed from him. "No!" He felt as if the room were a cauldron in which he would be reduced to his essence; he could almost feel his flesh beginning to melt.

Penniworth was saying, "I want, I want, I want, want," but he was vigorously shaking his head, trying to deny what he wanted. He was crying and trembling and sheet-white.

Peyser rose from his crouch and stepped away from the wall. He moved sinuously, swiftly, and although he could not stand entirely erect in his altered state, he was taller than Loman, simultaneously a frightening and seductive figure.

Sholnick shrieked.

Peyser bared his fierce teeth and hissed at Loman as if to say, *Either join us or die.*

With a cry composed partly of despair and partly of joy, Neil Penniworth dropped his 20-gauge and put his hands to his face. As if that contact had exerted an alchemical reaction, both his hands and face began to change.

Heat *exploded* in Loman, and he shouted wordlessly, but without the joy that Penniworth had expressed and without Sholnick's orgasmic cry. While he still had control of himself, he raised the shotgun and squeezed off a round point-blank at Peyser.

The blast took the regressive in the chest, blowing him backward against the bedroom wall in a tremendous spray of blood. Peyser went down, squealing, gasping for breath, wriggling on the floor like a half-stomped bug, but he was not dead. Maybe his heart and lungs had not sustained sufficient damage. If oxygen was still being conveyed to his blood and if blood was still being pumped throughout his body, he was already repairing the damage; his invulnerability was in some ways even greater than the supernatural imperviousness of a werewolf, for he could not be easily killed even with a *silver* bullet; in a moment he would be up, strong as ever.

Wave after wave of heat, each markedly hotter than the one before it washed through Loman. He felt pressure from within, not only in his chest but in every part of his body now. He had only seconds left in which his mind would be clear enough for him to act and his will strong enough to resist. He scuttled to Peyser, shoved the muzzle of the shotgun against the writhing regressive's chest, and pumped another round into him.

The heart *had* to have been pulverized by that round. The body leaped off the floor as the load tore through it. Peyser's monstrous face contorted, then froze with his eyes open and sightless, his lips peeled back from his inhumanly large, sharp, hooked teeth.

Someone screamed behind Loman.

Turning, he saw the Sholnick-thing coming for him. He fired a third round, then a fourth, hitting Sholnick in the chest and stomach.

The deputy went down hard, and began to crawl toward the hall, away from Loman.

Neil Penniworth was curled in the fetal position on the floor by the foot of the bed. He was chanting but not about blood and needs and being free; he was chanting his mother's name, over and over, as if it were a verbal talisman to protect him from the evil that wanted to claim him.

Loman's heart was pounding so hard that the sound of it seemed to have an external source, as if someone were thumping timpani in another room of the house. He was half-convinced that he could feel his entire body throbbing with his pulse, and that with each throb he was changing in some subtle yet hideous way.

Stepping in behind Sholnick, standing over him, Loman rammed the muzzle of the shotgun against the regressive's back, about where he thought the heart would be, and pulled the trigger. Sholnick let out a shrill scream when he felt the muzzle touch him, but he was too weak to roll over and grab the gun away from Loman. The scream was cut off forever by the blast.

The room steamed with blood. That complex scent was so sweet and compelling that it took the place of Peyser's seductive chanting, inducing Loman to regress.

He leaned against the dresser and squeezed his eyes shut, trying to establish a firmer grip on himself. He clung to the shotgun with both hands, clasping it tightly, not for its defensive value—it held no more rounds—but because it was an expertly crafted weapon, which was to say that it was a *tool*, an artifact of civilization, a reminder that he was a man, at the pinnacle of evolution, and that he must not succumb to the temptation to cast away all his tools and knowledge in exchange for the more primal pleasures and satisfactions of a beast.

But the blood smell was strong and so alluring. . . .

Desperately trying to impress himself with all that would be lost in this surrender, he thought of Grace, his wife, and remembered how much he once had loved her. But he was beyond love now, as were all of the New People. Thoughts of Grace could not save him. Indeed, images of their recent, bestial rutting flashed through his mind, and she was not Grace to him any more; she was simply *female*, and the recollection of their savage coupling excited him and drew him closer to the vortex of regression.

The intense desire to degenerate made him feel as though he were

in a whirlpool, being sucked down, down, and he thought that this was
how the nascent werewolf was supposed to feel when he looked up into
the night sky and saw, ascending at the horizon, a full moon. The conflict raged within him:

. . . blood . . .

. . . freedom . . .

—*no. Mind, knowledge—*

. . . hunt . . .

. . . kill . . .

—*no. Explore, learn—*

. . . eat . . .

. . . run . . .

. . . hunt . . .

. . . fuck . . .

. . . kill . . .

—*no, no! Music, art, language—*

His turmoil grew.

He was trying to resist the siren call of savagery with reason, but
that did not seem to be working, so he thought of Denny, his son. He
must hold fast to his humanity if only for Denny's sake. He tried to
summon the love he had once known for his boy, tried to let that love
rebuild in him until he could shout of it, but there was only a whisper
of remembered emotion deep in the darkness of his mind. His ability
to love had receded from him in much the way that matter had receded
from the center of existence following the Big Bang that created the
universe; his love for Denny was now so far away and long ago that it
was like a star at the outer edge of the universe, its light only dimly
perceived, with little power to illuminate and no power to warm. Yet
even that glimmer of feeling was something around which to build an
image of himself as human, human, first and always a man, not some
thing that ran on all fours or with its knuckles dragging on the ground,
but a man, a man.

His stentorian breathing slowed a little. His heartbeat fell from an
impossibly rapid *dubdubdubdubdubdubdub* to perhaps a hundred or
a hundred and twenty beats a minute, still fast, as if he were running,
but better. His head cleared, too, though not entirely, because the scent
of blood was an inescapable perfume.

He pushed away from the dresser and staggered to Penniworth.

The deputy was still curled in the tightest fetal position that a
grown man could achieve. Traces of the beast were in his hands and
face, but he was considerably more human than not. The chanting of

his mother's name seemed to be working nearly as well as the thread-thin lifeline of love had worked for Loman.

Letting go of his shotgun with one cramped hand, Loman reached down to Penniworth and took him by the arm. "Come on, let's get out of here, boy, let's get away from this smell."

Penniworth understood and got laboriously to his feet. He leaned against Loman and allowed himself to be led out of the room, away from the two dead regressives, along the hallway into the living room.

Here, the stink of urine completely smothered what trace of the blood scent might have ridden the currents of air outward from the bedroom. That was better. It was not a foul odor at all, as it had seemed previously, but acidic and cleansing.

Loman settled Penniworth in an armchair, the only upholstered item in the room that had not been torn to pieces.

"You going to be okay?"

Penniworth looked up at him, hesitated, then nodded. All signs of the beast had vanished from his hands and countenance, though his flesh was strangely lumpy, still in transition. His face appeared to be swollen with a disabling case of the hives, large round lumps from forehead to chin and ear to ear, and there were long, diagonal welts, too, that burned an angry red against his pale skin. However, even as Loman watched, those phenomena faded, and Neil Penniworth laid full claim to his humanity. To his *physical* humanity, at least.

"You sure?" Loman asked.

"Yes."

"Stay right there."

"Yes."

Loman went into the foyer and opened the front door. The deputy standing guard outside was so tense because of all the shooting and screaming in the house that he almost fired on his chief before he realized who it was.

"What the hell?" the deputy said.

"Get on the computer link to Shaddack," Loman said. "He has to come out here now. Right now. I have to see him *now*."

chapter fifty-five

Sam drew the heavy blue drapes, and Harry turned on one bedside lamp. Soft as it was, too dim to chase away more than half the shadows, the light nevertheless stung Tessa's eyes, which were already tired and bloodshot.

For the first time she actually saw the room. It was sparely furnished: the stool; the tall table beside the stool; the telescope; a long, modern-oriental, black lacquered dresser; a pair of matching nightstands; a small refrigerator in one corner; and an adjustable hospital-type bed, queen-size, without a spread but with plenty of pillows and brightly colored sheets patterned with splashes and streaks and spots of red, orange, purple, green, yellow, blue, and black, like a giant canvas painted by a demented and color-blind abstract artist.

Harry saw her and Sam's reaction to the sheets and said, "Now, *that's* a story, but first you've got to know the background. My housekeeper, Mrs. Hunsbok, comes in once a week, and she does most of my shopping for me. But I send Moose on errands every day, if only to pick up a newspaper. He wears this set of . . . well, sort of saddle-bags strapped around him, one hanging on each side. I put a note and some money in the bags, and he goes to the local convenience store—it's the only place he'll go when he's wearing the bags, unless I'm with him. The clerk at the little grocery, Jimmy Ramis, knows me real well. Jimmy reads the note, puts a quart of milk or some candy bars or whatever I want in the saddlebags, puts the change in there, too, and Moose brings it all back to me. He's a good, reliable service dog, the best. They train them real well at Canine Companions for Independence. Moose never chases after a cat with my newspaper and fresh milk in his backpack."

The dog raised his head off Tessa's lap, panted and grinned, as if acknowledging the praise.

"One day he came home with a few items I'd sent him for, and he also had a set of these sheets and pillow cases. I call up Jimmy Ramis, see, and ask him what's the idea, and Jimmy says he doesn't know what

I'm talking about, says he never saw any such sheets. Now, Jimmy's dad owns the convenience store, and he also owns Surplus Outlet, out on the county road. He gets all kinds of discontinued merchandise and stuff that didn't sell as well as the manufacturers expected, picks it up at ten cents on the dollar sometimes, and I figure these sheets were something he was having trouble unloading even at Surplus Outlet. Jimmy no doubt saw them, thought they were pretty silly, and decided to have some fun with me. But on the phone Jimmy says, 'Harry, if I knew anything about the sheets, I'd tell you, but I don't.' And I says, 'You trying to make me believe Moose went and bought them all on his own, with his own money?' And Jimmy says, 'Well, no, I'd guess he shoplifted them somewhere,' and I says, 'And just how did he manage to stuff them in his own backpack so neat,' and Jimmy says, 'I don't know, Harry, but that there is one hell of a clever dog—though it sounds like he doesn't have good taste.'"

Tessa saw how Harry relished the story, and she also saw why he was so pleased by it. For one thing, the dog was child and brother and friend, all rolled into one, and Harry was proud that people thought of Moose as clever. More important, Jimmy's little joke made Harry a part of his community, not just a homebound invalid but a participant in the life of his town. His lonely days were marked by too few such incidents.

"And you *are* a clever dog," Tessa told Moose.

Harry said, "Anyway, I decided to have Mrs. Hunsbok put them on the bed next time she came, as a joke, but then I sort of liked them."

After drawing the drapes at the second window, Sam returned to the stool, sat down, swiveled to face Harry, and said, "They're the loudest sheets I've ever seen. Don't they keep you awake at night?"

Harry smiled. "Nothing can keep me awake. I sleep like a baby. What keeps people awake is worry about the future, about what might happen to them. But the worst has *already* happened to me. Or they lie awake thinking about the past, about what might have been, but I don't do that because I just don't dare." His smile faded as he spoke. "So now what? What do we do next?"

Gently removing Moose's head from her lap, standing, and brushing a few dog hairs from her jeans, Tessa said, "Well, the phones aren't working, so Sam can't call the Bureau, and if we walk out of town we risk an encounter with Watkins's patrols or these Boogeymen. Unless you know a ham radio enthusiast who'd let us use his set to get a message relayed, then so as far as I can see, we've got to drive out."

"Roadblocks, remember," Harry said.

She said, "Well, I figure we'll have to drive out in a truck, something big and mean, ram straight through the damn roadblock, make it to the highway, then out of their jurisdiction. Even if we do get chased down by county cops, that's fine, because Sam can get them to call the Bureau, verify his assignment, then they'll be on our side."

"Who's the federal agent here, anyway?" Sam asked.

Tessa felt herself blush. "Sorry. See, a documentary filmmaker is almost always her own producer, sometimes producer and director and writer too. That means if the art part of it is going to work, the business part of it has to work first, so I'm used to doing a lot of planning, logistics. Didn't mean to step on your toes."

"Step on them any time."

Sam smiled, and she liked him when he smiled. She realized she was even attracted to him a little. He was neither handsome nor ugly, and not what most people meant by "plain," either. He was rather . . . nondescript but pleasant-looking. She sensed a darkness in him, something deeper than his current worries about events in Moonlight Cove— maybe sadness at some loss, maybe long-repressed anger related to some injustice he had suffered, maybe a general pessimism arising from too much contact in his work with the worst elements of society. But when he smiled, he was transformed.

"You really going to smash out in a truck?" Harry asked.

"Maybe as a last resort," Sam said. "But we'd have to find a rig big enough and then steal it, and that's an operation in itself. Besides, they might have riot guns at the roadblock, loaded with magnum rounds, maybe automatic weapons. I wouldn't want to run that kind of flak even in a Mack truck. You can ride into hell in a tank, but the devil will get his hands on you anyway, so it's best not to go there in the first place."

"So where *do* we go?" Tessa asked.

"To sleep," Sam said. "There's a way out of this, a way to get through to the Bureau. I can sort of see it out of the corner of my eye, but when I try to look directly at it, it goes away, and that's because I'm tired. I need a couple of hours in the sack to get fresh and think straight."

Tessa was exhausted, too, though after what had happened at Cove Lodge, she was somewhat surprised that she not only could sleep but wanted to. As she'd stood in her motel room, listening to the screams of the dying and the savage shrieks of the killers, she wouldn't have thought she'd ever sleep again.

chapter fifty-six

Shaddack arrived at Peyser's at five minutes till four in the morning. He drove his charcoal-gray van with heavily tinted windows, rather than his Mercedes, because a computer terminal was mounted on the console of the van, between the seats, where the manufacturer had originally intended to provide a built-in cooler. As eventful as the night had been thus far, it seemed a good idea to stay within reach of the data link that, like a spider, spun a silken web enmeshing all of Moonlight Cove. He parked on the wide shoulder of the two-lane rural blacktop, directly in front of the house.

As Shaddack walked across the yard to the front porch, distant rumbling rolled along the Pacific horizon. The hard wind that had harried the fog eastward had also brought a storm in from the west. During the past couple of hours, churning clouds had clothed the heavens, shrouding the naked stars that had burned briefly between the passing of the mist and the coming of the thunderheads. Now the night was very dark and deep. He shivered inside his cashmere topcoat, under which he still wore a sweat suit.

A couple of deputies were sitting in black-and-whites in the driveway. They watched him, pale faces beyond dusty car windows, and he liked to think they regarded him with fear and reverence, for he was in a sense their maker.

Loman Watkins was waiting for him in the front room. The place had been wrecked. Neil Penniworth sat on the only undamaged piece of furniture; he looked badly shaken and could not meet Shaddack's gaze. Watkins was pacing. A few spatters of blood marked his uniform, but he looked unhurt; if he'd sustained injuries, they had been minor and had already healed. More likely, the blood belonged to someone else.

"What happened here?" Shaddack asked.

Ignoring the question, Watkins spoke to his officer: "Go out to the car, Neil. Stay close to the other men."

"Yes, sir," Penniworth said. He was huddled in his chair, bent forward, looking down at his shoes.

"You'll be okay, Neil."

"I think so."

"It wasn't a question. It was a statement: You'll be okay. You have enough strength to resist. You've proven that already."

Penniworth nodded, got up, and headed for the door.

Shaddack said, "What's this all about?"

Turning toward the hallway at the other end of the room, Watkins said, "Come with me." His voice was as cold and hard as ice, informed by fear and anger, but noticeably devoid of the grudging respect with which he had spoken to Shaddack ever since he had been converted in August.

Displeased by that change in Watkins, uneasy, Shaddack frowned and followed him back down the hall.

The cop stopped at a closed door, turned to Shaddack. "You told me that what you've done to us is improve our biological efficiency by injecting us with these . . . these biochips."

"A misnomer, really. They're not chips at all, but incredibly small microspheres."

In spite of the regressives and a few other problems that had developed with the Moonhawk Project, Shaddack's pride of achievement was undiminished. Glitches could be fixed. Bugs could be worked out of the system. He was still *the* genius of his age; he not only felt this to be true, but knew it as well as he knew in which direction to look for the rising sun each morning.

Genius . . .

The ordinary silicon microchip that made possible the computer revolution had been the size of a fingernail, and had contained one million circuits etched onto it by photolithography. The smallest circuit on the chip had been one-hundredth as wide as a human hair. Breakthroughs in X-ray lithography, using giant particle accelerators called synchrotrons, eventually made possible the imprinting of one *billion* circuits on a chip, with features as small as one-thousandth the width of a human hair. Shrinking dimensions was the primary way to gain computer speed, improving both function and capabilities.

The microspheres developed by New Wave were one four-thousandth the size of a microchip. Each was imprinted with a quarter-million circuits. This had been achieved by the application of a radically new form of X-ray lithography that made it possible to etch circuits on amazingly small surfaces *and* without having to hold those surfaces perfectly still.

Conversion of Old People into New People began with the injection of hundreds of thousands of these microspheres, in solution, into the bloodstream. They were biologically interactive in function, but the material itself was biologically inert, so the immune system wasn't triggered. There were different kinds of microspheres. Some were heart-tropic, meaning they moved through the veins to the heart and took up residence there, attaching themselves to the walls of the blood vessels that serviced the cardiac muscle. Some spheres were liver-tropic, lung-tropic, kidney-tropic, bowel-tropic, brain-tropic, and so on. They settled in clusters at those sites and were designed in such a way that, when touching, their circuits linked.

Those clusters, spread throughout the body, eventually provided about fifty billion usable circuits that had the potential for data processing, considerably more than in the largest supercomputers of the 1980s. In a sense, by injection, a super-supercomputer had been put inside the human body.

Moonlight Cove and the surrounding area were constantly bathed in microwave transmissions from dishes on top of the main building at New Wave. A fraction of those transmissions involved the police computer system, and another fraction could be drawn upon to power-up the microspheres inside each of the New People.

A small number of spheres were of a different material and served as transducers and power distributors. When one of the Old People received his third injection of microspheres, the power spheres at once drew on those microwave transmissions, converting them into electrical current and distributing it throughout the network. The amount of current needed to operate the system was exceedingly small.

Other specialized spheres in each cluster were memory units. Some of those carried the program that would operate the system; that program was loaded the moment power entered the network.

To Watkins, Shaddack said, "Long ago I became convinced that the basic problem with the human animal is its extremely emotional nature. I've freed you from that burden. In so doing, I've made you not only mentally healthier but physically healthier as well."

"How? I know so little of how the Change is effected."

"You're a cybernetic organism now—that is, part man and part machine—but you don't *need* to understand it, Loman. You use a telephone, yet you've no idea of how to build a phone system from scratch. You don't know how a computer works, yet you can use one. And you don't have to know how the computer *in* you works in order to use it, either."

Watkins's eyes were clouded with fear. "Do I use it . . . or does it use me?"

"Of course, it doesn't use you."

"Of course . . ."

Shaddack wondered what had happened here tonight to have put Watkins in such a state of extreme anxiety. He was more curious than ever to see what was in the bedroom at the threshold of which they had halted. But he was acutely aware that Watkins was in a dangerously excited state and that it was necessary, if frustrating, to take the time to calm his fears.

"Loman, the clustered microspheres within you don't constitute a *mind*. The system's not in any way truly intelligent. It's a servant, your servant. It frees you from toxic emotions."

Strong emotions—hatred, love, envy, jealousy, the whole long list of human sensibilities—regularly destabilized the biological functions of the body. Medical researchers had proved that different emotions stimulated the production of different brain chemicals, and that those chemicals in turn induced the various organs and tissues of the body to either increase or reduce or alter their function in a less than productive fashion. Shaddack was convinced that a man whose body was ruled by his emotions could not be a totally healthy man and *never* entirely clear-thinking.

The microsphere computer within each of the New People monitored every organ in the body. When it detected the production of various amino-acid compounds and other chemical substances that were produced in response to strong emotion, it used electrical stimuli to override the brain and other organs, shutting off the flow, thus eliminating the physical consequences of an emotion if not the emotion itself. At the same time the microsphere computer stimulated the copious production of other compounds known to repress those same emotions, thereby treating not only the cause but the effect.

"I've released you from all emotions but fear," Shaddack said, "which is necessary for self-preservation. Now that the chemistry of your body is no longer undergoing wild swings, you'll think more clearly."

"So far as I've noticed, I've not suddenly become a genius."

"Well, you might not notice a greater mental acuity yet, but in time you will."

"When?"

"When your body is fully purged of the residue of a lifetime of emotional pollution. Meanwhile, your interior computer"—he lightly tapped Watkins's chest—"is also programmed to use complex electrical stimuli to induce the body to create wholly new amino-acid compounds that keep your blood vessels scoured and free of plaque and clots, kill cancerous cells the moment they appear, and perform a double score of other chores, keeping you far healthier than ordinary men, no doubt dramatically lengthening your life span."

Shaddack had expected the healing process to be accelerated in New People, but he had been surprised at the almost miraculous speed with which their wounds closed. He still could not entirely understand how new tissue could be formed so quickly, and his current work on Moonhawk was focused on discovering an explanation for that effect. The healing was not accomplished without a price, for the metabolism was fantastically accelerated; stored body fat was burned prodigiously in order to close a wound in seconds or minutes, leaving the healed man pounds lighter, sweat-drenched, and fiercely hungry.

Watkins frowned and wiped one shaky hand across his sweaty face. "I can maybe see that healing would be speeded up, but what gives us the ability to so completely reshape ourselves, to regress to another form? Surely not even buckets of these biological chemicals could tear down our bodies and rebuild them in just a minute or two. How can that be?"

For a moment Shaddack met the other man's gaze, then looked away, coughed, and said, "Listen, I can explain all of this to you later. Right now I want to see Peyser. I hope you were able to restrain him without doing much damage."

As Shaddack reached toward the door to push it open, Watkins seized his wrist, staying his hand. Shaddack was shocked. He did not allow himself to be touched.

"Take your hand off me."

"How can the body be so suddenly reshaped?"

"I told you, we'll discuss it later."

"Now." Watkins's determination was so strong that it carved deep lines in his face. "Now. I'm so scared I can't think straight. I can't function at this level of fear, Shaddack. Look at me. I'm shaking. I feel like I'm going to blow apart. A million pieces. You don't know what happened here tonight, or you'd feel the same way. I've got to know: How can our bodies change so suddenly?"

Shaddack hesitated. "I'm working on that."

Surprised, Watkins let go of his wrist and said, "You . . . you mean you don't know?"

"It's an unexpected effect. I'm beginning to understand it"—which was a lie—"but I've got a lot more work to do." First he had to understand the New People's phenomenal healing powers, which were no doubt an aspect of the same process that allowed them to completely metamorphose into subhuman forms.

"You subjected us to this without knowing what all it might do to us?"

"I knew it would be a benefit, a great gift," Shaddack said impatiently. "No scientist can ever predict all the side effects. He has to proceed with the confidence that whatever side effects arise will not outweigh the benefits."

"But they *do* outweigh the benefits," Watkins said, as close to anger as a New Man could get. "My God, how could you have done this to us?"

"I did this *for* you."

Watkins stared at him, then pushed open the bedroom door and said, "Have a look."

Shaddack stepped into the room, where the carpet was damp—and some of the walls festooned—with blood. He grimaced at the stink. He found all biological odors unusually repellent, perhaps because they were a reminder that human beings were far less efficient and clean than machines. After stopping at the first corpse—which lay facedown near the door—and studying it, he looked across the room at the second body. "Two of them? Two regressives, and you killed *both*? Two chances to study the psychology of these degenerates, and you threw away both opportunities?"

Watkins was unbowed by the criticism. "It was a life-or-death situation here. It couldn't have been handled differently."

He seemed angry to a degree inconsistent with the personality of a New Man, though perhaps the emotion sustaining his icy demeanor was less rage than fear. Fear was acceptable.

"Peyser was regressed when we got here," Watkins continued. "We searched the house, confronted him in this room."

As Watkins described that confrontation in detail, Shaddack was gripped by an apprehension that he tried not to reveal and to which he did not even want to admit. When he spoke he let only anger touch his voice, not fear: "You're telling me that your men, both Sholnick and Penniworth, are regressives, that even *you* are a regressive?"

"Sholnick was a regressive, yes. In my book Penniworth isn't—not yet anyway—because he successfully resisted the urge. Just as I resisted it." Watkins boldly maintained eye contact, not once glancing away, which further disturbed Shaddack. "What I'm telling you is the same thing I told you in so many words a few hours ago at your place: Each of us, every damned one of us, is potentially a regressive. It's not a rare sickness among the New People. It's in all of us. You've not created new and better men any more than Hitler's policies of genetic breeding could've created a master race. You're not God; you're Dr. Moreau."

"You will not speak to me like this," Shaddack said, wondering who this Moreau was. The name was vaguely familiar, but he could not place it. "When you talk to me, I'd suggest you remember who I am."

Watkins lowered his voice, perhaps realizing anew that Shaddack could extinguish the New People almost as easily as snuffing out a candle. But he continued to speak forcefully and with too little respect. "You still haven't responded to the worst of this news."

"And what's that?"

"Didn't you hear me? I said that Peyser was *stuck*. He couldn't remake himself."

"I doubt very much that he was trapped in an altered state. New Men have complete control of their bodies, more control than I ever anticipated. If he could not return to human form, that was strictly a psychological block. He didn't really want to return."

For a moment Watkins stared at him, then shook his head and said, "You aren't really that dense, are you? *It's the same thing.* Hell, it doesn't matter whether something went wrong with the microsphere network inside him or whether it was strictly psychological. Either way, the effect was the same, the result was the same: He was stuck, trapped, locked into that degenerate form."

"You will not speak to me like this," Shaddack repeated firmly, as if repetition of the command would work the same way it did when training a dog.

For all their physiological superiority and potential for mental superiority, New People were still dismayingly *people*, and to the degree they were people, they were that much less effective machines. With a computer, you only had to program a command once. The computer retained it and acted upon it always. Shaddack wondered if he would ever be able to perfect the New People to the point at which future generations functioned as smoothly and reliably as the average IBM PC.

Damp with sweat, pale, his eyes strange and haunted, Watkins was an intimidating figure. When the cop took two steps to reduce the gap between them, Shaddack was afraid and wanted to retreat, but he held his ground and continued to meet Watkins's eyes the way he would have defiantly met those of a dangerous German shepherd if he had been cornered by one.

"Look at Sholnick," Watkins said, indicating the corpse at their feet. He used the toe of his shoe to turn the dead man over.

Even riddled with shotgun pellets and soaked in blood, Sholnick's bizarre mutation was unmistakable. His sightlessly staring eyes were perhaps the most frightful thing about him: yellow with black irises, not the round irises of the human eye but elongated ovals as in the eyes of a snake.

Outside, thunder rolled across the night, a louder peal than the one Shaddack had heard when he'd been crossing Peyser's front lawn.

Watkins said, "The way you explained it to me—these degenerates undergo willful devolution."

"That's right."

"You said the whole history of human evolution is carried in our genes, that we still have in us traces of what the species once was, and that the regressives somehow tap that genetic material and devolve into creatures somewhere further back on the evolutionary ladder."

"What's your point?"

"That explanation made some sort of crazy sense when we trapped Coombs in the theater and got a good look at him back in September. He was more ape than man, something in between."

"It doesn't make crazy sense; it makes perfect sense."

"But, Jesus, look at Sholnick. *Look* at him! When I gunned him down, he'd halfway transformed himself into some goddamned creature that's part man, part . . . hell, I don't know, part lizard or snake. You telling me that we evolved from reptiles, we're carrying lizard genes from ten million years ago?"

Shaddack thrust both hands in his coat pockets, lest they betray his apprehension with a nervous gesture or tremble. "The first life on earth was in the sea, then something crawled onto the land—a fish with rudimentary legs—and the fish evolved into the early reptiles, and along the way mammals split off. If we don't contain actual fragments of the genetic material of those very early reptiles—and I believe we do—then at least we have racial memory of that stage of evolution encoded in us in some other way we don't really understand."

"You're jiving me, Shaddack."

"And you're *irritating* me."

"I don't give a damn. Come here, come with me, take a closer look at Peyser. He was a friend of yours from way back, wasn't he? Take a good, long look at what he was when he died."

Peyser was flat on his back, naked, right leg straight in front of him, left leg bent under him at an angle, one arm flung out at his side, the other across his chest, which had been shattered by a couple of shotgun blasts. The body and the face—with its inhuman muzzle and teeth, yet vaguely recognizable as Mike Peyser—were those of a shockingly horrific freak, a dog-man, a werewolf, something that belonged in either a carnival sideshow or an old horror movie. The skin was coarse. The patchy coat of hair was wiry. The hands looked powerful, the claws sharp.

Because his fascination exceeded his disgust and fear, Shaddack pulled up his topcoat to keep the hem of it from brushing the bloody corpse, and stooped beside Peyser's body for a closer look.

Watkins hunkered down on the other side of the cadaver.

While another avalanche of thunder rumbled down the night sky, the dead man stared at the bedroom ceiling with eyes that were too human for the rest of his twisted countenance.

"You going to tell me that somewhere along the way we evolved from dogs, wolves?" Watkins asked.

Shaddack did not reply.

Watkins pressed the issue. "You going to tell me that we've got dog genes in us that we can tap when we want to transform ourselves? Am I supposed to believe God took a rib from some prehistoric Lassie and made man from it before he took man's rib to make a woman?"

Curiously Shaddack touched one of Mike Peyser's hands, which was designed for killing as surely as was a soldier's bayonet. It felt like flesh, just cooler than that of a living man.

"This can't be explained biologically," Watkins said, glaring at Shaddack across the corpse. "This wolf form isn't something Peyser could dredge up from racial memory stored in his genes. So how could he change like this? It's not just your biochips at work here. It's something else . . . something stranger."

Shaddack nodded. "Yes." An explanation had occurred to him, and he was excited by it. "Something a great deal stranger . . . but perhaps I understand it."

"So tell me. *I'd* like to understand it. Damned if I wouldn't. I'd like to understand it real well. Before it happens to me."

"There's a theory that form is a function of consciousness."

"Huh?"

"It holds that we are what we think we are. I'm not talking pop psychology here, that you can be what you want to be if you'll only like yourself, nothing of that sort. I mean *physically*, we may have the potential to be whatever we think we are, to override the morphic stasis dictated by our genetic heritage."

"Gobbledegook," Watkins said impatiently.

Shaddack stood. He put his hands in his pockets again. "Let me put it this way: The theory says that consciousness is the greatest power in the universe, that it can bend the physical world to its desire."

"Mind over matter."

"Right."

"Like some talk-show psychic bending a spoon or stopping a watch," Watkins said.

"Those people are usually fakes, I suspect. But, yes, maybe that power is really in us. We just don't know how to tap it because for millions of years we've allowed the physical world to dominate us. By habit, by stasis, and by preference for order over chaos, we remain at the mercy of the physical world. But what we're talking about here," he said, pointing to Sholnick and Peyser, "is a lot more complex and exciting than bending a spoon with the mind. Peyser felt the urge to regress, for reasons I don't understand, perhaps for the sheer thrill of it—"

"For the thrill." Watkins's voice lowered, became quiet, almost hushed, and was filled with such intense fear and mental anguish that it deepened Shaddack's chill. "Animal power is thrilling. Animal need. You feel animal hunger, animal lust, bloodthirst—and you're drawn toward that because it seems so . . . so simple and powerful, so natural. It's freedom."

"Freedom?"

"Freedom from responsibility, from worry, from the pressure of the civilized world, from having to *think* too much. The temptation to regress is tremendously powerful because you feel life will be so much easier and exciting then," Watkins said, evidently speaking about what he had felt when drawn toward an altered state. "When you become a beast, life is all sensation, just pain and pleasure, with no need to intellectualize anything. That's part of it, anyway."

Shaddack was silent, unsettled by the passion with which Watkins—not ordinarily an expressive man—had spoken of the urge to regress.

Another detonation rocked the sky, more powerful than any before it. The first hard crack of thunder reverberated in the bedroom windows.

Mind racing, Shaddack said, "Anyway, the important thing is that when Peyser felt this urge to become a beast, a hunter, he didn't regress along the human genetic line. Evidently, in his opinion, a wolf is the greatest of all hunters, the most desirable form for a predatory beast, so he *willed* himself to become wolflike."

"Just like that," Watkins said skeptically.

"Yes, just like that. Mind over matter. The metamorphosis is mostly a *mental* process. Oh, certainly, there are physical changes. But we might not be talking complete alteration of matter . . . only of biological structures. The basic nucleotides remain the same, but the sequence in which they're read changes drastically. Structural genes are transformed into operator genes by a force of will. . . ."

Shaddack's voice trailed off as his excitement rose to match his fear and left him breathless. He'd done far more than he'd hoped to do with the Moonhawk Project. The stunning accomplishment was the source of both his sudden joy and escalating fear: joy, because he had given men the ability to control their physical form and, eventually, perhaps all matter, simply by the exercise of will; fear, because he was not sure that the New People could learn to control and properly use their power . . . or that he could continue to control them.

"The gift I've given to you—computer-assisted physiology and re-lease from emotion—unleashes the mind's power over matter. It allows consciousness to dictate form."

Watkins shook his head, clearly appalled by what Shaddack was suggesting. "Maybe Peyser willed himself to become what he did. Maybe Sholnick willed it too. But I'll be damned if I did. When I was overcome by the desire to change, I fought it like an ex-addict sweating out a craving for heroin. I didn't want it. It came over me . . . the way the force of the full moon comes over a werewolf."

"No," Shaddack said. "Subconsciously, you *did* want to change, Loman, and you no doubt partially wanted it even on a conscious level. You *must* have wanted it to some extent because you spoke so forcefully about how attractive regression was. You resisted using your power of mind over body only because you found metamorphosis marginally more frightening than appealing. If you lose some of your fear of it . . . or if an altered state becomes just a little more appealing . . . well, then your psychological balance will shift, and you'll remake yourself. But it won't be some outside force at work. It'll be your own mind."

"Then why couldn't Peyser come back?"

"As I said, and as *you* suggested, he didn't want to."

"He was trapped."

"Only by his own desire."

Watkins looked down at the grotesque corpse of the regressive. "What have you done to us, Shaddack?"

"Haven't you grasped what I've said?"

"What have you done to us?"

"This is a great gift!"

"To have no emotions but fear?"

"That's what frees your mind and gives you the power to control your very form," Shaddack said excitedly. "What I don't understand is why the regressives have all chosen a subhuman condition. Surely you have the power within you to undergo evolution rather than devolution, to lift yourself up from mere humanity to something higher, cleaner, purer. Perhaps you even have the power to become a being of pure consciousness, intellect without *any* physical form. Why have all these New People chosen to regress instead?"

Watkins raised his head, and his eyes had a half-dead look, as if they had absorbed death from the very sight of the corpse. "What good is it to have the power of a god if you can't also experience the simple pleasures of a man?"

"But you can do and experience anything you want," Shaddack said exasperatedly.

"Not love."

"What?"

"Not love or hate or joy or any emotion but fear."

"But you don't *need* them. Not having them has freed you."

"You're not thickheaded," Watkins said, "so I guess you don't understand because you're psychologically . . . twisted, warped."

"You must not speak to me like—"

"I'm trying to tell you why they all choose a subhuman form over a superhuman form. It's because, for a thinking creature of high intellect, there can be no pleasure separate from emotion. If you deny men emotions, you deny them pleasure, so they seek an altered state in which complex emotions and pleasure *aren't* linked—the life of an unthinking beast."

"Nonsense. You are—"

Watkins interrupted him again, sharply. "Listen to me, for God's sake! If I remember, even Moreau listened to his creatures."

His face was flushed now instead of pale. His eyes no longer looked half dead; a certain wildness had returned to them. He was only a step or two from Shaddack and seemed to loom over him, though he was the shorter of the two. He looked scared, badly scared—and dangerous.

He said, "Consider sex—a basic human pleasure. For sex to be *fully* satisfying, it has to be accompanied by love or at least some affection. To a psychologically damaged man, sex can still be good if it's linked to hate or pride of domination; even negative emotions can make the act pleasurable for a twisted man. But done with *no emotion at all*, it's pointless, stupid, just the breeding impulse of an animal, just the rhythmic function of a machine."

A flash of lightning burned the night and blazed briefly on the bedroom windows, followed by a crash of thunder that seemed to shake the house. That celestial flicker was, for an instant, brighter than the soft glow of the single bedroom lamp.

In that queer light Shaddack thought he saw something happen to Loman Watkins's face . . . a *shift* in the relationship of the features. But when the lightning passed, Watkins looked quite like himself, so it must have been Shaddack's imagination.

Continuing to speak with great force, with the passion of stark fear, Watkins said, "It's not just sex, either. The same goes for other physical pleasures. Eating, for example. Yeah, I still taste a piece of chocolate when I eat it. But the taste gives me only a tiny fraction of the satisfaction that it did before I was converted. Haven't you noticed?"

Shaddack did not reply, and he hoped that nothing in his demeanor would reveal that he had not undergone conversion himself. He was, of course, waiting until the process had been more highly refined through additional generations of the New People. But he suspected Watkins would not react well to the discovery that their maker had not chosen to submit himself to the blessing that he had bestowed on them.

Watkins said, "And do you know why there's less satisfaction? Before conversion, when we ate chocolate, the taste had thousands of associations for us. When we ate it, we subconsciously remembered the first time we ate it and all the times in between, and subconsciously we remembered how often that taste was associated with holidays and celebrations of all kinds, and because of all that the taste made us *feel good*. But now when I eat chocolate, it's just a taste, a good taste, but it doesn't make me feel good any more. I know it should; I remember that such a thing as 'feeling good' was part of it once, but not now. The taste of chocolate doesn't generate emotional echoes any more. It's an empty sensation, its richness has been stolen from me. The richness of everything but fear has been stolen from me, and everything is gray now—strange, gray, drab—as if I'm half dead."

The left side of Watkins's head bulged. His cheekbone enlarged. That ear began to change shape and draw toward a point.

Stunned, Shaddack backed away from him.

Watkins followed, raising his voice, speaking with a slight slur but with no less force, not with real anger but with fear and an unsettling touch of savagery: "Why the hell would any of us want to evolve to some higher form with even fewer pleasures of the body and the heart? Intellectual pleasures aren't enough, Shaddack. Life is more than that. A life that's *only* intellectual isn't tolerable."

As Watkins's brow gradually sloped backward, slowly melting away like a wall of snow in the sun, heavier accretions of bone began to build up around his eyes.

Shaddack backed into the dresser.

Still approaching, Watkins said, "Jesus! Don't you see yet? Even a man confined to a hospital bed, paralyzed from the neck down, has more in his life than intellectual interests; no one's stolen his emotions from him; no one's reduced him to fear and pure intellect. We need pleasure, Shaddack, pleasure, pleasure. Life without it is terrifying. Pleasure makes life worth living."

"Stop."

"You've made it impossible for us to experience the pleasurable release of emotion, so we can't fully experience pleasures of the flesh, either, because we're creatures of a high order and need the emotional aspect to truly enjoy physical pleasure. It's both or neither in human beings."

Watkins's hands, fisted at his sides, were becoming larger, with swollen knuckles and tobacco-brown, pointed nails.

"You're transforming," Shaddack said.

Ignoring him, speaking more thickly as the shape of his mouth began to change subtly, Watkins said, "So we revert to a savage, altered state. We retreat from our intellect. In the cloak of the beast, our *only* pleasure is the pleasure of the flesh, the flesh, flesh . . . but at least we're no longer aware of what we've lost, so the pleasure remains intense, so intense, deep and sweet, sweet, so sweet. You've made . . . made our lives intolerable, gray and dead, dead, all dead, dead . . . so we have to devolve in mind and in body . . . to find a worthwhile existence. We . . . we have to flee . . . from the horrible restrictions of this narrowed life . . . this very narrowed life you've given us. Men aren't machines. Men . . . men . . . men are not *machines!*"

"You're regressing. For God's sake, Loman!"

Watkins halted and seemed disoriented. Then he shook his head, as if to cast off his confusion as he might a veil. He raised his hands, looked at them, and cried out in terror. He glanced past Shaddack, at the dresser mirror, and his cry grew louder, shriller.

Abruptly Shaddack was acutely aware of the stench of blood, to which he had somewhat accustomed himself. Watkins must be even more affected by it, though not repulsed, no, not in the least repulsed, but excited.

Lightning flashed and thunder shook the night again, and rain suddenly came down in torrents, beating on the windows and drumming on the roof.

Watkins looked from the mirror to Shaddack, raised a hand as if to strike him, then turned and staggered out of the room, into the hall, away from the ripe stink of blood. Out there he dropped to his knees, then onto his side. He curled into a ball, shaking violently, gagging, whimpering, snarling, and intermittently chanting, "No, no, no, no."

chapter fifty-seven

When he pulled back from the brink and felt in control of himself once more, Loman sat up and leaned against the wall. He was wet with perspiration again, and shaky with hunger. The partial transformation and the energy expended to keep it from going all the way had left him drained. He was relieved but also felt unfulfilled, as if some great prize had been within his reach but then had been snatched away just as he had touched it.

A hollow, somewhat susurrant sound surrounded him. At first he thought it was an internal noise, all in his head, perhaps the soft boom and sizzle of brain cells flaring and dying from the strain of thwarting the regressive urge. Then he realized it was rain hammering on the roof of the bungalow.

When he opened his eyes, his vision was blurred. It cleared, and he was staring at Shaddack, who stood on the other side of the hall, just beyond the open bedroom door. Gaunt, long-faced, pale enough to pass for an albino, with those yellowish eyes, in his dark topcoat, the man looked like a visitation, perhaps Death himself.

If this *had* been Death, Loman might well have stood up and warmly embraced him.

Instead, while he waited for the strength to get up, he said, "No more conversions. You've got to stop the conversions."

Shaddack said nothing.

"You're not going to stop, are you?"

Shaddack merely stared at him.

"You're mad," Loman said. "You're stark, raving mad, yet I've no choice but to do what you want . . . or kill myself."

"Never talk to me like that again. Never. Remember who I am."

"I remember who you are," Loman said. He struggled to his feet at last, dizzy, weak. "You did this to me without my consent. And if the time comes when I can no longer resist the urge to regress, when I sink down into savagery, when I'm no longer scared shitless of you, I'll somehow hold on to enough of my mind to remember *where* you are, too, and I'll come for you."

"You threaten me?" Shaddack said, clearly amazed.

"No," Loman said. "Threat isn't the right word."

"It better not be. Because if anything happens to me, Sun is programmed to broadcast a command that'll be received by the clusters of microspheres inside you and—"

"—will instantly kill us all," Loman finished. "Yeah, I know. You've told me. If you go, we all go with you, just like people down there at Jonestown years ago, drinking their poisoned Kool-Aid and biting the big one right along with Reverend Jim. You're our Reverend Jim Jones, a Jim Jones for the high-tech age, Jim Jones with a silicon heart and tightly packed semiconductors between the ears. No, I'm not threatening you, Reverend Jim, because 'threat' is too dramatic a word for it. A man making a threat has to be feeling something powerful, has to be hot with anger. I'm a New Person. I'm only afraid. That's all I can be. Afraid. So it's not a threat. No such a thing. It's a *promise*."

Shaddack stepped through the bedroom doorway, into the hall. A draught of cold air seemed to come with him. Maybe it was Loman's imagination, but the hall seemed chillier with Shaddack in it.

They stared at each other for a long moment.

At last Shaddack said, "You'll continue to do what I say."

"I don't have a choice," Loman noted. "That's the way you made me—without a choice. I'm right there in the palm of your hand, Lord, but it isn't love that keeps me there—it's fear."

"Better," Shaddack said.

He turned his back on Loman and walked down the hall, into the living room, out of the house, and into the night, the rain.

part two

DAYBREAK IN HADES

I could not stop something I knew was wrong and terrible. I had an awful sense of powerlessness.

—Andrei Sakharov

Power dements even more than it corrupts, lowering the guard of foresight and raising the haste of action.

—Will and Ariel Durant

chapter one

Before dawn, having slept less than an hour, Tessa Lockland was awakened by a coldness in her right hand and then the quick, hot licking of a tongue. Her arm was draped over the edge of the mattress, hand trailing just above the carpet, and something down there was taking a taste of her.

She sat straight up in bed, unable to breathe.

She had been dreaming of the carnage at Cove Lodge, of half-seen beasts, shambling and swift, with menacing teeth and claws like curved and well-honed blades. Now she thought that the nightmare had become real, that Harry's house had been invaded by those creatures, and that the questing tongue was but the prelude to a sudden, savage bite.

But it was only Moose. She could see him vaguely in the dim glow that came through the doorway from the night-light in the second-floor hall, and at last she was able to draw breath. He put his forepaws on the mattress, too well trained to climb all the way onto the bed. Whining softly, he seemed only to want affection.

She was sure that she had closed the door before retiring. But she had seen enough examples of Moose's cleverness to suppose that he was able to open a door if he was determined. In fact, she suddenly realized that the interior doors of the Talbot house were fitted with hardware that made the task easier for Moose: not knobs but lever-action handles that would release the latch when depressed either by a hand or a paw.

"Lonely?" she asked, gently rubbing the Labrador behind the ears.

The dog whined again and submitted to her petting.

Fat drops of rain rattled against the window. It was falling with such force that she could hear it slashing through the trees outside. Wind pressed insistently against the house.

"Well, as lonely as you are, fella, I'm a thousand times that sleepy, so you're going to have to scoot."

When she stopped petting him, he understood. Reluctantly he

dropped to the floor, padded to the door, looked back at her for a moment, then went into the hall, glanced both ways, and turned left.

The light from the hall was minimal, but it bothered her. She got up and closed the door, and by the time she returned to bed in the dark, she knew she would not be able to go back to sleep right away.

For one thing, she was wearing all her clothes—jeans and T-shirt and sweater—having taken off only her shoes, and she was not entirely comfortable. But she hadn't the nerve to undress, for that would make her feel so vulnerable that she wouldn't sleep at all. After what had happened at Cove Lodge, Tessa wanted to be prepared to move fast.

Furthermore, she was in the only spare bedroom—there was another, but unfurnished—and the mattress and quilted spread had a musty odor from years of disuse. It had once been Harry's father's room, as the house had once been Harry's father's house, but the elder Talbot had died seventeen years ago, three years after Harry had been brought home from the war. Tessa had insisted she could do without sheets and just sleep on top of the spread or, if cold, slip under the spread and sleep on the bare mattress. After shooing Moose out and closing the door, she felt chilled, and when she got under the spread, the musty odor seemed to carry a new scent of mildew, faint but unpleasant.

Above the background patter and hiss of the rain, she heard the hum of the elevator ascending. Moose probably had called it. Was he usually so peripatetic at night?

Though she was grindingly weary, she was now too awake to shut her mind off easily. Her thoughts were deeply troubling.

Not the massacre at Cove Lodge. Not the grisly stories of dead bodies being shoveled like so much refuse into crematoriums. Not the Parkins woman being torn to pieces by some species unknown. Not the monstrous night stalkers. All of those macabre images no doubt helped determine the channel into which her thoughts flowed, but for the most part they were only a somber background for more personal ruminations about her life and its direction.

Having recently brushed against death, she was more aware than usual of her mortality. Life was finite. In the business and the busyness of daily life, that truth was often forgotten.

Now she was unable to escape thinking about it, and she wondered if she was playing too loose with life, wasting too many years. Her work was satisfying. She was a happy woman; it was damned hard for a Lockland to be unhappy, predisposed as they were to good humor. But in all honesty she had to admit she was not getting what she truly wanted. If she remained on her current course, she'd never get it.

What she wanted was a family, a place to belong. That came, of course, from her childhood and adolescence in San Diego, where she had idolized her big sister, Janice, and had basked in the love of her mother and father. The tremendous amount of happiness and security she'd known in her youth was what allowed her to deal with the misery, despair, and terror that she sometimes encountered when working on one of her more ambitious documentaries. The first two decades of her life had been so full of joy, they balanced anything that followed.

The elevator had arrived on the second floor, and now, with a soft thump and a renewed hum, it descended. She was intrigued that Moose, so accustomed to using the elevator for and with his master, used it himself at night, though the stairs would have been quicker. Dogs, too, could be creatures of habit.

They'd had dogs at home when she was a kid, first a great golden retriever named Barney, then an Irish Setter named Mickey Finn. . . .

Janice had married and moved away from home sixteen years ago, when Tessa was eighteen, and thereafter entropy, the blind force of dissolution, had pulled apart that cozy life in San Diego. Tessa's dad died three years later, and soon after his funeral Tessa hit the road to make her industrials and documentaries and travel films, and although she had remained in touch with her mother and sister on a regular basis, that golden time had passed.

Janice was gone now. And Marion wouldn't live forever, not even if she actually gave up skydiving.

More than anything, Tessa wanted to re-create that home life with a husband of her own and children. She had been married, at twenty-three, to a man who wanted kids more than he wanted her, and when they had learned that she could never have children, he had left. Adoption wasn't enough for him. He wanted children that were biologically his. Fourteen months from wedding day to divorce. She had been badly hurt.

Thereafter she had thrown herself into her work with a passion she'd not shown previously. She was insightful enough to know that through her art she was trying to reach out to all the world as if it were one big extended family. By boiling down complex stories and issues to thirty, sixty, or ninety minutes of film, she was trying to pull the world in, reduce it to essences, to the size of one family.

But, lying awake in Harry Talbot's spare bedroom, Tessa knew she was never going to be fully satisfied if she didn't radically shake up her life and more directly seek the thing she so much wanted. It was impossible to be a person of depth if you lacked a love for humankind, but that generalized love could swiftly become airy and meaningless if you didn't have a particular family close to you; for in your family you saw, day to day, those specific things in specific people that justified, by extension, a broader love of fellow men and women. She was a stickler for specificity in her art, but she lacked it in her emotional life.

Breathing dust and the faint odor of mildew, she felt as if her potential as a person had long been lying as unused as that bedroom. But not having dated for years, having sought refuge from heartbreak in hard work, how did a woman of thirty-four begin to open herself to that part of life she had so purposefully sealed off? Just then she felt more barren than at any time since first learning that she would never have children of her own. And at the moment, finding a way to remake her life seemed a more important issue than learning where the Boogeymen came from and what they were.

A brush with death could stir up peculiar thoughts.

In a while her weariness overcame her inner turmoil, and she drifted into sleep again. Just as she dropped off, she realized that Moose might have come to her room because he sensed something wrong in the house. Perhaps he had been trying to alert her. But surely he would have been more agitated and would have barked if there was danger.

Then she slept.

chapter two

From Peyser's, Shaddack returned to his ultramodern house on the north point of the cove, but he didn't stay long. He made three ham sandwiches, wrapped them, and put them in a cooler with several cans of Coke. He put the cooler in the van along with a couple of blankets and a pillow. From the gun cabinet in his study he fetched a Smith & Wesson .357 Magnum, a Remington 12-gauge semiautomatic pistol-grip shotgun, and plenty of ammunition for both. Thus equipped, he set out in the storm to cruise Moonlight Cove and immediate outlying areas, intending to keep on the move, monitoring the situation by computer until the first phase of Moonhawk was concluded at midnight, in less than nineteen hours.

Watkins's threat unnerved him. Staying mobile, he wouldn't be easy to find if Watkins regressed and, true to his promise, came after him. By midnight, when the last conversions were performed, Shaddack would have consolidated his power. Then he could deal with the cop.

Watkins would be seized and shackled before he transformed. Then Shaddack could strap him down in a lab and study his psychology and physiology to find an explanation for this plague of regression.

He did not accept Watkins's explanation. They weren't regressing to escape life as New People. To accept that theory, he would have to admit that the Moonhawk Project was an unmitigated disaster, that the Change was not a boon to mankind but a curse, and that all his work was not only misguided but calamitous in its effect. He could admit no such thing.

As maker and master of the New People, he had tasted godlike power. He was unwilling to relinquish it.

The rainswept, pre-dawn streets were deserted except for cars—some police cruisers, some not—in which pairs of men patrolled in the hope of spotting either Booker, Tessa Lockland, the Foster girl, or regressives on the prowl. Though they could not see through his van's heavily smoked windows, they surely knew to whom the vehicle belonged.

Shaddack recognized many of them, for they worked at New Wave and were among the contingent of one hundred that he had put on loan to the police department only a few hours ago. Beyond the rain-washed windshields, their pale faces floated like disembodied spheres in the dark interiors of their cars, so expressionless that they might have been mannequins or robots.

Others were patrolling the town on foot but were circumspect, keeping to the deeper shadows and alleyways. He saw none of them.

Shaddack also passed two conversion teams as they went quietly and briskly from one house to another. Each time a conversion was completed, the team keyed in that data on one of their car VDTs so the central system at New Wave could keep track of their progress.

When he paused at an intersection and used his own VDT to call the current roster onto the screen, he saw that only five people remained to be dealt with in the midnight-to-six-o'clock batch of conversions. They were slightly ahead of schedule.

Hard rain slanted in from the west, silvery as ice in his headlights. Trees shook as if in fear. And Shaddack kept on the move, circling through the night as if he were some strange bird of prey that preferred to hunt on storm winds.

chapter three

With Tucker leading, they had hunted and killed, bitten and torn, clawed and bitten, hunted and killed and eaten the prey, drunk blood, blood, warm and sweet, thick and warm, sweet and thick, blood, feeding the fire in their flesh, cooling the fire with food. Blood.

Gradually Tucker had discovered that the longer they stayed in their altered state, the less intensely the fire burned and the easier it was to *remain* in subhuman form. Something told him that he should be worried that it was increasingly easy to cling to the shape of a beast, but he could not raise much concern about it, partly because his mind no longer seemed able to focus on complex thoughts for more than a few seconds.

So they had raced over the fields and hills in the moonlight, raced and roamed, free, so free in moonlight and fog, in fog and wind, and Tucker had led them, pausing only to kill and eat, or to couple with the female, who took her own pleasure with an aggressiveness that was exciting, savage and exciting.

Then the rains came.

Cold.

Slashing.

Thunder, too, and blazing light in the sky.

Part of Tucker seemed to know what the long, jagged bolts of sky-ripping light were. But he could not quite remember, and he was frightened, dashing for the cover of trees when the light caught him in the open, huddling with the other male and the female until the sky went dark again and stayed that way for a while.

Tucker began to look for a place to take shelter from the storm. He knew that they should go back to where they had started from, to a place of light and dry rooms, but he could not remember where that had been exactly. Besides, going back would mean surrendering freedom and assuming their born identities. He did not want to do that. Neither did the other male and the female. They wanted to race and roam and kill and rut and be free, free. If they went back they could not be free, so they went ahead, crossing a hard-surface road, slinking up into higher hills, staying away from the few houses in the area.

Dawn was coming, not yet on the eastern horizon but coming, and Tucker knew that they had to find a haven, a den, before daylight, a place where they could curl up around one another, down in darkness, sharing warmth, darkness and warmth, safely curled up with memories of blood and rutting, darkness and warmth and blood and rutting. They would be out of danger there, safe from a world in which they were still alien, safe also from the necessity to return to human form. When night fell again, they could venture forth to roam and kill, kill, bite and kill, and maybe the day would come when there were so many of their kind in the world that they would no longer be outnumbered and could venture forth in bright daylight as well, but not now, not yet.

They came to a dirt road, and Tucker had a dim memory of where he was, a sense that the road would quickly lead him to a place that could provide the shelter that he and his pack needed. He followed it farther into the hills, encouraging his companions with low growls of reassurance. In a couple of minutes they came to a building, a huge old house fallen to ruin, with the windows smashed in and the front door hanging open on half-broken hinges. Other gray structures loomed out of the rain: a barn in worse shape than the house, several outbuildings that had mostly collapsed.

Large, hand-painted signs were nailed to the house, between two of the second-floor windows, one sign above the other, in different styles of lettering, as though a lot of time had passed between the hanging of the first and the second. He knew they had meaning, but he couldn't read them, though he strained to recall the lost language used by the species to which he had once belonged.

The two members of his pack flanked him. They, too, stared up at the dark letters on the white background. Murky symbols in the rain and gloom. Eerily mysterious runes.

ICARUS COLONY

And under that:

THE OLD ICARUS COLONY RESTAURANT
NATURAL FOODS

On the dilapidated barn was another sign—FLEA MARKET—but that meant nothing more to Tucker than the signs on the house, and after a while he decided it didn't matter if he understood them. The important thing was that no people were nearby, no fresh scent or vibration of human beings, so the refuge that he sought might be found here, a burrow, a den, a warm and dark place, warm and dark, safe and dark.

chapter four

With one blanket and pillow, Sam had made his bed on a long sofa in the living room, just off the front hall downstairs. He wanted to sleep on the ground floor so he might be awakened by the sound of an intruder. According to the schedule that Sam had seen on the VDT in the patrol car, Harry Talbot wouldn't be converted until the following evening. He doubted that they would accelerate their schedule simply because they knew an FBI man was in Moonlight Cove. But he was taking no unnecessary chances.

Sam often suffered from insomnia, but it did not trouble him that night. After he took off his shoes and stretched out on the sofa, he listened to the rain for a couple of minutes, trying not to think. Soon he slept.

His was not a dreamless sleep. It seldom was.

He dreamed of Karen, his lost wife, and as always in nightmares, she was spitting up blood and emaciated, in the final stages of her cancer, after the chemotherapy had failed. He knew that he must save her. He could not. He felt small, powerless, and terribly afraid.

But that nightmare did not wake him.

Eventually the dream shifted from the hospital to a dark and crumbling building. It was rather like a hotel designed by Salvador Dali: The corridors branched off randomly; some were very short and some were so long that the ends of them could not be seen; the walls and floors were at surreal angles to one another, and the doors to the rooms were of different sizes, some so small that only a mouse could have passed through, others large enough for a man, and still others on a scale suitable to a thirty-foot giant.

He was drawn to certain rooms. When he entered them he found in each a person from his past or current life.

He encountered Scott in several rooms and had unsatisfactory, disjointed conversations with him, all ending in unreasoning hostility on Scott's part. The nightmare was made worse by the variation in Scott's age: Sometimes he was a sullen sixteen-year-old and sometimes ten or just four or five. But in every incarnation he was alienated, cold, quick to anger, and seething with hatred. "This isn't right, this isn't true, you weren't like this when you were younger," Sam told a seven-year-old Scott, and the boy made an obscene reply.

In every room and regardless of his age, Scott was surrounded by huge posters of black-metal rockers dressed in leather and chains, displaying satanic symbols on their foreheads and in the palms of their hands. The light was flickering and strange. In a dark corner Sam saw something lurking, a creature of which Scott was aware, something the boy did not fear but which scared the hell out of Sam.

But that nightmare did not wake him, either.

In other chambers of that surreal hotel, he found dying men, the same ones every time—Arnie Taft and Carl Sorbino. They were two agents with whom he had worked and whom he had seen gunned down.

The entrance to one room was a car door—the gleaming door of a blue '54 Buick, to be exact. Inside he found an enormous, gray-walled chamber in which was the front seat, dashboard, and steering wheel, nothing else of the car, like parts of a prehistoric skeleton lying on a vast expanse of barren sand. A woman in a green dress sat behind the wheel, her head turned away from him. Of course, he knew who she was, and he wanted to leave the room at once, but he could not. In fact he was drawn to her. He sat beside her, and suddenly he was seven years old, as he had been on the day of the accident, though he spoke with his grown-up voice: "Hello, Mom." She turned to him, revealing that the right side of her face was caved in, the eye gone from the socket, bone punching through torn flesh. Broken teeth were exposed in her cheek, so she favored him with half of a hideous grin.

Abruptly they were in the *real* car, cast back in time. Ahead of them on the highway, coming toward them, was the drunk in the white pickup truck, weaving across the double yellow line, bearing down on them at high speed. Sam cried out—"Mom!"—but she couldn't evade the pickup this time any more than she had been able to avoid it thirty-five years ago. It came at them as if they were a magnet and slammed into them head-on. He thought it must be like that at the center of a bomb blast: a great roar pierced by the shriek of shredding metal. Everything went black. Then, when he swam up from that gloom, he found himself pinned in the wreckage. He was face-to-face with his dead mother, peering into her empty eye socket. He began to scream.

That nightmare also failed to wake him.

Now he was in a hospital, as he'd been after the accident, for that had been the first of the six times he'd nearly died. He was no longer a boy, however, but a grown man, and he was on the operating table, undergoing emergency surgery because he had been shot in the chest during the same gun battle in which Carl Sorbino had died. As the surgical team labored over him, he rose out of his body and watched them at work on his carcass. He was amazed but not afraid, which was just how he had felt when it had *not* been a dream.

Next he was in a tunnel, rushing toward dazzling light, toward the Other Side. This time he knew what he would find at the other end because he had been there before, in real life instead of in a dream. He was terrified of it, didn't want to face it again, didn't want to look Beyond. But he moved faster, faster, faster through the tunnel, *bulleted* through it, his terror escalating with his speed. Having to look again at what lay on the Other Side was worse than his dream confrontations with Scott, worse than the battered and one-eyed face of his mother, infinitely worse (faster, faster), intolerable, so he began to scream (faster) and scream (faster) and scream—

That one woke him.

He sat straight up on the sofa and pinched off the cry before it left his throat.

An instant later he became aware that he was not alone in the unlighted living room. He heard something move in front of him, and he moved simultaneously, snatching his .38 revolver from the holster, which he had taken off and laid beside the sofa.

It was Moose.

"Hey, boy."

The dog chuffed softly.

Sam reached out to pat the dark head, but already the Labrador was moving away. Because the night outside was marginally less black than the interior of the house, the windows were visible as fuzzy-gray rectangles. Moose went to one at the side of the house, putting his paws on the sill and his nose to the glass.

"Need to go out?" Sam asked, though they had let him out for ten minutes just before they'd gone to bed.

The dog made no response but stood at the window with a peculiar rigidity.

"Something out there?" Sam wondered, and even as he asked the question, he knew the answer.

Quickly and gingerly he crossed the dark room. He bumped into furniture but didn't knock anything down, and joined the dog at the window.

The rain-battered night seemed at its blackest in this last hour before dawn, but Sam's eyes were adjusted to darkness. He could see the side of the neighboring house, just thirty feet away. The steeply sloping property between the two structures was not planted with grass but with a variety of shrubs and several starburst pines, all of which swayed and shuddered in the gusty wind.

He quickly spotted the two Boogeymen because their movement was in opposition to the direction of the wind and therefore in sharp contrast to the storm dance of the vegetation. They were about fifteen feet from the window, heading downslope toward Conquistador. Though Sam could discern no details of them, he could see by their hunchbacked movement and shambling yet queerly graceful gait that they were not ordinary men.

As they paused beside one of the larger pines, one of them looked toward the Talbot house, and Sam saw its softly radiant, utterly alien amber eyes. For a moment he was transfixed, frozen not by fear so much as by amazement. Then he realized that the creature seemed to be staring straight at the window, as if it could see him, and suddenly it loped straight toward him.

Sam dropped below the sill, pressing against the wall under the window, and pulled Moose down with him. The dog must have had some sense of the danger, for he didn't bark or whine or resist in any way, but lay with his belly to the floor and allowed himself to be held there, still and silent.

A fraction of a second later, over the sounds of wind and rain, Sam heard furtive movement on the other side of the wall against which he crouched. A soft scuttling sound. Scratching.

He held his .38 in his right hand, ready in case the thing was bold enough to smash through the window.

A few seconds passed in silence. A few more.

Sam kept his left hand on Moose's back. He could feel the dog shivering.

Tick-tick-tick.

After long seconds of silence, the sudden ticking startled Sam, for he had just about decided that the creature had gone away.

Tick-tick-tick-tick.

It was tapping the glass, as if testing the solidity of the pane or calling to the man it had seen standing there.

Tick-tick. Pause. *Tick-tick-tick.*

chapter five

Tucker led his pack out of the mud and rain, onto the sagging porch of the decrepit house. The boards creaked under their weight. One loose shutter was banging in the wind; all the others had rotted and torn off long ago.

He struggled to speak of his intentions, but he found it very difficult to remember or produce the necessary words. Midst snarls and growls and low brute mutterings, he only managed to say, ". . . *here* . . . *hide* . . . *here* . . . *safe* . . ."

The other male seemed to have lost his speech entirely, for he could produce no words at all.

With considerable difficulty, the female said, ". . . *safe* . . . *here* . . . *home*. . . ."

Tucker studied his two companions for a moment and realized they had changed during their night adventures. Earlier, the female had possessed a feline quality—sleek, sinuous, with cat ears and sharply pointed teeth that she revealed when she hissed either in fear, anger, or sexual desire. Though something of the cat was still in her, she had become more like Tucker, wolfish, with a large head drawn forward into a muzzle more canine than feline. She had lupine haunches, as well, and feet that appeared to have resulted from the crossbreeding of man and wolf, not paws but not hands, either, tipped with claws longer and more murderous than those of a real wolf. The other male, once unique in appearance, combining a few insectile features with the general form of a hyena, had now largely conformed to Tucker's appearance.

By unspoken mutual agreement, Tucker had become the leader of the pack. Upon submitting to his rule, his followers evidently had used his appearance as a model for their own. He realized that this was an important turn of events, maybe even an ominous one.

He did not know why it should spook him, and he no longer had the mental clarity to concentrate on it until understanding came to him. The more pressing concern of shelter demanded his attention.

". . . *here* . . . *safe* . . . *here* . . ."

He led them through the broken, half-open door, into the front hall of the moldering house. The plaster was pocked and cracked, and in some places missing altogether, with lath showing through like the rib cage of a half-decomposed corpse. In the empty living room, long strips of wallpaper were peeling off, as if the place was shedding its skin in the process of a metamorphosis as dramatic as any that Tucker and his pack had undergone.

He followed scents through the house, and that was interesting, not exciting but definitely interesting. His companions followed as he investigated patches of mildew, toadstools growing in a dank corner of the dining room, colonies of vaguely luminescent fungus in a room on the other side of the hall, several deposits of rat feces, the mummified remains of a bird that had flown in through one of the glassless windows and broken a wing against a wall, and the still ripe carcass of a diseased coyote that had crawled into the kitchen to die.

During the course of that inspection, Tucker realized the house did not offer ideal shelter. The rooms were too large and drafty, especially with windows broken out. Though no human scent lingered on the air, he sensed that people still came here, not frequently but often enough to be troublesome.

In the kitchen, however, he found the entrance to the cellar, and he was excited by that subterranean retreat. He led the others down the creaking stairs into that deeper darkness, where cold drafts could not reach them, where the floor and walls were dry, and where the air had a clean, lime smell that came off the concrete-block walls.

He suspected that trespassers seldom ventured into the basement. And if they did . . . they would be walking into a lair from which they could not possibly escape.

It was a perfect, windowless den. Tucker prowled the perimeter of the room, his claws ticking and scraping on the floor. He sniffed in corners and examined the rusted furnace. He was satisfied they'd be safe. They could curl up secure in the knowledge that they would not be found and if, by some chance, they were found, they could cut off the only exit and dispense with an intruder quickly.

In such a deep, dark, secret place, they could become anything they wanted, and no one would see them.

That last thought startled Tucker. Become anything they wanted?

He was not sure where that thought originated or what it meant. He suddenly sensed that by regressing he had initiated some process that was now beyond his conscious control, that some more primitive part of his mind was permanently in charge. Panic seized him. He had shifted to an altered state many times before and had always been able to shift back again. But now . . . His fear was sharp only for a moment, because he could not concentrate on the problem, didn't even remember what he meant by "regressing," and was soon distracted by the female, who wanted to couple with him.

Soon the three of them were in a tangle, pawing at one another, thrusting and thrashing. Their shrill, excited cries rose through the abandoned house, like ghost voices in a haunted place.

chapter six

Tick-tick-tick.

Sam was tempted to rise, look through the window, and confront the creature face-to-face, for he was eager to see what one of them looked like close-up.

But as violent as these beings evidently were, a confrontation was certain to result in an attack and gunfire, which would draw the attention of the neighbors and then the police. He couldn't risk his current hiding place, for at the moment he had nowhere else to go.

He clutched his revolver and kept one hand on Moose and remained below the windowsill, listening. He heard voices, either wordless or so muffled that the words did not come clearly through the glass above his head. The second creature had joined the first at the side of the house. Their grumbling sounded like a low-key argument.

Silence followed.

Sam crouched there for a while, waiting for the voices to resume or for the amber-eyed beast to tap once more—*tick-tick*—but nothing happened. At last, as the muscles in his thighs and calves began to cramp, he took his hand off Moose and eased up to the window. He half expected the Boogeyman to be there, malformed face pressed to the glass, but it was gone.

With the dog accompanying him, he went from room to room on the ground floor, looking out all the windows on four sides of the house. He would not have been surprised to find those creatures trying to force entry somewhere.

But for the sound of rain drumming on the roof and gurgling in the downspouts, the house was silent.

He decided they were gone and that their interest in the house had been coincidental. They weren't looking for him in particular, just for prey. They very likely had glimpsed him at the window, and they didn't want to let him go if he had seen them. But if they had come to deal with him, they apparently had decided that they could no more risk the sound of breaking glass and a noisy confrontation than he could, not in the heart of town. They were secretive creatures. They might rarely cut loose with an eerie cry that would echo across Moonlight Cove, but only when in the grip of some strange passion. And thus far, for the most part, they had limited their attacks to people who had been relatively isolated.

Back in the living room he slipped the revolver into the holster again and stretched out on the sofa.

Moose sat watching him for a while, as if unable to believe that he could calmly lie down and sleep again after seeing what had been on the prowl in the rain.

"Some of my dreams are worse than what's out there tonight," he told the dog. "So if I spooked easily, I'd probably never want to go to sleep again."

The dog yawned and got up and went out into the dark hall, where he boarded the elevator. The motor hummed as the lift carried the Labrador upstairs.

As he waited for sleep to steal over him again, Sam attempted to shape his dreams into a more appealing pattern by concentrating on a few images he would not mind dreaming about: good Mexican food, barely chilled Guinness Stout, and Goldie Hawn. Ideally, he'd dream about being in a great Mexican restaurant with Goldie Hawn, who'd look even more radiant than usual, and they'd be eating and drinking Guinness and laughing.

Instead, when he did fall asleep, he dreamed about his father, a mean-tempered alcoholic, into whose hands he had fallen at the age of seven, after his mother had died in the car crash.

chapter seven

Nestled in the stack of grass-scented burlap tarps in the back of the gardener's truck, Chrissie woke when the automatic garage door ascended with a groan and clatter. She almost sat up in surprise, revealing herself. But remembering where she was, she pulled her head under the top half-dozen tarps, which she was using as blankets. She tried to shrink into the pile of burlap.

She heard rain striking the roof. It sliced into the gravel driveway just beyond the open door, making a sizzling noise like a thousand strips of bacon on an immense griddle. Chrissie was hungry. That sound made her hungrier.

"You got my lunch box, Sarah?"

Chrissie didn't know Mr. Eulane well enough to recognize his voice, but she supposed that was him, for Sarah Eulane, whose voice Chrissie did recognize, answered at once:

"Ed, I wish you'd just come back home after you drop me at the school. Take the day off. You shouldn't work in such foul weather."

"Well, I can't cut grass in this downpour," he said. "But I can do some other chores. I'll just pull on my vinyl anorak. Keeps me dry as bone. Moses could've walked through the Red Sea in that anorak and wouldn't have needed God's miracle to help him."

Breathing air filtered through the coarse, grass-stained cloth, Chrissie was troubled by a tickling sensation in her nose, all the way into her sinuses. She was afraid that she was going to sneeze.

STUPID YOUNG GIRL SNEEZES, REVEALING HERSELF TO RAVENOUS ALIENS; EATEN ALIVE; "SHE WAS A TASTY LITTLE MORSEL," SAYS ALIEN NEST QUEEN, "BRING US MORE OF YOUR ELEVEN-YEAR-OLD BLOND FEMALES."

Opening the passenger door of the truck, a couple of feet from Chrissie's hiding place, Sarah said, "You'll catch your death, Ed."

"You think I'm some delicate violet?" he asked playfully as he opened the driver's door and got into the truck.

"I think you're a withered old dandelion."

He laughed. "You didn't think so last night."

"Yes, I did. But you're *my* withered old dandelion, and I don't want you to just blow away on the wind."

One door slammed shut, then the other.

Certain that they could not see her, Chrissie pulled back the burlap, exposing her head. She pinched her nose and breathed through her mouth until the tickling in her sinuses subsided.

As Ed Eulane started the truck, let the engine idle a moment, then reversed out of the garage, Chrissie could hear them talking in the cab at her back. She couldn't make out everything they were saying, but they still seemed to be bantering with each other.

Cold rain struck her face, and she immediately pulled her head under the tarps again, leaving just a narrow opening by which a little fresh air might reach her. If she sneezed while in transit, the sound of the rain and the rumble of the truck's engine would cover it.

Thinking about the conversation she had overheard in the garage and listening to Mr. Eulane laughing now in the cab, Chrissie thought she could trust them. If they were aliens, they wouldn't be making dumb jokes and lovey talk. Maybe they would if they were putting on a show for non-aliens, trying to convince the world that they were still Ed and Sarah Eulane, but not when they were in private. When aliens were together without unconverted humans nearby, they probably talked about . . . well, planets they had sacked, the weather on Mars, the price of flying-saucer fuel, and recipes for serving human beings. Who knew? But surely they didn't talk as the Eulanes were talking.

On the other hand . . .

Maybe these aliens had only taken control of Ed and Sarah Eulane during the night, and maybe they were not yet comfortable in their human roles. Maybe they were practicing being human in private so they could pass for human in public. Sure as the devil, if Chrissie revealed herself, they'd probably sprout tentacles and lobster pincers from their chests and either eat her alive, without condiments, or freeze-dry her and mount her on a plaque and take her to their home world to hang on their den wall, or pop her brain out of her skull and plug it into their spaceship and use it as a cheap control mechanism for their in-flight coffeemaker.

In the middle of an alien invasion, you could give your trust only with reluctance and considerable deliberation. She decided to stick to her original plan.

The fifty-pound plastic sacks of fertilizer and mulch and snail bait, piled on both sides of her burlap niche, protected her from some rain, but enough reached her to soak the upper layers of tarps. She was relatively dry and toasty warm when they set out, but soon she was saturated with grass-scented rainwater, cold to the bone.

She peeked out repeatedly to determine where they were. When she saw that they were turning off the county route onto Ocean Avenue, she peeled back the soggy burlap and crawled out of her hiding place.

The wall of the truck cab featured a window, so the Eulanes would see her if they turned and looked back. Mr. Eulane might even see her in the rearview mirror of she didn't keep very low. But she had to get to the rear of the truck and be ready to jump off when they passed Our Lady of Mercy.

On her hands and knees, she moved between—and over—the supplies and gardening equipment. When she reached the tailgate, she huddled there, head down, shivering and miserable in the rain.

They crossed Shasta Way, the first intersection at the edge of town, and headed down through the business district of Ocean Avenue. They were only about four blocks from the church.

Chrissie was surprised that no people were on the sidewalks and that no cars traveled the streets. It was early—she checked her watch, 7:03—but not so early that everyone would still be home in bed. She supposed the weather also had something to do with the town's deserted look; no one was going to be out and about in that mess unless he absolutely had to be.

There was another possibility: Maybe the aliens had taken over such a large percentage of the people in Moonlight Cove that they no longer felt it necessary to enact the charade of daily life; with complete conquest only hours away, all their efforts were bent on seeking the last of the unpossessed. *That* was too unsettling to think about.

When they were one block from Our Lady of Mercy, Chrissie climbed onto the white-board tailgate. She swung one leg over the top, then the other leg, and clung to the outside of the gate with both hands, her feet on the rear bumper. She could see the backs of the Eulanes' heads through the rear window of the cab, and if they turned her way—or if Mr. Eulane glanced at his rearview mirror—she'd be seen.

She kept expecting to be spotted by a pedestrian who would yell, "Hey, you, hanging on that truck, are you nuts?" But there were no pedestrians, and they reached the next intersection without incident.

The brakes squealed as Mr. Eulane slowed for the stop sign.

As the truck came to a stop, Chrissie dropped off the tailgate.

Mr. Eulane turned left on the cross street. He was heading toward Thomas Jefferson Elementary School on Palomino, a few blocks south, where Mrs. Eulane worked and where, on an ordinary Tuesday morning, Chrissie would soon be going to her sixth-grade classroom.

She sprinted across the intersection, splashed through the dirty streaming water in the gutter, and ran up the steps to the front doors of Our Lady of Mercy. A flush of triumph warmed her, for she felt that she had reached sanctuary against all odds.

With one hand on the ornate brass handle of the carved-oak door, she paused to look uphill and down. The windows of shops, offices, and apartments were as frost-blank as cataracted eyes. Smaller trees leaned with the stiff wind, and larger trees shuddered, which was the only movement other than the driving rain. The wind was inconstant, blustery; sometimes it stopped pushing the rain relentlessly eastward and gathered it into funnels, whirling them up Ocean Avenue, so if she squinted her eyes and ignored the chill in the air, she could almost believe that she was standing in a desert ghost town, watching dust devils whirl along its haunted streets.

At the corner beside the church, a police car pulled up to the stop sign. Two men were in it. Neither was looking toward her.

She already suspected that the police were not to be trusted. Pulling open the church door, she quickly slipped inside before they glanced her way.

The moment she stepped into the oak-paneled narthex and drew in a deep breath of the myrrh- and spikenard-scented air, Chrissie felt safe. She stepped through the archway to the nave, dipped her fingers in the holy water that filled the marble font on the right, crossed herself, and moved down the center aisle to the fourth pew from the rear. She genuflected, crossed herself again, and took a seat.

She was concerned about getting water all over the polished oak pew, but there was nothing she could do about that. She was dripping.

Mass was under way. Besides herself, only two of the faithful were present, which seemed to be a scandalously poor turnout. Of course, to the best of her memory, though her folks always attended Sunday Mass, they had brought her to a weekday service only once in her life, many years ago, and she could not be sure that weekday Masses ever drew more worshipers. She suspected, however, that the alien presence—or demons, whatever—in Moonlight Cove was responsible for the low attendance. No doubt space aliens were godless or, worse yet, bowed to some dark deity with a name like Yahgag or Scogblatt.

She was surprised to see that the priest celebrating Mass, with the assistance of one altarboy, was not Father Castelli. It was the young priest—the curate, they called him—whom the archdiocese had assigned to Father Castelli in August. His name was Father O'Brien. His first name was Tom, and following his rector's lead, he sometimes insisted that parishioners call him Father Tom. He was nice—though not as nice or as wise or as amusing as Father Castelli—but she could no more bring herself to call him Father Tom than she could call the older priest Father Jim. Might as well call the Pope Johnny. Her parents sometimes talked about how much the church had changed, how less formal it had become over the years, and they spoke approvingly of those changes. In her conservative heart, Chrissie wished that she had been born and raised in a time when the Mass had been in Latin, elegant and mysterious, and when the service had not included the downright silly ritual of "giving peace" to worshipers around you. She had gone to Mass at a cathedral in San Francisco once, when they were on vacation, and the service had been a special one, in Latin, conducted according to the old liturgy, and she had *loved* it. Making ever faster airplanes, improving television from black and white to color, saving lives with better medical technology, junking those clumsy old records for compact discs—all those changes were desirable and good. But there were some things in life that shouldn't change, because it was their changelessness that you loved about them. If you lived in a world of constant, rapid change in *all* things, where did you turn for stability, for a place of peace and calm and quiet in the middle of all that buzz and clatter? That truth was so evident to Chrissie that she could not understand why grownups were not aware of it. Sometimes adults were thickheaded.

She sat through only a couple of minutes of the Mass, just long enough to say a prayer and beseech the Blessed Virgin to intercede on her behalf, and to be sure that Father Castelli was not somewhere in the nave—sitting in a pew like an ordinary worshiper, which he did sometimes—or perhaps at one of the confessionals. Then she got up, genuflected, crossed herself, and went back into the narthex, where candle-shaped electric bulbs flickered softly behind the amber-glass panes of two wall-mounted lamps. She opened the front door a crack, peeking out at the rain-washed street.

Just then a police car came down Ocean Avenue. It was not the same one she'd seen when she had gone into the church. It was newer, and only one officer was in it. He was driving slowly, scanning the streets as if looking for someone.

As the police cruiser reached the corner on which Our Lady of Mercy stood, another car passed it, coming uphill from the sea. That one wasn't a patrol car but a blue Chevy. Two men were in it, giving everything a slow looking over, peering left and right through the rain, as the policeman was doing. And though the men in the Chevy and the policeman did not wave to each other or signal in any way, Chrissie sensed that they were involved in the same pursuit. The cops had linked up with a civilian posse to search for something, someone.

Me, she thought.

They were looking for her because she knew too much. Because yesterday morning, in the upstairs hall, she had seen the aliens in her parents. Because she was the only obstacle to their conquest of the human race. And maybe because she would taste good if they cooked her up with some Martian potatoes.

Thus far, although she had learned that aliens were taking possession of some people, she had seen no evidence that they were actually eating others, yet she continued to believe that somewhere, right now, they were snacking on body parts. It just *felt* right.

When the patrol car and the blue Chevy passed, she pushed the heavy door open another few inches and stuck her head out in the rain. She looked left and right, then again, to be very sure that no one was in sight either in a car or on foot. Satisfied, she stepped outside and dashed east to the corner of the church. After looking both ways on the cross street, she turned the corner and hurried along the side of the church toward the rectory behind it.

The two-story house was all brick with carved granite lintels and a white-painted front porch with scalloped eaves, respectable-looking enough to be the perfect residence for a priest. The old plane trees along the front walk protected her from the rain, but she was already sodden. When she reached the porch and approached the front door, her tennis shoes made squelching-squeaking noises.

As she was about to put her finger on the doorbell button, she hesitated. She was concerned that she might be walking into an alien lair—an unlikely possibility but one that could not be lightly dismissed. She also realized that Father O'Brien might be saying Mass in order that Father Castelli, a hard worker by nature, could enjoy a rare sleep-in, and she was loath to disturb him if that was the case.

Young Chrissie, she thought, *undeniably courageous and clever, was nonetheless too polite for her own good. While standing on the priest's porch, debating the proper etiquette of an early-morning visit, she suddenly was snatched up by slavering, nine-eyed aliens and eaten on the spot. Fortunately she was too dead to hear the way they belched and farted after eating her, for surely her refined sensibilities would have been gravely offended.*

She rang the bell. Twice.

A moment later a shadowy and strangely lumpish figure appeared beyond the crackle-finished, diamond-shaped panes in the top half of the door. She almost turned and ran but told herself that the glass was distorting the image and that the figure beyond was not actually grotesque.

Father Castelli opened the door and blinked in surprise when he saw her. He was wearing black slacks, a black shirt, a Roman collar, and a tattered gray cardigan, so he hadn't been fast asleep, thank God. He was a shortish man, about five feet seven, and round but not really fat, with black hair going gray at the temples. Even his proud beak of a nose was not enough to dilute the effect of his otherwise soft features, which gave him a gentle and compassionate appearance.

He blinked again—this was the first time Chrissie had seen him without his glasses—and said, "Chrissie?" He smiled, and she knew that she had done the right thing by coming to him, because his smile was warm and open and loving. "Whatever brings you here at this hour, in this weather?" He looked past her to the rest of the porch and the walkway beyond. "Where're your parents?"

"Father," she said, not altogether surprised to hear her voice crack, "I have to see you."

His smile wavered. "Is something wrong?"

"Yes, Father. Very wrong. Terribly, awfully wrong."

"Come in, then, come in. You're soaked!" He ushered her into the foyer and closed the door. "Dear girl, what *is* this all about?"

"Aliens, F-f-father," she said, as a chill made her stutter.

"Come on back to the kitchen," he said. "It's the warmest room in the house. I was just fixing breakfast."

"I'll ruin the carpet," she said, indicating the oriental runner that lay the length of the hallway, with oak flooring on both sides.

"Oh, don't worry about that. It's an old thing, but it stands up well to abuse. Sort of like me! Would you like some hot cocoa? I was making breakfast, including a big pot of piping hot cocoa."

She followed him gratefully back the dimly lighted hall, which smelled of lemon oil and pine disinfectant and vaguely of incense.

The kitchen was homey. A well-worn, yellow linoleum floor. Pale yellow walls. Dark wood cabinets with white porcelain handles. Gray and yellow Formica counter tops. There were appliances—refrigerator, oven, microwave oven, toaster, electric can opener—as in any kitchen, which surprised her, though when she thought about it, she didn't know why she would have expected it to be any different. Priests needed appliances too. They couldn't just summon up a fiery angel to toast some bread or work a miracle to brew a pot of hot cocoa.

The place smelled wonderful. Cocoa was brewing. Toast was toasting. Sausages were sizzling over a low flame on the gas stove.

Father Castelli showed her to one of the four padded vinyl chairs at the chrome and Formica breakfast set, then scurried about, taking care of her as if she were a chick and he a mother hen. He rushed upstairs, returned with two clean, fluffy bath towels, and said, "Dry your hair and blot your damp clothes with one of them, then wrap the other one around you like a shawl. It'll help you get warm." While she was following his instructions, he went to the bathroom off the downstairs hall and fetched two aspirins. He put those on the table in front of her and said, "I'll get you some orange juice to take them with. Lots of vitamin C in orange juice. Aspirin and vitamin C are like a one-two punch; they'll knock a cold right out of you before it can take up residence." When he returned with the juice, he stood for a moment looking down at her, shaking his head, and she figured she must look bedraggled and pitiful. "Dear girl, what on *earth* have you been up to?" He seemed not to have heard what she'd said about aliens when she'd first crossed his threshold. "No, wait. You can tell me over breakfast. Would you like some breakfast?"

"Yes, please, Father. I'm starved. The only thing I've eaten since yesterday afternoon was a couple of Hershey bars."

"Nothing but Hershey bars?" He sighed. "Chocolate is one of God's graces, but it's also a tool the devil uses to lead us into temptation—the temptation of gluttony." He patted his round belly. "I, myself, have often partaken of this particular grace, but I would *never*"—he exaggerated the word "never" and winked at her—"never, not ever, heed the devil's call to overindulge! But, see here, if you've been eating only chocolate, your teeth will fall out. So . . . I've got plenty of sausages, plenty to share. I was about to cook a couple of eggs for myself too. Would you like a couple of eggs?"

"Yes, please."

"And toast?"

"Yes."

"We've got some wonderful cinnamon sweetrolls there on the table. And the hot chocolate, of course."

Chrissie washed down the two aspirins with orange juice.

As he carefully cracked eggs into the hot frying pan, Father Castelli glanced at her again. "Are you all right?"

"Yes, Father."

"Are you sure?"

"Yes. Now. I'm all right now."

"It'll be nice having company for breakfast," he said.

Chrissie drank the rest of her juice.

He said, "When Father O'Brien finishes saying Mass, he never wants to eat. Nervous stomach." He chuckled. "They all have bad stomachs when they're new. For the first few months they're scared to death up there on the altar. It's such a sacred duty, you see, offering the Mass, and the young priests are always afraid of flubbing up in some way that'll be . . . oh, I don't know . . . that'll be an insult to God, I guess. But God doesn't insult very easily. If He did, He'd have washed His hands of the human race a long time ago! All young priests come to that realization eventually, and then they're fine. Then they come back from saying Mass, and they're ready to run through the entire week's food budget in one breakfast."

She knew that he was talking just to soothe her. He had noticed how distraught she was. He wanted to settle her down so they could discuss it in a calm, reasonable manner. She didn't mind. She *needed* to be soothed.

Having cracked all four eggs, he turned the sausages with a fork, then opened a drawer and took out a spatula, which he placed on the counter near the egg pan. As he got plates, knives, and forks for the table, he said, "You look more than a little scared, Chrissie, like you'd just seen a ghost. You can calm down now. After so many years of schooling and training, if a young priest can be afraid of making a mistake at Mass, then anyone can be afraid of anything. Most fears are things we create in our own minds, and we can banish them as easily as we called them forth."

"Maybe not this one," she said.

"We'll see."

He transferred eggs and sausages from frying pans to plates.

For the first time in twenty-four hours, the world seemed *right*. As Father Castelli put the food on the table and encouraged her to dig in, Chrissie sighed with relief and hunger.

chapter eight

Shaddack usually went to bed after dawn, so by seven o'clock Tuesday morning he was yawning and rubbing at his eyes as he cruised through Moonlight Cove, looking for a place to hide the van and sleep for a few hours safely beyond Loman Watkins's reach. The day was overcast, gray and dim, yet the sunlight seared his eyes.

He remembered Paula Parkins, who'd been torn apart by regressives back in September. Her 1.5-acre property was secluded, at the most rural end of town. Though the dead woman's family—in Colorado—had put it up for sale through a local real-estate agent, it had not sold. He drove out there, parked in the empty garage, cut the engine, and pulled the big door down behind him.

He ate a ham sandwich and drank a Coke. Brushing crumbs from his fingers, he curled up on the blankets in the back of the van and drifted toward sleep.

He never suffered insomnia, perhaps because he was so sure of his role in life, his destiny, and he had no concern about tomorrow. He was absolutely convinced he would bend the future to his agenda.

All of his life Shaddack had seen signs of his uniqueness, omens that foretold his ultimate triumph in any pursuit he undertook.

Initially he had noticed those signs only because Don Runningdeer had pointed them out to him. Runningdeer had been an Indian—of what tribe, Shaddack had never been able to learn—who had worked for the judge, Shaddack's father, back in Phoenix, as a full-time gardener and all-around handyman. Runningdeer was lean and quick, with a weathered face, ropy muscles, and calloused hands; his eyes were bright and as black as oil, singularly powerful eyes from which you sometimes had to look away . . . and from which you sometimes could *not* look away, no matter how much you might want to. The Indian took an interest in young Tommy Shaddack, occasionally letting him help with some yard chores and household repairs, when neither the judge nor Tommy's mother was around to disapprove of their boy doing common labor or associating with "social inferiors." Which meant he hung out with Runningdeer almost constantly between the ages of five and twelve, the period during which the Indian had worked for the judge, because his parents were hardly ever there to see and object.

One of the earliest detailed memories he had was of Runningdeer and the sign of the self-devouring snake. . . .

He had been five years old, sprawled on the rear patio of the big house in Phoenix, among a collection of Tonka Toys, but he'd been more interested in Runningdeer than in the miniature trucks and cars. The Indian was wearing jeans and boots, shirtless in the bright desert sun, trimming shrubs with a large pair of wood-handled shears. The muscles in Runningdeer's back, shoulders, and arms worked fluidly, stretching and flexing, and Tommy was fascinated by the man's physical power. The judge, Tommy's father, was thin, bony, and pale. Tommy himself, at five, was already visibly his father's son, fair and tall for his age and painfully thin. By the day he showed Tommy the self-devouring snake, Runningdeer had been working for the Shaddacks two weeks,

and Tommy had been increasingly drawn to him without fully understanding why. Runningdeer often had a smile for him and told funny
stories about talking coyotes and rattlesnakes and other desert animals. Sometimes he called Tommy "Little Chief," which was the first
nickname anyone had given him. His mother always called him Tommy
or Tom; the judge called him Thomas. So he sprawled among his Tonka
Toys, playing with them less and less, until at last he stopped playing
altogether and simply watched Runningdeer, as if mesmerized.

He was not sure how long he lay entranced in the patio shade, in
the hot dry air of the desert day, but after a while he was surprised to
hear Runningdeer call to him.

"Little Chief, come look at this."

He was in such a daze that at first he could not respond. His arms
and legs would not work. He seemed to have been turned to stone.

"Come on, come on, Little Chief. You've *got* to see this."

At last Tommy sprang up and ran out onto the lawn, to the hedges
surrounding the swimming pool, where Runningdeer had been trimming.

"This is a rare thing," Runningdeer said in a somber voice, and he
pointed to a green snake that lay at his feet on the sun-warmed decking
around the pool.

Tommy began to pull back in fear.

But the Indian seized him by the arm, held him close, and said,
"Don't be afraid. It's only a harmless garden snake. It's not going to
hurt you. In fact it's been sent here as a sign to you."

Tommy stared wide-eyed at the eighteen-inch reptile, which was
curled to form an O, its own tail in its mouth, as if eating itself. The
serpent was motionless, glassy eyes unblinking. Tommy thought it was
dead, but the Indian assured him that it was alive.

"This is a great and powerful sign that all Indians know," said Runningdeer. He squatted in front of the snake and pulled the boy down
beside him. "It is a sign," he whispered, "a supernatural sign, sent from
the great spirits, and it's always meant for a young boy, so it must have
been meant for you. A very powerful sign."

Staring wonderingly at the snake, Tommy said, "Sign? What do you
mean? It's not a sign. It's a snake."

"An omen. A presentiment. A sacred sign," Runningdeer said.

As they hunkered before the snake, he explained such things to
Tommy in an intense, whispery voice, all the while holding him by one
arm. Sun glare bounced off the concrete decking. Shimmering waves of
heat rose from it too. The snake lay so motionless that it might have
been an incredibly detailed jeweled choker rather than a real snake—
each scale a chip of emerald, twin rubies for the eyes. After a while

Tommy drifted back into the queer trance that he'd been in while lying on the patio, and Runningdeer's voice slithered serpentlike into his head, deep inside his skull, curling and sliding through his brain.

Stranger still, it began to seem that the voice was not really Runningdeer's at all, but the snake's. He stared unwaveringly at the viper and almost forgot that Runningdeer was there, for what the snake said to him was so compelling and exciting that it filled Tommy's senses, demanded his entire attention, even though he did not fully understand what he was hearing. This is a sign of destiny, the snake said, a sign of power and destiny, and you will be a man of great power, far greater than your father, a man to whom others will bow down, a man who will be obeyed, a man who will never fear the future because he will *make* the future, and you will have anything you want, anything in the world. But for now, said the snake, this is to be our secret. No one must know that I've brought this message to you, that the sign has been delivered, for if they know that you are destined to hold power over them, they will surely kill you, slit your throat in the night, tear out your heart, and bury you in a deep grave. They must not know that you are the king-to-be, a god-on-earth, or they will smash you before your strength has fully flowered. Secret. This is our secret. I am the self-devouring snake, and I will eat myself and vanish now that I've delivered this message, and no one will know I've been here. Trust the Indian but no one else.

No one. Ever.

Tommy fainted on the pool decking and was ill for two days. The doctor was baffled. The boy had no fever, no detectable swelling of lymph glands, no nausea, no soreness in the joints or muscles, no pain whatsoever. He was merely gripped by a profound malaise, so lethargic that he did not even want to bother holding a comic book; watching TV was too much effort. He had no appetite. He slept fourteen hours a day and lay in a daze most of the rest of the time. "Perhaps mild sunstroke," the doctor said, "and if he doesn't snap out of it in a couple of days, we'll put him in the hospital for tests."

During the day, when the judge was in court or meeting with his investment associates, and when Tommy's mother was at the country club or at one of her charity luncheons, Runningdeer slipped into the house now and then to sit by the boy's bed for ten minutes. He told Tommy stories, speaking in that soft and strangely rhythmic voice.

Miss Karval, their live-in housekeeper and part-time nanny, knew that neither the judge nor Mrs. Shaddack would approve of the Indian's sickbed visits or any of his other associations with Tommy. But Miss Karval was kindhearted, and she disapproved of the lack of attention that the Shaddacks gave to their offspring. And she liked the Indian. She turned her head because she saw no harm in it—if Tommy promised not to tell his folks how much time he spent with Runningdeer.

Just when they decided to admit the boy to a hospital for tests, he recovered, and the doctor's diagnosis of sunstroke was accepted. Thereafter, Tommy tagged along with Runningdeer most days from the time his father and mother left the house until one of them returned. When he started going to school, he came right home after classes; he was never interested when other kids invited him to their houses to play, for he was eager to spend a couple of hours with Runningdeer before his mother or father appeared in the late afternoon.

And week by week, month by month, year by year, the Indian made Tommy acutely aware of signs that foretold his great—though as yet unspecified—destiny. A patch of four-leaf clovers under the boy's bedroom window. A dead rat floating in the swimming pool. A score of chirruping crickets in one of the boy's bureau drawers when he came home from school one afternoon. Occasionally coins appeared where he had not left them—a penny in every shoe in his closet; a month later, a nickel in every pocket of every pair of his pants; later still, a shiny silver dollar *inside* an apple that Runningdeer was peeling for him—and the Indian regarded the coins with awe, explaining that they were some of the most powerful signs of all.

"Secret," Runningdeer whispered portentously on the day after Tommy's ninth birthday, when the boy reported hearing soft bells ringing under his window in the middle of the night.

On arising, he had seen nothing but a candle burning on the lawn. Careful not to wake his parents, he sneaked outside to take a closer look at the candle, but it was gone.

"Always keep these signs secret, or they'll realize that you're a child of destiny, that one day you'll have tremendous power over them, and they'll kill you now, while you're still a boy, and weak."

"Who's 'they'?" Tommy asked.

"They, them, everyone," the Indian said mysteriously.

"But who?"

"Your father, for one."

"Not him."

"Him especially," Runningdeer whispered. "He's a man of power. He enjoys having power over others, intimidating, arm-twisting to get his way. You've seen how people bow and scrape to him."

Indeed, Tommy had noticed the respect with which everyone spoke to his father—especially his many friends in politics—and a couple of times had glimpsed the unsettling and perhaps more honest looks they gave the judge behind his back. They appeared to admire and even revere him to his face, but when he was not looking they seemed not only to fear but loathe him.

"He is satisfied only when he has all the power, and he won't let go of it easily, not for anyone, not even for his son. If he finds out that you're destined to be greater and more powerful than he is . . . no one can save you then. Not even me."

Perhaps if their family life had been marked by more affection, Tommy would have found the Indian's warning difficult to accept. But his father seldom spoke to him in more than a perfunctory way, and even more seldom touched him—never a real hug and *never* a kiss.

Sometimes Runningdeer brought a gift of homemade candy for the boy. "Cactus candy," he called it. There was always just one piece for each of them, and they always ate it together, either sitting on the patio when the Indian was on his lunch break, or as Tommy followed his mentor around the two-acre property on a series of chores. Soon after eating the cactus candy, the boy was overcome by a curious mood. He felt euphoric. When he moved, he seemed to float. Colors were brighter, prettier. The most vivid thing of all was Runningdeer: His hair was impossibly black, his skin a beautiful bronze, his teeth radiantly white, his eyes as dark as the end of the universe. Every sound—even the crisp *snick-snick-snick* of hedge clippers, the roar of a plane passing overhead on its way to Phoenix airport, the insect-hum of the pool motor— became music; the world was full of music, though the most musical of all things was Runningdeer's voice. Odors also became sharper: flowers, cut grass, the oil with which the Indian lubricated his tools. Even the stink of perspiration was pleasant. Runningdeer smelled like fresh-baked bread and hay and copper pennies.

Tommy seldom remembered what Runningdeer talked about after they ate their cactus candy, but he did recall that the Indian spoke to him with a special intensity. A lot of it had to do with the sign of the moonhawk. "If the great spirits send the sign of the moonhawk, you'll know you're to have tremendous power and be invincible. Invincible! But if you *do* see the moonhawk, it'll mean the great spirits want something from you in return, an act that will truly prove your worthiness." That much stuck with Tommy, but he remembered little else. Usually, after an hour, he grew weary and went to his room to nap; his dreams then were particularly vivid, more real than waking life, and always involved the Indian. They were simultaneously frightening and comforting dreams.

On a rainy Saturday in November, when Tommy was ten, he sat on a stool by the workbench at one end of the four-car garage, watching as Runningdeer repaired an electric carving knife that the judge always used to slice the turkey on Thanksgiving and Christmas. The air was pleasantly cool and unusually humid for Phoenix. Runningdeer and Tommy were talking about the rain, the upcoming holiday, and things that had happened at school recently. They didn't always talk about signs and destiny, or otherwise Tommy might not have liked the Indian so much; Runningdeer was a great listener.

When the Indian finished repairing the electric knife, he plugged it in and switched it on. The blade shivered back and forth so fast that the cutting edge was a blur.

Tommy applauded.

"You see this?" Runningdeer asked, raising the knife higher and squinting at it in the glow from the fluorescent bulbs overhead.

Bright glints flew from the shuttling blade, as if it were busily slicing up the light itself.

"What?" Tommy asked.

"This knife, Little Chief. It's a machine. A frivolous machine, not a really important machine like a car or airplane or electric wheelchair. My brother is . . . crippled . . . and must get around in an electric wheelchair. Did you know that, Little Chief?"

"No."

"One of my brothers is dead, the other crippled."

"I'm sorry."

"They are my half brothers, really, but the only ones I have."

"How did it happen? Why?"

Runningdeer ignored the questions. "Even if this knife's purpose is just to carve a turkey that could be carved as well by hand, it's still efficient and clever. Most machines are much more efficient and clever than people."

The Indian lowered the cutting instrument slightly and turned to face Tommy. He held the purring knife between them and looked past the shuttling blade into Tommy's eyes.

The boy felt himself slipping into a spell similar to that he'd experienced after eating cactus candy, though they had eaten none.

"The white man puts great faith in machines," Runningdeer said. "He thinks machines are ever so much more reliable and clever than people. If you want to be truly great in the white man's world, Little Chief, you must make yourself as much like a machine as you can. You must be efficient. You must be relentless like a machine. You must be determined in your goals, allowing no desires or emotions to distract you."

He moved the purring blade slowly toward Tommy's face, until the boy's eyes crossed in an attempt to focus on the cutting edge.

"With this I could lop away your nose, slice off your lips, carve away your cheeks and ears . . ."

Tommy wanted to slip off the workbench stool and run.

But he could not move.

He realized that the Indian was holding him by one wrist.

Even if he had not been held, he would have been unable to flee. He was paralyzed. Not entirely by fear, either. There was something seductive about the moment; the potential for violence was in an odd way . . . exciting.

". . . cut off the round ball of your chin, scalp you, lay bare the bone, and you'd bleed to death or die of one cause or another but . . ."

The blade was no more than two inches from his nose.

". . . *but* the machine would go on . . ."

One inch.

". . . the knife would still purr and slice, purr and slice . . ."

Half an inch.

". . . because machines don't die . . ."

Tommy could feel the faint, faint breeze stirred by the continuously moving electric blade.

". . . machines are efficient and reliable. If you want to do well in the white man's world, Little Chief, you must be like a machine."

Runningdeer switched off the knife. He put it down.

He did not let go of Tommy.

Leaning close, he said, "If you wish to be great, if you wish to please the spirits and do what they ask of you when they send you the sign of the moonhawk, then you must be determined, relentless, cold, single-minded, uncaring of consequences, just like *a machine*."

Thereafter, especially when they ate cactus candy together, they often talked of being as dedicated to a purpose and as reliable as a machine. As he approached puberty, Tommy's dreams were less often filled with sexual references than with images of the moonhawk and with visions of people who looked normal on the outside but who were all wires and transistors and clicking metal switches on the inside.

In the summer of his twelfth year, after seven years in the Indian's company, the boy learned what had happened to Runningdeer's half-brothers. At least he learned some of it. He surmised the rest.

He and the Indian were sitting on the patio, having lunch and watching the rainbows that appeared and faded in the mist thrown up by the lawn sprinklers. He had asked about Runningdeer's brothers a few times since that day at the workbench, more than a year and a half earlier, but the Indian had never answered him. This time, however, Runningdeer stared off toward the distant, hazy mountains and said, "This is a secret I tell you."

"All right."

"As secret as all the signs you've been given."

"Sure."

"Some white men, just college boys, got drunk and were cruising around, maybe looking for women, certainly looking for trouble. They met my brothers by accident, in a restaurant parking lot. One of my brothers was married, and his wife was with him, and the college boys started playing tease-the-Indians, but they also really liked the look of my brother's wife. They wanted her and were drunk enough to think they could just take her. There was a fight. Five against my two brothers, they beat one to death with a tire iron. The other will never walk again. They took my brother's wife with them, used her."

Tommy was stunned by this revelation.

At last the boy said, "I *hate* white men."

Runningdeer laughed.

"I really do," Tommy said. "What happened to those guys who did it? Are they in prison now?"

"No prison." Runningdeer smiled at the boy. A fierce, humorless smile. "Their fathers were powerful men. Money. Influence. So the judge let them off for 'insufficient evidence.'"

"My father should've been the judge. He wouldn't let them off."

"Wouldn't he?" the Indian said.

"Never."

"Are you so sure?"

Uneasily, Tommy said, "Well . . . sure I'm sure."

The Indian was silent.

"I hate white men," Tommy repeated, this time motivated more by a desire to curry favor with the Indian than by conviction.

Runningdeer laughed again and patted Tommy's hand.

Near the end of that same summer, Runningdeer came to Tommy late on a blazing August day and, in a portentous and ominous voice, said, "There will be a full moon tonight, Little Chief. Go into the backyard and watch it for a while. I believe that tonight the sign will finally come, the most important sign of all."

After moonrise, which came shortly after nightfall, Tommy went out and stood on the pool apron, where Runningdeer had shown him the self-devouring snake seven years earlier. He stared up at the lunar sphere for a long time, while an elongated reflection of it shimmered on the surface of the water in the swimming pool. It was a swollen yellow moon, still low in the sky and immense.

Soon the judge came out onto the patio, calling to him, and Tommy said, "Here."

The judge joined him by the pool. "What're you doing, Thomas?"

"Watching for . . ."

"For what?"

Just then Tommy saw the hawk silhouetted by the moon. For years he had been told he would see it one day, had been prepared for it and all that it would mean, and suddenly there it was, frozen for a moment in midflight against the round lunar lamp.

"There!" he said, for the moment having forgotten that he could trust no one but the Indian.

"There what?" the judge asked.

"Didn't you see it?"

"Just the moon."

"You weren't looking or you'd have seen it."

"Seen what?"

His father's blindness to the sign only proved to Tommy that he was, indeed, special and that the portent had been meant for his eyes only—which reminded him that he could not trust his own father. He said, "Uh . . . a shooting star."

"You're standing out here watching for shooting stars?"

"They're actually meteors," Tommy said, talking too fast. "See, to-night the earth's supposed to be passing through a meteor belt, so there'll be lots of them."

"Since when are you interested in astronomy?"

"I'm not." Tommy shrugged. "Just wondered what it'd look like. Pretty boring." He turned away from the pool and started back toward the house, and after a moment the judge accompanied him.

The next day, Wednesday, the boy told Runningdeer about the moonhawk. "But I didn't get any messages from it. I don't know what the great spirits want me to do to prove myself."

The Indian smiled and stared at him in silence for what began to be an uncomfortably long time. Then he said, "Little Chief, we'll talk about that at lunch."

Miss Karval had Wednesdays off, and Runningdeer and Tommy were at home alone. They sat side by side on patio chairs for lunch. The Indian seemed to have brought nothing but cactus candy, and Tommy had no appetite for anything else.

Long ago the boy had ceased to eat the candy for its flavor but devoured it eagerly for its effect. And over the years its impact on him had grown constantly more profound.

Soon the boy was in that much-desired dreamlike plane, where colors were bright and sounds were loud and odors were sharp and all things were comforting and appealing. He and the Indian talked for nearly an hour, and at the end of that time Tommy came to understand that the great spirits expected him to kill his father four days hence, Sunday morning. "That's my day off," said Runningdeer, "so I will not be here to offer you support. But in fact that's probably the spirits' intention—that you should have to prove yourself all on your own. At least we'll have the next few days to plan it together, so that when Sunday comes you'll be prepared."

"Yes," the boy said dreamily. "Yes. We'll plan it together."

Later that afternoon, the judge came home from a business meeting that had followed his court session. Complaining of the heat, he went straight upstairs to take a shower. Tommy's mother had come home half an hour earlier. She was in an armchair in the living room, feet on a low upholstered stool, reading the latest issue of *Town & Country* and sipping at what she called a "precocktail-hour cocktail." She barely looked up when the judge leaned in from the hall to announce his intention of showering.

As soon as his father went upstairs, Tommy went to the kitchen and got a butcher's knife from the rack by the stove.

Runningdeer was outside, mowing the lawn.

Tommy went into the living room, walked up to his mother, and kissed her on the cheek. She was surprised by the kiss but more surprised by the knife, which he rammed into her chest three times. He carried the same knife upstairs and buried it in the judge's stomach as he stepped out of the shower.

He went to his room and took off his clothes. There was no blood on his shoes, little on his jeans, but a lot on his shirt. After he quickly washed up in his bathroom sink and sluiced all traces of blood down the drain, he dressed in fresh jeans and shirt. He carefully bundled his bloody clothes in an old towel and carried them into the attic, where he hid them in a corner behind a seaman's trunk. He could dispose of them later.

Downstairs he passed the living room without looking in at his dead mother. He went straight to the desk in the judge's study and opened the right bottom drawer. From behind a stack of files, he withdrew the judge's revolver.

In the kitchen he turned off the overhead fluorescents, so the only light was what came through the windows, which was bright enough but left some parts of the room in cool shadows. He put the butcher's knife on the counter by the refrigerator, squarely in some of those shadows. He put the revolver on one of the chairs at the table, and pulled the chair only partway out, so the gun could be reached but not easily seen.

He went out through the French doors that connected the kitchen to the patio, and yelled for Runningdeer. The Indian did not hear the boy over the roar of the lawnmower, but happened to look up and see him waving. Frowning, he shut off the mower and crossed the half-cut lawn to the patio. "Yes, Thomas?" he said, because he knew that the judge and Mrs. Shaddack were at home.

"My mother needs your help with something," Tommy said. "She asked me to fetch you."

"My help?"

"Yeah. In the living room."

"What's she want?"

"She needs some help with . . . well, it's easier to show you than to talk about it."

The Indian followed him through the French doors, into the large kitchen, past the refrigerator, toward the hall door.

Tommy halted abruptly, turned, and said, "Oh, yeah, Mother says you'll need that knife, that one there behind you on the counter, by the refrigerator."

Runningdeer turned, saw the knife lying on the shadowed tile top of the counter, and picked it up. His eyes went very wide. "Little Chief, there's blood on this knife. There's blood—"

Tommy had already plucked the revolver off the kitchen chair. As the Indian turned toward him in surprise, Tommy held the gun in both hands and fired until he emptied the cylinder, though the recoil slammed painfully through his arm and shoulders, nearly knocking him off his feet. At least two of the rounds hit Runningdeer, and one of them tore out his throat.

The Indian went down hard. The knife clattered out of his hand and spun across the floor.

With one shoe, Tommy kicked the knife closer to the corpse, so it would definitely look as if the dying man had been wielding it.

The boy's understanding of the great spirits' message had been clearer than his mentor's. They wanted him to free himself at once from *everyone* who had more than a little power over him: the judge, his mother, and Runningdeer. Only then could he achieve his own lofty destiny of power.

He had planned the three murders with the coolness of a computer and had executed them with machinelike determination and efficiency. He felt nothing. Emotions had not interfered with his actions. Well, in truth, he was scared and a little excited—even exhilarated—but those feelings had not distracted him.

After staring for a moment at Runningdeer's body, Tommy went to the kitchen phone, dialed the police, and hysterically reported that the Indian, shouting of revenge, had killed his parents and that he, Tommy, had killed the Indian with his father's gun. But he didn't put it so succinctly. He was so hysterical, they had to pry it from him. In fact he was so shattered and disoriented by what had happened that they had to work patiently with him for three or four tedious minutes to get him to stop babbling and give them his name and address. In his mind he had practiced hysteria all afternoon, since lunch with the Indian. Now he was pleased that he sounded so convincing.

He walked out to the front of the house and sat in the driveway and wept until the police arrived. His tears were more genuine than his hysteria. He was crying with relief.

He'd seen the moonhawk twice again, later in life. He saw it when he needed to see it, when he wanted to be reassured that some course of action he wished to follow was correct.

But he never killed anyone again—because he never needed to.

His maternal grandparents took him into their home and raised him in another part of Phoenix. Because he had endured such tragedy, they more or less gave him everything that he wanted, as if to deny him anything would be unbearably cruel and, just possibly, might be the additional straw of burden that would break him at last. He was the sole heir of his father's estate, which was fattened by large life-insurance policies; therefore he was guaranteed a first-rate education and plenty of capital with which to start out in life after graduation from the university. The world lay before him, filled with opportunity. And thanks to Runningdeer, he had the additional advantage of knowing beyond a doubt that he had a great destiny and that the forces of fate and heaven wanted him to achieve tremendous power over other men.

Only a madman killed without a compelling need.

With but rare exception, murder simply was not an *efficient* method of solving problems.

Now, curled up in the back of the van in Paula Parkins's dark garage, Shaddack reminded himself that he was destiny's child, that he had seen the moonhawk three times. He put all fear of Loman Watkins and of failure out of his mind. He sighed and slipped over the edge of sleep.

He dreamed the familiar dream. The vast machine. Half metal and half flesh. Steel pistons stroking. Human hearts dependably pumping lubricants of all kinds. Blood and oil, iron and bone, plastic and tendon, wires and nerves.

chapter nine

Chrissie was amazed that priests ate so well. The table in the rectory kitchen was heavily laden with food: an immense plateful of sausages, eggs, a stack of toast, a package of sweetrolls, another of blueberry muffins, a bowl of hash-brown potatoes that had been warming in the oven, fresh fruit, and a bag of marshmallows for the hot cocoa. Father Castelli was pudgy, sure, but Chrissie had always thought of priests as abstemious in all things, denying themselves at least some of the pleasures of food and drink just as they denied themselves marriage. If Father Castelli consumed as much at every meal, he ought to weigh twice what he did. No, three times as much!

As they ate, she told him about the aliens taking over her folks. In deference to Father Castelli's predisposition toward spiritual answers, and as a means of keeping him hooked, she left the door open on demonic possession, though personally she much favored the alien-invasion explanation. She told him what she'd seen in the upstairs hall yesterday, how she'd been locked in the pantry and, later, had been pursued by her parents and Tucker in their strange new shapes.

The priest expressed astonishment and concern, and several times he demanded more details, but he did not once pause significantly in his eating. In fact he ate with such tremendous gusto that his table manners suffered. Chrissie was as surprised by his sloppiness as she was by the size of his appetite. A couple of times he had egg yolk on his chin, and when she got up the nerve to point it out to him, he made a joke about it and immediately wiped it off. But a moment later she looked up, and there was more egg yolk. He dropped a few miniature marshmallows and didn't seem to care. The front of his black shirt was speckled with toast crumbs, a couple of tiny pieces of sausage, flecks of potatoes, sweetroll crumbs, muffin crumbs. . . .

Really, she was beginning to think that Father Castelli was as guilty as any man had ever been of the sin of gluttony.

But she loved him in spite of his eating habits because he never once doubted her sanity or expressed a lack of belief in her wild story. He listened with interest and utmost seriousness, and seemed genuinely concerned, even frightened, by what she told him. "Well, Chrissie, they've made maybe a thousand movies about alien invasions, hostile creatures from other worlds, and they've written maybe ten thousand books about it, and I've always said that man's mind can't imagine anything that isn't possible in God's world. So who knows, hmmmm? Who's to say they might *not* have landed here in Moonlight Cove? I'm a film buff, and I've always liked scary movies best, but I never imagined that I'd find myself in the middle of a *real-life* scary movie." He was sincere. He never patronized her.

Although Father Castelli continued to eat with undiminished appetite, Chrissie finished breakfast and her story at the same time. Because the kitchen was warm, she was rapidly drying out, and only the seat of her pants and her running shoes were still really wet. She felt sufficiently reinvigorated to consider what lay ahead of her now that she had reached help. "What next? We've got to call in the Army, don't you think, Father?"

"Perhaps the Army *and* the Marines," he said after a moment of deliberation. "The Marines might be better at this sort of thing."

"Do you think . . ."

"What is it, dear girl?" .

"Do you think there's any chance . . . well, any chance of getting my folks back? The way they were, I mean?"

He put down a muffin that he had been raising to his mouth, and he reached across the table, between the plates and tins of food, to take her hand. His fingers were slightly greasy with butter, but she did not mind, for he was so reassuring and comforting; right now she needed a lot of reassuring and comforting.

"You'll be reunited with your parents," Father Castelli said with great sympathy. "I absolutely guarantee that you will."

She bit her lower lip, trying to hold back her tears.

"I guarantee it," he repeated.

Abruptly his face *bulged*. Not evenly like an inflating balloon. Rather, it bulged in some places and not others, rippled and pulsed, as if his skull had turned to mush and as if balls of worms were writhing and squirming just under the skin.

"*I guarantee it!*"

Chrissie was too terrified to scream. For a moment she could not move. She was paralyzed by fear, frozen in her chair, unable to summon even enough motor control to blink or draw a breath.

She could hear his bones loudly crackling-crunching-popping as they splintered and dissolved and reshaped themselves with impossible speed. His flesh made a disgusting, wet, oozing sound as it flowed into new forms almost with the ease of hot wax.

The priest's skull swelled upward and swept back in a bony crest, and his face was hardly human at all now but partly crustacean, partly insectile, vaguely wasplike, with something of the jackal in it, too, and with fiery hateful eyes.

At last Chrissie cried out explosively, "No!" Her heart was pounding so hard that each beat was painful. "No, go away, let me alone, let me go!"

His jaws lengthened, then split back nearly to his ears in a menacing grin defined by double rows of immense sharp teeth.

"No, no!"

She tried to get up.

She realized that he was still holding her left hand.

He spoke in a voice eerily reminiscent of those of her mother and Tucker when they had stalked her as far as the mouth of the culvert last night:

"... *need, need* ... *want* ... *give me* ... *give me* ... *need* ..."

He didn't look like her parents had looked when transformed. Why wouldn't all the aliens look the same?

He opened his mouth wide and hissed at her, and thick yellowish saliva was strung like threads of taffy from his upper to his lower teeth. Something stirred inside his mouth, a strange-looking tongue; it thrust out at her like a jack-in-the-box popping forth on its spring, and it proved to be a mouth *within* his mouth, another set of smaller and even sharper teeth on a stalk, designed to get into tight places and bite prey that took refuge there.

Father Castelli was becoming something startlingly familiar: the creature from the movie *Alien*. Not exactly that monster in every detail but uncannily similar to it.

She was trapped in a movie, just as the priest had said, a real-life horror flick: no doubt one of his favorites. Was Father Castelli able to assume whatever shape he wanted, and was he becoming this beast only because it pleased him to do so and because it would best fulfill Chrissie's expectations of alien invaders?

This was crazy.

Beneath his clothes, the priest's body was changing too. His shirt sagged on him in some places, as if the substance of him had melted away beneath it, but in other places it strained at the seams as his body acquired new bony extrusions and inhuman excrescences. Shirt buttons popped. Fabric tore. His Roman collar came apart and fell askew on his hideously resculpted neck.

Gasping, making a curious *uh-uh-uh-uh-uh* sound in the back of her throat but unable to stop, she tried to pull free of him. She stood up, knocking her chair over, but she was still held fast. He was very strong. She could not tear loose.

His hands also had begun to change. His fingers had lengthened. They were plated with a hornlike substance—smooth, hard, and shiny black—more like pincers with digits than like human hands.

"... *need ... want, want ... need ...*"

She plucked up her breakfast knife, swung it high over her head, and drove it down with all her might, stabbing him in the forearm, just above the wrist, where his flesh still looked more human than not. She had hoped that the blade would pin him to the table, but she didn't feel it bite all the way through him to the wood beneath.

His shriek was so shrill and piercing that it seemed to vibrate through Chrissie's bones.

His armored, demonic hand spasmed open. She yanked free of him. Fortunately she was quick, for his hand clamped shut again a fraction of a second later, pinching her fingertips but unable to hold her.

The kitchen door was on the priest's side of the table. She could not reach it without exposing her back to him.

With a cry that was half scream and half roar, he tore the knife from his arm and threw it aside. He knocked the dishes and food from the table with one sweep of his bizarrely mutated arm, which was now eight or ten inches longer than it had been. It protruded from the cuff of his black shirt in nightmarish gnarls and planes and hooks of the dark, chitinous stuff that had replaced his flesh.

Mary, Mother of God, pray for me; Mother most pure, pray for me; Mother most chaste, pray for me. *Please*, Chrissie thought.

The priest grabbed hold of the table and threw it aside, too, as if it weighed only ounces. It crashed into the refrigerator.

Now nothing separated her from him.

From *it*.

She feinted toward the kitchen door, taking a couple of steps in that direction.

The priest—not really a priest any more; a *thing* that sometimes masqueraded as a priest—swung to his right, intending to cut her off and snare her.

Immediately she turned, as she'd always intended, and ran in the opposite direction, toward the open door that led to the downstairs hall, leaping over scattered toast and links of sausage. The trick worked.

Wet shoes squishing and squeaking on the linoleum, she was past him before he realized she actually was going to his left.

She suspected that he was quick as well as strong. Quicker than she, no doubt. She could hear him coming behind her.

If she could only reach the front door, get out onto the porch and into the yard, she would probably be safe. She suspected that he would not follow her beyond the house, into the street, where others might see him. Surely not everyone in Moonlight Cove had already been possessed by these aliens, and until the last real person in town was taken over, they could not strut around in a transformed state, eating young girls with impunity.

Not far. Just the front door and a few steps beyond.

She had covered two-thirds of the distance, expecting to feel a claw snag her shirt from behind, when the door opened ahead of her. The other priest, Father O'Brien, stepped across the threshold and blinked in surprise.

At once she knew that she couldn't trust him, either. He could not have lived in the same house as Father Castelli without the alien seed having been planted in him. Seed, spoor, slimy parasite, spirit—whatever was used to effect possession, Father O'Brien undoubtedly had had it rammed or injected into him.

Unable to go forward or back, unwilling to swerve through the archway on her right and into the living room because that was a dead end—in every sense of the word—she grabbed hold of the newel post, which she was just passing, and swung herself onto the stairs. She ran pell-mell for the second floor.

The front door slammed below her.

By the time she turned at the landing and started up the second flight of stairs, she heard both of them climbing behind her.

The upper hall had white plaster walls, a dark wood floor, and a wood ceiling. Rooms lay on both sides.

She sprinted to the end of the hall and into a bedroom furnished only with a simple dresser, one nightstand, a double bed with a white chenille spread, a bookcase full of paperbacks, and a crucifix on the wall. She threw the door shut after her but didn't bother trying to lock or brace it. There was no time. They'd smash through it in seconds, anyway.

Repeating, "MarymotherofGod, MarymotherofGod," in a breathless and desperate whisper, she rushed across the room to the window that was framed by emerald-green drapes. Rain washed down the glass.

Her pursuers were in the upstairs hall. Their footsteps boomed through the house.

She grabbed the handles on the sash and tried to pull the window up. It would not budge. She fumbled with the latch, but it already was disengaged.

Farther back the hall toward the head of the stairs, they were throwing open doors, looking for her.

The window was either painted shut or perhaps swollen tight because of the high humidity. She stepped back from it.

The door behind her crashed inward, and something snarled.

Without glancing behind her, she tucked her head down and crossed her arms over her face and threw herself through the window, wondering if she could kill herself by jumping from the second story, figuring it depended where she landed. Grass would be good. Sidewalk would be bad. The pointed spires of a wrought-iron fence would be *real* bad.

The sound of shattering glass was still in the air when she hit a porch roof two feet below the window, which was virtually a miracle—she was uncut too—so she kept saying *MarymotherofGod* as she did a controlled roll through hammering rain toward the edge of the shingled expanse. When she reached the brink, she clung there for a moment, her left side on the roof, right side supported by a creaking and rapidly sagging rain gutter, and she looked back at the window.

Something wolfish and grotesque was coming after her.

She dropped. She landed on a walkway, on her left side, jarring her bones, clacking her teeth together so hard that she feared they'd fall out in pieces, and scraping one hand badly on the concrete.

But she didn't lie there pitying herself. She scrambled up and, huddled around her pain, turned from the house to run into the street.

Unfortunately she wasn't in front of the rectory. She was behind it, in the rear yard. The back wall of Our Lady of Mercy bordered the lawn on her right, and a seven-foot-high brick wall encircled the rest of the property.

Because of the wall and the trees on both sides of it, she could not see either the neighboring house to the south or the one to the west, on the other side of the alley that ran behind the property. If she couldn't see the rectory's neighbors, they couldn't see her, either, even if they happened to be looking out a window.

That privacy explained why the wolf-thing dared to come onto the roof, pursuing her in broad—if rather gray and dismal—daylight.

She briefly considered going into the house, through the kitchen, down the hall, out the front door, into the street, because that was the last thing they'd expect. But then she thought: Are you *insane*?

She did not bother to scream for help. Her thudding heart seemed to have swollen until her lungs had too little room to expand, so she could barely get enough air to remain conscious, on her feet, and moving. No breath was left for a scream. Besides, even if people heard her call for help, they wouldn't necessarily be able to tell where she was; by the time they tracked her down, she would be either torn apart or possessed, because the scream would have slowed her by a fateful second or two.

Instead, limping slightly to favor a pulled muscle in her left leg but losing no time, she hurried across the expansive rear lawn. She knew she could not scale a blank seven-foot wall fast enough to save herself, especially not with one stingingly abraded hand, so she studied the trees as she ran. She needed one close to the wall; maybe she could climb into it, crawl out on a branch, and drop into the alleyway or into the neighbor's yard.

Above the slosh and patter of the rain, she heard a low growl behind her, and she dared to glance over her shoulder. Wearing only tatters of a shirt, freed entirely from shoes and trousers, the wolf-thing that had been Father O'Brien leaped from the edge of the porch roof in pursuit.

She finally saw a suitable tree—but an instant later noticed a gate in the wall at the southwest corner. She hadn't seen it sooner because it had been screened from her by some shrubbery that she had just passed.

Gasping for air, she put her head down, tucked her arms against her sides, and ran to the gate. She hit the bar latch with her hand, popping it out of the slot in which it had been cradled, and burst through into the alley. Turning left, away from Ocean Avenue toward Jacobi Street, she ran through deep puddles nearly to the end of the block before risking a glance behind her.

Nothing had followed her out of the rectory gate.

Twice she had been in the hands of the aliens, and twice she had escaped. She knew she would not be so lucky if she were captured a third time.

chapter ten

Shortly before nine o'clock, after less than four hours of sleep altogether, Sam Booker woke to the quiet clink and clatter of someone at work in the kitchen. He sat up on the living-room sofa, wiped at his matted eyes, put on his shoes and shoulder holster, and went down the hall.

Tessa Lockland was humming softly as she lined up pans, bowls, and food on the wheelchair-low counter near the stove, preparing to make breakfast.

"Good morning," she said brightly when Sam came into the kitchen.

"What's good about it?" he asked.

"Just listen to that rain," she said. "Rain always makes me feel clean and fresh."

"Always depresses me."

"And it's nice to be in a warm, dry kitchen, listening to the storm but cozy."

He scratched at the stubble of beard on his unshaven cheeks. "Seems a little stuffy in here to me."

"Well, anyway, we're still alive, and *that's* good."

"I guess so."

"God in heaven!" She banged an empty frying pan down on the stove and scowled at him. "Are all FBI agents like you?"

"In what way?"

"Are they all sourpusses?"

"I'm not a sourpuss."

"You're a classic Gloomy Gus."

"Well, life isn't a carnival."

"It isn't?"

"Life is hard and mean."

"Maybe. But isn't it a carnival too?"

"Are all documentary filmmakers like you?"

"In what way?"

"Pollyannas?"

"That's ridiculous. I'm no Pollyanna."

"Oh, no?"

"No."

"Here we are trapped in a town where reality seems to have been temporarily suspended, where people are being torn apart by species unknown, where Boogeymen roam the streets at night, where some mad computer genius seems to have turned human biology inside out, where we're all likely to be killed or 'converted' before midnight tonight, and when I come in here you're grinning and sprightly and humming a Beatles tune."

"It wasn't the Beatles."

"Huh?"

"Rolling Stones."

"And that makes a difference?"

She sighed. "Listen, if you're going to help eat this breakfast, you're going to help make it, so don't just stand there glowering."

"All right, okay, what can I do?"

"First, get on the intercom there and call Harry, make sure he's awake. Tell him breakfast in . . . ummmm . . . forty minutes. Pancakes and eggs and shaved, fried ham."

Sam pressed the intercom button and said, "Hello, Harry," and Harry answered at once, already awake. He said he'd be down in about half an hour.

"Now what?" Sam asked Tessa.

"Get the eggs and milk from the refrigerator—but for God's sake don't look in the cartons."

"Why not?"

She grinned. "You'll spoil the eggs and curdle the milk."

"Very funny."

"I thought so."

While making pancake mix from scratch, cracking six eggs into glass dishes and preparing them so they could be quickly slipped into the frying pans when she needed them, directing Sam to set the table and help her with other small chores, chopping onions, and shaving ham, Tessa alternately hummed and sang songs by Patti La Belle and the Pointer Sisters. Sam knew whose music it was because she told him, announcing each song as if she were a disc jockey or as if she hoped to educate him and loosen him up. While she worked and sang, she danced in place, shaking her bottom, swiveling her hips, rolling her shoulders, sometimes snapping her fingers, really getting into it.

She was genuinely enjoying herself, but he knew that she was also needling him a little and getting a kick out of that too. He tried to hold fast to his gloom, and when she smiled at him, he did not return her smile, but *damn* she was cute. Her hair was tousled, and she wasn't wearing any makeup, and her clothes were wrinkled from having been slept in, but her slightly disheveled look only added to her allure.

Sometimes she paused in her soft singing and humming to ask him questions, but she continued to sing and dance in place even while he answered her. "You figured what we're going to do yet to get out of this corner we're in?"

"I have an idea."

"Patti La Belle, 'New Attitude,'" she said, identifying the song she was singing. "Is this idea of yours a deep, dark secret?"

"No. But I have to go over it with Harry, get some information from him, so I'll tell you both at breakfast."

At her direction he was hunched over the low counter, cutting thin slices of cheese from a block of Cheddar when she broke into her song long enough to ask, "Why did you say life is hard and mean?"

"Because it is."

"But it's also full of fun—"

"No."

"—and beauty—"

"No."

"—and hope—"

"Bullshit."

"It is."

"It isn't."

"Yes, it is."

"It isn't."

"Why are you so negative?"

"Because I want to be."

"But why do you want to be?"

"Jesus, you're relentless."

"Pointer Sisters, 'Neutron Dance.'" She sang a bit, dancing in place as she put eggshells and other scraps down the garbage disposal. Then she interrupted her tune to say, "What could've happened to you to make you feel that life's only mean and hard?"

"You don't want to know."

"Yes, I do."

He finished with the cheese and put down the slicer. "You really want to know?"

"I really do."

"My mother was killed in a traffic accident when I was just seven. I was in the car with her, nearly died, was actually trapped in the wreckage with her for more than an hour, face-to-face, staring into her eyeless socket, one whole side of her head bashed in. After that I had to go live with my dad, whom she'd divorced, and he was a mean-tempered son of a bitch, an alcoholic, and I can't tell you how many times he beat me or threatened to beat me or tied me to a chair in the kitchen and left me there for hours at a time, until I couldn't hold myself any more and peed in my pants, and then he'd finally come to untie me and he'd see what I'd done and he'd beat me for *that*."

He was surprised by how it all spilled from him, as if the floodgates of his subconscious had been opened, pouring forth all the sludge that had been pent up through long years of stoic self-control.

"So as soon as I graduated from high school, I got out of that house, worked my way through junior college, living in cheap rented rooms, shared my bed with armies of cockroaches every night, then applied to the Bureau as soon as I could, because I wanted to see justice in the world, be a part of *bringing* justice to the world, maybe because there'd been so little fairness or justice in my life. But I discovered that more than half the time justice doesn't triumph. The bad guys get away with it, no matter how hard you work to bring them down, because the bad guys are often pretty damned clever, and the good guys never allow themselves to be as mean as they have to be to get the job done. But at the same time, when you're an agent, mainly what you see is the sick underbelly of society, you deal with the scum, one kind of scum or another, and day by day it makes you more cynical, more disgusted with people and sick of them."

He was talking so fast that he was almost breathless.

She had stopped singing.

He continued with an uncharacteristic lack of emotional control, speaking so fast that his sentences sometimes ran together: "And my wife died, Karen, she was wonderful, you'd have liked her, everybody liked her, but she got cancer and she died, painfully, horribly, with a lot of suffering, not easy like Ali McGraw in the movies, not with just a sigh and a smile and a quiet goodbye, but in agony. And then I lost my son too. Oh, he's alive, sixteen, nine when his mother died and sixteen now, physically alive and mentally alive, but he's emotionally dead, burnt out in his heart, cold inside, so damned cold inside. He likes computers and computer games and television, and he listens to black metal. You know what black metal is? It's heavy-metal music with a twist of satanism, which he likes because it tells him there are no moral values, that everything is relative, that his alienation is right, that his coldness inside is *right*, it tells him that whatever feels good *is* good. You know what he said once?"

She shook her head.

"He said to me, 'People aren't important. People don't count. Only *things* are important. Money is important, liquor is important, my stereo is important, anything that makes me *feel* good is important, but I'm not important.' He tells me that nuclear bombs are important because they'll blow up all those nice things some day, not because they'll blow up people—after all, people are nothing, just polluting animals that spoil the world. That's what he says. That's what he tells me he believes. He says he can prove it's all true. He says that next time you see a bunch of people standing around a Porsche, admiring the car, look real hard at their faces and you'll see that they care more about that car than about each other. They're not admiring the workmanship, either, not in the sense that they're thinking about the people who *made* the car. It's as if the Porsche was organic, as if it grew or somehow made itself. They admire it for itself, not for what it represents of human engineering skills and craftsmanship. The car is more *alive* than they are. They draw energy from the car, from the sleek lines of it, from the thrill of imagining its power under their hands, so the car becomes more real and far more important than any of the people admiring it."

"That's bullshit," Tessa said with conviction.

"But that's what he tells me, and I know it's crap, and I try to reason with him, but he's got all the answers—or thinks he has. And sometimes I wonder . . . if I wasn't so soured on life myself, so sick of so many people, would I be able to argue with him more persuasively? If I wasn't who I am, would I be more able to save my son?"

He stopped.

He realized he was trembling.

They were both silent for a moment.

Then he said, "*That's* why I say life is hard and mean."

"I'm sorry, Sam."

"Not your fault."

"Not yours either."

He sealed the Cheddar in a piece of Saran Wrap and returned it to the refrigerator while she returned to the pancake mix she was making.

"But you had Karen," she said. "There's been love and beauty in your life."

"Sure."

"Well, then—"

"But it doesn't last."

"Nothing lasts forever."

"Exactly my point," he said.

"But that doesn't mean we can't enjoy a blessing while we have it.

If you're always looking ahead, wondering when this moment of joy is going to end, you can never know any real pleasure in life."

"Exactly my point," he repeated.

She left the wooden mixing spoon in the big metal bowl and turned to face him. "But that's *wrong*. I mean, life is filled with moments of wonder, pleasure, joy . . . and if we don't seize the moment, if we don't sometimes turn off thoughts of the future and relish the moment, then we'll have no memory of joy to carry us through the bad times—and no hope."

He stared at her, admiring her beauty and vitality. But then he began to think about how she would age, grow infirm, and die just as everything died, and he could no longer bear to look at her. Instead he turned his gaze to the rain-washed window above the sink. "Well, I'm sorry if I've upset you, but you'll have to admit you asked for it. You insisted on knowing how I could be such a Gloomy Gus."

"Oh, you're no Gloomy Gus," she said. "You go way beyond that. You're a regular Dr. Doom."

He shrugged.

They returned to their culinary labors.

chapter eleven

After escaping through the gate at the rear of the rectory yard, Chrissie stayed on the move for more than an hour while she tried to decide what to do next. She had planned to go to school and tell her story to Mrs. Tokawa if Father Castelli proved unhelpful. But now she was no longer willing to trust even Mrs. Tokawa. After her experience with the priests, she realized the aliens would probably have taken possession of all the authority figures in Moonlight Cove as a first step toward conquest. She already knew the priests were possessed. She was certain that the police had been taken over as well, so it was logical to assume that teachers also had been among the early victims.

As she moved from neighborhood to neighborhood, she alternately cursed the rain and was grateful for it. Her shoes and jeans and flannel shirt were sodden again, and she was chilled through and through. But the darkish-gray daylight and the rain kept people indoors and provided her with some cover. In addition, as the wind subsided, a thin cold fog drifted in from the sea, not a fraction as dense as it had been last night, just a beardlike mist that clung to the trees, but enough to further obscure the passage of one small girl through those unfriendly streets.

Last night's thunder and lightning were gone too. She was no longer in danger of being flash-roasted by a sudden bolt, which was at least some comfort.

YOUNG GIRL FRIED TO A CRISP BY LIGHTNING THEN EATEN BY ALIENS; SPACE CREATURES ENJOY HUMAN POTATO CHIPS; "IF WE CAN MAKE THEM WITH RUFFLES," SAYS ALIEN NEST QUEEN, "THEY'LL BE PERFECT WITH ONION DIP."

She moved as much as possible through alleyways and backyards, crossing streets only when necessary and always quickly, for out there she saw too many pairs of somber-faced, sharp-eyed men in slow-moving cars, obvious patrols. Twice she almost ran into them in alleys, too, and had to dive for cover before they spotted her. About a quarter of an hour after she fled through the rectory gate, she noticed more patrols in the area, a sudden influx of cars and men on foot. Foot patrols scared her the most. Pairs of men in rain slickers were better able to conduct a search and were more difficult to escape from than men in cars. She was terrified of walking into them unexpectedly.

Actually she spent more time in hiding than on the move. Once she huddled for a while behind a cluster of garbage cans in an alley. She took refuge under a brewer's spruce, the lower branches of which nearly touched the ground, like a skirt, providing a dark and mostly dry retreat. Twice she crawled under cars and lay for a while.

She never stayed in one place for more than five or ten minutes. She was afraid that some alien-possessed busybody would see her as she crawled into her hiding place and would call the police to report her, and that she would be trapped.

By the time she reached the vacant lot on Juniper Lane, beside Callan's Funeral Home, and curled up in the deepest brush—dry grass and bristly chaparral—she was beginning to wonder if she would ever think of someone to turn to for help. For the first time since her ordeal had begun, she was losing hope.

A huge fir spread its branches across part of the lot, and her clump of brush was within its domain, so she was sheltered from the worst of the rain. More important, in the deep grass, curled on her side, she could not be seen from the street or from the windows of nearby houses.

Nevertheless, every minute or so, she cautiously raised her head far enough to look quickly around, to be sure that no one was creeping up on her. During that reconnoitering, looking east past the alleyway at the back of the lot, toward Conquistador, she saw a part of the big redwood-and-glass house on the east side of that street. The Talbot place. At once she remembered the man in the wheelchair.

He had come to Thomas Jefferson to speak to the fifth- and sixth-grade students last year, during Awareness Days, a week-long program of studies that was for the most part wasted time, though *he* had been interesting. He had talked to them about the difficulties and the amazing abilities of disabled people.

At first Chrissie had felt so sorry for him, had just pitied him half to death, because he'd looked so pathetic, sitting there in his wheelchair, his body half wasted away, able to use only one hand, his head slightly twisted and tilted permanently to one side. But then as she listened to him she realized that he had a wonderful sense of humor and did not feel sorry for himself, so it seemed more and more absurd to pity him. They had an opportunity to ask him questions, and he had been so willing to discuss the intimate details of his life, the sorrows and joys of it, that she had finally come to admire him a whole lot.

And his dog Moose had been terrific.

Now, looking at the redwood-and-glass house through the tips of the rain-shiny stalks of high grass, thinking about Harry Talbot and Moose, Chrissie wondered if *that* was a place she could go for help.

She dropped back down in the brush and thought about it for a couple of minutes.

Surely a wheelchair-bound cripple was one of the last people the aliens would bother to possess—if they wanted him at all.

She immediately was ashamed of herself for thinking such a thing. A wheelchair-bound cripple was not a second-class human being. He had just as much to offer the aliens as anyone else.

On the other hand . . . would a bunch of aliens have an enlightened view of disabled people? Wasn't that a bit much to expect? After all, they were *aliens.* Their values weren't supposed to be the same as those of human beings. If they went around planting seeds—or spoors or slimy baby slugs or whatever—in people, and if they ate people, surely they couldn't be expected to treat disabled people with the proper respect any more than they would help old ladies to cross the street.

Harry Talbot.

The more she thought about him, the more certain Chrissie became that he had thus far been spared the horrible attention of the aliens.

chapter twelve

After she called him Dr. Doom, he sprayed the Jenn-Air griddle with Pam, so the pancakes wouldn't stick.

She turned on the oven and put a plate in there, to which she could transfer the cakes to keep them warm as she made them.

Then, in a tone of voice that immediately clued him to the fact that she was bent on persuading him to reconsider his bleak assessment of life, she said, "Tell me—"

"Can't you leave it alone *yet*?"

"No."

He sighed.

She said, "If you're this damned glum, why not . . ."

"Kill myself?"

"Why not?"

He laughed bitterly. "On the drive up here from San Francisco, I played a little game with myself—counted the reasons that life was worth living. I came up with just four, but I guess they're enough, because I'm still hanging around."

"What were they?"

"One—good Mexican food."

"I'll go along with that."

"Two—Guinness Stout."

"I like Heineken Dark myself."

"It's okay, but it's not a reason to live. *Guinness* is a reason to live."

"What's number three?"

"Goldie Hawn."

"You know Goldie Hawn?"

"Nope. Maybe I don't want to, 'cause maybe I'd be disappointed. I'm talking about her screen image, the idealized Goldie Hawn."

"She's your dream girl, huh?"

"More than that. She . . . hell, I don't know . . . she seems untouched by life, undamaged, vital and happy and innocent and . . . *fun*."

"Think you'll ever meet her?"

"You've got to be kidding."

She said, "You know what?"

"What?"

"If you *did* meet Goldie Hawn, if she walked up to you at a party and said something funny, something cute, and giggled in that way she has, you wouldn't even recognize her."

"Oh, I'd recognize her, all right."

"No, you wouldn't. You'd be so busy brooding about how unfair, unjust, hard, cruel, bleak, dismal, and stupid life is that you would not seize the moment. You wouldn't even *recognize* the moment. You'd be too shrouded in a haze of gloom to see who she was. Now, what's your fourth reason for living?"

He hesitated. "Fear of death."

She blinked at him. "I don't understand. If life's so awful, why is death to be feared?"

"I underwent a near-death experience. I was in surgery, having a bullet taken out of my chest, and I almost bought the farm. Rose out of my body, drifted up to the ceiling, watched the surgeons for a while, then found myself rushing faster and faster down a dark tunnel toward this dazzling light—the whole screwy scenario."

She was impressed and intrigued. Her clear blue eyes were wide with interest. "And?"

"I saw what lies beyond."

"You're serious, aren't you?"

"Damned serious."

"You're telling me that you *know* there's an afterlife?"

"Yes."

"A God?"

"Yes."

Astonished, she said, "But if you *know* there's a God and that we move on from this world, then you know life has purpose, meaning."

"So?"

"Well, it's doubt about the purpose of life that lies at the root of most people's spells of gloom and depression. Most of us, if we'd experienced what you'd experienced . . . well, we'd never worry again. We'd have the strength to deal with any adversity, knowing there was meaning to it and a life beyond. So what's wrong with you, mister? Why didn't you lighten up after that? Are you just a bullheaded dweeb or what?"

"Dweeb?"

"Answer the question."

The elevator kicked in and ascended from the first-floor hall.

"Harry's coming," Sam said.

"Answer the question," she repeated.

"Let's just say that what I saw didn't give me hope. It scared the hell out of me."

"Well? Don't keep me hanging. What'd you see on the Other Side?"

"If I tell you, you'll think I'm crazy."

"You've got nothing to lose. I already think you're crazy."

He sighed and shook his head and wished that he'd never brought it up. How had she gotten him to open himself so completely?

The elevator reached the third floor and halted.

Tessa stepped away from the kitchen counter, moving closer to him, and said, "Tell me what you saw, dammit."

"You won't understand."

"What am I—a moron?"

"Oh, you'd understand what I saw, but you wouldn't understand what it meant to me."

"Do *you* understand what it meant to you?"

"Oh, yes," he said solemnly.

"Are you going to tell me willingly, or do I have to take a meat fork from that rack and torture it out of you?"

The elevator had started down from the third floor.

He glanced toward the hall. "I really don't want to discuss it."

"You don't, huh?"

"No."

"You saw God but you don't want to discuss it."

"That's right."

"Most guys who see God—that's the *only* thing they ever want to discuss. Most guys who see God—they form whole religions based on the one meeting with Him, and they tell *millions* of people about it."

"But I—"

"Fact is, according to what I've read, most people who undergo a near-death experience are changed forever by it. And always for the better. If they were pessimists, they become optimists. If they were atheists, they become believers. Their values change, they learn to love life for itself, they're goddamned *radiant*! But not you. Oh, no, you become even more dour, even more grim, even more bleak."

The elevator reached the ground floor and fell silent.

"Harry's coming," Sam said.

"Tell me what you saw."

"Maybe I can tell *you*," he said, surprised to find that he was actually willing to discuss it with her at the right time, in the right place. "Maybe you. But later."

Moose padded into the kitchen, panting and grinning at them, and Harry rolled through the doorway a moment later.

"Good morning," Harry said chipperly.

"Did you sleep well?" Tessa asked, favoring him with a genuine smile of affection that Sam envied.

Harry said, "Soundly, but not as soundly as the dead—thank God."

"Pancakes?" Tessa asked him.

"Stacks, please."

"Eggs?"

"Dozens."

"Toast?"

"Loaves."

"I like a man with an appetite."

Harry said, "I was running all night, so I'm famished."

"Running?"

"In my dreams. Chased by Boogeymen."

While Harry got a package of dog food from under one of the counters and filled Moose's dish in the corner, Tessa went to the griddle, sprayed it with Pam again, told Sam that he was in charge of the eggs, and started to ladle out the first of the pancakes from the bowl of batter. After a moment she said, "Patti La Belle, 'Stir It Up,'" and began to sing and dance in place again.

"Hey," Harry said, "I can give you music if you want music."

He rolled to a compact under-the-counter-mounted radio that neither Tessa nor Sam had noticed, clicked it on, and moved the tuner across the dial until he came to a station playing "I Heard It Through the Grapevine" by Gladys Knight and the Pips.

"All *right*," Tessa said, and she began to sway and pump and grind with such enthusiasm that Sam couldn't figure out how she poured the pancake batter onto the griddle in such neat puddles.

Harry laughed and turned his motorized wheelchair in circles, as if dancing with her.

Sam said, "Don't you people know that the world is coming to an end around us?"

They ignored him, which he supposed was what he deserved.

chapter thirteen

By a roundabout route, cloaking herself in the rain and mist and whatever shadows she could find, Chrissie reached the alley to the east of Conquistador. She entered Talbot's backyard through a gate in a redwood fence and scurried from one clump of shrubbery to another, twice nearly stepping in dog poop—Moose was an amazing dog, but not without faults—until she reached the steps to the back porch.

She heard music playing inside. It was an oldie, from the days when her parents had been teenagers. And in fact it had been one of their favorites. Though Chrissie didn't remember the title, she did recall the name of the group—Junior Walker and the All-Stars.

Figuring that the music, combined with the drumming rain, would cover any sounds she made, she crept up the steps onto the redwood porch and, in a crouch, moved to the nearest window. She hunkered below the sill for a while, listening to them in there. They were talking, often laughing, sometimes singing along with the songs on the radio.

They didn't sound like aliens. They sounded pretty much like ordinary people.

Were aliens likely to enjoy the music of Stevie Wonder and the Four Tops and the Pointer Sisters? Hardly. To human ears, alien music probably sounded like knights in armor playing bagpipes while simultaneously falling down a long set of stairs amidst a pack of baying hounds. More like Twisted Sister than like the Pointer Sisters.

Eventually she rose up just far enough to peer over the sill, through a gap in the curtains. She saw Mr. Talbot in his wheelchair, Moose, and a strange man and woman. Mr. Talbot was beating time with his good hand on the arm of his wheelchair, and Moose was wagging his tail vigorously if out of synch with the music. The other man was using a spatula to scoop eggs out of a couple of frying pans and shift them onto plates, glowering at the woman now and then as he did so, maybe not approving of the way she abandoned herself to the song, but still tapping his right foot to the music. The woman was making flapjacks and transferring them to a warming platter in the oven, and as she worked she shimmied and swayed and dipped; she had good moves.

Chrissie crouched down again and thought about what she had seen. Nothing about their behavior was particularly odd if they were people, but if they were aliens they surely wouldn't be bopping to the radio while they made breakfast. Chrissie had a real hard time believing that aliens—like the thing masquerading as Father Castelli—could have either a sense of humor or rhythm. Surely, all that aliens cared about was taking possession of new hosts and finding new recipes for cooking tender children.

Nevertheless, she decided to wait until she had a chance to watch them eating. From what she'd heard her mother and Tucker say in the meadow last night, and from what she had seen at breakfast with the Father Castelli creature, she believed that aliens were ravenous, each with the appetite of half a dozen men. If Harry Talbot and his guests didn't make absolute hogs of themselves when they sat down to eat, she could probably trust them.

chapter fourteen

Loman had stayed at Peyser's house, supervising the cleanup and overseeing the transfer of the regressives' bodies to Callan's hearse. He was afraid to let his men handle it alone, for fear that the sight of the mutated bodies or the smell of blood would induce them to seek altered states of their own. He knew that all of them—not least of all himself—were walking a taut wire over an abyss. For the same reason, he followed the hearse to the funeral home and stayed with Callan and his assistant until Peyser's and Sholnick's bodies were fed into the white-hot flames of the crematorium.

He checked on the progress of the search for Booker, the Lockland woman, and Chrissie Foster, and he made a few changes in the pattern of the patrols. He was in the office when the report came in from Castelli, and he went directly to the rectory at Our Lady of Mercy to hear firsthand how the girl could have slipped away from them. They were full of excuses, mostly lame. He suspected they had regressed in order to toy with the girl, just for the thrill of it, and while playing with her had unintentionally given her a chance to escape. Of course they would not admit to regression.

Loman increased the patrols in the immediate area, but there was no sign of the girl. She had gone to ground. Still, if she had come into town instead of heading out to the freeway, they were more likely to catch her and convert her before the day was done.

At nine o'clock he returned to his house on Iceberry Way to get breakfast. Since he'd nearly degenerated in Peyser's blood-spattered bedroom, his clothes had felt loose on him. He had lost a few pounds as his catabolic processes had consumed his own flesh to generate the tremendous energy needed to regress—and to *resist* regression.

The house was dark and silent. Denny was no doubt upstairs, in front of his computer, where he had been last night. Grace had left for work at Thomas Jefferson, where she was a teacher; she had to keep up the pretense of an ordinary life until everyone in Moonlight Cove had been converted.

At the moment no children under twelve had been put through the Change, partly because of difficulties New Wave technicians had had in determining the correct dosage for younger converts. Those problems had been solved, and tonight the kids would be brought into the fold.

In the kitchen Loman stood for a moment, listening to the rain on the windows and the ticking of the clock.

At the sink he drew a glass of water. He drank it, another, then two more. He was dehydrated after the ordeal at Peyser's.

The refrigerator was chock full of five-pound hams, roast beef, a half-eaten turkey, a plate of porkchops, chicken breasts, sausages, and packages of bologna and dried beef. The accelerated metabolisms of the New People required a diet high in protein. Besides, they had a craving for meat.

He took a loaf of pumpernickel from the breadbox and sat down with that, the roast beef, the ham, and a jar of mustard. He stayed at the table for a while, cutting or ripping thick hunks of meat, wrapping them in mustard-slathered bread, and tearing off large bites with his teeth. Food offered him less subtle pleasure than when he'd been an Old Person; now the smell and taste of it raised in him an animal excitement, a thrill of greed and gluttony. He was to some degree repelled by the way he tore at his food and swallowed before he'd finished chewing it properly, but every effort that he made to restrain himself soon gave way to even more feverish consumption. He slipped into a half-trance, hypnotized by the rhythm of chewing and swallowing. At one point he became clearheaded enough to realize he had gotten the chicken breasts from the refrigerator and was eating them with enthusiasm, though they were uncooked. He let himself slip mercifully back into the half-trance again.

Finished eating, he went upstairs to look in on Denny.

When he opened the door to the boy's room, everything at first seemed to be just as it had been the last time he'd seen it, during the previous night. The shades were lowered, the curtains drawn, the room dark except for the greenish light from the VDT. Denny sat in front of the computer, engrossed in the data that flickered across the screen.

Then Loman saw something that made his skin prickle.

He closed his eyes.

Waited.

Opened them.

It was not an illusion.

He felt sick. He wanted to step back into the hall and close the door, forget what he'd seen, go away. But he could not move and could not avert his eyes.

Denny had unplugged the computer keyboard and put it on the floor beside his chair. He'd unscrewed the front cover plate from the data-processing unit. His hands were in his lap, but they weren't exactly hands any more. His fingers were wildly elongated, tapering not to points and fingernails but to metallic-looking wires, as thick as lamp cords, that snaked into the guts of the computer, vanishing there.

Denny no longer needed the keyboard.

He had become part of the system. Through the computer and its modem link to New Wave, Denny had become one with Sun.

"Denny?"

He had assumed an altered state, but nothing like that sought by the regressives.

"Denny?"

The boy did not answer.

"Denny!"

An odd, soft clicking and electronic pulsing sounds came from the computer.

Reluctantly, Loman entered the room and walked to the desk. He looked down at his son and shuddered.

Denny's mouth hung open. Saliva drooled down his chin. He had become so enraptured by his contact with the computer that he had not bothered to get up and eat or go to the bathroom; he had urinated in his pants.

His eyes were gone. In their place were what appeared to be twin spheres of molten silver as shiny as mirrors. They reflected the data that swarmed across the screen in front of them.

The pulsing sounds, soft electronic oscillations, were not coming from the computer but from Denny.

chapter fifteen

The eggs were good, the pancakes were better, and the coffee was strong enough to endanger the porcelain finish of the cups but not so strong that it had to be chewed. As they ate, Sam outlined the method he had devised for getting a message out of town to the Bureau.

"Your phone's still dead, Harry. I tried it this morning. And I don't think we can risk heading out to the interstate on foot or by car, not with the patrols and roadblocks they've established; that'll have to be a last resort. After all, as far as we know, we're the only people who realize that something truly . . . twisted is happening here and that the need to stop it is urgent. Us and maybe the Foster girl, the one the cops talked about in their VDT conversation last night."

"If she's literally a girl," Tessa said, "just a child, even if she's a teenager, she won't have much of a chance against them. We've got to figure they'll catch her if they haven't already."

Sam nodded. "And if they nail us, too, while we're trying to get out of town, there'll be no one left to do the job. So first we've got to try a low-risk course of action."

"Is *any* option low risk?" Harry wondered as he mopped up some egg yolk with a piece of toast, eating slowly and with a touching precision necessitated by his having only one useful hand.

Pouring a little more maple syrup over his pancakes, surprised by how much he was eating, attributing his appetite to the possibility that this was his last meal, Sam said, "See . . . this is a wired town."

"Wired?"

"Computer-linked. New Wave gave computers to the police, so they'd be tied into the web—"

"And the schools," Harry said. "I remember reading about it in the paper last spring or early summer. They gave a lot of computers and software to both the elementary and the high schools. A gesture of civic involvement, they called it."

"Seems more ominous than that now, doesn't it?" Tessa said.

"Sure as hell does."

Tessa said, "Seems now like maybe they wanted their computers in the schools for the same reason they wanted the cops computerized—to tie them all in tightly with New Wave, to monitor and control."

Sam put down his fork. "New Wave employs, what, about a third of the people in town?"

"Probably that," Harry said. "Moonlight Cove really grew after New Wave moved in ten years ago. In some ways it's an old-fashioned company town—life here isn't just dependent upon the main employer but pretty much socially centered around it too."

After sipping some coffee so strong it was nearly as bracing as brandy, Sam said, "A third of the people . . . which works out to maybe forty percent or so of the adults."

Harry said, "I guess so."

"And you've got to figure everyone at New Wave is part of the conspiracy, that they were among the first to be . . . converted."

Tessa nodded. "I'd say that's a given."

"And they're even more than usually interested in computers, of course, because they're working in that industry, so it's a good bet most or all of them have computers in their homes."

Harry agreed.

"And no doubt many if not all of their home computers can be tied by modem directly to New Wave, so they can work at home in the evening or on weekends if they have to. And now, with this conversion scheme nearing a conclusion, I'll bet they're working round the clock; data must be flying back and forth over their phone lines half the night. If Harry can tell me of someone within a block of here who works for New Wave—"

"There're several," Harry said.

"—then I could slip out in the rain, try their house, see if anyone's home. At this hour they'll probably be at work. If no one's there, maybe I can get a call out on their phone."

"Wait, wait," Tessa said. "What's all this about phones? The phones don't work."

Sam shook his head. "All we know is that the public phones are out of service, as is Harry's. But remember: New Wave controls the telephone-company computer, so they can probably be selective about what lines they shut down. I'll bet they haven't cut off the service of those who've already undergone this . . . conversion. They wouldn't deny *themselves* communication. Especially not now, in a crisis, and with this scheme of theirs nearly accomplished. There's a better than fifty-percent chance that the only lines they've shut down are the ones they figure we might get to—pay phones, phones in public places—like the motel—and the phones in the homes of people who haven't yet been converted."

chapter sixteen

Fear permeated Loman Watkins, saturated him so completely that if it had possessed substance, it could have been wrung from his flesh in quantities to rival the rivers currently pouring forth from the storm-racked sky outside. He was afraid for himself, for what he might yet become. He was afraid for his son, too, who sat at the computer in an utterly alien guise. And he was also afraid *of* his son, no use denying that, scared half to death of him and unable to touch him.

A flood of data coruscated across the screen in blurred green waves. Denny's glistening, liquid, silvery eyes—like puddles of mercury in his sockets—reflected the luminescent tides of letters, numbers, graphs, and charts. Unblinkingly.

Loman remembered what Shaddack had said at Peyser's house when he had seen that the man had regressed to a lupine form that could not have been a part of human genetic history. Regression was not merely—or even primarily—a physical process. It was an example of mind over matter, of consciousness dictating form. Because they could no longer be ordinary people, and because they simply could not tolerate life as emotionless New People, they were seeking altered states in which existence was more endurable. And the boy had sought *this* state, had willed himself to become this grotesque thing.

"Denny?"

No response.

The boy had fallen entirely silent. Not even electronic noises issued from him any longer.

The metallic cords, in which the boy's fingers ended, vibrated continuously and sometimes throbbed as if irregular pulses of thick, inhuman blood were passing through them, cycling between organic and inorganic portions of the mechanism.

Loman's heart was pounding as fast as his running footsteps would have been if he could have fled. But he was held there by the weight of his fear. He had broken out in a sweat. He struggled to keep from throwing up the enormous meal he had just eaten.

Desperately he considered what he must do, and the first thing that occurred to him was to call Shaddack and seek his help. Surely Shaddack would understand what was happening and would know how to reverse this hideous metamorphosis and restore Denny to human form.

But that was wishful thinking. The Moonhawk Project was now out of control, following dark routes down into midnight horrors that Tom Shaddack had never foreseen and could not avert.

Besides, Shaddack would not be frightened by what was happening to Denny. He would be delighted, exuberant. Shaddack would view the boy's transformation as an *elevated* altered state, as much to be desired as the degeneration of the regressives was to be avoided and scorned. Here was what Shaddack truly sought, the forced evolution of man into machine.

In memory even now, Loman could hear Shaddack talking agitatedly in Peyser's blood-spattered bedroom: *". . . what I don't understand is why the regressives have all chosen a subhuman condition. Surely you have the power within you to undergo evolution rather than devolution, to lift yourself up from mere humanity to something higher, cleaner, purer . . ."*

Loman was certain that Denny's drooling, silver-eyed incarnation was not a higher form than ordinary human existence, neither cleaner nor purer. In its way it was as much a degeneration as Mike Peyser's regression to a lupine shape or Coombs's descent into apelike primitiveness. Like Peyser, Denny had surrendered intellectual individuality to escape awareness of the emotionless life of a New Person; instead of becoming just one of a pack of subhuman beasts, he had become one of many data-processing units in a complex supercomputer network. He had relinquished the last of what was human in him—his mind—and had become something simpler than a gloriously complex human being.

A bead of drool fell from Denny's chin, leaving a wet circle on his denim-clad thigh.

Do you know fear now? Loman wondered. You can't love. Not any more than I can. But do you fear anything now?

Surely not. Machines could not feel terror.

Though Loman's conversion had left him unable to experience any emotion but fear, and though his days and nights had become one long ordeal of anxiety of varying intensity, he had in a perverse way come to love fear, to cherish it, for it was the only feeling that kept him in touch with the unconverted man he had once been. If his fear were taken from him, too, he would be only a machine of flesh. His life would have no human dimension whatsoever.

Denny had surrendered that last precious emotion. All he had left to fill his gray days were logic, reason, endless chains of calculations, the never-ending absorption and interpolation of facts. And if Shaddack was correct about the longevity of the New People, those days would mount into centuries.

Suddenly eerie electronic noises came from the boy again. They echoed off the walls.

Those sounds were as strange as the cold, mournful songs and cries of some species dwelling in the deepest reaches of the sea.

To call Shaddack and reveal Denny to him in this condition would be to encourage the madman in his insane and unholy pursuits. Once he saw what Denny had become, Shaddack might find a way to induce or force all of the New People to transform themselves into identical, thoroughgoing cybernetic entities. That prospect boosted Loman's fear to new heights.

The boy-thing fell silent again.

Loman drew his revolver from its holster. His hand was shaking badly.

Data rushed ever more frantically across the screen and swam simultaneously across the surface of Denny's molten eyes.

Staring at the creature that had once been his son, Loman dragged memories from the trunk of his pre-Change life, desperately trying to recall something of what he'd once felt for Denny—the love of father for son, the sweet ache of pride, hope for the boy's future. He remembered fishing trips they had taken together, evenings spent in front of the TV, favorite books shared and discussed, long hours during which they'd worked happily together on science projects for school, the Christmas that Denny had gotten his first bicycle, the kid's first date when he had nervously brought the Talmadge girl home to meet his folks. . . . Loman could summon forth images of those times, quite detailed memory-pictures, but they had no power to warm him. He knew he should *feel* something if he was going to kill his only child, something more than fear, but he no longer had that capacity. To hold fast to whatever remained of the human being in him, he ought to be able to squeeze out one tear, at least one, as he squeezed off the shot from the Smith & Wesson, but he remained dry-eyed.

Without warning, something erupted from Denny's forehead.

Loman cried out and stumbled backward two steps in surprise.

At first he thought the thing was a worm, for it was shiny-oily and segmented, as thick as a pencil. But as it continued to extrude, he saw that it was more metallic than organic, terminating in a fish-mouth plug three times the diameter of the "worm" itself. Like the feeler of a singularly repulsive insect, it weaved back and forth in front of Denny's face, growing longer and longer, until it touched the computer.

He is *willing* this to happen, Loman reminded himself.

This was mind over matter, not short-circuited genetics. Mental power made concrete, not merely biology run amok. This was what the boy wanted to become, and if this was the only life he could tolerate now, the only existence he desired, then why shouldn't he be allowed to have it?

The hideous wormlike extrusion probed the exposed mechanism, where the cover plate had once been. It disappeared inside, making some linkage that helped the boy achieve a more intimate bond with Sun than could be had solely through his mutated hands and mercuric eyes.

A hollow, electronic, blood-freezing wail came from the boy's mouth, though neither his lips nor tongue moved.

Loman's fear of taking action was at last outweighed by his fear of *not* acting. He stepped forward, put the muzzle of the revolver against the boy's right temple, and fired two rounds.

chapter seventeen

Crouching on the back porch, leaning against the wall of the house, rising up now and then to look cautiously through the window at the three people gathered around the kitchen table, Chrissie grew slowly more confident that they could be trusted. Above the dull roar and sizzle of the rain, through the closed window, she could hear only snatches of their conversation. After a while, however, she determined that they knew something was terribly wrong in Moonlight Cove. The two strangers seemed to be hiding out in Mr. Talbot's house and were on the run as much as she was. Apparently they were working on a plan to get help from authorities outside of town.

She decided against knocking on the door. It was solid wood, with no panes in the upper half, so they would not be able to see who was knocking. She had heard enough to know they were tense, maybe not as completely frazzle-nerved as she was herself, but definitely on edge. An unexpected knock at the door would give them all massive heart attacks—or maybe they'd pick up guns and blast the door to smithereens, and her with it.

Instead she rose up in plain sight and rapped on the window.

Mr. Talbot jerked his head in surprise and pointed, but even as he was pointing, the other man and the woman flew to their feet with the suddenness of marionettes snapped upright on strings. Moose barked once, twice. The three people—and the dog—stared in surprise at Chrissie. From the expression on their faces, she might have been not a bedraggled eleven-year-old girl but a chainsaw-wielding maniac wearing a leather hood to conceal a deformed face.

She supposed that right now, in alien-infested Moonlight Cove, even a pathetic, rain-soaked, exhausted little girl could be an object of terror to those who didn't know that she was still human. In hope of allaying their fear, she spoke through the windowpane:

"Help me. Please, help me."

chapter eighteen

The machine screamed. Its skull shattered under the impact of the two slugs, and it was blown out of its seat, toppling to the floor of the bedroom and pulling the chair with it. The elongated fingers tore loose of the computer on the desk. The segmented wormlike probe snapped in two, halfway between the computer and the forehead from which it had sprung. The thing lay on the floor, twitching, spasming.

Loman had to think of it as a machine. He could not think of it as his son. That was too terrifying.

The face was misshapen, wrenched into an asymmetrical, surreal mask by the impact of the bullets as they'd torn through the cranium.

The silvery eyes had gone black. Now it appeared as if puddles of oil, not mercury, were pooled in the sockets in the thing's skull.

Between plates of shattered bone, Loman saw not merely the gray matter he had expected but what appeared to be coiled wire, glinting shards that looked almost ceramic, odd geometrical shapes. The blood that seeped from the wounds was accompanied by wisps of blue smoke.

Still, the machine screamed.

The electronic shrieks no longer came from the boy-thing but from the computer on the desk. Those sounds were so bizarre that they were as out of place in the machine half of the organism as they had been in the boy half.

Loman realized these were not entirely electronic wails. They also had a tonal quality and character that were unnervingly human.

The waves of data ceased flowing across the screen. One word was repeated hundreds of times, filling line after line on the display:

NO NO NO NO NO NO NO NO NO NO NO NO NO NO NO . . .

He suddenly knew that Denny was only half dead. The part of the boy's mind that had inhabited his body was extinguished, but another fragment of his consciousness still lived somehow within the computer, kept alive in silicon instead of brain tissue. *That* part of him was screaming in this machine-cold voice.

On the screen:

WHERE'S THE REST OF ME WHERE'S THE REST OF ME WHERE'S THE REST OF ME NO NO NO NO NO NO NO NO. . . .

Loman felt as if his blood was icy sludge pumped by a heart as jellid as the meat in the freezer downstairs. He had never known a chill that penetrated as deep as this one.

He stepped away from the crumpled body, which at last stopped twitching, and turned his revolver on the computer. He emptied the gun into the machine, first blowing out the screen. Because the blinds and drapes were closed, the room was nearly dark. He blasted the circuitry to pieces. Thousands of sparks flared in the blackness, spraying out of the data-processing unit. But with a final sputter and crackle, the machine died, and the gloom closed in again.

The air stank of scorched insulation. And worse.

Loman left the room and walked to the head of the stairs. He stood there a moment, leaning against the railing. Then he descended to the front hall.

He reloaded his revolver, holstered it.

He went out into the rain.

He got in his car and started the engine.

"Shaddack," he said aloud.

chapter nineteen

Tessa immediately took charge of the girl. She led her upstairs, leaving Harry and Sam and Moose in the kitchen, and got her out of her wet clothes.

"Your teeth are chattering, honey."

"I'm lucky to have any teeth to chatter."

"Your skin's positively blue."

"I'm lucky to have skin," the girl said.

"I noticed you're limping too."

"Yeah. I twisted an ankle."

"Sure it's just sprained?"

"Yeah. Nothing serious. Besides—"

"I know," Tessa said, "you're lucky to *have* ankles."

"Right. For all I know, aliens find ankles particularly tasty, the same way some people like pig's feet. Yuch."

She sat on the edge of the bed in the guest room, a wool blanket pulled around her nakedness, and waited while Tessa got a sheet from the linen supplies and several safety pins from a sewing box that she noticed in the same closet.

Tessa said, "Harry's clothes are much too big for you, so we'll wrap you in a sheet temporarily. While your clothes are in the dryer, you can come downstairs and tell Harry and Sam and me all about it."

"It's been quite an adventure," the girl said.

"Yes, you look as if you've been through a lot."

"It'd make a great book."

"You like books?"

"Oh, yes, I love books."

Blushing but evidently determined to be sophisticated, she threw back the blanket and stood and allowed Tessa to drape the sheet around her. Tessa pinned it in place, fashioning a toga of sorts.

As Tessa worked, Chrissie said, "I think I'll write a book about all of this one day. I'll call it *The Alien Scourge* or maybe *Nest Queen*, although naturally I won't title it *Nest Queen* unless it turns out there really is a nest queen somewhere. Maybe they don't reproduce like insects or even like animals. Maybe they're basically a vegetable life-form. Who knows? If they're basically a vegetable life-form, then I'd have to call the book something like *Space Seeds* or *Vegetables of the Void* or maybe *Murderous Martian Mushrooms*. It's sometimes good to use alliteration in titles. Alliteration. Don't you like that word? It sounds so nice. I like words. Of course, you could always go with a more poetic title, haunting, like *Alien Roots, Alien Leaves*. Hey, if they're vegetables, we may be in luck, because maybe they'll eventually be killed off by aphids or tomato worms, since they won't have developed protection against earth pests, just like a few tiny germs killed off the mighty Martians in *War of the Worlds*."

Tessa was reluctant to disclose that their enemies were not from the stars, for she was enjoying the girl's precocious chatter. Then she noticed that Chrissie's left hand was injured. The palm had been badly abraded; the center of it looked raw.

"I did that when I fell off the porch roof at the rectory," the girl said.

"You fell off a roof?"

"Yeah. Boy, *that* was exciting. See, the wolf-thing was coming through the window after me, and I didn't have anywhere else to go. Twisted my ankle in the same fall and then had to run across the yard to the back gate before he caught me. You know, Miss Lockland—"

"Please call me Tessa."

Apparently Chrissie was unaccustomed to addressing adults by their Christian names. She frowned and was silent for a moment, struggling with the invitation to informality. Evidently she decided it would be rude not to use first names when asked to do so. "Okay . . . Tessa. Well, anyway, I can't decide what the aliens are most likely to do if they catch us. Maybe eat our kidneys? Or don't they eat us at all? Maybe they just shove alien pill bugs in our ears, and the bugs crawl into our brains and take over. Either way, I figure it's worth falling off a roof to avoid them."

Having finished pinning the toga, Tessa led Chrissie down the hall to the bathroom and looked in the medicine cabinet for something with which to treat the scraped palm. She found a bottle of iodine with a faded label, a half-empty roll of adhesive tape, and a package of gauze pads so old that the paper wrapper around each bandage square was yellow with age. The gauze itself looked fresh and white, and the iodine was undiluted by time, still strong enough to sting.

Barefoot, toga-clad, with her blond hair frizzing and curling as it dried, Chrissie sat on the lowered lid of the toilet seat and submitted stoically to the treatment of her wound. She didn't protest in any way, didn't cry out—or even hiss—in pain.

But she *did* talk: "That's the second time I've fallen off a roof, so I guess I must have a guardian angel looking over me. About a year and a half ago, in the spring, these birds—starlings, I think they were—built a nest on the roof of one of our stables at home, and I just *had* to see what baby birds looked like in the nest, so when my folks weren't around, I got a ladder and waited for the mama bird to fly off for more food, and then I real quick climbed up there to have a peek. Let me tell you, before they get their feathers, baby birds are just about the ugliest things you'd want to see—except for aliens, of course. They're withered little wrinkled things, all beaks and eyes, and stumpy little wings like deformed arms. If human babies looked that bad when they were born, the first people back a few million years ago would've flushed their newborns down the toilet—if they'd *had* toilets—and wouldn't have *dared* have any more of them, and the whole race would've died out before it even really got started."

Still painting the wound with iodine, trying without success to repress a grin, Tessa looked up and saw that Chrissie was squeezing her eyes tightly shut, wrinkling her nose, struggling very hard to be brave.

"Then the mama and papa bird came back," the girl said, "and saw me at the nest and flew at my face, shrieking. I was so startled that I slipped and fell off the roof. Didn't hurt myself at all that time—though I did land in some horse manure. Which isn't a thrill, let me tell you. I love horses, but they'd be ever so much more lovable if you could teach them to use a litterbox like a cat."

Tessa was crazy about this kid.

chapter twenty

Sam leaned forward with his elbows on the kitchen table and listened attentively to Chrissie Foster. Though Tessa had heard the Boogeymen in the middle of a kill at Cove Lodge and had glimpsed one of them under the door of her room, and though Harry had watched them at a distance in night and fog, and though Sam had spied two of them last night through a window in Harry's living room, the girl was the only one present who had seen them close up and more than once.

But it was not solely her singular experience that held Sam's attention. He also was captivated by her sprightly manner, good humor, and articulateness. She obviously had considerable inner strength, real toughness, for otherwise she would not have survived the previous night and the events of this morning. Yet she remained charmingly innocent, tough but not hard. She was one of those kids who gave you hope for the whole damn human race.

A kid like Scott used to be.

And that was why Sam was fascinated by Chrissie Foster. He saw in her the child that Scott had been. Before he . . . changed. With regret so poignant that it manifested itself as a dull ache in his chest and a tightness in his throat, he watched the girl and listened to her, not only to hear what information she had to impart but with the unrealistic expectation that by studying her he would at last understand why his own son had lost both innocence and hope.

chapter twenty-one

Down in the darkness of the Icarus Colony cellar, Tucker and his pack did not sleep, for they did not require it. They lay curled in the deep blackness. From time to time, he and the other male coupled with the female, and they tore at one another in savage frenzy, gashing flesh that began to heal at once, drawing one another's blood simply for the pleasure of the scent—immortal freaks at play.

The darkness and the barren confines of their concrete-walled burrow contributed to Tucker's growing disorientation. By the hour he remembered less of his existence prior to the past night's exciting hunt. He ceased to have much sense of self. Individuality was not to be encouraged in the pack when hunting, and in the burrow it was even a less desirable trait; harmony in that windowless, claustrophobic space required the relinquishment of self to group.

His waking dreams were filled with images of dark, wild shapes creeping through night-clad forests and across moon-washed meadows. When occasionally a memory of human form flickered through his mind, its origins were a mystery to him; more than that, he was frightened by it and quickly shifted his fantasies back to running-hunting-killing-coupling scenes in which he was just a part of the pack, one aspect of a single shadow, one extension of a larger organism, free from the need to think, having no desire but to *be*.

At one point he became aware that he had slipped out of his wolf-like form, which had become too confining. He no longer wanted to be the leader of a pack, for that position carried with it too much responsibility. He didn't want to think at all. Just be. *Be*. The limitations of all rigid physical forms seemed insufferable.

He sensed that the other male and the female were aware of his degeneration and were following his example.

He felt his flesh flowing, bones dissolving, organs and vessels surrendering form and function. He devolved beyond the primal ape, far beyond the four-legged thing that laboriously had crawled out of the ancient sea millennia ago, beyond, beyond, until he was but a mass of pulsing tissue, protoplasmic soup, throbbing in the darkness of the Icarus Colony cellar.

chapter twenty-two

Loman rang the doorbell at Shaddack's house on the north point, and Evan, the manservant, answered.

"I'm sorry, Chief Watkins, but Mr. Shaddack isn't here."

"Where's he gone?"

"I don't know."

Evan was one of the New People. To be sure of dispatching him, Loman shot him twice in the head and then twice in the chest while he lay on the foyer floor, shattering both brain and heart. Or data-processor and pump. Which was needed now—biological or mechanical terminology? How far had they progressed toward becoming machines?

Loman closed the door behind him and stepped over Evan's body. After replenishing the expended rounds in the revolver's cylinder, he searched the huge house room by room, floor by floor, looking for Shaddack.

Though he wished that he could be driven by a hunger for revenge,

could be consumed by anger, and could take satisfaction in bludgeon-
ing Shaddack to death, that depth of feeling was denied him. His son's
death had not melted the ice in his heart. He couldn't feel grief or rage.

Instead he was driven by fear. He wanted to kill Shaddack before the
madman made them into something worse than they'd already become.

By killing Shaddack—who was always linked to the supercomputer
at New Wave by a simple cardiac telemetry device—Loman would activate a program in Sun that would broadcast a microwave death order.
That transmission would be received by all the microsphere computers
wedded to the innermost tissues of the New People. Upon receiving the
death order, each biologically interactive computer in each New Person
would instantly still the heart of its host. Every one of the converted in
Moonlight Cove would die. He, too, would die.

But he no longer cared. His fear of death was outweighed by his
fear of living, especially if he had to live either as a regressive or as that
more hideous thing that Denny had become.

In his mind he could see himself in that wretched condition—
gleaming mercurial eyes, a wormlike probe bursting bloodlessly from
his forehead to seek obscene conjugation with the computer. If skin
actually could crawl, his own would have crept off his body.

When he could not find Shaddack at home, he set out for New Wave,
where the maker of the new world was no doubt in his office busily
designing neighborhoods for this hell that he called paradise.

chapter twenty-three

Shortly after eleven o'clock, as Sam was leaving, Tessa stepped out onto
the back porch with him and closed the door, leaving Harry and Chrissie in the kitchen. The trees at the rear of the property were just tall
enough to prevent neighbors, even those uphill, from looking into the
yard. She was sure they could not be seen in the deeper shadows of the
porch.

"Listen," she said, "it makes no sense for you to go alone."

"It makes perfect sense."

The air was chilly and damp. She hugged herself.

She said, "I could ring the front doorbell, distract anyone inside, while you went in the back."

"I don't want to have to worry about you."

"I can take care of myself."

"Yeah, I believe you can," he said.

"Well?"

"But I work alone."

"You seem to do everything alone."

He smiled thinly. "Are we going to get into another argument about whether life is a tea party or hell on earth?"

"That wasn't an argument we had. It was a discussion."

"Well, anyway, I've shifted to undercover assignments for the very reason that I can pretty much work alone. I don't want a partner any more, Tessa, because I don't want to see any more of them die."

She knew he was referring not only to the other agents who had been killed in the line of duty with him but also to his late wife.

"Stay with the girl," he said. "Take care of her if anything happens. She's like you, after all."

"What?"

"She's one of those who knows how to love life. How to really, deeply love it, no matter what happens. It's a rare and precious talent."

"You know too," she said.

"No. I've never known."

"Dammit, everyone is born with a love of life. You still have it, Sam. You've just lost touch with it, but you can find it again."

"Take care of her," he said, turning away and descending the porch steps into the rain.

"You better come back, damn you. You promised to tell me what you saw at the other end of that tunnel, on the Other Side. You just better come back."

Sam departed through silver rain and thin patches of gray fog.

As she watched him go, Tessa realized that even if he never told her about the Other Side, she wanted him to come back for many other reasons both complex and surprising.

chapter twenty-four

The Coltrane house was two doors south of the Talbot place, on Conquistador. Two stories. Weathered cedar siding. A covered patio instead of a rear porch.

Moving quickly along the back of the house, where rain drizzled off the patio cover with a sound inaptly like crackling fire, Sam peered through sliding glass doors into a gloomy family room and then through French windows into an unlighted kitchen. When he reached the kitchen door, he withdrew his revolver from the holster under his leather jacket and held it down at his side, against his thigh.

He could have walked around front and rung the bell, which might have seemed less suspicious to the people inside. But that would mean going out to the street, where he was more likely to be seen not only by neighbors but by the men Chrissie said were patrolling the town.

He knocked on the door, four quick raps. When no one responded, he knocked again, louder, and then a third time, louder still. If anyone was home, the knock would have been answered.

Harley and Sue Coltrane must be at New Wave, where they worked.

The door was locked. He hoped it had no dead bolt.

Though he had left his other tools at Harry's, he had brought a thin, flexible metal loid. Television dramas had popularized the notion that any credit card made a convenient and unincriminating loid, but those plastic rectangles too often got wedged in the crack or snapped before the latch bolt was slipped. He preferred time-proven tools. He worked the loid between the door and frame, below the lock, and slid it up, applying pressure when he met resistance. The lock popped. He tried the door, and there was no dead bolt; it opened with a soft creak.

He stepped inside and quietly closed the door, making sure that the lock did not engage. If he had to get out fast, he did not want to fumble with a latch.

The kitchen was illuminated only by the dismal light of the rain-darkened day that barely penetrated the windows. Evidently the vinyl flooring, wall-covering, and tile were of the palest hues, for in that dimness everything seemed to be one shade of gray or another.

He stood for almost a minute, listening intently.

A kitchen clock ticked.

Rain drummed on the patio cover.

His soaked hair was pasted to his forehead. He pushed it aside, out of his eyes.

When he moved, his wet shoes squished.

He went directly to the phone, which was mounted on the wall above a corner secretary. When he picked it up, he got no dial tone, but the line was not dead, either. It was filled with strange sounds: clicking, low beeping, soft oscillations—all of which blended into mournful and alien music, an electronic threnody.

The back of Sam's neck went cold.

Carefully, silently, he returned the handset to its cradle.

He wondered what sounds could be heard on a telephone that was being used as a link between two computers, with a modem. Was one of the Coltranes at work elsewhere in the house, tied in by a home computer to New Wave?

Somehow he sensed that what he had heard on the line was not as simply explained as that. It had been damned eerie.

A dining room lay beyond the kitchen. The two large windows were covered with gauzy sheers, which further filtered the ashen daylight. A hutch, buffet, table, and chairs were revealed as blocks of black and slate-gray shadows.

Again he stopped to listen. Again he heard nothing unusual.

The house was laid out in a classic California design, with no downstairs hall. Each room led directly to the next in an open and airy floorplan. Through an archway he entered the large living room, grateful that the house had wall-to-wall carpeting, on which his wet shoes made no sound.

The living room was less shadowy than any other part of the house that he had seen thus far, yet the brightest color was a pearly gray. The west windows were sheltered by the front porch, but rain streamed over those facing north. Leaden daylight, passing through the panes, speckled the room with the watery-gray shadows of the hundreds of beads that tracked down the glass, and Sam was so edgy that he could almost feel those small ameboid phantoms crawling over him.

Between the lighting and his mood, he felt as if he were in an old black-and-white movie. One of those bleak exercises in *film noir*.

The living room was deserted, but abruptly a sound came from the last room downstairs. At the southwest corner. Beyond the foyer. The den, most likely. It was a piercing trill that made his teeth ache, followed by a forlorn cry that was neither the voice of a man nor that of a machine but something in between, a semimetallic voice wrenched by fear and twisted with despair. That was followed by low electronic pulsing, like a massive heartbeat.

Then silence.

He had brought up his revolver, holding it straight out in front of him, ready to shoot anything that moved. But everything was as still as it was silent.

The trill, the eerie cry, and the base throbbing surely could not be associated with the Boogeymen that he'd seen last night outside of Harry's house, or with the other shape-changers Chrissie described. Until now, an encounter with one of them had been the thing he feared most. But suddenly the unknown entity in the den was more frightening.

Sam waited.

Nothing more.

He had the queer feeling that something was listening for his movements as tensely as he was listening for it.

He considered returning to Harry's to think of some other way to send a message to the Bureau, because Mexican food and Guinness Stout and Goldie Hawn movies—even *Swing Shift*—now seemed precious beyond value, not pathetic reasons to live but pleasures so exquisite that no words existed to adequately describe them.

The only thing that kept him from getting the hell out of there was Chrissie Foster. The memory of her bright eyes. Her innocent face. The enthusiasm and animation with which she had recounted her adventures. Perhaps he had failed Scott, and perhaps it was too late for the boy to be hauled back from the brink. But Chrissie was still alive in every vital sense of the word—physically, intellectually, emotionally— and she was dependent on him. No one else could save her from conversion.

Midnight was little more than twelve hours away.

He edged through the living room and quietly crossed the foyer. He stood with his back against the wall beside the half-open door to the room from which the weird sounds had come.

Something clicked in there.

He stiffened.

Low, soft clicks. Not the *tick-tick-tick* of claws like those he had heard tapping on the window last night. More like a long series of relays being tripped, scores of switches being closed, dominoes falling against one another: *click-click-click-clickety-clickety-click-click-clickety*. . . .

Silence once more.

Holding the revolver in both hands, Sam stepped in front of the door and pushed it open with one foot. He crossed the threshold and assumed a shooter's stance just inside the room.

The windows were covered by interior shutters, and the only light was from two computer screens. Both were fitted with filters that resulted in black text on an amber background. Everything in the room not wrapped in shadows was touched by that golden radiance.

Two people sat before the terminals, one on the right side of the room, the other on the left, their backs to each other.

"Don't move," Sam said sharply.

They neither moved nor spoke. They were so still that at first he thought they were dead.

The peculiar light was brighter yet curiously less revealing than the half-burnt-out daylight that vaguely illuminated the other rooms. As his eyes adjusted, Sam saw that the two people at the computers were not only unnaturally still but were not really people any more. He was drawn forward by the icy grip of horror.

Oblivious of Sam, a naked man, probably Harley Coltrane, sat in a wheeled, swivel-based chair at the computer to the right of the door, against the west wall. He was connected to the VDT by a pair of inch-thick cables that looked less metallic than organic, glistening wetly in the amber glow. They extended from within the bowels of the data-processing unit—from which the cover plate had been removed—and into the man's bare torso below his rib cage, melding bloodlessly with the flesh. They throbbed.

"Dear God," Sam whispered.

Coltrane's lower arms were utterly fleshless, just golden bones. The meat of his upper arms ended smoothly two inches above the elbows; from those stumps, bones thrust out as cleanly as robotic extrusions from a metal casing. The skeletal hands were locked tightly around the cables, as if they were merely a pair of clamps.

When Sam stepped nearer to Coltrane and looked closer, he saw the bones were not as well differentiated as they should have been but had half melted together. Furthermore, they were veined with metal. As he watched, the cables pulsed with such vigor that they began to vibrate wildly. If not held fast by the clamping hands, they might have torn loose either from the man or the machine.

Get out.

A voice spoke within him, telling him to flee, and it was his own voice, though not that of the adult Sam Booker. It was the voice of the child he had once been and to which his fear was encouraging him to revert. Extreme terror is a time machine a thousand times more efficient than nostalgia, hurtling us backward through the years, into that forgotten and intolerable condition of helplessness in which so much of childhood is spent.

Get out, run, run, get out!

Sam resisted the urge to bolt.

He wanted to understand. What was happening? What had these people become? *Why?* What did this have to do with the Boogeymen who prowled the night? Evidently through microtechnology Thomas Shaddack had found a way to alter, radically and forever, human biology. That much was clear to Sam, but knowing just that and nothing else was like sensing that something lived within the sea without ever having seen a fish. So much more lay beneath the surface, mysterious.

Get out.

Neither the man before him nor the woman across the room seemed remotely aware of him. Apparently he was in no imminent danger.

Run, said the frightened boy within.

Rivers of data—words, numbers, charts and graphs of myriad types—flowed in a floodlike rampage across the amber screen, while Harley Coltrane stared unwaveringly at that darkly flickering display. He could not have seen it as an ordinary man would have, for he had no eyes. They'd been torn from his sockets and replaced by a cluster of other sensors: tiny beads of ruby glass, small knots of wire, wafflesurfaced chips of some ceramic material, all bristling and slightly recessed in the deep black holes in his skull.

Sam was holding the revolver in only one hand now. He kept his finger on the trigger guard rather than on the trigger itself, for he was shaking so badly that he might unintentionally let off a shot.

The man-machine's chest rose and fell. His mouth hung open, and bitterly foul breath rushed from him in rhythmic waves.

A rapid pulse was visible in his temples and in the gruesomely swollen arteries in his neck. But other pulses throbbed where none should have been: in the center of his forehead; along each jawline; at four places in his chest and belly; in his upper arms, where dark ropy vessels had thickened and risen above subcutaneous fat, sheathed now only by his skin. His circulatory system seemed to have been redesigned and augmented to assist new functions that his body was being called upon to perform. Worse yet, those pulses beat in a strange syncopation, as if at least two hearts pounded within him.

A shriek erupted from the thing's gaping mouth, and Sam twitched and cried out in surprise. This was akin to the unearthly sounds that he had heard while in the living room, that had drawn him here, but he had thought they'd come from the computer.

Grimacing as the electronic wail spiraled higher and swelled into painful decibels, Sam let his gaze rise from the man-machine's open mouth to its "eyes." The sensors still bristled in the sockets. The beads of ruby glass glowed with inner light, and Sam wondered if they registered him on the infrared spectrum or by some other means. Did Coltrane see him at all? Perhaps the man-machine had traded the human world for a different reality, moving from this physical plane to another level, and perhaps Sam was an irrelevancy to him, unnoticed.

The shriek began to fade, then cut off abruptly.

Without realizing what he'd done, Sam had raised his revolver and, from a distance of about eighteen inches, pointed it at Harley Coltrane's face. He was startled to discover that he also had slipped his finger off the guard and onto the trigger itself and that he was going to destroy this thing.

He hesitated. Coltrane was, after all, still a man—at least to some extent. Who was to say that he didn't desire his current state more than life as an ordinary human being? Who was to say that he was not happy like this? Sam was uneasy in the role of judge, but an even uneasier executioner. As a man who believed that life was hell on earth, he had to consider the possibility that Coltrane's condition was an improvement, an escape.

Between man and computer, the glistening, semiorganic cables *thrummed*. They rattled against the skeletal hands in which they were clamped.

Coltrane's rank breath was redolent with both the stench of rotting meat and overheated electronic components.

Sensors glistened and moved within the lidless eye sockets.

Tinted gold by the light from the screen, Coltrane's face seemed to be frozen in a perpetual scream. The vessels pulsing in his jaws and temples looked less like reflections of his own heartbeat than like parasites squirming under his skin.

With a shudder of revulsion, Sam squeezed the trigger. The blast was thunderous in that confined space.

Coltrane's head snapped back with the impact of the point-blank shot, then dropped forward, chin on his chest, smoking and bleeding.

The repulsive cables continued to swell and shrink and swell as if with the rhythmic passage of inner fluid.

Sam sensed that the man was not entirely dead. He turned the gun on the computer screen.

One of Coltrane's skeletal hands released the cable around which it had been firmly clamped. With a *click-snick-snack* of bare bones, it whipped up and seized Sam's wrist.

Sam cried out.

The room filled with electronic clicks and snaps and beeps and warblings.

The hellish hand held him fast and with such tremendous strength that the bony fingers pinched his flesh, then began to cut through it. He felt warm blood trickle down his arm, under his shirt sleeve. With a flash of panic he realized that the unhuman power of the man-machine was ultimately sufficient to crush his wrist and leave him crippled. At best his hand would swiftly go numb from lack of circulation, and the revolver would drop from his grasp.

Coltrane was struggling to raise his half-shattered head.

Sam thought of his mother in the wreckage of the car, face torn open, grinning at him, grinning, silent and unmoving but grinning. . . .

Frantically he kicked at Coltrane's chair, hoping to send it rolling and spinning away. The wheels had been locked.

The bony hand squeezed tighter, and Sam screamed. His vision blurred.

Still, he saw that Coltrane's head was coming up slowly, slowly.

Jesus, I don't want to see that ruined face!

With his right foot, putting everything he had into the kick, Sam struck once, twice, three times at the cables between Coltrane and the computer. They tore loose from Coltrane, popping out of his flesh with a hideous sound, and the man slumped in his chair. Simultaneously the skeletal hand opened and fell away from Sam's wrist. With a cold rattle it struck the hard plastic mat under the chair.

Bass electronic pulses thumped like soft drumbeats and echoed off the walls, while under them a thin bleat wavered continuously through three notes.

Gasping and half in shock, Sam clamped his left hand around his bleeding wrist, as if that would still the stinging pain.

Something brushed against his leg.

He looked down and saw the semiorganic cables, like pale headless snakes, still attached to the computer and full of malevolent life. They seemed to have grown, as well, until they were twice the length they had been when linking Coltrane to the machine. One snared his left ankle, and the other curled sinuously around his right calf.

He tried to tear loose.

They held him fast.

They twined up his legs.

Instinctively he knew they were seeking bare flesh on the upper half of his body, and that upon contact they would burrow into him and make him part of the system.

He was still holding the revolver in his blood-slicked right hand. He aimed at the screen.

Data was no longer flowing across that amber field. Instead, Coltrane's face looked out from the display. His eyes had been restored, and it seemed as if he could see Sam, for he was looking directly at him and speaking to him:

"... need ... need ... want, need. ..."

Without understanding a damned thing about it, Sam knew Coltrane was still alive. He had not died—or at least not all of him had perished—with his body. He was there, in the machine somehow.

As if to confirm that insight, Coltrane influenced the glass screen of the VDT to relinquish the convex plane of its surface and adapt to the contours of his face. The glass became as flexible as gelatin, thrusting outward, as if Coltrane actually existed within the machine, physically, and was now pushing his face out of it.

This was impossible. Yet it was happening. Harley Coltrane seemed to be controlling matter with the power of his mind, a mind not even any longer linked to a human body.

Sam was mesmerized by fear, frozen, paralyzed. His finger lay immovable against the trigger.

Reality had been ripped, and through that tear a nightmare world of infinite malign possibilities seemed to be rushing into the world that Sam knew and—suddenly—loved.

One of the snakelike cables had reached his chest and found its way under his sweater to bare skin. He felt as if he'd been touched by a white-hot-brand, and the pain broke his trance.

He fired two rounds into the computer, shattering the screen first, which was the second face of Coltrane's into which he'd pumped a .38 slug. Though Sam half expected it to absorb the bullet without effect, the cathode-ray tube imploded as if still made of glass. The other round scrambled the guts of the data-processing unit, at last finishing off the thing that Coltrane had become.

The pale, oily tentacles fell away from him. They blistered, began to bubble, and seemed to be putrefying before his eyes.

Eerie electronic beeps, crackles, and oscillations, not ear-torturingly loud but uncannily piercing, still filled the room.

When Sam looked toward the woman who had been seated at the other computer, against the east wall, he saw that the mucus-slick cables between her and the machine had lengthened, allowing her to turn in her chair to face him. Aside from those semiorganic connections and her nakedness, she was in a different but no less hideous condition from her husband. Her eyes were gone, but her sockets did not bristle with a host of sensors. Rather, two reddish orbs, three times the size of ordinary eyes, filled enlarged sockets in a face redesigned to accommodate them; they were less eyes than eye-shaped receptors, no doubt designed to see in many spectrums of light, and in fact Sam became aware of an image of himself in each red lens, reversed. Her legs, belly, breasts, arms, throat, and face were heavily patterned with swollen blood vessels that lay just beneath her skin and that seemed to stretch it to the breaking point, so she looked as if she were a design board for branch-pattern circuitry. Some of those vessels might, indeed, have carried blood, but some of them throbbed with waves of radiumlike illumination, some green and some sulfurous yellow.

A segmented, wormlike probe, the diameter of a pencil, erupted from her forehead, as if shot from a gun, and streaked toward Sam, closing the ten feet between them in a split second, striking him above the right eye before he could duck. The tip bit into his skin on contact. He heard a whirring sound, as of tiny blades spinning at maybe a thousand revolutions a minute. Blood ran down his brow and along the side of his nose. But he was squeezing off the last two rounds in his gun even as the probe came at him. Both shots found their mark. One slammed into the woman's upper body, and one took out the computer behind her in a blaze of sparks and crackling electrical bolts that jumped to the ceiling and snaked briefly across the plaster before dissipating. The probe went limp and fell away from him before it could link his brain to hers, which evidently had been its intention.

Except for gray daylight that entered through the paper-thin cracks between the slats of the shutters, the room was dark.

Crazily, Sam remembered something a computer specialist had said at a seminar for agents, when explaining how the Bureau's new system worked: *Computers can perform more effectively when linked, allowing parallel processing of data.*

Bleeding from the forehead and the right wrist, he stumbled backward to the door and flicked the light switch, turning on a floor lamp. He stood there—as far as he could get from the two grotesque corpses and still see them—while he began to reload the revolver with rounds he dug out of the pockets of his jacket.

The room was preternaturally silent.

Nothing moved.

Sam's heart was hammering with such force that his chest ached dully with each blow.

Twice he dropped cartridges because his hands were shaking. He didn't stoop to retrieve them. He was half convinced that the moment he wasn't in a position to fire with accuracy or to run, one of the dead creatures would prove not to be dead, after all, and like a flash would come at him, spitting sparks, and would seize him before he could rise and scramble out of its way.

Gradually he became aware of the sound of rain. After losing half of its force during the morning, it was now falling harder than at any time since the storm had first broken the previous night. No thunder shook the day, but the furious drumming of the rain itself—and the insulated walls of the house—had probably muffled the gunfire enough to prevent it being heard by neighbors. He hoped to God that was the case. Otherwise, they were coming even now to investigate, and they would prevent his escape.

Blood continued to trickle down from the wound on his forehead, and some of it got into his right eye. It stung. He wiped at his eye with his sleeve and blinked away the tears as best he could.

His wrist hurt like hell. But if he had to, he could hold the revolver with his left hand and shoot well enough in close quarters.

When the .38 was reloaded, Sam edged back into the room, to the smoking computer on the worktable along the west wall, where Harley Coltrane's mutated body was slumped in a chair, trailing its bone-metal arms. Keeping one eye on the dead man-machine, he took the phone off the modem and hung it up. Then he lifted the receiver and was relieved to hear a dial tone.

His mouth was so dry that he wasn't sure he'd be able to speak clearly when his call got through.

He punched out the number of the Bureau office in Los Angeles.

The line clicked.

A pause.

A recording came on: "We are sorry that we are unable to complete your call at this time."

He hung up, then tried again.

"We are sorry that we are unable to complete—"

He slammed the phone down.

Not all of the telephones in Moonlight Cove were operable. And evidently, even from those in service, calls could be placed only to certain numbers. Approved numbers. The local phone company had been reduced to an elaborate intercom to serve the converted.

As he turned away from the phone, he heard something move behind him. Stealthy and quick.

He swung around, and the woman was three feet away. She was no longer connected to the ruined computer, but one of those organic-looking cables trailed across the floor from the base of her spine and into an electrical socket.

Free-associating in his terror, Sam thought: So much for your clumsy kites, Dr. Frankenstein, so much for the need for storms and lightning; these days we just plug the monsters into the wall, give them a jolt of the juice direct, courtesy of Pacific Power & Light.

A reptilian hiss issued from her, and she reached for him. Instead of fingers, her hand had three multiple-pronged plugs similar to the couplings with which the elements of a home computer were joined, though these prongs were as sharp as nails.

Sam dodged to the side, colliding with the chair in which Harley Coltrane still slumped, and nearly fell, firing at the woman-thing as he went. He emptied the five-round .38.

The first three shots knocked her backward and down. The other two tore through vacant air and punched chunks of plaster out of the walls because he was too panicked to stop pulling the trigger when she fell out of his line of fire.

She was trying to get up.

Like a goddamn vampire, he thought.

He needed the high-tech equivalent of a wooden stake, a cross, a silver bullet.

The artery-circuits that webbed her naked body were still pulsing with light, although in places she was sparking, just as the computers themselves had done when he had pumped a couple of slugs into them.

No rounds were left in the revolver.

He searched his pockets for cartridges.

He had none.

Get out.

An electronic wail, not deafening but more nerve-splintering than a thousand sharp fingernails scraped simultaneously down a blackboard, shrilled from her.

Two segmented, wormlike probes burst from her face and flew straight at him. Both fell inches short of him—perhaps a sign of her waning energy—and returned to her like splashes of quicksilver streaming back into the mother mass.

But she *was* getting up.

Sam scrambled to the doorway, stooped, and snatched up the two cartridges he had dropped when he had reloaded the gun. He broke open the cylinder, shook out the empty brass casings, jammed in the last two rounds.

". . . *neeeeeeeeeeeeeeed . . . neeeeeeeeeeeeeeeed . . .*"

She was on her feet, coming toward him.

This time he held the Smith & Wesson in both hands, aimed carefully, and shot her in the head.

Take out the data processor, he thought with a flash of black humor. Only way to stop a determined machine. Take out its data processor, and it's nothing but a tangle of junk.

She crumpled to the floor. The red light went out of her unhuman eyes; they were black now. She was perfectly still.

Suddenly flames erupted from her bullet-cracked skull, spurting from the wound, from her eyes, nostrils, and gaping mouth.

He moved quickly to the socket to which she was still tethered, and he kicked at the semiorganic plug that she had extruded from her body, knocking it loose.

The flames still leaped from her.

He could not afford a house fire. The bodies would be found, and the neighborhood, Harry's house included, would be searched door-to-door. He looked around for something to throw over her to smother the flames, but already the blaze within her skull was subsiding. In a moment it burned itself out.

The air reeked of a dozen foul odors, some of which did not bear contemplation.

He was mildly dizzy. Nausea stole over him. He gagged, clenched his teeth, and forced back his gorge.

Though he wanted desperately to get out of there, he took time to unplug both computers. They were inoperable and damaged beyond repair, but he was irrationally afraid that, like Dr. Frankenstein's home-built man in movie sequel after sequel, they would somehow come to life if exposed to electricity.

He hesitated at the doorway, leaned against the jamb to take some of the weight off his weak and trembling legs, and studied the strange corpses. He had expected them to revert to their normal appearance when they were dead, the way werewolves in the movies, upon taking a silver bullet in the heart or being beaten with a silver-headed cane, always metamorphosed one last time, becoming their tortured, too-human selves, finally released from the curse. Unfortunately this was not lycanthropy. This was not a supernatural affliction, but something worse that men had brought upon themselves with no help from demons or spirits or other things that went bump in the night. The Coltranes remained as they had been, monstrous half-breeds of flesh and metal, blood and silicon—human and machine.

He could not comprehend *how* they had become what they had become, but he half remembered that a word existed for them, and in a moment he recalled it. *Cyborg*: a person whose physiological functioning was aided by or dependent on a mechanical or electronic device. People wearing pacemakers to regulate arrhythmic hearts were cyborgs, and that was a good thing. Those whose kidneys had both failed—and who received dialysis on a regular basis—were cyborgs, and that was good too. But with the Coltranes the concept had been carried to extremes. They were the nightmare side of advanced cybernetics, in whom not merely physiological but mental function had become aided by and almost certainly dependent on a machine.

Sam began to gag again. He turned quickly away from the smoke-hazed den and backtracked through the house to the kitchen door, by which he had entered.

Every step of the way, he was certain that he would hear a voice behind him, half human and half electronic—"*neeeeeeeeeeed*"—and would look back to see one of the Coltranes lumbering toward him, reanimated by a last small supply of current stored in battery cells.

chapter twenty-five

At the main gate of New Wave Microtechnology, on the highlands along the northern perimeter of Moonlight Cove, the guard, wearing a black rain slicker with the corporate logo on the breast, squinted at the oncoming police cruiser. When he recognized Loman, he waved him through without stopping him. Loman had been well known there even before he and they had become New People.

New Wave power, prestige, and profitability were not hidden in an unassuming corporate headquarters. The place had been designed by a leading architect who favored rounded corners, gentle angles, and the interesting juxtaposition of curved walls—some concave, some convex. The two large three-story buildings—one erected four years after the other—were faced with buff-colored stone, had huge tinted windows, and blended well with the landscape.

Of the fourteen hundred people employed there, nearly a thousand lived in Moonlight Cove. The rest resided in outlying communities elsewhere in the county. All of them, of course, lived within the effective reach of the microwave broadcasting dish on the roof of the main structure.

As he followed the entrance road around the big buildings toward the parking area behind, Loman thought: Sure as hell, Shaddack's our very own Reverend Jim Jones. Needs to be sure he can take every last one of his devoted followers with him any time he wants. A modern pharaoh. When he dies, those attending him die, too, as if he expects them to continue to attend him in the next world. Shit. Do we even believe in a next world any more?

No. Religious faith was akin to hope, and it required emotional commitment.

New People did not believe in God any more than they believed in Santa Claus. The only thing they believed in was the power of the machine and the cybernetic destiny of humanity.

Maybe some of them didn't even believe in that.

Loman didn't. He no longer believed in anything at all—which scared him because he had once believed in so many things.

The ratio of New Wave's gross sales and profits to its number of employees was high even for the microtechnology industry, and its ability to pay for the best talent in its field was reflected in the percentage of high-ticket cars in the two enormous lots. Mercedes. BMW. Porsche. Corvette. Cadillac Seville. Jaguar. High-end Japanese imports with every bell and whistle.

Only half the usual number of cars were in the lot. It looked as if a high percentage of the staff was at home, working by modem. How many were already like Denny?

Side by side on the rainswept macadam, those cars reminded Loman of the orderly ranks of tombstones in a cemetery. All those quiescent engines, all that cold metal, all those hundreds of wet windshields reflecting the flat gray autumn sky, suddenly seemed a presentiment of death. To Loman, that parking lot represented the future of the entire town: silence, stillness, the terrible eternal peace of the graveyard.

If the authorities outside of Moonlight Cove tumbled to what was happening there, or if it turned out that virtually every one of the New People *was* a regressive—or worse—and the Moonhawk Project was a disaster, the remedy would not be poisoned Kool-Aid this time, like Reverend Jim Jones used down there in Jonestown, but lethal commands broadcast in bursts of microwaves, received by microsphere computers inside the New People, instantly translated into the language of the governing program, and acted upon. Thousands of hearts would stop as one. The New People would fall, as one, and Moonlight Cove would in an instant become a graveyard of the unburied.

Loman drove through the first parking lot, into the second, and headed toward the row of spaces reserved for the top executives.

If I wait for Shaddack to see that Moonhawk's gone bad and to take us with him, Loman thought, he won't be doing it because he cares about cleaning up the messes he makes, not that damn albino-spider-of-a-man. He'll take us with him just for the bloody hell of it, just so he can go out with a big bang, so the world will stand in awe of his power, a man of such incredible power that he could command thousands to die simultaneously with him.

More than a few sickos would see him as a hero, idolize him. Some budding young genius might want to emulate him. That was no doubt what Shaddack had in mind. At best, if Moonhawk succeeded and all of mankind was eventually converted, Shaddack literally would be master of his world. At worst, if it all went bad and he had to kill himself to avoid falling into the hands of the authorities, he would become a nearly mythic figure of dark inspiration, whose malign legend would encourage legions of the mad and power-mad, a Hitler for the silicon age.

Loman braked at the end of the row of cars.

He wiped at his greasy face. His hand was shaking.

He was filled with a longing to abandon this responsibility and seek the pressure-free existence of the regressive.

But he resisted.

If Loman killed Shaddack first, before Shaddack had a chance to kill himself, the legend would be tarnished. Loman would die a few seconds after Shaddack died, as would all the New People, but at least the legend would have to incorporate the fact that this high-tech Jim Jones had perished at the hands of one of the creatures he'd created. His power would be shown to be finite; he would be seen as clever but not clever enough, a flawed god, sharing both the hubris and the fate of Wells's Moreau, and his work more universally would be viewed as folly.

Loman turned right, drove to the row of executive parking spaces, and was disappointed to see that neither Shaddack's Mercedes nor his charcoal-gray van was in his reserved slot. He might still be there. He could have been driven to the office by someone else or could have parked elsewhere.

Loman swung his cruiser into Shaddack's reserved space. He cut the engine.

He was carrying his revolver in a hip holster. He had checked twice before to be sure it was fully loaded. He checked again.

Between Shaddack's house and New Wave, Loman had parked along the road to write a note, which he would leave on Shaddack's body, clearly explaining that he had killed his maker. When authorities entered Moonlight Cove from the unconverted world beyond, they would find the note and know.

He would execute Shaddack not because he was motivated by noble purpose. Such high-minded self-sacrifice required a depth of feeling he could no longer achieve. He would murder Shaddack strictly because he was terrified that Shaddack would learn about Denny, or would discover that others had become what Denny had become, and would find a way to make *all* of them enter into an unholy union with machines.

Molten silver eyes . . .

Drool spilling from the gaping mouth . . .

The segmented probe bursting from the boy's forehead and seeking the vaginal heat of the computer . . .

Those blood-freezing images, and others, played through Loman's mind on an endless loop of memory.

He'd kill Shaddack to save himself from being forced to become what Denny had become, and the destruction of Shaddack's legend would just be a beneficial side-effect.

He holstered his gun and got out of the car. He hurried through the rain to the main entrance, pushed through the etched-glass doors into the marble-floored lobby, turned right, away from the elevators, and approached the main reception desk. In corporate luxury, the place rivaled the most elaborate headquarters of high-tech companies in the more famous Silicon Valley, farther south. Detailed marble moldings, polished brass trim, fine crystal sconces, and modernistic crystal chandeliers were testament to New Wave's success.

The woman on duty was Dora Hankins. He had known her all of his life. She was a year older than he. In high school he had dated her sister a couple of times.

She looked up as he approached, said nothing.

"Shaddack?" he said.

"Not in."

"You sure?"

"Yes."

"When's he due?"

"His secretary will know."

"I'll go up."

"Fine."

As he boarded an elevator and pushed the 3 on the control board, Loman reflected on the small talk in which he and Dora Hankins would have engaged in the days before they had been put through the Change. They would have bantered with each other, exchanged news about their families, and commented on the weather. Not now. Small talk was a pleasure of their former world. Converted, they had no use for it. In fact, though he recalled that small talk had once been a part of civilized life, Loman could no longer quite remember why he ever had found it worthwhile or what kind of pleasure it had given him.

Shaddack's office suite was on the northwest corner of the third floor. The first room off the hall was the reception lounge, plushly carpeted in beige Edward Fields originals, impressively furnished in plump Roche-Bobois leather couches and brass tables with inch-thick glass tops. The single piece of art was a painting by Jasper Johns—an original, not a print.

What happens to artists in the new world coming? Loman wondered.

But he knew the answer. There would be none. Art was emotion embodied in paint on a canvas, words on a page, music in a symphony hall. There would be no art in the new world. And if there was, it would be the art of fear. The writer's most frequently used words would all be synonyms of darkness. The musician would write dirges of one form or another. The painter's most used pigment would be black.

Vicky Lanardo, Shaddack's executive secretary, was at her desk. She said, "He's not in."

Behind her the door to Shaddack's enormous private office stood open. No lights were on in there. It was illuminated only by the light of the storm-torn day, which came through the blinds in ash-gray bands.

"When will he be in?" Loman asked.

"I don't know."

"No appointments?"

"None."

"Do you know where he is?"

"No."

Loman walked out. For a while he prowled the half-deserted corridors, offices, labs, and tech rooms, hoping to spot Shaddack.

Before long, however, he decided that Shaddack was not lurking about the premises. Evidently the great man was staying mobile on this last day of Moonlight Cove's conversion.

Because of me, Loman thought. Because of what I said to him last night at Peyser's. He's afraid of me, and he's either staying mobile or gone to ground somewhere, making himself difficult to find.

Loman left the building, returned to his patrol car, and set out in search of his maker.

chapter twenty-six

In the downstairs half-bath off the kitchen, naked from the waist up, Sam sat on the closed lid of the commode, and Tessa performed the same kind of nursely duties she'd performed earlier for Chrissie. But Sam's wounds were more serious than the girl's.

In a dime-size circle on his forehead, above his right eye, the skin had been flensed off, and in the center of the circle the flesh had been entirely eaten away, revealing a speck of bared bone about an eighth of an inch in diameter. Stanching the flow of blood from those tiny, severed capillaries required a few minutes of continuous pressure, followed by the application of iodine, a liberal coating of NuSkin, and a tightly taped gauze bandage. But even after all these efforts, the gauze slowly darkened with red stain.

As Tessa worked on him, Sam told them what had happened:

". . . so if I hadn't shot her in the head, just then . . . if I'd been a second or two slower, I think that damn thing, that probe, whatever it was, it would have bored right through my skull and sunk into my brain, and she'd have connected with me the way she was connected with that computer."

Her toga forsaken in favor of dry jeans and blouse, Chrissie stood just inside the bathroom, white-faced but wanting to hear all.

Harry had pulled his wheelchair into the doorway.

Moose was lying at Sam's feet, rather than at Harry's. The dog seemed to realize that at the moment the visitor needed comforting more than Harry did.

Sam was colder to the touch than could be explained by his time in the chilly rain. He was trembling, and periodically the shivers that passed through him were so powerful that his teeth chattered.

The more Sam talked, the colder Tessa became, too, and in time his shivers were communicated to her.

His right wrist had been cut on both sides, when Harley Coltrane had gripped him with a powerful bony hand. No major blood vessels had been severed; neither gash required stitches, and Tessa quickly stopped the bleeding there. The bruises, which had barely begun to appear and would not fully flower for hours yet, were going to be worse than the cuts. He complained of pain in the joint, and his hand was weak, but she did not think that any bones had been broken or crushed.

". . . as if they'd somehow been given the ability to control their physical form," Sam said shakily, "to make anything they wanted of themselves, mind over matter, just like Chrissie said when she told us about the priest, the one who started to become the creature from that movie. . . ."

The girl nodded.

"I mean, they changed *before my eyes*, grew these probes, tried to spear me. Yet with this incredible control of their bodies, of their physical substance, all they apparently wanted to make of themselves was . . . something out of a bad dream."

The wound on his abdomen was the least of the three. As on his forehead, the skin was stripped away in a dime-size circle, though the probe that had struck him there seemed to have been meant to burn rather than cut its way into him. His flesh was scorched, and the wound itself was pretty much cauterized.

From his wheelchair Harry said, "Sam, do you think they're really people who control themselves, who have *chosen* to become machine-like, or are they people who've somehow been taken over by machines, against their will?"

"I don't know," Sam said. "It could be either, I guess."

"But how could they be taken over, how could this happen, how could such a change in the human body be accomplished? And how does what's happened to the Coltranes tie in with the Boogeymen?"

"Damned if I know," Sam said. "Somehow it's all related to New Wave. Got to be. And none of us here knows anything much about the cutting edge of that kind of technology, so we don't even have the basic knowledge required to speculate intelligently. It might as well be magic to us, supernatural. The only way we'll ever really understand what's happened is to get help from outside, quarantine Moonlight Cove, seize New Wave's labs and records, and reconstruct it the way fire marshals reconstruct the history of a fire from what they sift out of the ashes."

"Ashes?" Tessa asked as Sam stood up and as she helped him into his shirt. "This talk about fires and ashes—and other things you've said—make it sound as if you think whatever's going on in Moonlight Cove is building real fast toward an explosion or something."

"It is," he said.

At first he tried to button his shirt with one hand, but then he allowed Tessa to do it for him. She noticed that his skin was still cold and that his shivers were not subsiding with time.

He said, "All these murders they've got to cover up, these things that stalk the night . . . there's a sense that a collapse has begun, that whatever they tried to do here isn't turning out like they expected, and that the collapse is accelerating." He was breathing too quickly, too shallowly. He paused, took a deeper breath. "What I saw in the Coltranes' house . . . that didn't look like anything anyone could have planned, not something you'd *want* to do to people or that they'd want for themselves. It looked like an experiment out of control, biology run amok, reality turned inside out, and I swear to God that if *those* kinds of secrets are hidden in the houses of this town, then the whole project has to be collapsing on New Wave right now, coming down fast and hard on their heads, whether they want to admit it or not. It's all blowing up now, right now, one hell of an explosion, and we're in the middle of it."

From the moment he'd stumbled through the kitchen door, dripping rain and blood, throughout the time Tessa had cleaned and bandaged his wounds, she had noticed something that frightened her more than his paleness and shivering. He kept touching them. He had embraced Tessa in the kitchen when she gasped at the sight of the bleeding hole in his forehead; he'd held her and leaned against her and assured her that he was okay. Primarily he seemed to be reassuring himself that she and Harry and Chrissie were okay, as if he had expected to come back and find them . . . changed. He hugged Chrissie, too, as if she were his own daughter, and he said, "It'll be all right, everything'll be all right," when he saw how frightened she was. Harry held out a hand in concern, and Sam grasped it and was reluctant to let go. In the bathroom, while Tessa dressed his wounds, he had repeatedly touched her hands, her arms, and had once put a hand against her cheek as if wondering at the softness and warmth of her skin. He reached out to touch Chrissie, too, where she stood inside the bathroom door, patting her shoulder, holding her hand for a moment and giving it a reassuring squeeze. Until now he had not been a toucher. He had been reserved, self-contained, cool, even distant. But during the quarter of an hour he'd spent in the Coltrane house, he had been so profoundly shaken by what he had seen that his shell of self-imposed isolation had cracked wide open; he had come to want and need the human contact that, only a short while ago, he had not even ranked as desirable as good Mexican food, Guinness Stout, and Goldie Hawn films.

When she contemplated the intensity of the horror necessary to transform him so completely and abruptly, Tessa was more frightened than ever because Sam Booker's redemption seemed akin to that of a sinner who, on his deathbed, glimpsing hell, turns desperately to the god he once shunned, seeking comfort and reassurance. Was he less sure now of their chances of escaping? Perhaps he was seeking human contact because, having denied it to himself for so many years, he believed that only hours remained in which to experience the communion of his own kind before the great, deep endless darkness settled over them.

chapter twenty-seven

Shaddack awoke from his familiar and comforting dream of human and machine parts combined in a world-spanning engine of incalculable power and mysterious purpose. He was, as always, refreshed as much by the dream as by sleep itself.

He got out of the van and stretched. Using tools he found in the garage, he forced open the connecting door to the late Paula Parkins's house. He used her bathroom, then washed his hands and face.

Upon returning to the garage, he raised the big door. He pulled the van out into the driveway, where it could better transmit and receive data by microwave.

Rain was still falling, and depressions in the lawn were filled with water. Already wisps of fog stirred in the windless air, which probably meant the banks that rolled in from the sea later in the day would be even denser than those last night.

He took another ham sandwich and a Coke from the cooler and ate while using the van's VDT to check on the progress of Moonhawk. The 6:00 A.M. to 6:00 P.M. schedule for four hundred and fifty conversions was still under way. Already, at 12:50, slightly less than seven hours into the twelve-hour program, three hundred and nine had been injected with full-spectrum microspheres. The conversion teams were well ahead of schedule.

He checked on the progress of the search for Samuel Booker and the Lockland woman. Neither had been found.

Shaddack should have been worried about their disappearance. But he was unconcerned. He had seen the moonhawk, after all, not once but three times, and he had no doubt that ultimately he would achieve all of his goals.

The Foster girl was still missing too. He didn't trouble himself about her, either. She had probably encountered something deadly in the night. At times regressives could be useful.

Perhaps Booker and the Lockland woman had fallen victim to those same creatures. It would be ironic if the regressives—the only flaw in the project, and a potentially serious one—should prove to have preserved the secret of Moonhawk.

Through the VDT, he tried to reach Tucker at New Wave, then at his home, but the man was at neither place. Could Watkins be correct? Was Tucker a regressive and, like Peyser, unable to find his way back to human form? Was he out there in the woods right now, trapped in an altered state?

Clicking off the computer, Shaddack sighed. After everyone had been converted at midnight, this first phase of Moonhawk would not be finished. Not quite. They'd evidently have a few messes to mop up.

chapter twenty-eight

In the cellar of the Icarus Colony, three bodies had become one. The resultant entity was without rigid shape, boneless, featureless, a mass of pulsing tissue that lived in spite of lacking a brain and heart and blood vessels, without organs of any kind. It was primal, a thick protein soup, brainless but aware, eyeless but seeing, earless but hearing, without a gut but hungry.

The agglomerations of silicon microspheres had dissolved within it. That inner computer could no longer function in the radically altered substance of the creature, and in turn the beast had no use any more for the biological assistance that the microspheres had been designed to provide. Now it was not linked to Sun, the computer at New Wave. If the microwave transmitter there sent a death order, it would not receive the command—and would live.

It had become the master of its physiology by reducing itself to the uncomplicated essence of physical existence.

Their three minds also had become one. The consciousness now dwelling in that darkness was as lacking in complex form as the amorphous, jellid body it inhabited.

It had relinquished its memory because memories were inevitably of events and relationships that had consequences, and consequences—good or bad—implied that one was responsible for one's actions. Flight from responsibility had driven the creature to regression in the first place. Pain was another reason for shedding memory—the pain of recalling what had been lost.

Likewise, it had surrendered the capacity to consider the future, to plan, to dream.

Now it had no past of which it was aware, and the concept of a future was beyond its ken. It lived only for the moment, unthinking, unfeeling, uncaring.

It had one need. To survive.

And to survive, it needed only one thing. To feed.

chapter twenty-nine

The breakfast dishes had been cleared from the table while Sam was at the Coltranes' house, battling monsters that apparently had been part human and part computer and part zombies—and maybe, for all they knew, part toaster oven. After Sam was bandaged, Chrissie gathered with him and Tessa and Harry around the kitchen table again, to listen to them discuss what action to take next.

Moose stayed at Chrissie's side, regarding her with soulful brown eyes, as if he adored her more than life itself. She couldn't resist giving him all the petting and scratching-behind-the-ears that he wanted.

"The greatest problem of our age," Sam said, "is how to keep technological progress accelerating, how to use it to improve the quality of life—without being overwhelmed by it. Can we employ the computer to redesign our world, to remake our lives, without one day coming to worship it?" He blinked at Tessa and said, "It's not a silly question."

Tessa frowned. "I didn't say it was. Sometimes we have a blind trust in machines, a tendency to believe that whatever a computer tells us is gospel—"

"To forget the old maxim," Harry injected, "which says—'garbage in, garbage out.'"

"Exactly," Tessa agreed. "Sometimes, when we get data or analyses from computers, we treat it as if the machines were all infallible. Which is dangerous because a computer application can be conceived, designed, and implemented by a madman, perhaps not as easily as by a benign genius but certainly as effectively."

Sam said, "Yet people have a tendency—no, even a deep desire—to *want* to depend on the machines."

"Yeah," Harry said, "that's our sorry damn need to shift responsibility whenever we possibly can. A spineless desire to get out from under responsibility is in our genes, I swear it is, and the only way we get anywhere in this world is by constantly fighting our natural inclination to be utterly irresponsible. Sometimes I wonder if *that's* what we got from the devil when Eve listened to the serpent and ate the apple—this aversion to responsibility. Most evil has it roots there."

Chrissie noticed this subject energized Harry. With his one good arm and a little help from his half-good leg, he levered himself higher in his wheelchair. Color seeped into his previously pale face. He made a fist of one hand and stared at it intently, as if holding something precious in that tight grip, as if he held the idea there and didn't want to let go of it until he had fully explored it.

He said, "Men steal and kill and lie and cheat because they feel no responsibility for others. Politicians want power, and they want acclaim when their policies succeed, but they seldom stand up and take the responsibility for failure. The world's full of people who want to tell you how to live your life, how to make heaven right here on earth, but when their ideas turn out half-baked, when it ends in Dachau or the Gulag or the mass murders that followed our departure from Southeast Asia, they turn their heads, avert their eyes, and pretend they had no responsibility for the slaughter."

He shuddered, and Chrissie shuddered, too, though she was not entirely sure that she entirely understood everything he was saying.

"Jesus," he continued, "if I've thought about this once, I've thought about it a thousand times, ten thousand, maybe because of the war."

"Vietnam, you mean?" Tessa said.

Harry nodded. He was still staring at his fist. "In the war, to survive, you had to be responsible every minute of every day, unhesitatingly responsible for yourself, for your every action. You had to be responsible for your buddies, too, because survival wasn't something that could be achieved alone. That's maybe the one positive thing about fighting in a war—it clarifies your thinking and makes you realize that a sense of responsibility is what separates good men from the damned. I don't regret the war, not even considering what happened to me there. I learned that great lesson, learned to be responsible in all things, and I still feel responsible to the people we were fighting for, always will, and sometimes when I think of how we abandoned them to the killing fields, the mass graves, I lie awake at night and cry because they depended on me, and to the extent that I was a part of the process, I'm responsible for failing them."

They were all silent.

Chrissie felt a peculiar pressure in her chest, the same feeling she always got in school when a teacher—any teacher, any subject—began to talk about something that had been previously unknown to her and that so impressed her that it changed the way she looked at the world. It didn't happen often, but it was always both a scary and wonderful sensation. She felt it now, because of what Harry had said, but the sensation was ten times or a hundred times stronger than it had ever been when some new insight or idea had been passed to her in geography or math or science.

Tessa said, "Harry, I think your sense of responsibility in this case is excessive."

He finally looked up from his fist. "No. It can never be. Your sense of responsibility to others can never be excessive." He smiled at her. "But I know you just well enough to suspect you're already aware of that, Tessa, whether you realize it or not." He looked at Sam and said, "Some of those who came out of the war saw no good at all in it. When I meet up with them, I always suspect they were the ones who never learned the lesson, and I avoid them—though I suppose that's unfair. Can't help it. But when I meet a man from the war and see he learned the lesson, then I'd trust him with my life. Hell, I'd trust him with my soul, which in this case seems to be what they want to steal. You'll get us out of this, Sam." At last he opened his fist. "I've no doubt of that."

Tessa seemed surprised. To Sam she said, "You were in Vietnam?"

Sam nodded. "Between junior college and the Bureau."

"But you never mentioned it. This morning, when we were making breakfast, when you told me all the reasons you saw the world so differently from the way I saw it, you mentioned your wife's death, the murder of your partners, your situation with your son, but not that."

Sam stared at his bandaged wrist for a while and finally said, "The war is the most personal experience of my life."

"What an odd thing to say."

"Not odd at all," Harry said. "The most intense and the most personal."

Sam said, "If I'd not come to terms with it, I'd probably still talk about it, probably run on about it all the time. But I *have* come to terms with it. I've understood. And now to talk about it casually with someone I've just met would . . . well, cheapen it, I guess."

Tessa looked at Harry and said, "But you knew he was in Vietnam?"

"Yes."

"Just *knew* it somehow."

"Yes."

Sam had been leaning over the table. Now he settled back in his chair. "Harry, I swear I'll do my best to get us out of this. But I wish I had a better grasp of what we're up against. It all comes from New Wave. But exactly what have they done, and how can it be stopped? And how can I hope to deal with it when I don't even *understand* it?"

To that point Chrissie had felt that the conversation had been way over her head, even though all of it had been fascinating and though some of it had stirred the learning feeling in her. But now she felt that she had to contribute: "Are you really *sure* it's not aliens?"

"We're sure," Tessa said, smiling at her, and Sam ruffled her hair.

"Well," Chrissie said, "what I mean is, maybe what went wrong at New Wave is that aliens landed *there* and used it as a base, and maybe they want to turn us all into machines, like the Coltranes, so we can serve them as slaves—which, when you think about it, is more sensible than wanting to eat us. They're aliens, after all, which means they have alien stomachs and alien digestive juices, and we'd probably be real hard to digest, give them heartburn, maybe even diarrhea."

Sam, who was sitting in the chair beside Chrissie, took both her hands and held them gently in his, as aware of her abraded palm as he was aware of his own injured wrist. "Chrissie, I don't know if you've been paying too much attention to what Harry's been saying—"

"Oh, yes," she said at once. "All of it."

"Well, then you'll understand when I tell you that wanting to blame all these horrors on aliens is yet another way of shifting the responsibility from where it really belongs—on us, on people, on our very real and very great capacity to do harm to one another. It's hard to believe that anybody, even crazy men, would want to make the Coltranes into what they became, but somebody evidently did want just that. If we try to blame it on aliens—or the devil or God or trolls or whatever—we won't be likely to see the situation clearly enough to figure out how to save ourselves. You understand?"

"Sort of."

He smiled at her. He had a very nice smile, though he didn't flash it much. "I think you understand it more than sort of."

"More than sort of," Chrissie agreed. "It'd sure be nice if it was aliens, because we'd just have to find their nest or their hive or whatever, burn them out real good, maybe blow up their spaceship, and it would be over and done with. But if it's not aliens, if it's us—people like us—who did all this, then maybe it's never quite over and done with."

chapter thirty

With increasing frustration, Loman Watkins cruised from one end of Moonlight Cove to the other, back and forth, around and around in the rain, seeking Shaddack. He had revisited the house on the north point to be sure Shaddack had not returned there, and also to check the garage to see which vehicle was missing. Now he was looking for Shaddack's charcoal-gray van with tinted windows, but he was unable to locate it.

Wherever he went, conversion teams and search parties were at work. Though the unconverted were not likely to notice anything too unusual about those men's passage through town, Loman was constantly aware of them.

At the north and south roadblocks on the county route and at the main blockade on the eastern end of Ocean Avenue, out toward the interstate, Loman's officers were continuing to deal with outsiders wanting to enter Moonlight Cove. Exhaust plumes rose from the idling patrol cars, mingling with the wisps of fog that had begun to slither through the rain. The red and blue emergency beacons were reflected in the wet macadam, so it seemed as if streams of blood, oxygenated and oxygen-depleted, flowed along the pavement.

There weren't many would-be visitors because the town was neither the county seat nor a primary shopping center for people in outlying communities. Furthermore, it was close to the end of the county road, and there were no destinations beyond it, so no one wanted to pass through on the way to somewhere else. Those who did want to come into town were turned away, if at all possible, with a story about a toxic spill at New Wave. Those who seemed at all skeptical were arrested, conveyed to the jail, and locked in cells until a decision could be made either to kill or convert them. Since the establishment of the quarantine in the early hours of the morning, only a score of people had been stopped at the blockades, and only six had been jailed.

Shaddack had chosen his proving ground well. Moonlight Cove was relatively isolated and therefore easier to control.

Loman was of a mind to order the roadblocks dismantled, and to drive over to Aberdeen Wells, where he could spill the whole story to the county sheriff. He wanted to blow the Moonhawk Project wide open.

He was no longer afraid of Shaddack's rage or of dying. Well . . . not true. He was afraid of Shaddack and of death, but they held less fear for him than the prospect of becoming something like Denny had become. He would have as soon entrusted himself to the mercies of the sheriff in Aberdeen and the federal authorities—even scientists who, cleaning up the mess in Moonlight Cove, might be sorely tempted to dissect him—than stay in town and inevitably surrender the last few fragments of his humanity either to regression or to some nightmare wedding of his body and mind with a computer.

But if he ordered his officers to stand down, they would be suspicious, and their loyalty lay more with Shaddack than with him, for they were bound to Shaddack by terror. They were still more frightened of their New Wave master than of anything else, for they had not seen what Denny had become and did not yet realize that their future might hold in store something even worse than regression to a savage state. Like Moreau's beastmen, they kept the Law as best they could, not daring—at least for now—to betray their maker. They would probably try to stop Loman from sabotaging the Moonhawk Project, and he might wind up dead or, worse, locked in a jail cell.

He couldn't risk revealing his counterrevolutionary commitment, for then he might never have a chance to deal with Shaddack. In his mind's eye he saw himself caged at the jail, with Shaddack smiling coldly at him through the bars, as they wheeled in a computer with which they somehow intended to fuse him.

Molten silver eyes . . .

He kept on the move in the rain-hammered day, squinting through the streaked windshield. The wipers thumped steadily, as though ticking off time. He was acutely aware that midnight was drawing nearer.

He was the puma-man, on the prowl, and Moreau was out there in the island jungle that was Moonlight Cove.

chapter thirty-one

Initially the protean creature was content to feed on the things it found when it extended thin tendrils of itself down the drain in the cellar floor or through fine cracks in the walls and into the moist surrounding earth. Beetles. Grubs. Earthworms. It no longer knew the names of those things, but it avidly consumed them.

Soon, however, it depleted the supply of insects and worms within ten yards of the house. It needed a more substantial meal.

It churned, seethed, perhaps striving to marshal its amorphous tissues into a shape in which it could leave the cellar and seek prey. But it had no memory of previous forms and no desire whatsoever to impose structural order on itself.

The consciousness that inhabited that jellid mass no longer had more than the dimmest sense of self-awareness, yet it was still able to remake itself to an extent that would satisfy its needs. Suddenly a score of lipless, toothless mouths opened in that fluid form. A blast of sound, mostly beyond the range of human hearing, erupted from it.

Throughout the moldering structure above the shapeless beast, dozens of mice were scurrying, nibbling at food, nest-building, and grooming themselves. They stopped, as one, when the call blared up from the cellar.

The creature could sense them above, in the crumbling walls, though it thought of them not as mice but as small warm masses of living flesh. Food. Fuel. It wanted them. It *needed* them.

It attempted to express that need in the form of a wordless but compelling summons.

In every corner of the house, mice twitched. They brushed at their faces with forepaws, as if they'd scurried through cobwebs and were trying to scrape those clingy, gossamer strands out of their fur.

A small colony of eight bats lived in the attic, and they also reacted to the urgent call. They dropped from the rafters on which they hung, and flew in frenzied, random patterns in the long upper room, repeat-

edly swooping within a fraction of an inch of the walls and one another.

But nothing came to the creature in the basement. Though the call
had reached the small animals for which it had been intended, it did
not have the desired effect.

The shapeless thing fell silent.

Its many mouths closed.

One by one the bats returned to their perches in the attic.

The mice sat as if in shock for a moment, then resumed their usual
activities.

A couple of minutes later, the protean beast tried again with a different pattern of sounds, still pitched beyond human hearing but more
alluring than before.

The bats flung themselves from their perches and roiled through the
attic in such turmoil that an observer might have thought they num-
bered a hundred instead of only eight. The beating of their wings was
louder than the rush of rain on the leaky roof.

Everywhere, mice rose on their hind feet, sitting at attention, ears
pricked. Those in the lower reaches of the house, nearer the source of the
summons, shivered violently, as though they saw before them a crouched
and grinning cat.

Screeching, the bats swooped through a hole in the attic floor, into
an empty room on the second story, where they circled and soared and
dove ceaselessly.

Two mice on the ground floor began to creep toward the kitchen,
where the door to the basement stood open. But both stopped on the
threshold of that room, frightened and confused.

Below, the shapeless entity tripled the power of its call.

One of the mice in the kitchen suddenly bled from the ears and fell
dead.

Upstairs, the bats began to bounce off walls, their radar shot.

The cellar dweller cut back somewhat on the force of its summons.

The bats immediately swooped out of the upstairs room, into the
hallway, down the stairwell, and along the ground-floor hall. As they
went, they flew over a double score of scurrying mice.

Below, the creature's many mouths had connected, forming one
large orifice in the center of the pulsing mass.

In swift succession the bats flew straight into that gaping maw like
black playing cards being tossed one at a time into a waste can. They
embedded themselves in the oozing protoplasm and were swiftly dissolved by powerful digestive acids.

An army of mice and four rats—even two chipmunks that eagerly abandoned their nest inside the dining-room wall—swarmed down the steep cellar steps, falling over one another, squeaking excitedly. They fed themselves to the waiting entity.

After that flurry of movement, the house was still.

The creature stopped its siren song. For the moment.

chapter thirty-two

Officer Neil Penniworth was assigned to patrol the northwest quadrant of Moonlight Cove. He was alone in the car because even with the hundred New Wave employees detailed to the police department during the night, their manpower was stretched thin.

Right now, he preferred to work without a partner. Since the episode at Peyser's house, when the smell of blood and the sight of Peyser's altered form had enticed Penniworth to regress, he had been afraid to be around other people. He had avoided total degeneration last night . . . but only by the thinnest of margins. If he witnessed someone else in the act of regression, the urge might stir within him, too, and this time he was not sure that he could successfully repress that dark yearning.

He was equally afraid to be alone. The struggle to hold fast to his remaining shreds of humanity, to resist chaos, to be responsible, was wearying, and he longed to escape this new, hard life. Alone, with no one to see him if he began to surrender the very form and substance of himself, with no one to talk him out of it or even to protest his degeneration, he would be lost.

The weight of his fear was as real as a slab of iron, crushing the life out of him. At times he had difficulty drawing breath, as though his lungs were banded by steel and restricted from full expansion.

The dimensions of the black-and-white seemed to shrink, until he felt almost as confined as he would have been in a straitjacket. The metronomic thump of the windshield wipers grew louder, at least to his ears, until the volume was as thunderous as an endless series of cannon volleys. Repeatedly during the morning and early afternoon, he pulled off the road, flung open the door, and scrambled out into the rain, drawing deep breaths of the cool air.

As the day progressed, however, even the world outside of the car began to seem smaller than it had been. He stopped on Holliwell Road, half a mile west of New Wave's headquarters, and got out of the cruiser, but he felt no better. The low roof of gray clouds denied him the sight of the limitless sky. Like semitransparent curtains of tinsel and thinnest silk, the rain and fog hung between him and the rest of the world. The humidity was cloying, stifling. Rain overflowed gutters, churned in muddy torrents through roadside ditches, dripped from every branch and leaf of every tree, pattered on the macadam pavement, tapped hollowly on the patrol car, sizzled, gurgled, chuckled, snapped against his face, beat upon him with such force that it seemed he was being driven to his knees by thousands of tiny hammers, each too small to be effective in itself but with brutal cumulative effect.

Neil clambered back into the car with as much eagerness as he had scrambled out of it.

He understood that it was neither the claustrophobic interior of the cruiser nor the enervating enwrapment of the rain that he was desperately trying to escape. The actual oppressor was his life as a New Person. Able to feel only fear, he was locked in an emotional closet of such unendurably narrow dimensions that he could not move at all. He was not suffocating because of external entanglements and constrictions; rather, he was bound from within, because of what Shaddack had made of him.

Which meant there was no escape.

Except, perhaps, by regression.

Neil could not bear life as he must now live it. On the other hand he was repelled and terrified by the thought of devolution into some subhuman form.

His dilemma appeared irresoluble.

He was as distressed by his inability to stop thinking about his predicament as he was by the predicament itself. It pried constantly at his mind. He could find no surcease.

The closest he came to being able to put his worry—and some of his fear—out of mind was when he was working with the mobile VDT in the patrol car. When he checked the computer bulletin board to see if messages awaited him, when he accessed the Moonhawk schedule to learn how conversions were progressing, or undertook any other task with the computer, his attention became so focused on the interaction with the machine that briefly his anxiety subsided and his nagging claustrophobia faded.

From adolescence, Neil had been interested in computers, though he had never become a hacker. His interest was less obsessive than that. He'd started with computer games, of course, but later had been given an inexpensive PC. Later still he had bought a modem with some of the money earned at a summer job. Though he could not afford much long-distance telephone time and never spent leisurely hours using the modem to reach far from the backwaters of Moonlight Cove into the fascinating data nets available in the outside world, he found his forays into online systems engrossing and fun.

Now, as he sat in the parked car along Holliwell Road, using the VDT, he thought that the inner world of the computer was admirably clean, comparatively simple, predictable, and sane. So unlike human existence—whether that of New People or Old. In there, logic and reason ruled. Cause and effect and side-effect were always analyzed and made perfectly clear. In there, all was black and white—or, when gray, the gray was carefully measured, quantified and qualified. Cold facts were easier to deal with than feelings. A universe formed purely of data, abstracted from matter and event, seemed so much more desirable than the real universe of cold and heat, sharp and blunt, smooth and rough, blood and death, pain and fear.

Calling up menu after menu, Neil probed ever deeper into the Moonhawk research files within Sun. He needed none of the data that he summoned forth but found solace in the process of obtaining it.

He began to see the terminal screen not as a cathode-ray tube on which information was displayed, but as a window into another world. A world of facts. A world free of troubling contradictions . . . and responsibility. In there, nothing could be felt; there was only the known and the unknown, either an abundance of facts about a particular subject or a dearth of them, but not *feeling*; never feeling; feeling was the curse of those whose existence was dependent upon flesh and bone.

A window into another world.

Neil touched the screen.

He wished the window could be opened and that he could climb through it to that place of reason, order, peace.

With the fingertips of his right hand, he traced circles across the warm glass screen.

Strangely, he thought of Dorothy, swept up from the plains of Kansas with her dog Toto, spun high into the tornado, and dropped out of that depression-era grayness into a world far more intriguing. If only some electronic tornado could erupt from the VDT and carry him to a better place . . .

His fingers passed through the screen.

He snatched his hand back in astonishment.

The glass had not ruptured. Chains of words and numbers glowed on the tube, as before.

At first he tried to convince himself that what he had seen had been a hallucination. But he did not believe that.

He flexed his fingers. They appeared unhurt.

He looked out at the storm-swept day. The windshield wipers were not switched on. Rain rippled down the glass, distorting the world beyond; everything out there looked twisted, mutated, strange. There could never be order, sanity, and peace in such a place as that.

Tentatively he touched the computer screen once more. It felt solid.

Again, he thought of how desirable the clean, predictable world of the computer would be—and as before his hand slipped through the glass, up to the wrist this time. The screen had opened around him and sealed tight to him, as if it were an organic membrane. The data continued to blaze on the tube, the words and numbers forming lines around his intruding hand.

His heart was racing. He was afraid but also excited.

He tried to wiggle his fingers in that mysterious, inner warmth. He could not feel them. He began to think they had dissolved or been cut off, and that when he withdrew his hand from the machine, the stump of his wrist would spout blood.

He withdrew it anyway.

His hand was whole.

But it was not quite a hand any more. The flesh on the upper side, from the tips of his fingernails to his wrist, appeared to be veined with copper and threads of glass. In those glass filaments beat a steady and luminous pulse.

He turned his hand over. The undersides of his fingers and his palm resembled the surface of a cathode-ray tube. Data burned there, green letters on a background glassy and dark. When he compared the words and numbers on his hand to those on the car's VDT, he saw they were identical. The information on the VDT changed; simultaneously, so did that on his hand.

Abruptly, he understood that regression into bestial form was not the only avenue of escape open to him, that he could enter into the world of electronic thought and magnetic memory, of knowledge without fleshly desire, of awareness without feeling. This was not an insight strictly—or even primarily—intellectual in nature. It wasn't just instinctive understanding, either. On some level more profound than either intellect or instinct, he knew that he could remake himself more thoroughly than even Shaddack had remade him.

He lowered his hand from the tilted computer screen to the data-processing unit in the console between the seats. As easily as he had penetrated the glass, he let his hand slide through the keyboard and cover plate, into the guts of the machine.

He was like a ghost, able to pass through walls, ectoplasmic.

A coldness crept up his arm.

The data on the screen was replaced by cryptic patterns of light.

He leaned back in his seat.

The coldness had reached his shoulder. It flowed into his neck.

He sighed.

He felt something happening to his eyes. He wasn't sure what. He could have looked at the rearview mirror. He didn't care. He decided to close his eyes and let them become whatever was necessary as part of this second and more complete conversion.

This altered state was infinitely more appealing than that of the regressive. Irresistible.

The coldness was in his face now. His mouth was numb.

Something also was happening inside his head. He was becoming as aware of the inner geography of his brain circuits and synapses as he was of the exterior world. His body was not as much a part of him as it had once been; he sensed less through it, as if his nerves had been mostly abraded away; he could not even tell if it was warm or chilly in the car unless he concentrated on accumulating that data. His body was just a machine casing, after all, and a rack for sensors, designed to protect and serve the inner him, the calculating mind.

The coldness was inside his skull.

It felt like scores, then hundreds, then thousands of ice-cold spiders scurrying over the surface of his brain, burrowing into it.

Suddenly he remembered that Dorothy had found Oz to be a living nightmare and ultimately had wanted desperately to find her way back to Kansas. Alice, too, had found madness and terror down the rabbit hole, beyond the looking-glass. . . .

A million cold spiders.

Inside his skull.

A billion.

Cold, cold.

Scurrying.

chapter thirty-three

Still circling through Moonlight Cove, seeking Shaddack, Loman saw two regressives sprint across the street.

He was on Paddock Lane, at the southern end of town, where the properties were big enough for people to keep horses. Ranch houses lay on both sides, with small private stables beside or behind them. The homes set back from the street, behind split-rail or white ranch fencing, beyond deep and lushly landscaped lawns.

The pair of regressives erupted from a dense row of mature three-foot-high azaleas that were still bushy but flowerless this late in the season. They streaked on all fours across the roadway, leaped a ditch, and crashed through a hedgerow, vanishing behind it.

Although immense pines were lined up along both sides of Paddock Lane, adding their shadows to the already darkish day, Loman was sure of what he had seen. They had been modeled after dream creatures rather than any single animal of the real world: part wolf, perhaps, part cat, part reptile. They were swift and looked powerful. One of them had turned its head toward him, and in the shadows its eyes had glowed as pink-red as those of a rat.

He slowed but did not stop. He no longer cared about identifying and apprehending regressives. For one thing, he'd already identified them to his satisfaction: all of the converted. He knew that stopping them could be accomplished only by stopping Shaddack. He was after much bigger game.

However, he was unnerved to see them brazenly on the prowl in daylight, at two-thirty in the afternoon. Heretofore, they had been secretive creatures of the night, hiding the shame of their regression by seeking their altered states only well after sunset. If they were prepared to venture forth before nightfall, the Moonhawk Project was disintegrating into chaos even faster than he had expected. Moonlight Cove was not merely teetering on the brink of hell but had already tipped over the edge and into the pit.

chapter thirty-four

They were in Harry's third-floor bedroom again, where they had passed the last hour and a half, brainstorming and urgently discussing their options. No lamps were on. Watery afternoon light washed the room, contributing to the somber mood.

"So we're agreed there are two ways we might send a message out of town," Sam said.

"But in either case," Tessa said uneasily, "you have to go out there and cover a lot of ground to get where you need to go."

Sam shrugged.

Tessa and Chrissie had taken off their shoes and sat on the bed, their backs against the headboard. The girl clearly intended to stay close to Tessa; she seemed to have imprinted on her the way a baby chick, freshly hatched from the egg, imprints on the nearest adult bird, whether it's the mother or not.

Tessa said, "It's not going to be as easy as slipping two doors south to the Coltrane house. Not in daylight."

"You think I ought to wait until it gets dark?" Sam asked.

"Yes. The fog will come in more heavily, too, as the afternoon fades."

She meant what she said, though she was worried about the delay. During the hours that they bided their time, more people would be converted. Moonlight Cove would become an increasingly alien, dangerous, and surprise-filled environment.

Turning to Harry, Sam said, "What time's it get dark?"

Harry was in his wheelchair. Moose had returned to his master, thrusting his burly head under the arm of the chair and onto Harry's lap, content to sit for long stretches in that awkward posture in return for just a little petting and scratching and an occasional reassuring word.

Harry said, "These days, twilight comes before six o'clock."

Sam was sitting at the telescope, though at the moment he was not using it. A few minutes ago he had surveyed the streets and reported seeing more activity than earlier—plenty of car and foot patrols. As steadily fewer local residents remained unconverted, the conspirators behind Moonhawk were growing bolder in their policing actions, less concerned than they'd once been about calling attention to themselves.

Glancing at his watch, Sam said, "I can't say I like the idea of wasting three hours or more. The sooner we get the word out, the more people we'll save from . . . from whatever's being done to them."

"But if you get caught because you didn't wait for nightfall," Tessa said, "then the chances of saving *anyone* become a hell of a lot slimmer."

"The lady has a point," Harry said.

"A good one," Chrissie said. "Just because they're not aliens doesn't mean they're going to be any easier to deal with."

Because even the working telephones would allow a caller to dial only approved numbers within town, they'd given up on that hope. But Sam had realized that any PC connected by modem with the supercomputer at New Wave—Harry said they called it Sun—might provide a way out of town, an electronic highway on which they could circumvent the current restrictions on the phone lines and the roadblocks.

As Sam had noted last night while using the VDT in the police car, Sun maintained direct contacts with scores of other computers—including several FBI data banks, both those approved for wide access and those supposedly sealed to all but Bureau agents. If he could sit at a VDT, link in to Sun, and through Sun link to a Bureau computer, then he could transmit a call for help that would appear on Bureau computer screens and spew out in hard copy from the laser printers in their offices.

They were assuming, of course, that the restrictions on outside contact that applied to all other phone lines in town did *not* apply to the lines by which Sun maintained its linkages with the broader world. If Sun's routes out of Moonlight Cove were clipped off, too, they were utterly without hope.

Understandably, Sam was reluctant to enter the houses of those who worked for New Wave, afraid that he would encounter more people like the Coltranes. That left only two ways to attain access to a PC that could be linked to Sun.

First, he could try to get into a black-and-white and use one of their mobile terminals, as he'd done last night. But they were alert to his presence now, making it harder to sneak into an unused patrol car. Furthermore, all of the cars were probably now in use, as the cops searched diligently for him and, no doubt, for Tessa as well. And even if a cruiser were parked behind the municipal building, that area was at the moment bound to be a lot busier than the last time he had been there.

Second, they could use the computers at the high school on Roshmore Way. New Wave had donated them not out of a noble concern for the educational quality of local schools but as one more means of tying the community to it. Sam believed, and Tessa agreed, that the school's terminals probably had the capacity to link with Sun.

But Moonlight Cove Central, as the combination junior-senior high was called, stood on the west side of Roshmore Way, two blocks west of Harry's house and a full block south. In ordinary times it was a pleasant five-minute walk. But with the streets under surveillance and every house potentially a watchtower occupied by enemies, reaching Central School now without being seen was about as easy as crossing a minefield.

"Besides," Chrissie said, "they're still in class at Central. You couldn't just walk in there and use a computer."

"Especially," Tessa said, "since you can figure the teachers were among the first converted."

"What time are classes over?" Sam asked.

"Well, at Thomas Jefferson we get out at three o'clock, but they go an extra half hour at Central."

"Three-thirty," Sam said.

Checking his watch, Harry said, "Forty-seven minutes yet. But even then, there'll be after-school activities, won't there?"

"Sure," Chrissie said. "Band, probably football practice, a few other clubs that don't meet during regular activity period."

"What time would all that be done with?"

"I know band practice is from a quarter to four till a quarter to five," Chrissie said, "because I'm friends with a kid one year older than me who's in the band. I play a clarinet. I want to be in the band, too, next year. If there is a band. If there is a next year."

"So, say . . . by five o'clock the place is cleared out."

"Football practice runs later than that."

"Would they practice today, in pouring rain?"

"I guess not."

"If you're going to wait until five or five-thirty," Tessa said, "then you might as well wait just a little while longer and head down there after dark."

Sam nodded. "I guess so."

"Sam, you're forgetting," Harry said.

"What?"

"Sometime shortly after you leave here, maybe as early as six o'clock sharp, they'll be coming to convert me."

"Jesus, that's right!" Sam said.

Moose slipped his head off his master's lap and from beneath the arm of the wheelchair. He sat erect, black ears pricked, as if he understood what had been said and was already anticipating the doorbell or listening for a knock downstairs.

"I believe you *do* have to wait for nightfall before you go, to have a better chance," Harry said, "but then you'll have to take Tessa and Chrissie with you. It won't be safe to leave them here."

"We'll have to take you too," Chrissie said at once. "You and Moose. I don't know if they convert dogs, but we have to take Moose just to be sure. We wouldn't want to have to worry about him being turned into a machine or something."

Moose chuffed.

"Can he be trusted not to bark?" Chrissie asked. "We wouldn't want him to yap at something at a crucial moment. I guess we could always wind a long strip of gauze bandage around his snout, muzzle him, which is sort of cruel and would probably hurt his feelings, since muzzling him would mean we don't entirely trust him, but it wouldn't hurt him physically, of course, and I'm sure we could make it up to him later with a juicy steak or—"

Suddenly recognizing an unusual solemnity in the silence of her companions, the girl fell silent too. She blinked at Harry, at Sam, and frowned at Tessa, who still sat on the bed beside her.

Darker clouds had begun to plate the sky since they had come upstairs, and the room was receding deeper into shadows. But at the moment Tessa could see Harry Talbot's face almost too clearly in the gray dimness. She was aware of how he was striving to conceal his fear, succeeding for the most part, managing a genuine smile and an unruffled tone of voice, betrayed only by his expressive eyes.

To Chrissie, Harry said, "I won't be going with you, honey."

"Oh," the girl said. She looked at him again, her gaze slipping down from Harry to the wheelchair on which he sat. "But you came to our school that day to talk to us. You leave the house sometimes. You must have a way to get out."

Harry smiled. "The elevator goes down to the garage on the cellar level. I don't drive any more, so there's no car down there, and I can easily roll out into the driveway, to the sidewalk."

"Well, then!" Chrissie said.

Harry looked at Sam and said, "But I can't go anywhere on these streets, steep as they are in some places, without someone along. The chair has brakes, and the motor has quite a lot of pull, but half the time not enough for these slopes."

"We'll be with you," Chrissie said earnestly. "We can help."

"Dear girl, you can't sneak quickly through three blocks of occupied territory and drag me with you at the same time," Harry said firmly. "For one thing, you'll have to stay off the streets as much as possible, move from yard to yard and between houses as much as you can, while I can only roll on pavement, especially in this weather, with the ground so soggy."

"We can carry you."

"No," Sam said. "We can't. Not if we hope to get to the school and get a message out to the Bureau. It's a short distance but full of danger, and we've got to travel light. Sorry, Harry."

"No need to apologize," Harry said. "I wouldn't have it any other way. You think I want to be dragged or shoulder-carried like a bag of cement across half the town?"

In obvious distress, Chrissie got off the bed and stood with her small hands fisted at her sides. She looked from Tessa to Sam to Tessa again, silently pleading with them to think of a way to save Harry.

Outside the gray sky was mottled now with ugly clouds that were nearly black.

The rain eased up, but Tessa sensed that they were entering a brief lull, after which the downpour would continue with greater force than ever.

Both the spiritual and the physical gloom deepened.

Moose whined softly.

Tears shimmered in Chrissie's eyes, and she seemed unable to bear looking at Harry. She went to a north window and stared down at the house next door and at the street beyond—staying just far enough back from the glass to avoid being spotted by anyone outside.

Tessa wanted to comfort her.

She wanted to comfort Harry too.

More than that . . . she wanted to make everything *right*.

As writer-producer-director, she was a mover and shaker, good at taking charge, making things happen. She always knew how to solve a problem, what to do in a crisis, how to keep the cameras rolling once a project had begun. But now she was at a loss. She could not always script reality with the assurance she brought to the writing of her films; sometimes the real world resisted conforming to her demands. Maybe that was why she had chosen a career over a family, even after having enjoyed a wonderful family atmosphere as a child. The real world of daily life and struggle was sloppy, unpredictable, full of loose ends; she couldn't count on being able to tie it all up the way she could when she took aspects of it and reduced them to a neatly structured film. Life was life, broad and rich . . . but film was only essences. Maybe she dealt better with essences than with life in all its gaudy detail.

Her genetically received Lockland optimism, previously as bright as a spotlight, had not deserted her, though it definitely had dimmed for the time being.

Harry said, "It's going to be all right."

"How?" Sam asked.

"I'm probably last on their list," Harry said. "They wouldn't be worried about cripples and blind people. Even if we learn something's up, we can't try to get out of town and get help. Mrs. Sagerian—she lives over on Pinecrest—she's blind, and I'll bet she and I are the last two on the schedule. They'll wait to do us until near midnight. You see if they don't. Bet on it. So what you've got to do is go to the high school and get through to the Bureau, bring help in here pronto, before midnight comes, and then I'll be all right."

Chrissie turned away from the window, her cheeks wet with tears. "You really think so, Mr. Talbot? You really, honestly think they won't come here until midnight?"

With his head tilted to one side in a perpetual twist that was, depending on how you looked at it, either jaunty or heart-wrenching, Harry winked at the girl, though she was farther away from him than Tessa and probably didn't see the wink. "If I'm jiving you, honey, may God strike me with lightning this instant."

Rain fell but no lightning struck.

"See?" Harry said, grinning.

Though the girl clearly wanted to believe the scenario that Harry had painted for her, Tessa knew that they could not count on his being the last or next to last on the final conversion schedule. What he'd said made a little sense, actually, but it was just too neat. Like a narrative development in a film script. Real life, as she had just reminded herself, was sloppy, unpredictable. She desperately wanted to believe that Harry would be safe until a few minutes till midnight, but the reality was that he would be at extreme risk as soon as the clock struck six and the final series of conversions was under way.

chapter thirty-five

Shaddack remained in Paula Parkins's garage through most of the afternoon.

Twice he put up the big door, switched on the van's engine, and pulled into the driveway to better monitor Moonhawk's progress on the VDT. Both times, satisfied with the data, he rolled back into the garage and lowered the door again.

The mechanism was clicking away. He had designed it, built it, wound it up, and pushed the start button. Now it could go through its paces without him.

He passed the hours sitting behind the wheel, daydreaming about the time when the final stage of Moonhawk would be completed and all the world would be brought into the fold. When no Old People existed, he would have redefined the word "power," for no man before him in all of history would have known such total control. Having remade the species, he could then program its destiny to his own desires. All of humankind would be one great hive, buzzing industriously, serving his vision. As he daydreamed, his erection grew so hard that it began to ache dully.

Shaddack knew many scientists who genuinely seemed to believe that the purpose of technological progress was to improve the lot of humanity, lift the species up from the mud and carry it, eventually, to the stars. He saw things differently. To his way of thinking, the sole purpose of technology was to concentrate power in his hands. Previous would-be remakers of the world had relied on political power, which always ultimately meant the power of the legal gun. Hitler, Stalin, Mao, Pol Pot, and others had sought power through intimidation and mass murder, wading to the throne through lakes of blood, and all of them had ultimately failed to achieve what silicon circuitry was in the process of bestowing upon Shaddack. The pen was not mightier than the sword, but the microprocessor was mightier than vast armies.

If they knew what he had undertaken and what dreams of conquest still preoccupied him, virtually all other men of science would say that he was bent, sick, deranged. He didn't care. They were wrong, of course. Because they didn't realize who he was. The child of the moonhawk. He had destroyed those who had posed as his parents, and he had not been discovered or punished, which was proof that the rules and laws governing other men were not meant to apply to him. His *true* mother and father were spirit forces, disembodied, powerful. They had protected him from punishment because the murders that he'd committed in Phoenix so long ago were a sacred offering to his real progenitors, a statement of his faith and trust in them. Other scientists would misunderstand him because they could not know that all of existence centered around him, that the universe itself existed only because *he* existed, and that if he ever died—which was unlikely—then the universe would simultaneously cease to exist. He was the center of creation. He was the only man who mattered. The great spirits had told him this. The great spirits had whispered these truths in his ear, waking and sleeping, for more than thirty years.

Child of the moonhawk . . .

As the afternoon waned, he became ever more excited about the approaching completion of the first stage of the project, and he could no longer endure temporary exile in the Parkins garage. Though it had seemed wise to absent himself from places in which Loman Watkins might find him, he was having increasing difficulty justifying the need to hide out. Events at Mike Peyser's house last night no longer seemed so catastrophic to him, merely a minor setback; he was confident that the problem of the regressives would eventually be solved. His genius resulted from the direct line between him and higher spiritual forces, and no difficulty was beyond resolution when the great spirits desired his success. The threat he'd felt from Watkins steadily diminished in his memory, too, until the police chief's promise to find him seemed empty, even pathetic.

He was the child of the moonhawk. He was surprised that he had forgotten such an important truth and had run scared. Of course, even Jesus had spent his time in the garden, briefly frightened, and had wrestled with his demons. The Parkins garage was, Shaddack saw, his own Gethsemane, where he had taken refuge to cast out those last doubts that plagued him.

He was the child of the moonhawk.

At four-thirty he put up the garage door.

He started the van and pulled down the driveway.

He was the child of the moonhawk.

He turned onto the county road and headed toward town.

He was the child of the moonhawk, heir to the crown of light, and at midnight he would ascend the throne.

chapter thirty-six

Pack Martin—his name was actually Packard because his mother named him after a car that had been her father's pride—lived in a house trailer on the southeast edge of town. It was an old trailer, its enameled finish faded and crackled like the glaze on an ancient vase. It was rusted in a few spots, dented, and set on a concrete-block foundation in a lot that was mostly weeds. Pack knew that many people in Moonlight Cove thought his place was an eyesore, but he just plain did not give a damn.

The trailer had electrical hookup, an oil furnace, and plumbing, which was enough to meet his needs. He was warm, dry, and had a place to keep his beer. It was a veritable palace.

Best of all, the trailer had been paid for twenty-five years ago, with money he had inherited from his mother, so no mortgage hung over him. He had a little of the inheritance left, too, and rarely touched the principal. The interest amounted to nearly three hundred dollars a month, and he also had his disability check, earned by virtue of a fall he had taken three weeks after being inducted into the Army. The only real work in which Pack had ever engaged was all the reading and studying he had done to learn and memorize all of the subtlest and most complex symptoms of serious back injury, before reporting per the instructions on his draft notice.

He was born to be a man of leisure. He had known that much about himself from a young age. Work and him had nothing for each other. He figured he'd been scheduled to be born into a wealthy family, but something had gotten screwed up and he'd wound up as the son of a waitress who'd been just sufficiently industrious to provide him with a minimum inheritance.

But he envied no one. Every month he bought twelve or fourteen cases of cheap beer at the discount store out on the highway, and he had his TV, and with a bologna and mustard sandwich now and then, maybe some Fritos, he was happy enough.

By four o'clock that Tuesday afternoon, Pack was well into his second six-pack of the day, slumped in his tattered armchair, watching a game show on which the prize girl's prime hooters, always revealed in low-cut dresses, were a lot more interesting than the MC, the contestants, or the questions.

The MC said, "So what's your choice? Do you want what's behind screen number one, screen number two, or screen number three?"

Talking back to the tube, Pack said, "I'll take what's in that cutie's Maidenform, thank you very much," and he swigged more beer.

Just then someone knocked on the door.

Pack did not get up or in any way acknowledge the knock. He had no friends, so visitors were of no interest to him. They were always either community do-gooders bringing him a box of food that he didn't want, or offering to cut down his weeds and clean up his property, which he didn't want, either, because he liked his weeds.

They knocked again.

Pack responded by turning up the volume on the TV.

They knocked harder.

"Go away," Pack said.

They really *pounded* on the door, shaking the whole damn trailer.

"What the hell?" Pack said. He clicked off the TV and got up.

The pounding was not repeated, but Pack heard a strange scraping noise against the side of the trailer.

And the place creaked on its foundation, which it sometimes did when the wind was blowing hard. Today, there was no wind.

"Kids," Pack decided.

The Aikhorn family, which lived on the other side of the county road and two hundred yards to the south, had kids so ornery they ought to have been put to sleep with injections, pickled in formaldehyde, and displayed in some museum of criminal behavior. Those brats got a kick out of pushing cherry bombs through chinks in the foundation blocks, under the trailer, waking him with a bang in the middle of the night.

The scraping at the side of the trailer stopped, but now a couple of kids were walking around on the roof.

That was too much. The metal roof didn't leak, but it had seen better days, and it was liable to bend or even separate at the seams under the weight of a couple of kids.

Pack opened the door and stepped out into the rain, shouting obscenities at them. But when he looked up, he didn't see any kids on the roof. What he saw, instead, was something out of a fifties bug movie, big as a man, with clacking mandibles and multifaceted eyes, and a mouth framed by small pincers. The weird thing was that he also saw a few features of a human face in that monstrous countenance, just enough so he thought he recognized Daryl Aikhorn, father of the brats.

"*Neeeeeeeeeed,*" it said, in a voice half Aikhorn's and half an insectile keening. It leaped at him, and as it came, a wickedly sharp stinger telescoped from its repulsive body. Even before that yard-long, serrated spear skewered his belly and thrust all the way through him, Pack knew that the days of beer and bologna sandwiches and Fritos and disability checks and game-show girls with perfect hooters were over.

•

Randy Hapgood, fourteen, sloshed through the dirty calf-deep water in an overflowing gutter and sneered contemptuously, as if to say that nature would have to come up with an obstacle a thousand times more formidable than that if she hoped to daunt him. He refused to wear a raincoat and galoshes because such gear was not fashionably cool. You didn't see rad blondes hanging on the arms of nerds who carried umbrellas, either. There were no rad girls hanging on Randy, as far as that went, but he figured they just hadn't yet noticed how cool he was, how indifferent to weather and everything else that humbled other guys.

He was soaked and miserable—but whistling jauntily to conceal it—when he got home from Central at twenty minutes till five, after band practice, which had been cut short because of the bad weather. He stripped out of his wet denim jacket and hung it on the back of the pantry door. He slipped out of his soggy tennis shoes, as well.

"I'm *heeeeerrreeeee,*" he shouted, parodying the little girl in *Poltergeist.*

No one answered him.

He knew his parents were home, because lights were on, and the door was unlocked. Lately they'd been working at home more and more. They were in some sort of product research at New Wave, and they were able to put in a full day on their dual terminals upstairs, in the back room, without actually going in to the office.

Randy got a Coke out of the refrigerator, popped the tab, took a swig, and headed upstairs to dry out while he told Pete and Marsha about his day. He didn't call them Mom and Dad, and that was all right with them; they were cool. Sometimes he thought they were even too cool. They drove a Porsche, and their clothes were always six months ahead of what everyone else was wearing, and they'd talk about anything with him, *anything*, including sex, as frankly as if they were his pals. If he ever *did* find a rad blonde who wanted to hang on him, he'd be afraid to bring her home to meet his folks, for fear she'd think his dad was infinitely cooler than he was. Sometimes he wished Pete and Marsha were fat, frumpy, dressed out of date, and stuffily insisted on being called Mom and Dad. Competition in school for grades and popularity was fierce enough without having to feel that he was also in competition at home with his parents.

As he reached the top of the stairs, he called out again, "In the immortal words of the modern American intellectual, John Rambo: 'Yo!'"

They still didn't answer him.

Just as Randy reached the open door to the workroom at the back of the hall, a case of the creeps hit him. He shivered and frowned but didn't stop, however, because his self-image of ultimate coolth did not allow him to be spooked.

He stepped across the threshold, ready with a wisecrack about their failure to respond to his calls. Too late, he was flash-frozen in place by fear.

Pete and Marsha were sitting on opposite sides of the large worktable, where their computer terminals stood back to back. No, they were not exactly sitting there; they were wired into the chairs and the computers by scores of hideous, segmented cables that grew out of them— or out of the machine; it was hard to tell which—and not only anchored them to their computers but to their chairs and, finally, to the floor, into which the cables disappeared. Their faces were still vaguely recognizable, though wildly altered, half pale flesh and half metal, with a slightly melted look.

Randy could not breathe.

But abruptly he could move, and he scrambled backward.

The door slammed behind him.

He whirled.

Tentacles—half organic, half metallic—erupted from the wall. The entire room seemed weirdly, malevolently alive, or maybe the walls were filled with alien machinery. The tentacles were quick. They lashed around him, pinned his arms, thoroughly snared him, and turned him toward his parents.

They were still in their chairs but were no longer facing their computers. They stared at him with radiant green eyes that appeared to be boiling in their sockets, bubbling and churning.

Randy screamed. He thrashed, but the tentacles held him.

Pete opened his mouth, and half a dozen silvery spheres, like large ball bearings, shot from him and struck Randy in the chest.

Pain exploded through the boy. But it didn't last more than a couple of seconds. Instead, the hot pain became an icy-cold, crawling sensation that worked through his entire body and up into his face.

He tried to scream again. No sound escaped him.

The tentacles shrank back into the wall, pulling him with them, until his back was pinned tightly against the plaster.

The coldness was in his head now. Crawling, crawling.

Again, he tried to scream. This time a sound came from him. A thin, electronic oscillation.

•

Tuesday afternoon, wearing warm wool slacks and a sweatshirt and a cardigan over the sweatshirt because she found it hard to stay warm these days, Meg Henderson sat at the kitchen table by the window, with a glass of chenin blanc, a plate of onion crackers, a wedge of Gouda, and a Nero Wolfe novel by Rex Stout. She had read all of the Wolfe novels ages ago, but she was rereading them. Returning to old novels was comforting because the people in them never changed. Wolfe was still a genius and gourmet. Archie was still a man of action. Fritz still ran the best private kitchen in the world. None of them had aged since last she'd met them, either, which was a trick she wished she had learned.

Meg was eighty years old, and she looked eighty, every minute of it; she didn't kid herself. Occasionally, when she saw herself in a mirror, she stared in amazement, as if she had not lived with that face for the better part of a century and was looking at a stranger. Somehow she expected to see a reflection of her youth because inside she was still that girl. Fortunately she didn't *feel* eighty. Her bones were creaky, and her muscles had about as much tone as those of Jabba the Hut in the third *Star Wars* movie she'd watched on the VCR last week, but she was free of arthritis and other major complaints, thank God. She still lived in her bungalow on Concord Circle, an odd little half-moon street that began and ended from Serra Avenue on the east end of town. She and Frank had bought the place forty years ago, when they had both been teachers at Thomas Jefferson School, in the days when it had been a combined school for all grades. Moonlight Cove had been much smaller then. For fourteen years, since Frank died, she had lived in the bungalow alone. She could get around, clean, and cook for herself, for which she was grateful.

She was even more grateful for her mental acuity. More than physical infirmity, she dreaded senility or a stroke that, while leaving her physically functional, would steal her memory and alter her personality. She tried to keep her mind flexible by reading a lot of books of all different kinds, by renting a variety of videos for her VCR, and by avoiding at all costs the mind-numbing slop that passed for entertainment on television.

By four-thirty Tuesday afternoon, she was halfway through the novel, though she paused at the end of each chapter to look out at the rain. She liked rain. She liked whatever weather God chose to throw at

the world—storms, hail, wind, cold, heat—because the variety and extremes of creation were what made it so beautiful.

While looking at the rain, which earlier had declined from a fierce
downpour to a drizzle but was once more falling furiously, she saw
three large, dark, and utterly fantastic creatures appear out of the stand
of trees at the rear of her property, fifty feet from the window at which
she sat. They halted for a moment as a thin mist eddied around their
feet, as if they were dream monsters that had taken shape from those
scraps of fog and might melt away as suddenly as they had arisen. But
then they raced toward her back porch.

As they drew swiftly nearer, Meg's first impression of them was reinforced. They were like nothing on this earth . . . unless perhaps gargoyles could come alive and climb down from cathedral roofs.

She knew at once that she must be in the early stages of a truly
massive stroke, because that was what she had always feared would at
last claim her. But she was surprised that it would begin like this, with
such a weird hallucination.

That was all it could be, of course—hallucination preceding the
bursting of a cerebral blood vessel that must be already swelling and
pressing on her brain. She waited for a painful exploding sensation
inside her head, waited for her face and body to twist to the left or right
as one side or the other was paralyzed.

Even when the first of the gargoyles crashed through the window,
showering the table with glass, spilling the chenin blanc, knocking Meg
off her chair, and falling to the floor atop her, all teeth and claws, she
marveled that a stroke could produce such vivid, convincing illusions,
though she was not surprised by the intensity of the pain. She'd always
known that death would hurt.

•

Dora Hankins, the receptionist in the main lobby at New Wave, was
accustomed to seeing people leave work as early as four-thirty. Though
the official quitting time was five o'clock, a lot of workers put in hours
at home, on their own PCs, so no one strictly enforced the eight-hour
office day. Since they'd been converted, there had been no need for
rules, anyway, because they were all working for the same goal, for the
new world that was coming, and the only discipline they needed was
their fear of Shaddack, of which they had plenty.

By 4:55, when no one at all had passed through the lobby, Dora
was apprehensive. The building was oddly silent, though hundreds of
people were working there in offices and labs farther back on the ground
floor and in the two floors overhead. In fact the place seemed deserted.

At five o'clock no one had yet left for the day, and Dora had decided to see what was going on. She abandoned her post at the main reception desk, walked to the end of the large marble lobby, through a brass door, into a less grand corridor floored with vinyl tile. Offices lay on both sides. She went into the first room on the left, where eight women served as a secretarial pool for minor department heads who had no personal secretaries of their own.

The eight were at their VDTs. In the fluorescent light, Dora had no trouble seeing how intimately flesh and machine had joined.

Fear was the only emotion Dora had felt in weeks. She thought she had known it in all its shades and degrees. But now it fell over her with greater force, darker and more intense, than anything she had experienced before.

A glistening probe erupted from the wall to Dora's right. It was more metallic than not, yet it dripped what appeared to be yellowish mucus. The thing shot straight to one of the secretaries and bloodlessly pierced the back of her head. From the top of one of the other women's heads, another probe erupted, rose like a snake to the music of a charmer's flute, hesitated, then with tremendous speed snapped to the ceiling, piercing the acoustic tile without disturbing it, and vanished toward rooms above.

Dora sensed that all of the computers and people of New Wave had somehow linked into a single entity and that the building itself was swiftly being incorporated into it. She wanted to run but couldn't move—maybe because she knew any escape attempt would prove futile.

A moment later they plugged her into the network.

•

Betsy Soldonna was carefully taping up a sign on the wall behind the front desk at the Moonlight Cove Town Library. It was part of Fascinating Fiction Week, a campaign to get kids to read more fiction.

She was the assistant librarian, but on Tuesdays, when her boss, Cora Danker, was off, Betsy worked alone. She liked Cora, but Betsy also liked being by herself. Cora was a talker, filling every free minute with gossip or her boring observations on the characters and plots of her favorite TV programs. Betsy, a lifelong bibliophile obsessed with books, would have been delighted to talk endlessly about what she'd read, but Cora, though head librarian, hardly read at all.

Betsy tore a fourth piece of Scotch tape off the dispenser and fixed the last corner of the poster to the wall. She stepped back to admire her work.

She had made the poster herself. She was proud of her modest artistic talent. In the drawing, a boy and a girl were holding books and staring bug-eyed at the open pages before them. Their hair was standing on end. The girl's eyebrows appeared to have jumped off her face, as had the boy's ears. Above them was the legend BOOKS ARE PORTABLE FUNHOUSES, FILLED WITH THRILLS AND SURPRISES.

From back in the stacks at the other end of the library came a curious sound—a grunt, a choking cough, and then what might have been a snarl. Next came the unmistakable clatter of a row of books falling from a shelf to the floor.

The only person in the library, other than Betsy, was Dale Foy, a retiree who'd been a cashier at Lucky's supermarket until three years ago when he'd turned sixty-five. He was always searching for thriller writers he had never read before and complaining that none of them was as good as the really old-time tale-spinners, by which he meant John Buchan rather than Robert Louis Stevenson.

Betsy suddenly had the terrible feeling that Mr. Foy had suffered a heart attack in one of the aisles, that she had heard him gurgling for help, and that he had pulled the books to the floor when he'd grabbed at a shelf. In her mind she could see him writhing in agony, unable to breathe, his face turning blue and his eyes bulging, a bloody foam bubbling at his lips. . . .

Years of heavy reading had stropped Betsy's imagination until it was as sharp as a straight razor made from fine German steel.

She hurried around the desk and along the head of the aisles, looking into each of the narrow corridors, which were flanked by nine-foot-high shelves. "Mr. Foy? Mr. Foy, are you all right?"

In the last aisle she found the fallen books but no sign of Dale Foy. Puzzled, she turned to go back the way she had come, and *there* was Foy behind her. But changed. And even Betsy Soldonna's sharp imagination could not have conceived of the thing that Foy had become—or of the things that he was about to do to her. The next few minutes were as filled with surprises as any hundred books she had ever read, though there was not a happy ending.

•

Because of the dark storm clouds that clotted the sky, an early twilight crept over Moonlight Cove, and the entire town seemed to be celebrating Fascinating Fiction Week at the library. The dying day was, for many, filled with thrills and surprises, just like a funhouse in the most macabre carnival that had ever pitched its tents.

chapter thirty-seven

Sam swept the beam of the flashlight around the attic. It had a rough board floor but no light fixture. Nothing was stored there except dust, spider webs, and a multitude of dead, dry bees that had built nests in the rafters during the summer and had died either due to the work of an exterminator or at the end of their span.

Satisfied, he returned to the trapdoor and went backward down the wooden rungs, into the closet of Harry's third-floor bedroom. They had removed many of the hanging clothes to be able to open the trap and draw down the collapsible ladder.

Tessa, Chrissie, Harry, and Moose were waiting for him just outside the closet door, in the steadily darkening bedroom.

Sam said, "Yeah, it'll do."

"I haven't been up there since before the war," Harry said.

"A little dirty, a few spiders, but you'll be safe. If you're not at the end of their list, if they *do* come for you early, they'll find the house empty, and they'll never think of the attic. Because how could a man with two bad legs and one bad arm drag himself up there?"

Sam was not sure that he believed what he was saying. But for his own peace of mind as well as Harry's, he wanted to believe.

"Can I take Moose up there with me?"

"Take that handgun you mentioned," Tessa said, "but not Moose. Well-behaved as he is, he might bark at just the wrong moment."

"Will Moose be safe down here . . . when *they* come?" Chrissie wondered.

"I'm sure he will be," Sam said. "They don't want dogs. Only people."

"We better get you up there, Harry," Tessa said. "It's twenty past five. We've got to be out of here soon."

The bedroom was filling with shadows almost as rapidly as a glass filling with blood-dark wine.

part three

THE NIGHT
BELONGS TO THEM

Montgomery told me that the Law . . . became oddly weakened about nightfall; that then the animal was at its strongest; a spirit of adventure sprang up in them at the dusk; they would dare things they never seemed to dream about by day.
—H. G. Wells, *The Island of Dr. Moreau*

chapter one

In the scrub-covered hills that surrounded the abandoned Icarus Colony, gophers and field mice and rabbits and a few foxes scrambled out of their burrows and shivered in the rain, listening. In the two nearest stands of pine, sweet gum, and autumn-stripped birch, one just to the south and one immediately east of the old colony, squirrels and raccoons stood to attention.

The birds were the first to respond. In spite of the rain, they flew from their sheltered nests in the trees, in the dilapidated old barn, and in the crumbling eaves of the main building itself. Cawing and screeching, they spiraled into the sky, darted and swooped, then streaked directly to the house. Starlings, wrens, crows, owls, and hawks all came in shrill and flapping profusion. Some flew against the walls, as if struck blind, battering insistently until they broke their necks, or until they snapped their wings and fell to the ground where they fluttered and squeaked until they were exhausted or had perished. Others, equally frenzied, found open doorways and windows through which they entered without damaging themselves.

Though wildlife within a two-hundred-yard radius had heard the call, only the nearer animals responded obediently. Rabbits leaped, squirrels scurried, coyotes loped, foxes dashed, and raccoons waddled in that curious way of theirs, through wet grass and rain-bent weeds and mud, toward the source of the siren song. Some were predators and some, by nature, were timid prey, but they moved side by side without conflict. It might have been a scene from an animated Disney film—the neighborly and harmonious folk of field and forest responding to the sweet guitar or harmonica music of some elderly black man who, when they gathered around him, would tell them stories of magic and great adventure. But there was no kindly, tale-spinning Negro where they were going, and the music that drew them was dark, cold, and without melody.

chapter two

While Sam struggled to lift Harry up the ladder and into the attic, Tessa and Chrissie took the wheelchair to the basement garage. It was a heavy-duty motorized model, not a light collapsible chair, and would not fit through the trap. Tessa and Chrissie parked it just inside the big garage door, so it looked as if Harry had gotten this far in his chair and had left the house, perhaps in a friend's car.

"You think they'll fall for it?" Chrissie asked worriedly.

"There's a chance," Tessa said.

"Maybe they'll even think Harry left town yesterday before the roadblocks went up."

Tessa agreed, but she knew—and suspected Chrissie knew—that the chance of the ruse working was slim. If Sam and Harry really had been as confident in the attic trick as they pretended, they would have wanted Chrissie to be tucked up there, too, instead of sent out into the storm-lashed, nightmare world of Moonlight Cove.

They rode the elevator back to the third floor, where Sam was just folding the ladder and pushing the trapdoor into place. Moose watched him curiously.

"Five forty-two," Tessa said, checking her watch.

Sam snatched up the closet pole, which he'd had to remove to pull down the trap, and he reinserted it into its braces. "Help me put the clothes back."

Shirts and slacks, still on hangers, had been transferred to the bed. Working together, passing the garments like amateur firemen relaying pails of water, they quickly restored the closet to its former appearance.

Tessa noticed that traces of fresh blood were soaking through the thick gauze bandage on Sam's right wrist. His wounds were pulling open from the exertion. Although they weren't mortal injuries, they must hurt a lot, and anything that weakened or distracted him during the ordeal ahead decreased their chances of success.

Closing the door, Sam said, "God, I hate to leave him there."

"Five forty-six," Tessa reminded him.

While Tessa pulled on a leather jacket, and while Chrissie slipped into a too-large but waterproof blue nylon windbreaker that belonged to Harry, Sam reloaded his revolver. He had used up all the rounds in his pockets while at the Coltranes'. But Harry owned a .45 revolver and a .38 pistol, both of which he had taken with him into the attic, and he had a box of ammunition for each, so Sam had taken a score or so of the .38 cartridges.

Holstering the gun, he went to the telescope and studied the streets that lay west and south toward Central School. "Still lots of activity," he reported.

"Patrols?" Tessa asked.

"But also lots of rain. And fog's coming in faster, thicker."

Thanks to the storm, an early twilight was upon them and already fading. Although some bleak light still burned above the churning clouds, night might as well have fallen, for cloaks of gloom lay over the wet and huddled town.

"Five fifty," Tessa said.

Chrissie said, "If Mr. Talbot's at the top of their list, they could be here any minute."

Turning from the telescope, Sam said, "All right. Let's go."

Tessa and Chrissie followed him out of the bedroom. They took the stairs down to the first floor.

Moose used the elevator.

chapter three

Shaddack was a child tonight.

Circling repeatedly through Moonlight Cove, from the sea to the hills, from Holliwell Road on the north to Paddock Lane on the south, he could not remember ever having been in a better mood. He altered the patterns of his patrol, largely to be sure that eventually he would cover every block of every street in town; the sight of each house and every citizen on foot in the storm affected him in a way they never had previously, because soon they would be his to do with as he pleased.

He was filled with excitement and anticipation, the likes of which he had not felt since Christmas Eve when he was a young boy. Moonlight Cove was a huge toy, and in a few hours, when midnight struck, when this dark eve ticked over into the holiday, he would be able to have so much fun with his marvelous toy. He would indulge in games that he had long wanted to play but had denied himself. Henceforth, no urge or desire would be denied, for despite the bloodiness or outrageousness of whatever game he chose, there would be no referees, no authorities, to penalize him.

And like a child sneaking into a closet to filch coins from his father's coat to buy ice cream, he was so completely transported by contemplation of the rewards that he had virtually forgotten there was a potential for disaster. Minute by minute, the threat of the regressives faded from his awareness. He did not entirely forget about Loman Watkins, but he no longer was able to remember exactly why he had spent the day hiding from the police chief in the garage at the Parkins house.

More than thirty years of unrelenting self-control, strenuous and undeviating application of his mental and physical resources, beginning with the day he had murdered his parents and Runningdeer, thirty years of repressing his needs and desires and of sublimating them in his work, had at last led him to the brink of his dream's realization. *He could not doubt.* To doubt his mission or worry about its outcome would be to question his sacred destiny and insult the great spirits who had favored him. He was now incapable of even seeing a downside; he turned his mind away from any incipient thought of disaster.

He sensed the great spirits in the storm.

He sensed them moving secretly through his town.

They were there to witness and approve his ascension to the throne of destiny.

He had eaten no cactus candy since the day he had killed his mother, father, and the Indian, but over the years he had been subject to vivid flashbacks. They came upon him unexpectedly. One moment he would be in this world, and the next instant he would be in that other place, the eerie world parallel to this one, where the cactus candy had always conveyed him, a reality in which colors were simultaneously more vivid and more subtle, where every object seemed to have more angles and dimensions than in the ordinary world, where he seemed to be strangely weightless—buoyant as a helium-filled balloon—and where the voices of spirits spoke to him. The flashbacks had been frequent during the year following the murders, striking him about twice a week, then had gradually declined in number—though not in intensity—through his teenage years. Those dreamy, fuguelike spells, which usually lasted an hour or two but could occasionally last half a day, were responsible in part for his reputation, with family and teachers, of being a somewhat detached child. They all had sympathy for him, naturally, because they assumed that whatever detachment he displayed was a result of the shattering trauma that he had endured.

Now, cruising in his van, he was phasing slowly into that cactus-candy condition. This flashback was unexpected, too, but it didn't *snap* upon him as all the others had. He sort of . . . drifted into it, deeper, deeper. And the further he went, the more he suspected that this time he would not be pulled rudely back from that realm of higher consciousness. From now on he would be a resident of both worlds, which was how the great spirits themselves lived, with awareness of both the higher and the lower states of existence. He even began to think that what he was undergoing now, spiritually, was a conversion of his own, a thousand times more profound than that the citizens of Moonlight Cove had undergone.

In this exalted state, everything was special and wondrous to Shaddack. The twinkling lights of the rain-swept town seemed like jewels sprinkled through the descending darkness. The molten, silvery beauty of the rain itself astonished him, as did the swiftly dimming, gorgeously turbulent gray sky.

As he braked at the intersection of Paddock Lane and Saddleback Drive, he touched his breast, feeling the telemetry device he wore from a chain around his neck, unable for a moment to remember what it was, and *that* seemed mysterious and wonderful, as well. Then he recalled that the device monitored and broadcast his heartbeat, which was received by a unit at New Wave. It was effective over a distance of five miles, and worked even when he was indoors. If the reception of his heartbeat was interrupted for more than one minute, Sun was programmed to feed a destruct order, via microwave, to the microsphere computers in all of the New People.

A few minutes later, on Bastenchurry Road, when he touched the device, the memory of its purpose again proved elusive. He sensed that it was a powerful object, that whoever wore it held the lives of others in his hands, and the fantasy-tripping child in him decided that it must be an amulet, bestowed upon him by the great spirits, one more sign that he stood astride the two worlds, one foot in the ordinary plane of ordinary men and one foot in the higher realm of the great spirits, the gods of the cactus candy.

His slowly phased-in flashback, like time-released medication, had carried him back into the condition of his youth, at least to those seven years when he'd been in the thrall of Runningdeer. He was a child. And he was a demigod. He was the favored child of the moonhawk, so he could do anything he wanted to anyone, *anyone*, and as he continued to drive, he fantasized about just what he might want to do . . . and to whom.

Now and then he laughed softly and slightly shrilly, and his eyes gleamed like those of a cruel and twisted boy studying the effects of fire on captive ants.

chapter four

As Moose padded around them and wagged his tail so hard it seemed in danger of flying off, Chrissie waited in the kitchen with Tessa and Sam until more light bled out of the dying day.

At last Sam said, "All right. Stay close. Do what I say every step of the way."

He looked at Chrissie and Tessa for a long moment before actually opening the door; without any of them speaking a word, they hugged one another. Tessa kissed Chrissie on the cheek, then Sam kissed her, and Chrissie returned their kisses. She didn't have to be told why they all suddenly felt so affectionate. They were people, *real* people, and expressing their feelings was important, because before the night was out they might not be real people any more. Maybe they wouldn't ever again feel the kinds of things real people felt, so those feelings were more precious by the second.

Who knew what those weird shape-changers felt? Who would *want* to know?

Besides, if they didn't reach Central, it would be because one of the search parties or a couple of the Boogeymen nailed them along the way. In that case this might be their last chance to say goodbye to one another.

Finally Sam led them onto the porch.

Carefully, Chrissie closed the door behind them. Moose didn't try to get out. He was too good and noble a dog for such cheap stunts. But he did stick his snout in the narrowing crack, sniffing at her and trying to lick her hand, so she was afraid she was going to pinch his nose. He pulled back at the last moment, and the door clicked shut.

Sam led them down the steps and across the yard toward the house to the south of Harry's. No lights were on there. Chrissie hoped no one was home, but she figured some monstrous creature was at one of the dark windows right now, peering out at them and licking its chops.

The rain seemed colder than when she'd been on the run last night, but that might have been because she had just come out of the warm, dry house. Only the palest gray glow still illuminated the sky to the west. The icy, slashing droplets seemed to be tearing the last of that light out of the clouds and driving it into the earth, pulling down a deep, damp darkness. Before they had even reached the fence separating Harry's property from the next, Chrissie was grateful for the hooded nylon windbreaker, even though it was so big on her that it made her feel as if she was a little kid playing dress-up in her parents' clothes.

It was a picket fence, easy to clamber over. They followed Sam across the neighbor's backyard to another fence. Chrissie was over that one, too, and into yet another yard, with Tessa close behind her, before she realized they had reached the Coltranes' place.

She looked at the blank windows. No lights on here, either, which was a good thing, because if there *had* been lights, that would mean someone had found what was left of the Coltranes after their battle with Sam.

Crossing the yard toward the next fence, Chrissie was overcome by the fear that the Coltranes had somehow reanimated themselves after Sam had fired all of those bullets into them, that they were standing in the kitchen and looking out the windows right this minute, that they had seen their nemesis and his two companions, and that they were even now opening the back door. She expected two robot-things to come clanking out with metal arms and working massive metal hands, sort of like tin versions of the walking dead in old zombie movies, miniature radar-dish antennae whirling around and around on their heads, steam hissing from body vents.

Her fear must have slowed her, because Tessa almost stumbled into her from behind and gave her a gentle push to urge her along. Chrissie crouched and hurried to the south side of the yard.

Sam helped her over a wrought-iron fence with spearlike points on the staves. She would probably have gored herself if she'd had to scale it alone. Chrissie shishkebab.

People were home at the next house, and Sam took refuge behind some shrubbery to study the lay of things before continuing. Chrissie and Tessa quickly joined him there.

While clambering over the last fence, she'd rubbed the abraded palm of her left hand, even though it was bandaged. It hurt, but she gritted her teeth and made no complaint.

Parting the branches of what appeared to be a mulberry bush, Chrissie peered at the house, which was only twenty feet away. She saw four people through the kitchen windows. They were preparing dinner together. A middle-aged couple, a gray-haired man, and a teenage girl.

She wondered if they had been converted yet. She suspected not, but there was no way to be sure. And since the robots and Boogeymen sometimes hid in clever human disguises, you couldn't trust anyone, not even your best friend . . . or your parents. Pretty much the same as when aliens were taking over.

"Even if they look out, they won't see us," Sam said. "Come on."

Chrissie followed him from the cover of the mulberry bush and across the open lawn toward the next property line, thanking God for the fog, which was getting denser by the minute.

Eventually they reached the house at the end of the block. The south side of that lawn fronted the cross street, Bergenwood Way, which led down to Conquistador.

When they were two-thirds of the way across the lawn, less than twenty feet from the street, a car turned the corner a block and a half uphill and started down. Following Sam's lead, Chrissie threw herself flat on the soggy lawn because there was no nearby shrubbery behind which to take refuge. If they tried to scramble too far, the driver of the approaching car might get close enough to spot them while they were still scuttling for cover.

No streetlamps flanked Bergenwood, which was in their favor. The last of the ashen light was gone from the western sky—another boon.

As the car drew nearer, moving slowly either because of the bad weather or because its occupants were part of a patrol, its headlights were diffused by the fog, which seemed not to be reflecting that light but glowing with a radiance of its own. Objects in the night for yards on both sides of the car were half revealed and weirdly distorted by those slowly churning, ground-hugging, luminous clouds.

When the car was less than a block away, someone riding in the back seat switched on a handheld spotlight. He directed it out his side window, playing it over the front lawns of the houses that faced on Bergenwood and the side lawns of houses facing the cross streets. At the moment the beam was pointed in the opposite direction, south, toward the other side of Bergenwood. But by the time they had driven this far, they might decide to spotlight the properties to the north of Bergenwood.

"Backtrack," Sam said fiercely. "But stay down and crawl, *crawl*." The car reached the intersection, half a block uphill.

Chrissie crawled after Sam, not straight back the way they had come but toward the nearby house. She didn't see anywhere he could hide, because the back-porch railing was pretty open and there were no large shrubs. Maybe he figured to slip around the side of the house until the patrol passed, but she didn't think she and Tessa would make it to the corner in time.

When she glanced over her shoulder, she saw that the spotlight was still sweeping the front lawns and between the houses on the south flank of the street. However, there was also the side-glow effect of the headlights to worry about, and that was going to wash across *this* lawn in a few seconds.

She was half crawling and half slithering on her belly, moving fast, though no doubt squashing lots of snails and earthworms that had come out to bask on the wet grass, which didn't bear thinking about. She came to a concrete walkway close to the house—and realized that Sam had disappeared.

She halted on her hands and knees, looking left and right.

Tessa appeared at her side. "Cellar steps, honey. Hurry!"

Scrambling forward, she discovered a set of exterior concrete steps leading down to a cellar entrance. Sam was crouched at the bottom, where collected rainwater gurgled softly as it trickled into a drain in front of the closed cellar door. Chrissie joined him in that haven, slipping below ground level, and Tessa followed. About four seconds later a spotlight swept across the wall of the house and even played for a moment inches above their heads, on the concrete lip of the stairwell.

They huddled in silence, unmoving, for a minute or so after the spotlight swung away from them and the car passed. Chrissie was sure that something inside the house had heard them, that the door at Sam's back would fly open at any second, that something would leap at them, a creature part werewolf and part computer, snarling and beeping, its mouth bristling with both teeth and programming keys, saying something like, "To be killed, please press ENTER and proceed."

She was relieved when at last Sam whispered, "Go."

They recrossed the lawn toward Bergenwood Way. This time the street remained conveniently deserted.

As Harry promised, a stone-lined drainage channel ran alongside Bergenwood. According to Harry, who had played in it when he was a kid, the channel was about three feet wide and maybe five feet deep. Judging by those dimensions, a foot or more of runoff surged through it at the moment. Those currents were swift, almost black, revealed at the bottom of the shadow-pooled trench only by an occasional dark glint and chuckle of roiling water.

The channel offered a considerably less conspicuous route than the open street. They moved uphill a few yards until they found the mortared, iron handholds that Harry had promised they'd find every hundred feet along the open sections of the channel. Sam climbed down first, Chrissie went second, and Tessa brought up the rear.

Sam hunched over to keep his head below street level, and Tessa hunched a bit less than he did. But Chrissie didn't have to hunch at all. Being eleven had its advantages, especially when you were on the run from werewolves or ravenous aliens or robots or Nazis, and at one time or another during the past twenty-four hours, she had been on the run from the first three, but not from Nazis, too, thank God, though who knew what might happen next.

The churning water was cold around her feet and calves. She was surprised to discover that although it only reached her knees it had considerable force. It pushed and tugged relentlessly, as if it were a living thing with a mean desire to topple her. She was not in any danger of falling as long as she stood in one place with feet widely planted, but she was not sure how long she could maintain her balance while walking. The watercourse sloped steeply downhill. The old stone floor, after several decades of rainy seasons, was well polished by runoff. Because of that combination of factors, the channel was the next best thing to an amusement-park flume ride.

If she fell, she'd be swept all the way downhill, to within half a block of the bluff, where the channel widened and dropped straight down into the earth. Harry had said something about safety bars dividing the passage into narrow slots just before the downspout, but she figured that if she were swept down there and had to rely on those bars, they would prove to be missing or rusted out, leaving a straight shot to the bottom. The system came out again at the base of the cliffs, then led part of the way across the beach, discharging the runoff onto the sand or, at high tide, into the sea.

She had no difficulty picturing herself tumbling and twisting helplessly, choking on filthy water, desperately but unsuccessfully grabbing at the stone channel for purchase, suddenly plummeting a couple of hundred feet straight down, banging against the walls of the shaft when it went vertical, breaking bones, smashing her head to bits, hitting the bottom with . . .

Well, yes, she *could* easily picture it, but suddenly she didn't see any wisdom in doing so.

Fortunately Harry had warned them of this problem, so Sam had come prepared. From under his jacket and around his waist, he unwound a length of rope that he had removed from a long-unused pulley system in Harry's garage. Though the rope was old, Sam said it was still strong, and Chrissie hoped he was right. He had tied one end around his waist before leaving the house. Now he looped the other end through Chrissie's belt and finally tied it around Tessa's waist, leaving approximately eight feet of play between each of them. If one of them fell—well, face it, Chrissie was far and away the one most likely to fall and most likely to be swept to a wet and bloody death—the others could stand fast until she had time to regain her footing.

That was the plan, anyway.

Securely linked, they started down the channel. Sam and Tessa hunched over so no one in a passing car would see their heads bobbling above the stone rim of the watercourse, and Chrissie hunched over a bit, too, keeping her feet wide apart, sort of troll-walking as she had done last night in the tunnel under the meadow.

Per Sam's instructions, she held on to the line in front of her with both hands, taking up the slack when she drew close to him, to avoid tripping on it, then paying it out again when she fell back a couple of feet. Behind her, Tessa was doing the same thing; Chrissie felt the subtle tug of the rope on her belt.

They were heading toward a culvert half a block downhill. The channel went underground at Conquistador and stayed subterranean not just through the intersection but for two entire blocks, surfacing again at Roshmore.

Chrissie kept glancing up, past Sam at the mouth of the pipe, not liking what she saw. It was round, concrete rather than stone. It was wider than the rectangular channel, about five feet in diameter, no doubt so workmen could get into it easily and clean it out if it became choked with debris. However, neither the shape nor the size of the culvert made her uneasy; it was the absolute blackness of it that prickled the nape of her neck, for it was darker even than the essence of night at the bottom of the drainage channel itself—absolutely, absolutely black, and it seemed as if they were marching into the gaping mouth of some prehistoric behemoth.

A car cruised by slowly on Bergenwood, another on Conquistador. Their headlights were refracted by the incoming bank of fog, so the night itself seemed to glow, but little of that queer luminosity reached down into the watercourse, and none of it penetrated the mouth of the culvert.

When Sam crossed the threshold of that tunnel and, within two steps, disappeared entirely from sight, Chrissie followed without hesitation, although not without trepidation. They proceeded at a slower pace, for the floor of the culvert was not merely steeply sloped but curved, as well, and even more treacherous than the stone drainage channel.

Sam had a flashlight, but Chrissie knew he didn't want to use it near either end of the tunnel. The backsplash of the beam might be visible from outside and draw the attention of one of the patrols.

The culvert was as utterly lightless as the inside of a whale's belly. Not that she knew what a whale's belly was like, inside, but she doubted it was equipped with a lamp or even a Donald Duck night-light, like the one she'd had when she was years younger. The whale's belly image seemed fitting because she had the creepy feeling that the pipe was really a stomach and that the rushing water was digestive juice, and that already her tennis shoes and the legs of her jeans were dissolving in that corrosive flood.

Then she fell. Her feet slipped on something, perhaps a fungus that was growing on the floor and attached so tightly to the concrete that the runoff had not torn it away. She let go of the line and windmilled her arms, trying to keep her balance, but she went down with a tremendous splash, and instantly found herself borne away by the water.

She had enough presence of mind not to scream. A scream would draw one of the search teams—or worse.

Gasping for breath, spluttering as water slopped into her mouth, she collided with Sam's legs, knocking him off balance. She felt him falling. She wondered how long they'd all lie, dead and decomposing, at the bottom of the long vertical drain, out at the foot of the bluff, before their bloated, purple remains were found.

chapter five

In the tomb-perfect darkness, Tessa heard the girl fall, and she immediately halted, planting her legs as wide and firm as she could on that sloped and curved floor, keeping both hands on the security line. Within a second that rope pulled taut as Chrissie was swept away by the water.

Sam grunted, and Tessa realized that the girl had been carried into

him. Slack developed on the line for an instant, but then it went taut
again, pulling her forward, which she took to mean that Sam was staggering ahead, trying to stay on his feet, with the girl pressing against his
lower legs and threatening to knock them out from under him. If Sam
had been brought down, too, and seized by tumultuous currents, the
line would not have been merely taut; the drag would have been great
enough to wrench Tessa off her feet.

She heard a lot of splashing ahead. A soft curse from Sam.

The water was creeping higher. At first she thought she was imagining it, but then she realized the torrent had risen to above her knees.

The damned darkness was the worst of it, not being able to see
anything, virtually blind, unable to be sure what was happening.

Abruptly she was jerked forward again. Two, three—oh, God—half
a dozen steps.

Sam, don't fall!

Stumbling, almost losing her balance, realizing that they were on
the edge of disaster, Tessa leaned backward on the line, using its taut-
ness to steady herself instead of rushing forward with the hope of developing slack again. She hoped to God she didn't resist too much and
get yanked off her feet.

She swayed. The line pulled hard at her waist. Without slack to
loop through her hands, she was unable to take most of the strain with
her arms.

The pressure of water against the back of her legs was growing.

Her feet skidded.

Like videotape fast-forwarded through an editing machine, strange
thoughts flew through her mind, scores of them in a few seconds, all
unbidden, and some of them surprised her. She thought about living,
surviving, about not wanting to die, and that wasn't so surprising, but
then she thought about Chrissie, about not wanting to fail the girl, and
in her mind she saw a detailed image of her and Chrissie together, in a
cozy house somewhere, living as mother and daughter, and she was
surprised at how much she *wanted* that, which seemed wrong because
Chrissie's parents were not dead, as far as anyone knew, and might not
even be hopelessly changed, because the conversion—whatever it was—
just might be reversible. Chrissie's family might be put back together
again. Tessa couldn't see a picture of that in her mind. It didn't seem as
much a possibility as she and Chrissie together. But it might happen.
Then she thought of Sam, of never having a chance to make love to
him, and *that* startled her, because although he was sort of attractive,
she truly hadn't realized she was drawn to him in any romantic way.
Of course his grit in the face of spiritual despair was appealing, and his

perfectly serious four-reasons-for-living shtick made him an intriguing challenge. Could she give him a fifth? Or supplant Goldie Hawn as the fourth? But until she found herself tottering on the brink of a watery death, she didn't realize how very much he had attracted her in such a short time.

Her feet skidded again. Beneath the surging water, the floor was much more slippery than it had been in the stone channel, as if moss grew on the concrete. Tessa tried to dig in her heels.

Sam cursed under his breath. Chrissie made a coughing-choking sound.

The depth of water in the center of the tunnel had risen to about eighteen or twenty inches.

A moment later the line jerked hard, then went completely slack.

The rope had snapped. Sam and Chrissie had been swept down into the tunnel.

The gurgle-slosh-slap of gushing water echoed off the walls, and echoes of the echoes overlaid previous echoes, and Tessa's heart was pounding so loud she could hear it, but still she should have heard their cries, too, as they were carried away. Yet for one awful moment they were silent.

Then Chrissie coughed again. Only a few feet away.

A flashlight snapped on. Sam was hooding most of the lens with his hand.

Chrissie was sideways in the passage, pressed up out of the worst of the flow, her back and the palms of both hands braced against the side of the tunnel.

Sam stood with his feet planted wide part. Water churned and foamed around his legs. He had gotten turned around. He was facing uphill now.

The rope hadn't snapped, after all; the tension had been released because both Sam and Chrissie had regained their equilibrium.

"You all right?" Sam whispered to the girl.

She nodded, still gagging on the dirty water she had swallowed. She wrinkled her face in distaste, spat once, twice, and said, "Yuch."

Looking at Tessa, Sam said, "Okay?"

She couldn't speak. A rock-hard lump had formed in her throat. She swallowed a few times, blinked. A delayed wave of relief passed through her, reducing the almost unbearable pressure in her chest, and at last she said, "Okay. Yeah. Okay."

chapter six

Sam was relieved when they got to the end of the culvert without another fall. He stood for a moment, just outside the lower mouth of the drain, happily looking up at the sky. Because of the thick fog, he couldn't actually see the sky, but that was a technicality; he still felt relieved to be out in the open air again, if still knee-deep in muddy water.

They were virtually in a river now. Either the rain was falling harder in the hills, at the far east end of town, or some breakwater in the system had collapsed. The level had swiftly risen well past midthigh on Sam and nearly to Chrissie's waist, and the deluge poured from the conduit at their back with impressive power. Keeping their footing in those cataracts was getting more difficult by the second.

He turned, reached for the girl, drew her close, and said, "I'm going to hold tight to your arm from here on."

She nodded.

The night was grave-deep, and even inches from her face, he could see only a shadowy impression of her features. When he looked up at Tessa, who stood a few feet behind the girl, she was little more than a black shape and might not have been Tessa at all.

Holding fast to the girl, he turned and looked again at the way ahead.

The tunnel had extended for two blocks before pouring the flood forth into another one-block length of open drainage channel, just as Harry had remembered from the days when he had been a kid and, against every admonition of his parents, had played in the drainage system. Thank God for disobedient children.

One block ahead of them, this new section of stone watercourse fed into another concrete culvert. *That* pipe, according to Harry, terminated at the mouth of the long vertical drain at the west end of town. Supposedly, in the last ten feet of the main sloping line, a row of sturdy, vertical iron bars was set twelve inches apart and extended floor to ceiling, creating a barrier through which only water and smaller objects could pass. There was virtually no chance of being carried all the way into that two-hundred-foot drop.

But Sam didn't want to risk it. There must be no more falls. After being washed to the end and crashing against the safety barrier, if they were not suffering from myriad broken bones, if they were able to get to their feet and move, climbing back up that long culvert, on a steep slope, against the onrushing force of the water, was not an ordeal he was willing to contemplate, let alone endure.

All of his life he had felt he'd failed people. Though he had been only seven when his mother had died in the accident, he'd always been eaten by guilt related to her death, as if he ought to have been able to save her in spite of his tender age and in spite of having been pinned in the wreckage of the car with her. Later, Sam had never been able to please his drunken, mean, sorry son-of-a-bitch of a father—and had suffered grievously for that failure. Like Harry, he felt that he had failed the people of Vietnam, though the decision to abandon them had been made by authorities who far outranked him and with whom he could have had no influence. Neither of the Bureau agents who had died with him had died *because* of him, yet he felt he had failed them too. He had failed Karen, somehow, though people told him he was mad to think that he had any responsibility for her cancer; it was just that he couldn't help thinking that if he had loved her more, loved her harder, she would have found the strength and will to pull through. God knew, he had failed his own son, Scott.

Chrissie squeezed his hand.

He returned the squeeze.

She seemed so small.

Earlier in the day, gathered in Harry's kitchen, they'd had a conversation about responsibility. Now, suddenly, he realized that his sense of responsibility was so highly developed that it bordered on obsession, but he still agreed with what Harry had said: A man's commitment to others, especially to friends and family, could never be excessive. He had never imagined that one of the key insights of his life would come to him while he was standing nearly waist-deep in muddy water in a drainage canal, on the run from enemies both human and inhuman, but that was where he received it. He realized that his problem was not the alacrity with which he shouldered responsibility or the unusual weight of it that he was willing to carry. No, hell no, his problem was that he had allowed his sense of responsibility to obstruct his ability to cope with failure. All men failed from time to time, and often the fault lay not in the man himself but in the role of fate. When he failed, he had to learn not only to go on but to *enjoy* going on. Failure could not be allowed to bleed him of the very pleasure of life. Such a turning away from life was blasphemous, if you believed in God—and just plain stupid if you didn't. It was like saying, "Men fail, but *I* shouldn't fail, because I'm more than just a man, I'm somewhere up there between the angels and God." He saw why he had lost Scott: because he had lost his own love of life, his sense of fun, and had ceased to be able to share anything meaningful with the boy—or to halt Scott's own descent into nihilism when it had begun.

At the moment, if he had tried to count his reasons for living, the list would have had more than four items. It would have had hundreds. *Thousands*.

All of this understanding came to him in an instant, while he was holding Chrissie's hand, as if the flow of time had been stretched by some quirk of relativity. He realized that if he failed to save the girl or Tessa, but got out of this mess himself, he would nevertheless have to rejoice at his own salvation and get *on* with life. Although their situation was dark and their hope slim, his spirits soared, and he almost laughed aloud. The living nightmare they were enduring in Moonlight Cove had profoundly shaken him, rattling important truths into him, truths that were simple and should have been easy to see during his long years of torment, but that he received gratefully in spite of their simplicity and his own previous thickheadedness. Maybe the truth was always simple when you found it.

Yeah, okay, maybe he could go on now even if he failed in his responsibilities to others, even if he lost Chrissie and Tessa—but, shit, he wasn't *going* to lose them. Damned if he was.

Damned if he was.

He held Chrissie's hand and cautiously edged along the stone channel, grateful for the comparative unevenness of that pavement and the moss-free traction it provided. The water was just deep enough to give him a slight buoyant feeling, which made it harder to put each foot down after he lifted it, so instead of walking, he dragged his feet along the bottom.

In less than a minute they reached a set of iron rungs mortared into the masonry of the channel wall. Tessa moved in, and for a while they all just hung there, gripping iron, grateful for the solid feel of it and the anchor it provided.

A couple of minutes later, when the rain abruptly slacked off, Sam was ready to move again. Being careful not to step on Tessa's and Chrissie's hands, he climbed a couple of rungs and looked out at the street.

Nothing moved but the fog.

This section of open watercourse flanked Moonlight Cove Central School. The athletic field was just a few feet from him, and, sitting beyond that open space, barely visible in the darkness and mist, was the school itself, illuminated only by a couple of dim security lamps.

The property was encircled by a nine-foot-high chain-link fence. But Sam wasn't daunted by that. Fences always had gates.

chapter seven

Harry waited in the attic, hoping for the best, expecting the worst.

He was propped against the outer wall of the long, unlighted chamber, tucked in the corner at the extreme far end from the trapdoor through which he had been lifted. There was nothing in that upper room behind which he could hide.

But if someone went so far as to empty out the master-bedroom closet, pull down the trap, open the folding stairs, and poke his head up to look around, maybe he wouldn't be diligent about probing every corner of the place. When he saw bare boards and a flurry of spiders on his first sweep of the flash, maybe he would click off the beam and retreat.

Absurd, of course. Anyone who went to the trouble to look into the attic at all would look into it properly, exploring every corner. But whether that hope was absurd or not, Harry clung to it; he was good at nurturing hope, making hearty stew from the thinnest broth of it, because for half his life, hope was mostly what had sustained him.

He was not uncomfortable. As preparation for the unheated attic, with Sam's help to speed the dressing process, he had put on wool socks, warmer pants than what he had been wearing, and two sweaters.

Funny, how a lot of people seemed to think that a paralyzed man could feel nothing in his unresponsive extremities. In some cases, that was true; all nerves were blunted, all feeling lost. But spinal injuries came in myriad types; short of a total severing of the cord, the range of sensations left to the victim varied widely.

In Harry's case, though he had lost all use of one arm and one leg and nearly all use of the other leg, he could still feel heat and cold. When something pricked him, he was aware—if not of pain—at least of a blunt pressure.

Physically, he felt much less than when he'd been a whole man; no argument about that. But all feelings were not physical. Though he was sure that few people would believe him, his handicap actually had enriched his emotional life. Though by necessity something of a recluse, he had learned to compensate for a dearth of human contact. Books had helped. Books opened the world to him. And the telescope. But mostly his unwavering will to lead as full a life as possible was what had kept him whole in mind and heart.

If these were his final hours, he would blow out the candle with no bitterness when the time came to extinguish it. He regretted what he had lost, but more important, he treasured what he had kept. In the last analysis, he felt that he had lived a life that was in the balance good, worthwhile, precious.

He had two guns with him. A .45 revolver. A .38 pistol. If they came into the attic after him, he would use the pistol on them until it was empty. Then he would make them eat all but one of the rounds in the revolver. That last cartridge would be for himself.

He had brought no extra bullets. In a crisis, a man with one good hand could not reload fast enough to make the effort more than a comic finale.

The drumming of rain on the roof had subsided. He wondered if this was just another lull in the storm or if it was finally ending.

It would be nice to see the sun again.

He worried more about Moose than about himself. The poor damn dog was down there alone. When the Boogeymen or their makers came at last, he hoped they wouldn't harm old Moose. And if they came into the attic and forced him to kill himself, he hoped that Moose would not be long without a good home.

chapter eight

To Loman, as he cruised, Moonlight Cove seemed both dead and teeming with life.

Judged by the usual signs of life in a small town, the burg was an empty husk, as defunct as any sun-dried ghost town in the heart of the Mohave. The shops, bars, and restaurants were closed. Even the usually crowded Perez Family Restaurant was shuttered, dark; no one had showed up to open for business. The only pedestrians out walking in the aftermath of the storm were foot patrols or conversion teams. Likewise, the police units and two-man patrols in private cars had the streets to themselves.

However, the town seethed with perverse life. Several times he saw strange, swift figures moving through the darkness and fog, still secretive but far bolder than they had been on other nights. When he stopped or slowed to study those marauders, some of them paused in deep shadows to gaze at him with baleful yellow or green or smoldering red eyes, as if they were contemplating their chances of attacking his black-and-white and pulling him out of it before he could take his foot off the brake pedal and get out of there. Watching them, he was filled with a longing to abandon his car, his clothes, and the rigidity of his human form, to join them in their simpler world of hunting, feeding, and rutting. Each time he quickly turned away from them and drove on before they—or he—could act upon such impulses. Here and there he passed houses in which eerie lights glowed, and against the windows of which moved shadows so grotesque and unearthly that his heart quickened and his palms went damp, though he was well removed from them and probably beyond their reach. He did not stop to investigate what creatures might inhabit those places or what tasks they were engaged upon, for he sensed that they were kin to the thing Denny had become and that they were more dangerous, in many ways, than the prowling regressives.

He now lived in a Lovecraftian world of primal and cosmic forces, of monstrous entities stalking the night, where human beings were reduced to little more than cattle, where the Judeo-Christian universe of a love-motivated God had been replaced by the creation of the old gods who were driven by dark lusts, a taste for cruelty, and a never-satisfied thirst for power. In the air, in the eddying fog, in the shadowed and dripping trees, in the unlighted streets, and even in the sodium-yellow glare of the lamps on the main streets, there was the pervasive sense that nothing good could happen that night . . . but that anything *else* could happen, no matter how fantastical or bizarre.

Having read uncounted paperbacks over the years, he was familiar with Lovecraft. He had not liked him a hundredth as much as Louis L'Amour, largely because L'Amour had dealt with reality, while H.P. Lovecraft had traded in the impossible. Or so it had seemed to Loman at the time. Now he knew that men could create, in the real world, hells equal to any that the most imaginative writer could dream up.

Lovecraftian despair and terror flooded through Moonlight Cove in greater quantities than those in which the recent rain had fallen. As he drove through those transmuted streets, Loman kept his service revolver on the car seat beside him, within easy reach.

Shaddack.

He must find Shaddack.

Going south on Juniper, he stopped at the intersection with Ocean Avenue. At the same time another black-and-white braked at the stop sign directly opposite Loman, headed north.

No traffic was moving on Ocean. Rolling his window down, Loman pulled slowly across the intersection and braked beside the other cruiser, with no more than a foot separating them.

From the number on the door, above the police-department shield, Loman knew it was Neil Penniworth's patrol car. But when he looked through the side window, he did not see the young officer. He saw something that might once have been Penniworth, still vaguely human, illuminated by the gauge and speedometer lights but more directly by the glow of the mobile VDT in there. Twin cables, like the one that had erupted from Denny's forehead to join him more intimately with his PC, had sprouted from Penniworth's skull; and although the light was poor, it appeared as if one of those extrusions snaked through the steering wheel and into the dashboard, while the other looped down toward the console-mounted computer. The shape of Penniworth's skull had changed dramatically, too, drawing forward, bristling with spiky features that must have been sensors of some kind and that gleamed softly like burnished metal in the light of the VDT; his shoulders were larger, queerly scalloped and pointed; he appeared earnestly to have sought the form of a baroque robot. His hands were not on the steering wheel, but perhaps he did not even have hands any more; Loman suspected that Penniworth had not just become one with his mobile computer terminal but with the patrol car itself.

Penniworth slowly turned his head to face Loman.

In his eyeless sockets, crackling white fingers of electricity wiggled and jittered ceaselessly.

Shaddack had said that the New People's freedom from emotion had given them the ability to make far greater use of their innate brain power, even to the extent of exerting mental control over the form and function of matter. Their consciousness now dictated their form; to escape a world in which they were not permitted emotion, they could become whatever they chose—though they could not return to the Old People they had been. Evidently life as a cyborg was free of angst, for Penniworth had sought release from fear and longing—perhaps some kind of obliteration, as well—in this monstrous incarnation.

But what did he feel now? What purpose did he have? And did he remain in that altered state because he truly preferred it? Or was he like Peyser—trapped either for physical reasons or because an aberrant aspect of his own psychology would not permit him to reassume the human form to which, otherwise, he desired to return?

Loman reached for the revolver on the seat beside him.

A segmented cable burst from the driver's door of Penniworth's car, without shredding metal, extruding as if a part of the door had melted and re-formed to produce it—except that it looked at least semiorganic. The probe struck Loman's side window with a snap.

The revolver eluded Loman's sweaty hand, for he could not take his eyes off the probe to look for the gun.

The glass did not crack, but a quarter-size patch bubbled and melted in an instant, and the probe weaved into the car, straight at Loman's face. It had a fleshy sucker mouth, like an eel, but the tiny, sharply pointed teeth within it looked like steel.

He ducked his head, forgot about the revolver, and tramped the accelerator to the floor. The Chevy almost seemed to rear back for a fraction of a second; then with a surge of power that pressed Loman into the seat, it shot forward, south on Juniper.

For a moment the probe between the cars stretched to maintain contact, brushed the bridge of Loman's nose—and abruptly was gone, reeled back into the vehicle from which it had come.

He drove fast all the way to the end of Juniper before slowing down to make a turn. The wind of his passage whistled at the hole that the probe had melted in his window.

Loman's worst fear seemed to be unfolding. Those New People

who didn't choose regression were going to transform themselves—or be transformed at the demand of Shaddack—into hellish hybrids of man and machine.

Find Shaddack. Murder the maker and release the anguished monsters he had made.

chapter nine

Preceded by Sam and followed by Tessa, Chrissie squelched through the mushy turf of the athletic field. In places the soggy grass gave way to gluey mud, which pulled noisily at her shoes, and she thought she sounded like a sort of goofy alien herself, plodding along on big, sucker-equipped feet. Then it occurred to her that in a way she *was* an alien in Moonlight Cove tonight, a different sort of creature from what the majority of the citizens had become.

They were two-thirds of the way across the field when they were halted by a shrill cry that split the night as cleanly as a sharp ax would split a dry cord of wood. That unhuman voice rose and fell and rose again, savage and uncanny but familiar, the call of one of those beasts that she'd thought were invading aliens. Though the rain had stopped, the air was laden with moisture, and in that humidity, the unearthly shriek carried well, like the bell-clear notes of a distant trumpet.

Worse, the call at once was answered by the beast's excited kin. At least half a dozen equally chilling shrieks arose from perhaps as far south as Paddock Lane and as far north as Holliwell Road, from the high hills in the east end of town and from the beach-facing bluffs only a couple of blocks to the west.

All of a sudden Chrissie longed for the cold, lightless culvert churning with waist-deep water so filthy that it might have come from the devil's own bathtub. This open ground seemed wildly dangerous by comparison.

A new cry arose as the others faded, and it was closer than any that had come before it. Too close.

"Let's get inside," Sam said urgently.

Chrissie was beginning to admit to herself that she might not make a good Andre Norton heroine, after all. She was scared, cold, grainy-eyed with exhaustion, starting to feel sorry for herself, and hungry again. She was sick and tired of adventure. She yearned for warm rooms and lazy days with good books and trips to movie theaters and wedges of double-fudge cake. By this time a true adventure-story heroine would have worked out a series of brilliant stratagems that would have brought the beasts in Moonlight Cove to ruin, would have found a way to turn the robot-people into harmless car-washing machines, and would be well on her way to being crowned princess of the kingdom by acclamation of the respectful and grateful citizenry.

They hurried to the end of the field, rounded the bleachers, and crossed the deserted parking lot to the back of the school.

Nothing attacked them.

Thank you, God. Your friend, Chrissie.

Something howled again.

Sometimes even God seemed to have a perverse streak.

There were six doors at different places along the back of the school. They moved from one to another, as Sam tried them all and examined the locks in the hand-hooded beam of his flashlight. He apparently couldn't pick any of them, which disappointed her, because she'd imagined FBI men were so well trained that in an emergency they could open a bank vault with spit and a hairpin.

He also tried a few windows and spent what seemed a long time peering through the panes with his flashlight. He was examining not the rooms beyond but the inner sills and frames of the windows.

At the last door—which was the only one that had glass in the top of it, the others being blank rectangles of metal—Sam clicked off the flashlight, looked solemnly at Tessa, and spoke to her in a low voice. "I don't think there's an alarm system here. Could be wrong. But there's no alarm tape on the glass and, as far as I can see, no hard-wired contacts along the frames or at the window latches."

"Are those the only two kinds of alarms they might have?" Tessa whispered.

"Well, there're motion-detection systems, either employing sonic transmitters or electric eyes. But they'd be too elaborate for just a school, and probably too sensitive for a building like this."

"So now what?"

"Now I break a window."

Chrissie expected him to withdraw a roll of masking tape from a pocket of his coat and tape one of the panes to soften the sound of shattering glass and to prevent the shards from falling noisily to the floor inside. That was how they usually did it in books. But he just turned sideways to the door, drew his arm forward, then rammed it back and drove his elbow through the eight-inch-square pane in the lower-right corner of the window grid. Glass broke and clattered to the floor with an awful racket. Maybe he had forgotten to bring his tape.

He reached through the empty pane, felt for the locks, disengaged them, and went inside first. Chrissie followed him, trying not to step on the broken glass.

Sam switched on the flashlight. He didn't hood it quite so much as he had done outside, though he was obviously trying to keep the back-wash of the beam off the windows.

They were in a long hallway. It was full of the cedar-pine smell that came from the crumbly green disinfectant and dust-attractor that for years the janitors had sprinkled on the floors and then swept up, until the tiles and walls had become impregnated with the scent. The aroma was familiar to her from Thomas Jefferson Elementary, and she was disappointed to find it here. She had thought of high school as a special, mysterious place, but how special or mysterious could it be if they used the same disinfectant as at the grade school?

Tessa quietly closed the outside door behind them.

They stood listening for a moment.

The school was silent.

They moved down the hall, looking into classrooms and lavatories and supply closets on both sides, searching for the computer lab. In a hundred and fifty feet they reached a junction with another hall. They stood in the intersection for a moment, heads cocked, listening again.

The school was still silent.

And dark. The only light in any direction was the flashlight, which Sam still held in his left hand but which he no longer hooded with his right. He had withdrawn his revolver from his holster and needed his right hand for that.

After a long wait, Sam said, "Nobody's here."

Which did seem to be the case.

Briefly Chrissie felt better, safer.

On the other hand, if he really believed they were the only people in the school, why didn't he put his gun away?

chapter ten

As he drove through his domain, impatient for midnight, which was still five hours away, Thomas Shaddack had largely regressed to a child-like condition. Now that his triumph was at hand, he could cast off the masquerade of a grown man, which he had so long sustained, and he was relieved to do so. He had never been an adult, really, but a boy whose emotional development had been forever arrested at the age of twelve, when the message of the moonhawk had not only come to him but been *embedded* in him; he had thereafter faked emotional ascension into adulthood to match his physical growth.

But it was no longer necessary to pretend.

On one level, he had always known this about himself, and had considered it to be his great strength, an advantage over those who had put childhood behind them. A boy of twelve could harbor and nurture a dream with more determination than could an adult, for adults were constantly distracted by conflicting needs and desires. A boy on the edge of puberty, however, had the single-mindedness to focus on and dedicate himself unswervingly to a single Big Dream. Properly bent, a twelve-year-old boy was the perfect monomaniac.

The Moonhawk Project, his Big Dream of godlike power, would not have reached fruition if he had matured in the usual way. He owed his impending triumph to arrested development.

He was a boy again, not secretly any more but openly, eager to satisfy his every whim, to take whatever he wanted, to do anything that broke the rules. Twelve-year-old boys reveled in breaking the rules, challenging authority. At their worst, twelve-year-old boys were naturally lawless, on the verge of hormonal-induced rebellion.

But he was more than lawless. He was a boy flying on cactus candy that had been eaten long ago but that had left a psychic if not a physical residue. He was a boy who knew that he was a god. *Any* boy's potential for cruelty paled in comparison to the cruelty of gods.

To pass the time until midnight, he imagined what he would do with his power when the last of Moonlight Cove had fallen under his command. Some of his ideas made him shiver with a strange mixture of excitement and disgust.

He was on Iceberry Way when he realized the Indian was with him. He was surprised when he turned his head and saw Runningdeer sitting in the passenger seat. Indeed he stopped the van in the middle of the street and stared in disbelief, shocked and afraid.

But Runningdeer did not menace him. In fact, the Indian didn't even speak to him or look at him, but stared straight ahead, through the windshield.

Slowly understanding came to Shaddack. The Indian's spirit was his now, his possession as surely as was the van. The great spirits had given him the Indian as an advisor, as a reward for having made a success of Moonhawk. But *he*, not Runningdeer, was in control this time, and the Indian would speak only when spoken to.

"Hello, Runningdeer," he said.

The Indian looked at him. "Hello, Little Chief."

"You're mine now."

"Yes, Little Chief."

For just a brief flicker of time, it occurred to Shaddack that he was mad and that Runningdeer was an illusion coughed up by a sick mind. But monomaniacal boys do not have the capacity for an extended examination of their mental condition, and the thought passed out of his mind as quickly as it had entered.

To Runningdeer, he said, "You'll do what I say."

"Always."

Immensely pleased, Shaddack let up on the brake pedal and drove on. The headlights revealed an amber-eyed thing of fantastic shape, drinking from a puddle on the pavement. He refused to regard it as a thing of consequence, and when it loped away, he let it vanish from his memory as swiftly as it disappeared from the night-mantled street.

Casting a sly glance at the Indian, he said, "You know one thing I'm going to do some day?"

"What's that, Little Chief?"

"When I've converted everyone, not just the people in Moonlight Cove but everyone in the world, when no one stands against me, then I'll spend some time tracking down your family, all of your remaining brothers, sisters, even your cousins, and I'll find all of *their* children, and all their wives and husbands, and all their *children's* wives and husbands . . . and I'll make them pay for your crimes, I'll really, really make them pay." A whining petulance had entered his voice. He disapproved of the tone he heard himself using, but he could not lose it. "I'll kill all the men, hack them to bloody bits and pieces, do it myself. I'll let them know that it's because of their relation to you that they've got to suffer, and they'll despise you and curse your name, they'll be sorry you ever existed. And I'll rape all the women and hurt them, hurt them all, really bad, and then I'll kill them too. What do you think of that? Huh?"

"If it's what you want, Little Chief."

"Damn right it's what I want."

"Then you may have it."

"Damn right I may have it."

Shaddack was surprised when tears came to his eyes. He stopped at an intersection and didn't move on. "It wasn't right what you did to me."

The Indian said nothing.

"Say it wasn't right!"

"It wasn't right, Little Chief."

"It wasn't right at all."

"It wasn't right."

Shaddack pulled a handkerchief from his pocket and blew his nose. He blotted his eyes. Soon his tears dried up.

He smiled at the nightscape revealed through the windshield. He sighed. He glanced at Runningdeer.

The Indian was staring forward, silent.

Shaddack said, "Of course, without you, I might never have been a child of the moonhawk."

chapter eleven

The computer lab was on the ground floor, in the center of the building, near a confluence of corridors. Windows looked out on a courtyard but could not be seen from any street, which allowed Sam to switch on the overhead lights.

It was a large chamber, laid out like a language lab, with each VDT in its own three-sided cubicle. Thirty computers—upper end, hard-disk systems—were lined up along three walls and in a back-to-back row down the middle of the room.

Looking around at the wealth of hardware, Tessa said, "New Wave sure was generous, huh?"

"Maybe 'thorough' is a better word," Sam said.

He walked along a row of VDTs, looking for telephone lines and modems, but he found none.

Tessa and Chrissie stayed back by the open lab door, peering out at the dark hallway.

Sam sat down at one of the machines and switched it on. The New Wave logo appeared in the center of the screen.

With no telephones, no modems, maybe the computers really had been given to the school for student training, without the additional intention of tying the kids to New Wave during some stage of the Moonhawk Project.

The logo blinked off, and a menu appeared on the screen. Because they were hard-disk machines with tremendous capacity, their programs were already loaded and ready to go as soon as the system was powered up. The menu offered him five choices:

A.   TRAINING 1
B.   TRAINING 2
C.   WORD PROCESSING
D.   ACCOUNTING
E.   OTHER

He hesitated, not because he couldn't decide what letter to push but because he was suddenly afraid of using the machine. He vividly remembered the Coltranes. Though it had seemed to him that they had elected to meld with their computers, that their transformation began within them, he had no way of knowing for sure that it had not been the other way around. Maybe the computers had somehow reached out and *seized* them. That seemed impossible. Besides, thanks to Harry's observations, they knew that people in Moonlight Cove were being converted by an injection, not by some insidious force that passed semimagically through computer keys into the pads of their fingers. He was hesitant nevertheless.

Finally he pressed E and got a list of school subjects:

A.   ALL LANGUAGES
B.   MATH
C.   ALL SCIENCES
D.   HISTORY

E.   ENGLISH
F.   OTHER

He pressed F. A third menu appeared, and the process continued until he finally got a menu on which the final selection was NEW WAVE. When he keyed in that choice, words began to march across the screen.

HELLO, STUDENT.
YOU ARE NOW IN CONTACT
WITH THE SUPERCOMPUTER
AT NEW WAVE MICROTECHNOLOGY.
MY NAME IS SUN.
I AM HERE TO SERVE YOU.

The school machines were wired directly to New Wave. Modems were unnecessary.

WOULD YOU LIKE TO SEE MENUS?
OR WILL YOU SPECIFY INTEREST?

Considering the wealth of menus in the police department's system alone, which he had reviewed last night in the patrol car, he figured he could sit here all evening just looking at menu after menu after submenu before he found what he wanted. He typed in: MOONLIGHT COVE POLICE DEPARTMENT.

THIS FILE RESTRICTED.
PLEASE DO NOT ATTEMPT TO PROCEED
WITHOUT
THE ASSISTANCE OF YOUR TEACHER.

He supposed that the teachers had individual code numbers that, depending on whether or not they were converted, would allow them to access otherwise restricted data. The only way to hit on one of their codes was to begin trying random combinations of digits, but since he didn't even know how many numbers were in a code, there were millions if not billions of possibilities. He could sit there until his hair turned white and his teeth fell out, and not luck into a good number.

Last night he had used Officer Reese Dorn's personal computer-access code, and he wondered whether it worked only on a designated police-department VDT or whether any computer tied to Sun would accept it. Nothing lost for trying. He typed in 262699.

The screen cleared. Then: HELLO, OFFICER DORN.
Again he requested the police-department data system.
This time it was given to him.

CHOOSE ONE
A. DISPATCHER
B. CENTRAL FILES
C. BULLETIN BOARD
D. OUTSYSTEM MODEM

He pressed D.

He was shown a list of computers nationwide with which he could link through the police-department's modem.

His hands were suddenly damp with sweat. He was sure something was going to go wrong, if only because nothing had been easy thus far, not from the minute he had driven into town.

He glanced at Tessa. "Everything okay?"

She squinted at the dark hallway, then blinked at him. "Seems to be. Any luck?"

"Yeah . . . maybe." He turned to the computer again and said softly, "Please . . ."

He scanned the long roster of possible outsystem links. He found FBI KEY, which was the name of the latest and most sophisticated of the Bureau's computer networks—a highly secure, interoffice data-storage, -retrieval, and -transmission system housed at headquarters in Washington, which had been installed only within the past year. Supposedly no one but approved agents at the home office and in the Bureau's field offices, accessing with their own special codes, were able to use FBI KEY.

So much for high security.

Still expecting trouble, Sam selected FBI KEY. The menu disappeared. The screen remained blank for a moment. Then, on the display, which proved to be a full-color monitor, the FBI shield appeared in blue and gold. The word KEY appeared below it.

Next, a series of questions was flashed on the screen—WHAT IS YOUR BUREAU ID NUMBER? NAME? DATE OF BIRTH? DATE OF BUREAU INDUCTION? MOTHER'S MAIDEN NAME?—and when he answered those, he was rewarded with access.

"Bingo!" he said, daring to be optimistic.

Tessa said, "What's happened?"

"I'm in the Bureau's main system in D.C."

"You're a hacker," Chrissie said.

"I'm a fumbler. But I'm in."

"Now what?" Tessa asked.

"I'll ask for the current operator in a minute. But first I want to send greetings to every damned office in the country, make them all sit up and take notice."

"Greetings?"

From the extensive FBI KEY menu, Sam called up item G—IMMEDIATE INTEROFFICE TRANSMISSION. He intended to send a message to every Bureau field office in the country, not just to San Francisco, which was the closest and the one from which he hoped to obtain help. There was one chance in a million that the night operator in San Francisco would overlook the message among reams of other transmissions, in spite of the ACTION ALERT heading he would tag on to it. If that happened, if someone was asleep at the wheel at this most inopportune of moments, they wouldn't be asleep for long, because every office in the country would be asking HQ for more details about the Moonlight Cove bulletin and requesting an explanation of why they had been fed an alert about a situation outside their regions.

He did not understand half of what was happening in this town. He could not have explained, in the shorthand of a Bureau bulletin, even as much as he *did* understand. But he quickly crafted a summary that he believed was as accurate as it had to be—and that he hoped would get them off their duffs and running.

ACTION ALERT
MOONLIGHT COVE, CALIFORNIA

* SCORES DEAD. CONDITION DETERIORATING.
  HUNDREDS MORE COULD DIE WITHIN HOURS.
* NEW WAVE MICROTECHNOLOGY ENGAGED IN ILLICIT EXPER-
  IMENTS ON HUMAN SUBJECTS, WITHOUT THEIR KNOWL-
  EDGE. CONSPIRACY OF WIDEST SCOPE.
* THOUSANDS OF PEOPLE CONTAMINATED.
* REPEAT, ENTIRE POPULATION OF TOWN CONTAMINATED.
* SITUATION EXTREMELY DANGEROUS.
* CONTAMINATED CITIZENS SUFFER LOSS OF FACULTIES, EX-
  HIBIT TENDENCY TO EXTREME VIOLENCE.
* REPEAT, EXTREME VIOLENCE.
* REQUEST IMMEDIATE QUARANTINE BY ARMY SPECIAL
  FORCES. ALSO REQUEST IMMEDIATE, MASSIVE, ARMED
  BACKUP BY BUREAU PERSONNEL.

He gave his position at the high school on Roshmore, so incoming support would have a place to start looking for him, though he was not certain that he, Tessa, and Chrissie could safely continue to take refuge there until reinforcements arrived. He signed off with his name and Bureau ID number.

That message was not going to prepare them for the shock of what they would find in Moonlight Cove, but at least it would get them on the move and encourage them to come prepared for anything.

He typed TRANSMIT, but then he had a thought and wiped the word from the screen. He typed REPEAT TRANSMISSION.

The computer asked NUMBER OF REPEATS?

He typed 99.

The computer acknowledged the order.

Then he typed TRANSMIT again and pressed the ENTER button. WHAT OFFICES?

He typed ALL.

The screen went blank. Then: TRANSMITTING.

At the moment every KEY laser printer in every Bureau field office in the country was printing out the first of ninety-nine repeats of his message. Night staffers everywhere soon would be climbing the walls.

He almost whooped with delight.

But there was more to be done. They were not out of this mess yet.

Sam quickly returned to the KEY menu and tapped selection A–NIGHT OPERATOR. Five seconds later he was in touch with the agent manning the KEY post at the Bureau's central communications room in Washington. A number flashed on the screen—the operator's ID—followed by a name, ANNE DENTON. Taking immense satisfaction in using high technology to bring the downfall of Thomas Shaddack, New Wave, and the Moonhawk Project, Sam entered into a long-distance, unspoken, electronic conversation with Anne Denton, intending to spell out the horrors of Moonlight Cove in more detail.

chapter twelve

Though Loman no longer was interested in the activities of the police department, he switched on the VDT in his car every ten minutes or so to see if anything was happening. He expected Shaddack to be in touch with members of the department from time to time. If he was lucky enough to catch a VDT dialogue between Shaddack and other cops, he might be able to pinpoint the bastard's location from something that was said.

He didn't leave the computer on all the time because he was afraid of it. He didn't think it would jump at him and suck out his brains or anything, but he did recognize that working with it too long might induce in him a temptation to become what Neil Penniworth and Denny had become—in the same way that being around the regressives had given rise to a powerful urge to devolve.

He had just pulled to the side of Holliwell Road, where his restless cruising had taken him, had switched on the machine, and was about to call up the dialogue channel to see if anyone was engaged in conversation, when the word ALERT appeared in large letters on the screen. He pulled his hand back from the keyboard as if something had nipped at him.

The computer said, SUN REQUESTS DIALOGUE.

Sun? The supercomputer at New Wave? Why would it be accessing the police department's system?

Before another officer at headquarters or in another car could query the machine, Loman took charge and typed DIALOGUE APPROVED.

REQUEST CLARIFICATION, Sun said.

Loman typed YES, which could mean GO AHEAD.

Structuring its questions from its own self-assessment program, which allowed it to monitor its own workings as if it were an outside observer, Sun said, ARE TELEPHONE CALLS TO AND FROM UNAPPROVED NUMBERS IN MOONLIGHT COVE AND ALL NUMBERS OUTSIDE STILL RESTRICTED?

YES.

ARE SUN'S RESERVED TELEPHONE LINES INCLUDED IN AFOREMEN-TIONED PROHIBITION? the New Wave computer asked, speaking of it-self in third person.

Confused, Loman typed UNCLEAR.

Patiently leading him through it step by step, Sun explained that it had its own dedicated phone lines, outside the main directory, by which its users could call other computers all over the country and access them.

He already knew this, so he typed YES.

ARE SUN'S RESERVED TELEPHONE LINES INCLUDED IN AFOREMEN-TIONED PROHIBITION? it repeated.

If he'd had Denny's interest in computers, he might have tumbled immediately to what was happening, but he was still confused. So he typed WHY?—meaning WHY DO YOU ASK?

OUTSYSTEM MODEM NOW IN USE.

BY WHOM?

SAMUEL BOOKER.

Loman would have laughed if he had been capable of glee. The agent had found a way out of Moonlight Cove, and now the shit was going to hit the fan at last.

Before he could query Sun as to Booker's activities and where-abouts, another name appeared on the upper left corner of the screen—SHADDACK—indicating that New Wave's own Moreau was watching the dialogue on his VDT and was cutting in. Loman was content to let his maker and Sun converse uninterrupted.

Shaddack asked for more details.

Sun responded: FBI KEY SYSTEM ACCESSED.

Loman could imagine Shaddack's shock. The beast master's de-mand appeared on the screen: OPTIONS. Which meant he desperately wanted a menu of options from Sun to deal with the situation.

Sun presented him with five choices, the fifth of which was SHUT DOWN, and Shaddack chose that one.

A moment later Sun reported: FBI KEY SYSTEM LINK SHUT DOWN.

Loman hoped that Booker had gotten enough of a message out to blow Shaddack and Moonhawk out of the water.

On the screen, from Shaddack to Sun: BOOKER'S TERMINAL?

YOU REQUIRE LOCATION?

YES.

MOONLIGHT COVE CENTRAL SCHOOL, COMPUTER LAB.

Loman was three minutes from Central.

He wondered how close Shaddack was to the school. It didn't matter. Near or far, Shaddack would bust his ass to get there and prevent Booker from compromising the Moonhawk Project—or to take vengeance if it had already been compromised.

At last Loman knew where he could find his maker.

chapter thirteen

When Sam was only six exchanges into his dialogue with Anne Denton in Washington, the link was cut off. The screen went blank.

He wanted to believe that he had been disconnected by ordinary line problems somewhere along the way. But he knew that wasn't the case.

He got up from his chair so fast that he knocked it over.

Chrissie jumped up in surprise, and Tessa said, "What is it? What's wrong?"

"They know we're here," Sam said. "They're coming."

chapter fourteen

Harry heard the doorbell ring down in the house below him.

His stomach twisted. He felt as if he were in a roller coaster, just pulling away from the boarding ramp.

The bell rang again.

A long silence followed. They knew he was crippled. They would give him time to answer.

Finally it rang again.

He looked at his watch. Only 7:24. He took no comfort in the fact that they had not put him at the end of their schedule.

The bell rang again. Then again. Then insistently.

In the distance, muffled by the two intervening floors, Moose began barking.

chapter fifteen

Tessa grabbed Chrissie's hand. With Sam, they hurried out of the computer lab. The batteries in the flashlight must not have been fresh, for the beam was growing dimmer. She hoped it would last long enough for them to find their way out. Suddenly the school's layout—which had been uncomplicated when they had not been in a life-or-death rush to negotiate its byways—seemed like a maze.

They crossed a junction of four halls, entered another corridor, and went about twenty yards before Tessa realized they were going the wrong direction. "This isn't how we came in."

"Doesn't matter," Sam said. "Any door out will do."

They had to go another ten yards before the failing flashlight beam was able to reach all the way to the end of the hall, revealing that it was a dead end.

"This way," Chrissie said, pulling loose of Tessa and turning back into the darkness from which they'd come, forcing them either to follow or abandon her.

chapter sixteen

Shaddack figured they wouldn't have tried to break into Central on any side that faced a street, where they might be seen—and the Indian agreed—so he drove around to the back. He passed metal doors that would have provided too formidable a barrier, and studied the windows, trying to spot a broken pane.

The last rear door, the only one with glass in the top, was in an angled extension of the building. He was driving toward it for a moment, just before the service road swung to the left to go around that wing, and from a distance of only a few yards, with all the other panes reflecting the glare of his headlights, his attention was caught by the missing glass at the bottom right.

"There," he told Runningdeer.

"Yes, Little Chief."

He parked near the door and grabbed the loaded Remington 12-gauge semiautomatic pistol-grip shotgun from the van's floor behind him. The box of extra shells was on the passenger seat. He opened it, grabbed four or five, stuffed them in a coat pocket, grabbed four or five more, then got out of the van and headed toward the door with the broken window.

chapter seventeen

Four soft thuds reverberated through the house, even into the attic, and Harry thought he heard glass breaking far away.

Moose barked furiously. He sounded like the most vicious attack dog ever bred, not a sweet black Lab. Maybe he would prove willing to defend home and master in spite of his naturally good temperament.

Don't do it, boy, Harry thought. Don't try to be a hero. Just crawl away in a corner somewhere and let them pass, lick their hands if they offer them, and don't—

The dog squealed and fell silent.

No, Harry thought, and a pang of grief tore through him. He had lost not just a dog but his best friend.

Moose, too, had a sense of duty.

Silence settled over the house. They would be searching the ground floor now.

Harry's grief and fear receded as his anger grew. Moose. Dammit, poor harmless Moose. He could feel the flush of rage in his face. He wanted to kill them all.

He picked up the .38 pistol in his one good hand and held it on his lap. They wouldn't find him for a while, but he felt better with the gun in his hand.

In the service he had won competition medals for both rifle sharp-shooting and performance with a handgun. That had been a long time ago. He had not fired a gun, even in practice, for more than twenty years, since that faraway and beautiful Asian land, where on a morning of exceptionally lovely blue skies, he had been crippled for life. He kept the .38 and the .45 cleaned and oiled, mostly out of habit; a soldier's lessons and routines were learned for life—and now he was glad of that.

A clank.

A rumble-purr of machinery.

The elevator.

chapter eighteen

Halfway down the correct hallway, holding the dimming flashlight in his left hand and the revolver in his other, just as he caught up with Chrissie, Sam heard a siren approaching outside. It was not on top of them, but it was too close. He couldn't tell if the patrol car was actually closing in on the back of the school, toward which they were headed, or coming to the front entrance.

Apparently Chrissie was uncertain too. She stopped running and said, "Where, Sam? Where?"

From behind them Tessa said, "Sam, the doorway!"

For an instant he didn't understand what she meant. Then he saw the door swinging open at the end of the hall, about thirty yards away, the same door by which they had entered. A man stepped inside. The siren was still wailing, drawing nearer, so there were more of them on the way, a whole platoon of them. The guy who'd come through the door was just the first—tall, six feet five if he was one inch, but otherwise only a shadow, minimally backlighted by the security lamp outside and to the right of the door.

Sam squeezed off a shot with his .38, not bothering to determine if this man was an enemy, because they were all enemies, every last one of them—their name was legion—and he knew the shot was wide. His marksmanship was lousy because of his injured wrist, which hurt like hell after their misadventures in the culvert. With the recoil, pain burst out of that joint and all the way back to his shoulder, then back again, Jesus, pain sloshing around like acid inside him, from shoulder to fingertips. Half the strength went out of his hand. He almost dropped the gun.

As the roar of Sam's shot slammed back to him from the walls of the corridor, the guy at the far end opened fire with a weapon of his own, but he had heavy artillery. A shotgun. Fortunately he was not good with it. He was aiming too high, not aware of how the kick would throw the muzzle up. Consequently the first blast went into the ceiling only ten yards ahead of him, tearing out one of the unlit fluorescent fixtures and a bunch of acoustic tiles. His reaction confirmed his lack of experience with guns; he overcompensated for the kick, swinging the muzzle too far down as he pulled the trigger a second time, so the follow-up round struck the floor far short of target.

Sam did not remain an idle observer of the misdirected gunfire. He seized Chrissie and pushed her to the left, across the corridor and through a door into a dark room, even as the second flock of buckshot gouged chunks out of the vinyl flooring. Tessa was right behind them. She threw the door shut and leaned against it, as if she thought that she was Superwoman and that any pellets penetrating the door would bounce harmlessly from her back.

Sam shoved the woefully dim flashlight at her. "With my wrist, I'm going to need both hands to manage the gun."

Tessa swept the weak yellow beam around the chamber. They were in the band room. To the right of the door, tiered platforms—full of chairs and music stands—rose up to the back wall. To the left was a large open area, the band director's podium, a blond-wood and metal desk. And two doors. Both standing open, leading to adjoining rooms.

Chrissie needed no urging to follow Tessa toward the nearer of those doors, and Sam brought up the rear, moving backward, covering the hall door through which they had come.

Outside, the siren had died. Now there would be more than one man with a shotgun.

chapter nineteen

They had searched the first two floors. They were in the third-floor bedroom.

Harry could hear them talking. Their voices rose to him through their ceiling, his floor. But he couldn't quite make out what they were saying.

He almost hoped they would spot the attic trap in the closet and would decide to come up. He wanted a chance to blow a couple of them away. For Moose. After twenty long years of being a victim, he was sick to death of it; he wanted a chance to let them know that Harry Talbot was still a man to be reckoned with—and that although Moose was only a dog, his was nevertheless a life taken only with serious consequences.

chapter twenty

In the eddying fog, Loman saw the single patrol car parked beside Shaddack's van. He braked next to it just as Paul Amberlay got out from behind the wheel. Amberlay was lean and sinewy and very bright, one of Loman's best young officers, but he looked like a high-school boy now, too small to be a cop—and scared.

When Loman got out of his car, Amberlay came to him, gun in hand, visibly shaking. "Only you and me? Where the hell's everybody else? This is a major alert."

"Where's everybody else?" Loman asked. "Just listen, Paul. Just listen."

From every part of town, scores of wild voices were lifted in eerie song, either calling to one another or challenging the unseen moon that floated above the wrung-out clouds.

Loman hurried to the back of the patrol car and opened the trunk. His unit, like every other, carried a 20-gauge riot gun for which he'd never had use in peaceable Moonlight Cove. But New Wave, which had generously equipped the force, did not stint on equipment even if it was perceived as unnecessary. He pulled the shotgun from its clip mounting on the back wall of the trunk.

Joining him, Amberlay said, "You telling me they've regressed, all of them, everyone on the force, except you and me?"

"Just listen," Loman repeated as he leaned the 20-gauge against the bumper.

"But that's crazy!" Amberlay insisted. "Jesus, God, you mean this whole thing is coming down on us, the whole damn thing?"

Loman grabbed a box of shells that was in the right wheel-well of the trunk, tore off the lid. "Don't *you* feel the yearning, Paul?"

"No!" Amberlay said too quickly. "No, I don't feel it, I don't feel anything."

"I feel it," Loman said, putting five rounds in the 20-gauge—one in the chamber, four in the magazine. "Oh, Paul, I sure as hell feel it. I want to tear off my clothes and change, *change*, and just run, be free, go with them, hunt and kill and run with them."

"Not me, no, never," Amberlay said.

"Liar," Loman said. He brought up the loaded gun and fired at Amberlay point-blank, blowing his head off.

He couldn't have trusted the young officer, couldn't have turned his back on him, not with the urge to regress so strong in him, and those voices in the night singing their siren songs.

As he stuffed more shells into his pockets, he heard a shotgun blast from inside the school.

He wondered if that gun was in the hands of Booker or Shaddack. Struggling to control his raging terror, fighting off the hideous and powerful urge to shed his human form, Loman went inside to find out.

chapter twenty-one

Tommy Shaddack heard another shotgun, but he didn't think much about that because, after all, they were in a war now. You could hear what a war it was by just stepping out in the night and listening to the shrieks of the combatants echoing down through the hills to the sea. He was more focused on getting Booker, the woman, and the girl he'd seen in the hall, because he knew the woman must be the Lockland bitch and the girl must be Chrissie Foster, though he couldn't figure how they had joined up.

War. So he handled it the way soldiers did in the good movies, kicking the door open, firing a round into the room before entering. No one screamed. He guessed he hadn't hit anyone, so he fired again, and still no one screamed, so he figured they were already gone from there. He crossed the threshold, fumbled for the light switch, found it, and discovered he was in the deserted band room.

Evidently they had left by one of the two other doors, and when he saw that, he was angry, really angry. The only time in his life that he had fired a gun was in Phoenix, when he had shot the Indian with his father's revolver, and that had been close-up, where he could not miss. But still he had expected that he would be *good* with a gun. After all, jeez, he had watched a lot of war movies, cowboy movies, cop shows on television, and it didn't look hard, not hard at all, you just pointed the muzzle and pulled the trigger. But it hadn't been that easy, after all, and Tommy was angry, furious, because they shouldn't make it look so easy in the movies and on the boob tube when, in fact, the gun jumped in your hands as if it was alive.

He knew better now, and he was going to brace himself when he fired, spread his legs and brace himself, so his shots wouldn't be blowing holes in the ceiling or bouncing off the floor any more. He would nail them cold the next time he got a whack at them, and they'd be sorry for making him chase them, for not just lying down and being dead when he *wanted* them to be dead.

chapter twenty-two

The door out of the band room had led into a hall that served ten sound-proofed practice rooms, where student musicians could mutilate fine music for hours at a time without disturbing anyone. At the end of that narrow corridor, Tessa pushed through another door and coaxed just enough out of the flashlight to see that they were in a chamber as large as the band room. It also featured tiered platforms rising to the back. A student-drawn sign on one wall, complete with winged angels singing, proclaimed this the home of The World's Best Chorus.

As Chrissie and Sam followed her into the room, a shotgun roared in the distance. It sounded as if it was outside. But even as the door to the corridor of practice rooms swung shut behind them, another shotgun discharged, closer than the first, probably back at the door to the band room. Then a second blast from the same location.

Just like in the band room, two more doors led out of the choral chamber, but the first one she tried was a dead end; it went into the chorus director's office.

They dashed to the other exit, beyond which they found a corridor illuminated only by a red, twenty-four-hour-a-day emergency sign—STAIRS—immediately to their right. Not EXIT, just STAIRS, which meant this was an interior well with no access to the outside. "Take her up," Sam urged Tessa.

"But—"

"Up! They're probably coming in the ground floor by every entrance, anyway."

"What're you—"

"Gonna make a little stand here," he said.

A door crashed open and a shotgun exploded back in the chorus room.

"Go!" Sam whispered.

chapter twenty-three

Harry heard the closet door open in the bedroom below.

The attic was cold, but he was streaming sweat as if in a sauna. Maybe he hadn't needed the second sweater.

Go away, he thought. Go away.

Then he thought, Hell, no, come on, come and get it. You think I want to live forever?

chapter twenty-four

Sam went down on one knee in the hall outside the chorus room, taking a stable position to compensate somewhat for his weak right wrist. He held the swinging door open six inches, both arms thrust through the gap, the .38 gripped in his right hand, his left hand clamped around his right wrist.

He could see the guy across the room, silhouetted in the lights of the band-room corridor behind him. Tall. Couldn't see his face. But something about him struck a chord of familiarity.

The gunman didn't see Sam. He was only being cautious, laying down a spray of pellets before he entered. He pulled the trigger. The click was loud in the silent room. He pumped the shotgun. *Clackety-clack*. No ammo.

That meant a change in Sam's plans. He surged to his feet and through the swinging door, back into the chorus room, no longer able to wait for the guy to switch on the overhead lights or step farther across the threshold, because now was the time to take him, before he reloaded. Firing as he went, Sam squeezed off the four remaining rounds in the .38, trying his damnedest to make every slug count. On the second or third shot, the guy in the doorway squealed, God, he squealed like a kid, his voice high-pitched and quaverous, as he threw himself back into the practice-room corridor, out of sight.

Sam kept moving, fumbling in his jacket pocket with his left hand, grabbing at the spare cartridges, while with his right hand he snapped open the revolver's cylinder and shook out the expended brass casings. When he reached the closed door to the narrow hall that connected chorus room to band room, the door through which the tall man had vanished, he pressed his back to the wall and jammed fresh rounds into the Smith & Wesson, snapped the cylinder shut.

He kicked the door open and looked into the hall, where the overhead fluorescents were lit.

It was deserted.

No blood on the floor.

Damn. His right hand was half numb. He could feel his wrist swelling tight under the bandage, which was now soaked with fresh blood. At the rate his shooting was deteriorating, he was going to have to walk right up to the bastard and ask him to bite on the muzzle in order to make the shot count.

The doors to the ten practice rooms, five on each side, were closed. The door at the far end, where the hall led into the band room, was open, and the lights were on there. The tall guy could be there or in any of the ten practice rooms. But wherever he was, he had probably slipped at least a couple of shells into that shotgun, so the moment to pursue him had passed.

Sam backed up, letting the door between the hall and the chorus room slip shut. Even as he let go of it, as it was swinging back into place, he glimpsed the tall man stepping through the open door of the band room about forty feet away.

It was Shaddack himself.

The shotgun boomed.

The soundproofed door, gliding shut at the crucial moment, was thick enough to stop the pellets.

Sam turned and ran across the chorus room, into the hall, and up the stairs, where he had sent Tessa and Chrissie.

When he reached the top flight, he found them waiting for him in the upper hall, in the soft red glow of another STAIRS sign.

Below, Shaddack entered the stairwell.

Sam turned, stepped back onto the landing and descended the first step. He leaned over the railing, looked down, glimpsed part of his pursuer, and squeezed off two shots.

Shaddack squealed like a boy again. He ducked back against the wall, away from the open center of the well, where he could not be seen.

Sam didn't know whether he'd scored a hit or not. Maybe. What he *did* know was that Shaddack wasn't mortally wounded; he was still coming, easing up step by step, staying against the outer wall. And when that geek reached the lower landing, he would take the turn suddenly, firing the shotgun repeatedly at whoever waited above.

Silently Sam retreated from the upper landing, into the hall once more. The scarlet light of the STAIRS sign fell on Chrissie's and Tessa's faces . . . an illusion of blood.

chapter twenty-five

A clink. A scraping sound.

Clink-scrape. Clink-scrape.

Harry knew what he was hearing. Clothes hangers sliding on a metal rod.

How could they have known? Hell, maybe they had smelled him up here. He was sweating like a horse, after all. Maybe the conversion improved their senses.

The clinking and scraping stopped.

A moment later he heard them lifting the closet rod out of its braces so they could lower the trap.

chapter twenty-six

The fading flashlight kept winking out, and Tessa had to shake it, jarring the batteries together, to get a few more seconds of weak and fluttery light from it.

They had stepped out of the hall, into what proved to be a chemistry lab with black marble lab tables and steel sinks and high wooden stools. Nowhere to hide.

They checked the windows, hoping there might be a roof just under them. No. A two-story drop to a concrete walk.

At the end of the chemistry lab was a door, through which they passed into a ten-foot-square storage room full of chemicals in sealed tins and bottles, some labeled with skulls and crossbones, some with DANGER in bright red letters. She supposed there were ways to use the contents of that closet as a weapon, but they didn't have time to inventory the contents, looking for interesting substances to mix together. Besides, she'd never been a great science student, recalled nothing whatsoever of her chemistry classes, and would probably blow herself up with the first bottle she opened. From the expression on Sam's face, she knew that he saw no more hope there than she did.

A rear door in the storage closet opened into a second lab that seemed to double as a biology classroom. Anatomy charts hung on one wall. The room offered no better place to hide than had the previous lab.

Holding Chrissie close against her side, Tessa looked at Sam and whispered, "Now what? Wait here and hope he can't find us . . . or keep moving?"

"I think it's safer to keep moving," Sam said. "Easier to be cornered if we sit still."

She nodded agreement.

He eased past her and Chrissie, leading the way between the lab benches, toward the door to the hall.

From behind them, either in the dark chemical-storage room or in the unlighted chemistry lab beyond it, came a soft but distinct *clink*.

Sam halted, motioned Tessa and Chrissie ahead of him, and turned to cover the exit from the storage room.

With Chrissie at her side, Tessa stepped to the hall door, turned the knob slowly, quietly, and eased the door outward.

Shaddack came from the darkness in the corridor, into the pale and inconstant pulse of light from her flash, and rammed the barrel of his shotgun into her stomach. "You're gonna be sorry now," he said excitedly.

chapter twenty-seven

They pulled the trapdoor down. A shaft of light from the closet shot up to the rafters, but it didn't illuminate the far corner in which Harry sat with his useless legs splayed out in front of him.

His bad hand was curled in his lap, while his good hand fiercely clasped the pistol.

His heart was hammering harder and faster than it had in twenty years, since the battlefields of Southeast Asia. His stomach was churning. His throat was so tight he could barely breathe. He was dizzy with fear. But, God in heaven, he sure felt *alive*.

With a squeak and clatter, they unfolded the ladder.

chapter twenty-eight

Tommy Shaddack shoved the muzzle into her belly and almost blew her guts out, almost wasted her, before he realized how *pretty* she was, and then he didn't want to kill her any more, at least not right away, not until he'd made her do some things with him, do some things *to* him.

She'd have to do whatever he wanted, anything, whatever he told her to do, or he could just smear her across the wall, yeah, she was his, and she better realize that, or she'd be sorry, he'd make her sorry.

Then he saw the girl beside her, a pretty *little* girl, only ten or twelve, and she excited him even more. He could have her first, and then the older one, have them any which way he wanted them, make them *do* things, all sorts of things, and then hurt them, that was his right, they couldn't deny him, not him, because all the power was in his hands now, he had seen the moonhawk *three* times.

He pushed through the open door, into the room, keeping the gun in the woman's belly, and she backed up to accommodate him, pulling the girl with her. Booker was behind them, a startled expression on his face. Tommy Shaddack said, "Drop your gun and back away from it, or I'll make raspberry jelly out of this bitch, I swear I will, you can't move fast enough to stop me."

Booker hesitated.

"Drop it!" Tommy Shaddack insisted.

The agent let go of the revolver and sidestepped away from it.

Keeping the muzzle of the Remington hard against the woman's belly, he made her edge around until she could reach the light switch and click on the fluorescents. The room leaped out of shadows.

"Okay, now, all of you," Tommy Shaddack said, "sit down on those three stools, by that lab bench, yeah, there, and don't do anything funny."

He stepped back from the woman and covered them all with the shotgun. They looked scared, and that made him laugh.

Tommy was getting excited now, really excited, because he had decided he would kill Booker in front of the woman and the girl, not swift and clean but slowly, the first shot in the legs, let him lie on the floor and wriggle a while, the second shot in the gut but not from such a close range that it finished him instantly, make him hurt, make the woman and the girl watch, show them what a customer they had in Tommy Shaddack, what a damned tough customer, make them grateful for being spared, so grateful they'd get on their knees and let him *do* things to them, do all the things he had wanted to do for thirty years but that he had denied himself, let off thirty years of steam right here, right now, tonight. . . .

chapter twenty-nine

Beyond the house, filtering into the attic through vents in the eaves, came eerie howling, point and counterpoint, first solo and then chorus. It sounded as if the gates of hell had been thrown open, letting denizens of the pit pour forth into Moonlight Cove.

Harry worried about Sam, Tessa, and Chrissie.

Below him, the unseen conversion team locked the collapsible ladder in place. One of them began to climb into the attic.

Harry wondered what they would look like. Would they be just ordinary men—old Doc Fitz with a syringe and a couple of deputies to assist him? Or would they be Boogeymen? Or some of the machine-men Sam had talked about?

The first one ascended through the open trap. It was Dr. Worthy, the town's youngest physician.

Harry considered shooting him while he was still on the ladder. But he hadn't fired a gun in twenty years, and he didn't want to waste his limited ammunition. Better to wait for a closer shot.

Worthy didn't have a flashlight. Didn't seem to need one. He looked straight toward the darkest corner, where Harry was propped, and said, "How did you know we were coming, Harry?"

"Cripple's intuition," Harry said sarcastically.

Along the center of the attic, there was plenty of headroom to allow Worthy to walk upright. He rose from a crouch as he came out from under the sloping rafters near the trap, and when he had taken four steps forward, Harry fired twice at him.

The first shot missed, but the second hit low in the chest.

Worthy was flung backward, went down hard on the bare boards of the attic floor. He lay there for a moment, twitching, then sat up, coughed once, and got to his feet.

Blood glistened all over the front of his torn white shirt. He had been hit hard, yet he had recovered in seconds.

Harry remembered what Sam had said about how the Coltranes had refused to stay dead. *Go for the data processor.*

He aimed for Worthy's head and fired twice again, but at that distance—about twenty-five feet—and at that angle, shooting up from the floor, he couldn't hit anything. He hesitated with only four rounds left in the pistol's clip.

Another man was climbing through the trap.

Harry shot at him, trying to drive him back down.

He came on, unperturbed.

Three rounds in the pistol.

Keeping his distance, Dr. Worthy said, "Harry, we're not here to harm you. I don't know what you've heard or *how* you've heard about the project, but it isn't a bad thing. . . ."

His voice trailed off, and he cocked his head as if to listen to the unhuman cries that filled the night outside. A peculiar look of longing, visible even in the dim wash of light from the open trap, crossed Worthy's face.

He shook himself, blinked, and remembered that he had been trying to sell his elixir to a reluctant customer. "Not a bad thing at all, Harry. Especially for you. You'll walk again, Harry, walk as well as anyone. You'll be whole again. Because after the Change, you'll be able to heal yourself. You'll be free of paralysis."

"No, thanks. Not at that price."

"What price, Harry?" Worthy asked, spreading his arms, palms up. "Look at me. What price have I paid?"

"Your soul?" Harry said.

A third man was coming up the ladder.

The second man was listening to the ululant cries that came in through the attic vents. He gritted his teeth, ground them together forcefully, and blinked very fast. He raised his hands and covered his face with them, as if he were suddenly anguished.

Worthy noticed his companion's situation. "Vanner, are you all right?"

Vanner's hands . . . *changed*. His wrists swelled and grew gnarly with bone, and his fingers lengthened, all in a couple of seconds. When he took his hands from his face, his jaw was thrusting forward like that of a werewolf in midtransformation. His shirt tore at the seams as his body reconfigured itself. He snarled, and teeth flashed.

". . . *need,*" Vanner said, ". . . *need, need, want, need . . .*"

"No!" Worthy shouted.

The third man, who had just come out of the trap, rolled onto the floor, changing as he did so, flowing into a vaguely insectile but thoroughly repulsive form.

Before he quite knew what he was doing, Harry emptied the .38 at the insect-thing, pitched it away, snatched the .45 revolver off the board floor beside him, also fired three rounds from that, evidently striking the thing's brain at least once. It kicked, twitched, fell back down through the trap, and did not clamber upward again.

Vanner had undergone a complete lupine metamorphosis and seemed to have patterned himself after something that he had seen in a movie, because he looked familiar to Harry, as if Harry had seen that same movie, though he could not quite remember it. Vanner shrieked in answer to the creatures whose cries pealed through the night outside.

Tearing frantically at his clothes, as if the pressure of them against his skin was driving him mad, Worthy was changing into a beast quite different from either Vanner or the third man. Some grotesque physical incarnation of his own mad desires.

Harry had only three rounds left, and he had to save the last one for himself.

chapter thirty

Earlier, after surviving the ordeal in the culvert, Sam had promised himself that he would learn to accept failure, which had been all well and good until now, when failure was again at hand.

He could *not* fail, not with both Chrissie and Tessa depending on him. If no other opportunity presented itself, he would at least leap at Shaddack the moment before he believed the man was ready to pull the trigger.

Judging that moment might be difficult. Shaddack looked and sounded insane. The way his mind was short-circuiting, he might pull the trigger in the middle of one of those high, quick, nervous, boyish laughs, without any indication that the moment had come.

"Get off your stool," he said to Sam.

"What?"

"You heard me, dammit, get off your stool. Lay on the floor, over there, or I'll make you sorry, I sure will, I'll make you very sorry." He gestured with the muzzle of the shotgun. "Get off your stool and lay on the floor *now*."

Sam didn't want to do it because he knew Shaddack was separating him from Chrissie and Tessa only to shoot him.

He hesitated, then slid off the stool because there was nothing else he could do. He moved between two lab benches, to the open area that Shaddack had indicated.

"Down," Shaddack said. "I want to see you down there on the floor, groveling."

Dropping to one knee, Sam slipped a hand into an inner pocket of his leather jack, fished out the metal loid that he had used to pop the lock at the Coltranes' house, and flicked it away from himself, with the same snap of his wrist that he would have used to toss a playing card at a hat.

The loid sailed low across the floor, toward the windows, until it clattered through the rungs of a stool and clinked off the base of a marble lab bench.

The madman swung the Remington toward the sound.

With a shout of rage and determination, Sam came up fast and threw himself at Shaddack.

chapter thirty-one

Tessa grabbed Chrissie and hustled her away from the struggling men, to the wall beside the hall door. They crouched there, where she hoped they would be out of the line of fire.

Sam had come up under the shotgun before Shaddack could swing back from the distraction. He grabbed the barrel with his left hand and Shaddack's wrist with his weakened right hand, and pressed him backward, pushing him off balance, slamming him against another lab bench.

When Shaddack cried out, Sam snarled with satisfaction, as if *he* might turn into something that howled in the night.

Tessa saw him ram a knee up between Shaddack's legs, hard into his crotch. The tall man screamed.

"All *right*, Sam!" Chrissie said approvingly.

As Shaddack gagged and spluttered and tried to double over in an involuntary reaction to the pain in his damaged privates, Sam tore the shotgun out of his hands and stepped back—

—and a man in a police uniform came into the room from the chemistry storage closet, carrying a shotgun of his own. "No! Drop your weapon. Shaddack is *mine*."

chapter thirty-two

The thing that had been Vanner moved toward Harry, growling low in its throat, drooling yellowish saliva. Harry fired twice, struck it both times, but failed to kill it. The gaping wounds seemed to close up before his eyes.

One round left.

"...*need, need*..."

Harry put the barrel of the .45 in his mouth, pressed the muzzle against his palate, gagging on the hot steel.

The hideous, wolfish thing loomed over him. The swollen head was three times as big as it ought to have been, out of proportion to its body. Most of the head was mouth, and most of the mouth was teeth, not even the teeth of a wolf but the inward-curving teeth of a shark. Vanner had not been satisfied to model himself entirely after just one of nature's predators, but wanted to make himself something more murderous and efficiently destructive than anything nature had contemplated.

When Vanner was only three feet from him, leaning in to bite, Harry pulled the gun out of his own mouth, said, "Hell, no," and shot the damn thing in the head. It toppled back, landed with a crash, and stayed down.

Go for the data-processor.

Elation swept through Harry, but it was short-lived. Worthy had completed his transformation and seemed to have been thrown into a frenzy by the carnage in the room and the escalating shrieks that came through the attic vents from the world beyond. He turned his lantern eyes on Harry, and in them was a look of unhuman hunger.

No more bullets.

chapter thirty-three

Sam was squarely under the cop's gun, with no room to maneuver. He had to drop the Remington that he'd taken off Shaddack.

"I'm on your side," the cop repeated.

"No one's on our side," Sam said.

Shaddack was gasping for breath and trying to stand up straight. He regarded the officer with abject terror.

With the coldest premeditation Sam had ever seen, with no hint of emotion whatsoever, not even anger, the cop turned his 20-gauge shotgun on Shaddack, who was no longer a threat to anyone, and fired four rounds. As if punched by a giant, Shaddack flew backward over two stools and into the wall.

The cop threw the gun aside and moved quickly to the dead man. He tore open the sweat-suit jacket that Shaddack wore under his coat and ripped loose a strange object, a largish rectangular medallion, that had hung from a gold chain around the man's neck.

Holding up that curious artifact, he said, "Shaddack's dead. His heartbeat isn't being broadcast any more, so Sun is even now putting the final program into effect. In half a minute or so we'll all know peace. Peace at last."

At first Sam thought the cop was saying they were all going to die, that the thing in his hand was going to kill them, that it was a bomb or something. He backed quickly toward the door and saw that Tessa evidently had the same expectation. She had pulled Chrissie up from where they'd been crouching, and had opened the door.

But if there was a bomb, it was a silent one, and the radius of its small explosion remained within the police officer. Suddenly his face contorted. Between clenched teeth, he said, "God." It was not an exclamation but a plea or perhaps an inadequate description of something he had just seen, for in that moment he fell down dead from no cause that Sam could see.

chapter thirty-four

When they stepped out through the back door by which they had entered, the first thing Sam noticed was that the night had fallen silent. The shrill cries of the shape-changers no longer echoed across the fog-bound town.

The keys were in the van's ignition.

"You drive," he told Tessa.

His wrist was swollen worse than ever. It was throbbing so hard that each pulse of pain reverberated through every fiber of him.

He settled in the passenger seat.

Chrissie curled in his lap, and he wrapped his arms around her. She was uncharacteristically silent. She was exhausted, on the verge of collapse, but Sam knew the cause of her silence was more profound than weariness.

Tessa slammed her door and started the engine. She didn't have to be told where to go.

On the drive to Harry's place, they discovered that the streets were littered with the dead, not the corpses of ordinary men and women but—as their headlights revealed beyond a doubt—of creatures out of a painting by Hieronymus Bosch, twisted and phantasmagorical forms. She drove slowly, maneuvering around them, and a couple of times she had to pull up on the sidewalk to get past a pack of them that had gone down together, apparently felled by the same unseen force that had dropped the policeman back at Central.

Shaddack's dead. His heartbeat isn't being broadcast any more, so Sun is even now putting the final program into effect. . . .

After a while Chrissie lowered her head against Sam's chest and would not look out the windshield.

Sam kept telling himself that the fallen creatures were phantoms, that no such things could have actually come into existence, either by the application of the highest of high technology or by sorcery. He expected them to vanish every time a shroud of fog briefly obscured them, but when the fog moved off again, they were still huddled on the pavement, sidewalks, and lawns.

Immersed in all that horror and ugliness, he could not believe that he had been so foolish as to pass years of precious life in gloom, unwilling to see the beauty of the world. He'd been a singular fool. When the dawn came, he would never thereafter fail to look upon a flower and appreciate the wonder of it, the beauty that was beyond man's abilities of creation.

"Tell me now?" Tessa asked as they pulled within a block of Harry's redwood house.

"Tell you what?"

"What you saw. Your near-death experience. What did you see on the Other Side that scared you so?"

He laughed shakily. "I was an idiot."

"Probably," she said. "Tell me and let me judge."

"Well, I can't tell you exactly. It was more an *understanding* than a seeing, a spiritual rather than visual perception."

"So what did you understand?"

"That we go on from this world," he said. "That there's either life for us on another plane, one life after another on an endless series of planes . . . or that we live again on this plane, reincarnate. I'm not sure which, but I felt it deeply, *knew* it when I reached the end of that tunnel and saw the light, that brilliant light."

She glanced at him. "And *that's* what terrified you?"

"Yes."

"That we live again?"

"Yes. Because I found life so bleak, you see, just a series of tragedies, just pain. I'd lost the ability to appreciate the beauty of life, the joy, so I didn't want to die and have to start in all over again, not any sooner than absolutely necessary. At least in *this* life I'd become hardened, inured to the pain, which gave me an advantage over starting out as a child again in some new incarnation."

"So your fourth reason for living wasn't technically a fear of death," she said.

"I guess not."

"It was a fear of having to live again."

"Yes."

"And now?"

He thought a moment. Chrissie stirred in his lap. He stroked her damp hair. At last he said, "Now, I'm *eager* to live again."

chapter thirty-five

Harry heard noises downstairs—the elevator, then someone in the third-floor bedroom. He tensed, figuring two miracles were one too many to hope for, but then he heard Sam calling to him from the bottom of the ladder.

"Here, Sam! Safe! I'm okay."

A moment later Sam climbed into the attic.

"Tessa? Chrissie?" Harry asked anxiously.

"They're downstairs. They're both all right."

"Thank God." Harry let out a long breath, as if it had been pent up in him for hours. "Look at these brutes, Sam."

"Rather not."

"Maybe Chrissie was right about alien invaders after all."

"Something stranger," Sam said.

"What?" Harry said as Sam knelt beside him and gingerly pushed Worthy's mutated body off his legs.

"Damned if I know," Sam said. "Not even sure I want to know."

"We're entering an age when we make our own reality, aren't we? Science is giving us that ability, bit by bit. Used to be only madmen could do that."

Sam said nothing.

Harry said, "Maybe making our own reality isn't wise. Maybe the natural order is the best one."

"Maybe. On the other hand, the natural order could do with some perfecting here and there. I guess we've got to try. We just have to hope to God that the men who do the tinkering aren't like Shaddack. You okay, Harry?"

"Pretty good, thanks." He smiled. "Except, of course, I'm still a cripple. See this hulking thing that was Worthy? He was leaning in to rip my throat out, I had no more bullets, he had his claws at my neck, and then he just fell dead, bang. Is that a miracle or what?"

"Been a miracle all over town," Sam said. "They all seemed to have died when Shaddack died . . . linked somehow. Come on, let's get you down from here, out of this mess."

"They killed Moose, Sam."

"The hell they did. Who do you think Chrissie and Tessa are fussing over downstairs?"

Harry was stunned. "But I heard—"

"Looks like maybe somebody kicked him in the head. He's got this bloody, skinned-up spot along one side of his skull. Might've been knocked unconscious, but he doesn't seem to've suffered a concussion."

chapter thirty-six

Chrissie rode in the back of the van with Harry and Moose, with Harry's good arm around her and Moose's head in her lap. Slowly she began to feel better. She was not herself, no, and maybe she never would feel like her old self again, but she was better.

They went to the park at the head of Ocean Avenue, at the east end of town. Tessa drove right up over the curb, bouncing them around, and parked on the grass.

Sam opened the rear doors of the van so Chrissie and Harry could sit side by side in their blankets and watch him and Tessa at work.

Braver than Chrissie would have been, Sam went into the nearby residential areas, stepping over and around the dead things, and jump-started cars that were parked along the streets. One by one, he and Tessa drove them into the park and arranged them in a huge ring, with the engines running and the headlights pointing in toward the middle of the circle.

Sam said that people would be coming in helicopters, even in the fog, and that the circle of light would mark a proper landing pad for them. With twenty cars, their headlights all blazing on high beam, the inside of that ring was as bright as noon.

Chrissie liked the brightness.

Even before the landing pad was fully outlined, a few people began to appear in the streets, live people, and not weird looking at all, without fangs and stingers and claws, standing fully erect—altogether normal, judging by appearances. Of course, Chrissie had learned that you could never confidently judge anyone by appearances because they could be anything inside; they could be something inside that would astonish even the editors of the *National Enquirer*. You couldn't even be sure of your own parents.

But she couldn't think about that.

She didn't *dare* think about what had happened to her folks. She knew that what little hope she still held for their salvation was probably false hope, but she wanted to hold on to it for just a while longer, anyway.

The few people who appeared in the streets began to gravitate toward the park while Tessa and Sam finished pulling the last few cars into the ring. They all looked dazed. The closer they approached, the more uneasy Chrissie became.

"They're all right," Harry assured her, cuddling her with his one good arm.

"How can you be sure?"

"You can see they're scared shitless. Oops. Maybe I shouldn't say 'shitless,' teach you bad language."

"'Shitless' is okay," she said.

Moose made a mewling sound and shifted in her lap. He probably had the kind of headache that only karate experts usually got from smashing bricks with their heads.

"Well," Harry said, "look at them—they're scared plenty bad, which probably tags them as our kind. You never saw one of those others acting scared, did you?"

She thought about it a moment. "Yeah. I did. That cop who shot Mr. Shaddack at the school. He was scared. He had more fear in his eyes, a lot more, than I've ever seen in anybody else's."

"Well, these people are all right, anyway," Harry told her as the dazed stragglers approached the van. "They're some of the ones who were scheduled to be converted before midnight, but nobody got around to them. Must be others in their houses, barricaded in there, afraid to come out, think the whole world's gone crazy, probably think aliens are on the loose, like you thought. Besides, if these people were more of those shape-changers, they wouldn't be staggering up to us so hesitantly. They'd have loped right up the hill, leaped in here, and eaten our noses, plus whatever other parts of us they consider to be delicacies."

That explanation appealed to her, even made her smile thinly, and she relaxed a little.

But just a second later, Moose jerked his burly head off her lap, yipped, and scrambled to his feet.

Outside, the people approaching the van cried out in surprise and fear, and Chrissie heard Sam say, "What the blazing *hell*?"

She threw aside her warm blankets and scrambled out of the back of the van to see what was happening.

Behind her, alarmed in spite of the reassurances that he had just given her, Harry said, "What is it? What's wrong?"

For a moment she wasn't sure what had startled everyone, but then she saw the animals. They swarmed through the park—scores of mice, a few grungy rats, cats of all descriptions, half a dozen dogs, and maybe a couple of dozen squirrels that had scampered down from the trees. More mice and rats and cats were racing out of the mouths of the streets that intersected Ocean Avenue, pouring up that main drag, running pell-mell, frenzied, cutting through the park and angling over to the county road. They reminded her of something she'd read about once, and she only had to stand there for a few seconds, watching them pour by her, before she remembered: lemmings. Periodically, when the lemming population became too great in a particular area, the little creatures ran and ran, straight toward the sea, into the surf, and drowned themselves. All these animals were acting like lemmings, tearing off in the same direction, letting nothing stand in their way, drawn by nothing apparent and therefore evidently following an inner compulsion.

Moose jumped out of the van and joined the fleeing multitudes.

"Moose, no!" she shouted.

He stumbled, as if he had tripped over the cry that she had flung after him. He looked back, then snapped his head toward the county road again, as if he had been jerked by an invisible chain. He took off at top speed.

"*Moose!*"

He stumbled once more and actually fell this time, rolled, and scrambled onto his feet.

Somehow Chrissie knew that the image of lemmings was apt, that these animals were rushing to their graves, though away from the sea, toward some other and more hideous death that was part of all the rest that had happened in Moonlight Cove. If she did not stop Moose, they would never see him again.

The dog ran.

She sprinted after him.

She was bone weary, burnt out, aching in every muscle and joint, and afraid, but she found the strength and will to pursue the Labrador because no one else seemed to understand that he and the other animals were running toward death. Tessa and Sam, smart as they were, didn't get it. They were just standing, gaping at the spectacle. So Chrissie tucked her arms against her sides, pumped her legs, and ran for all she was worth, picturing herself as Chrissie Foster, World's Youngest Olympic Marathon Champion, pounding around the course, with thousands cheering her from the sidelines. *("Chrissie, Chrissie, Chrissie, Chrissie . . .")* And as she ran, she screamed at Moose to stop, because every time he heard his name, he faltered, hesitated, and she gained a little ground on him. Then they were through the park, and she nearly fell in the deep ditch alongside the county road, leaped it at the last instant, not because she saw it in time but because she had her eye on Moose and saw *him* leap something. She landed perfectly, not losing a stride. The next time Moose faltered in response to his name, she was on him, grabbing at him, seizing his collar. He growled and nipped at her, and she said, "Moose," in such a way as to shame him. That was the only time he tried to bite her but, Lord, he strained mightily to pull loose. Hanging on to him took everything she had, and he even dragged her, big as she was, about fifty or sixty feet along the road. His big paws scrabbled at the blacktop as he struggled to follow the wave of small animals that was receding into the night and fog.

By the time the dog calmed down enough to be willing to go back toward the park, Tessa and Sam joined Chrissie. "What's happening?" Sam asked.

"They're all running to their deaths," Chrissie said. "I just couldn't let Moose go with them."

"To their deaths? How do you know?"

"I don't know. But . . . what else?"

They stood on the dark and foggy road for a moment, looking after the animals, which had vanished into the blackness.

Tessa said, "What else indeed?"

chapter thirty-seven

The fog was thinning, but visibility was still no more than about a quarter of a mile.

Standing with Tessa in the middle of the circle of cars, Sam heard the choppers shortly after ten o'clock, before he saw their lights. Because the mist distorted sound, he could not tell from which direction they were approaching, but he figured they were coming in from the south, along the coast, staying a couple of hundred yards out to sea, where there were no hills to worry about in the fog. Packed with the most sophisticated instruments, they could virtually fly blind. The pilots would be wearing night-vision goggles, coming in under five hundred feet in respect of the poor weather.

Because the FBI maintained tight relationships with the armed services, especially the Marines, Sam pretty much knew what to expect. This would be a Marine Reconnaissance force composed of the standard elements required by such a situation: one CH-46 helicopter carrying the recon team itself—probably twelve men detached from a Marine Assault Unit—accompanied by two Cobra gunships.

Turning around, looking in every direction, Tessa said, "I don't see them."

"You won't," Sam said. "Not until they're almost on top of us."

"They fly without lights?"

"No. They're equipped with blue lights, which can't be seen well from the ground, but which give them a damned good view through their night-vision goggles."

Ordinarily, when responding to a terrorist threat, the CH-46—called the "Sea Knight," officially, but referred to as "The Frog" by grunts—would have gone, with its Cobra escorts, to the north end of town. Three fire teams, composed of four men each, would have disembarked and swept through Moonlight Cove from north to south, checking out the situation, rendezvousing at the other end for evacuation as necessary.

But because of the message Sam had sent to the Bureau before Sun's links to the outside world had been cut off, and because the situation did not involve terrorists and was, in fact, singularly strange, SOP was discarded for a bolder approach. The choppers overflew the town repeatedly, descending to within twenty or thirty feet of the treetops. At times their strange bluish-green lights were visible, but nothing whatsoever could be seen of their shape or size; because of their Fiberglas blades, which were much quieter than the old metal blades that once had been used, the choppers at times seemed to glide silently in the distance and might have been alien craft from a far world even stranger than this one.

At last they hovered near the circle of light in the park.

They did not put down at once. With the powerful rotors flinging the fog away, they played a searchlight over the people in the park who stood outside the illuminated landing pad, and they spent minutes examining the grotesque bodies in the street.

Finally, while the Cobras remained aloft, the CH-46 gentled down almost reluctantly in the ring of cars. The men who poured from the chopper were toting automatic weapons, but otherwise they didn't look like soldiers because, thanks to Sam's message, they were dressed in biologically secure white suits, carrying their own air-supply tanks on their backs. They might have been astronauts instead of Marines.

Lieutenant Ross Dalgood, who looked baby-faced behind the face-plate of his helmet, came straight to Sam and Tessa, gave his name and rank, and greeted Sam by name, evidently because he'd been shown a photograph before his mission had gotten off the ground. "Biological hazard, Agent Booker?"

"I don't think so," Sam said, as the chopper blades cycled down from a hard rhythmic cracking to a softer, wheezing chug.

"But you don't know?"

"I don't know," he admitted.

"We're the advance," Dalgood said. "Lots more on the way—regular Army and your Bureau people are coming in by highway. Be here soon."

The three of them—Dalgood, Sam, and Tessa—moved between two of the encircling cars, to one of the dead things that lay on a sidewalk bordering the park.

"I didn't believe what I saw from the air," Dalgood said.

"Believe it," Tessa said.

"What the hell?" Dalgood said.

Sam said, "Boogeymen."

chapter thirty-eight

Tessa worried about Sam. She and Chrissie and Harry returned to Harry's house at one in the morning, after being debriefed three times by men in decontamination suits. Although they had terrible nightmares, they managed to get a few hours' sleep. But Sam was gone all night. He had not returned by the time they finished breakfast at eleven o'clock Wednesday morning.

"He may think he's indestructible," she said, "but he's not."

"You care about him," Harry said.

"Of course I care about him."

"I mean *care* about him."

"Well . . . I don't know."

"I know."

"I know too," Chrissie said.

Sam returned at one o'clock, grimy and gray-faced. She'd made up the spare bed with fresh sheets, and he tumbled into it still half dressed.

She sat in a chair by the bed, watching him sleep. Occasionally he groaned and thrashed. He called her name and Chrissie's—and sometimes Scott's—as if he had lost them and was wandering in search of them through a dangerous and desolate place.

Bureau men in decontamination suits came for him at six o'clock, Wednesday evening, after he'd slept less than five hours. He went away for the rest of that night.

By then all the bodies, in their multitudinous biologies, had been collected from where they had fallen, tagged, sealed in plastic bags, and put into cold storage for the attention of the pathologists.

That night Tessa and Chrissie shared the same bed. Lying in the half-dark room, where a towel had been thrown over a lamp to make a night-light, the girl said, "They're gone."

"Who?"

"My mom and dad."

"I think they are."

"Dead."

"I'm sorry, Chrissie."

"Oh, I know. I know you are. You're very nice." Then for a while she cried in Tessa's arms.

Much later, nearer sleep, she said, "You talked to Sam a little. Did he say if they figured out . . . about those animals last night . . . where they were all running to?"

"No," Tessa said. "They haven't got a clue yet."

"That spooks me."

"Me too."

"I mean, that they haven't got a clue."

"I know," Tessa said. "That's what I mean too."

chapter thirty-nine

By Thursday morning, teams of Bureau technicians and outside consultants from the private sector had pored through enough of the Moonhawk data in Sun to determine that the project had dealt strictly with the implantation of a nonbiological control mechanism that had resulted in profound physiological changes in the victims. No one yet had the glimmer of an idea as to how it worked, as to how the microspheres could have resulted in such radical metamorphoses, but they were certain no bacterium, virus, or other engineered organism had been involved. It was purely a matter of machines.

The Army troops, enforcing the quarantine against news-media interlopers and civilian curiosity-seekers, still had their work to do, but they were grateful to be able to strip out of their hot and clumsy decon suits. So were the hundreds of scientists and Bureau agents who were bivouacked throughout town.

Although Sam would surely be returning in the days ahead, he and Tessa and Chrissie were cleared for evacuation early Friday morning. A sympathetic court, with the counsel of a host of federal and state officials, had already granted Tessa temporary custody of the girl. The three of them said see-you-soon to Harry, not goodbye, and were lifted out by one of the Bureau's Bell JetRanger executive helicopters.

To keep onsite researchers from having their views colored by sensationalistic and inaccurate news accounts, a media blackout was in force in Moonlight Cove, and Sam did not fully realize the impact of the Moonhawk story until they flew over the Army roadblock near the interstate. Hundreds of press vehicles were strewn along the road and parked in fields. The pilot flew low enough for Sam to see all the cameras turned upward to shoot them as they passed over the mob.

"It's almost as bad on the county route, north of Holliwell Road," the chopper pilot said, "where they set up the other block. Reporters from all over the world, sleeping on the ground 'cause they don't want to go away to some motel and wake up to find that Moonlight Cove was opened to the press while they were snoozing."

"They don't have to worry," Sam said. "It's not going to be opened to the press—or to anyone but researchers—for weeks."

The JetRanger transported them to San Francisco International Airport, where they had reservations for three seats on a PSA flight south to Los Angeles. In the terminal, scanning the news racks, Sam read a couple of headlines:

ARTIFICIAL INTELLIGENCE BEHIND COVE TRAGEDY
SUPERCOMPUTER RUNS AMOK

That was nonsense, of course. New Wave's supercomputer, Sun, was not an artificial intelligence. No such thing had yet been built anywhere on earth, though legions of scientists were racing to be the first to father a true, thinking, electronic mind. Sun had not run amok; it had only served, as all computers do.

Paraphrasing Shakespeare, Sam thought: the fault lies not in our technology but in ourselves.

These days, however, people blamed screwups in the system on computers—just as, centuries ago, members of less sophisticated cultures had blamed the alignment of celestial bodies.

Tessa quietly pointed out another headline:

SECRET PENTAGON EXPERIMENT BEHIND
MYSTERIOUS DISASTER

The Pentagon was a favorite Boogeyman in some circles, almost beloved for its real and imagined evils because believing it was the root of all malevolence made life simpler and easier to understand. To those who felt that way, the Pentagon was almost the bumbling old Frankenstein monster in his clodhopper shoes and too-small black suit, scary but understandable, perverse and to be shunned yet comfortably predictable and preferable to consideration of worse and more complex villains.

Chrissie pulled from the rack a rare special edition of a major national tabloid, filled with stories about Moonlight Cove. She showed them the main headline:

ALIENS LAND ON CALIFORNIA COAST
RAVENOUS FLESH-EATERS SACK TOWN

They looked at one another solemnly for a moment, then smiled. For the first time in a couple of days, Chrissie laughed. It was not a hearty laugh, just a chuckle, and there might have been a touch of irony in it that was too sharp for an eleven-year-old girl, not to mention a trace of melancholy, but it *was* a laugh. Hearing her laugh, Sam felt better.

chapter forty

Joel Ganowicz, of United Press International, had been on the perimeter of Moonlight Cove, at one roadblock or another, since early Wednesday morning. He bunked in a sleeping bag on the ground, used the woods as a toilet, and paid an unemployed carpenter from Aberdeen Wells to bring meals to him. Never in his career had he been so committed to a story, willing to rough it to this extent. And he was not sure why. Yes, certainly, it was the biggest story of the decade, maybe bigger than that. But why did he feel this need to hang in there, to learn every scrap of the truth? Why was he obsessed? His behavior was a puzzle to him.

He wasn't the only one obsessed.

Though the story of Moonlight Cove had been leaked to the media in piecemeal fashion over three days and had been explored in detail during a four-hour press conference on Thursday evening, and though reporters had exhaustively interviewed many of the two hundred survivors, no one had had enough. The singular horror of the deaths of the victims—and the number, nearly three thousand, many times the number at Jonestown—stunned newspaper and TV audiences no matter how often they heard the specifics. By Friday morning the story was hotter than ever.

Yet Joel sensed that it wasn't even the grisliness of the facts or the spectacular statistics that gripped the public interest. It was something deeper than that.

At ten o'clock Friday morning, Joel was sitting on his bedroll in a field alongside the county route, just ten yards away from the police checkpoint north of Holliwell, basking in a surprisingly warm October morning and thinking about that very thing. He was starting to believe that maybe this news hit home hard because it was about not just the relatively modern conflict of man and machine but about the eternal human conflict, since time immemorial, between responsibility and irresponsibility, between civilization and savagery, between contradictory human impulses toward faith and nihilism.

Joel was still thinking about that when he got up and started to walk. Somewhere along the way he stopped thinking about much of anything, but he started walking more briskly.

He was not alone. Others at the roadblock, fully half the two hundred who had been waiting there, turned almost as one and walked east into the fields with sudden deliberation, neither hesitating along the way nor wandering in parabolic paths, but cutting straight up across a sloped meadow, over scrub-covered hills, and through a stand of trees.

The walkers startled those who had not felt the abrupt call to go for a stroll, and some reporters tagged along for a while, asking questions, then shouting questions. None of the walkers answered.

Joel was possessed by a feeling that there was a place he must go to, a special place, where he would never again have to worry about anything, a place where all would be provided, where he would have no need to worry about the future. He didn't know what that magic place looked like, but he knew he'd recognize it when he saw it. He hurried forward excitedly, compelled, *drawn*.

•

Need.

The protean thing in the basement of the Icarus Colony was in the grip of need. It had not died when the other children of Moonhawk had perished, for the microsphere computer within it had dissolved when it had first sought the freedom of utter shapelessness; it had not been able to receive the microwave-transmitted death order from Sun. Even if the command had been received, it would not have been acted upon, for the cellar-dwelling creature had no heart to stop.

Need.

Its need was so intense that it pulsed and writhed. This need was more profound than mere desire, more terrible than any pain.

Need.

Mouths had opened all over its surface. The thing called out to the world around it in a voice that seemed silent but was not, a voice that spoke not to the ears of its prey but to their minds.

And they were coming.

Its needs would soon be fulfilled.

•

Colonel Lewis Tarker, commanding officer at the Army field headquarters in the park at the eastern end of Ocean Avenue, received an urgent call from Sergeant Sperlmont, who was in charge of the county-route roadblock. Sperlmont reported losing six of his twelve men when they just walked off like zombies, with maybe a hundred reporters who were in the same strange condition.

"Something's up," he told Tarker. "This isn't over yet, sir."

•

Tarker immediately got hold of Oren Westrom, the Bureau man who was heading the investigation into Moonhawk and with whom all of the military aspects of the operation had to be coordinated.

"It isn't over," Tarker told Westrom. "I think those walkers are even weirder than Sperlmont described them, weird in some way he can't quite convey. I know him, and he's more spooked than he thinks he is."

•

Westrom, in turn, ordered the Bureau's JetRanger into the air. He explained the situation to the pilot, Jim Lobbow, and said, "Sperlmont's going to have some of his men track them on the ground, see where the hell they're going—and why. But in case that gets difficult, I want you spotting from the air."

"On my way," Lobbow said.

"You filled up on fuel recently?"

"Tanks are brimming."

"Good."

•

Nothing worked for Jim Lobbow but flying a chopper.

He had been married three times, and every marriage had ended in divorce. He'd lived with more women than he could count; even without the pressure of marriage weighing him down, he could not sustain a relationship. He had one child, a son, by his second marriage, but he saw the boy no more than three times a year, never for longer than a day at a time. Though he'd been brought up in the Catholic Church, and though all his brothers and sisters were regulars at Mass, that did not work for Jim. Sunday always seemed to be the only morning he could sleep in, and when he considered going to a weekday service it seemed like too much trouble. Though he dreamed of being an entrepreneur, every small business he started seemed doomed to failure; he was repeatedly startled to find how much work went into a business, even one that seemed designed for absentee management, and sooner or later it always became too much trouble.

But nobody was a better chopper pilot than Jim Lobbow. He could take one up in weather that grounded everyone else, and he could set down or pick up in any terrain, any conditions.

He took the JetRanger up at Westrom's orders and swung out over the county-route roadblock, getting there in no time because the day was blue and clear, and the roadblock was just a mile and a quarter from the park where he kept the chopper. On the ground, a handful of regular Army troops, still at the barricade, were waving him due east, up into the hills.

Lobbow went where they told him, and in less than a minute he found the walkers toiling busily up scrub-covered hills, scuffing their shoes, tearing their clothes, but scrambling forward in a frenzy. It was definitely weird.

A funny buzzing filled his head. He thought something was wrong with his radio headphones, and he pulled them off for a moment, but that wasn't it. The buzzing didn't stop. Actually it wasn't a buzzing at all, not a sound, but a *feeling*.

And what do I mean by that? he wondered.

He tried to shrug it off.

The walkers were circling east-southeast as they went, and he flew ahead of them, looking for some landmark, anything unusual toward which they might be headed. He came almost at once to the decaying Victorian house, the tumbledown barn, and the collapsed outbuildings.

Something about the place drew him.

He circled it once, twice.

Though it was a complete dump, he suddenly had the crazy idea that he would be happy there, free, with no worries any more, no ex-wives nagging at him, no child-support to pay.

Over the hills to the northwest, the walkers were coming, all hundred or more of them, not walking any more but running. They stumbled and fell but got up and ran again.

And Jim knew why they were coming. He circled over the house again, and it was the most appealing place he had ever seen, a source of surcease. He wanted that freedom, that release, more than he had ever wanted anything in his life. He took the JetRanger up in a steep climb, leveled out, swooped south, then west, then north, then east, coming all the way around again, back toward the house, the wonderful house, he had to be there, had to go there, had to go, and he took the chopper straight in through the front porch, directly at the door that hung open and half off its hinges, through the wall, plowing straight into the heart of the house, burying the chopper in the heart—

•

Need.

The creature's many mouths sang of its need, and it knew that momentarily its needs would be met. It throbbed with excitement.

Then vibrations. Hard vibrations. Then heat.

It did not recoil from the heat, for it had surrendered all the nerves and complex biological structures required to register pain.

The heat had no meaning for the beast-except that heat was not food and therefore did not fulfill its needs.

Burning, dwindling, it tried to sing the song that would draw what it required, but the roaring flames filled its mouths and soon silenced it.

•

Joel Ganowicz found himself standing two hundred feet from a ramshackle house that had exploded in flames. It was a tremendous blaze, fire shooting a hundred feet into the clear sky, black smoke beginning to billow up, the old walls of the place collapsing in upon themselves with alacrity, as if eager to give up the pretense of usefulness. The heat washed over him, forcing him to squint and back away, even though he was not particularly close to it. He couldn't understand how a little dry wood could burn that intensely.

He realized that he could not remember how the fire had started. He was just suddenly *there*, in front of it.

He looked at his hands. They were abraded and filthy.

The right knee was torn out of his corduroys, and his Rockports were badly scuffed.

He looked around and was startled to see scores of people in his same condition, tattered and dirty and dazed. He couldn't remember how he had gotten there, and he definitely didn't recall setting out on a group hike.

The house sure was burning, though. Wouldn't be a stick of it left, just a cellarful of ashes and hot coals.

He frowned and rubbed his forehead.

Something had happened to him. Something . . . He was a reporter, and his curiosity was gradually reasserting itself. Something had happened, and he ought to find out what. Something disturbing. *Very* disturbing. But at least it was over now.

He shivered.

chapter forty-one

When they entered the house in Sherman Oaks, the music on Scott's stereo, upstairs, was turned so loud that the windows were vibrating.

Sam climbed the steps to the second floor, motioning for Tessa and Chrissie to follow. They were reluctant, probably embarrassed, feeling out of place, but he was not certain he could do what had to be done if he went up there alone.

The door to Scott's room was open.

The boy was lying on his bed, wearing black jeans and a black denim shirt. His feet were toward the headboard, his head at the foot of the mattress, propped up on pillows, so he could stare at all of the posters on the wall behind the bed: black-metal rockers wearing leather and chains, some of them with bloody hands, some with bloody lips as if they were vampires who had just fed, others holding skulls, one of them french-kissing a skull, another holding out cupped hands filled with glistening maggots.

Scott didn't hear Sam enter. With the music at that volume, he wouldn't have heard a thermonuclear blast in the adjacent bathroom.

At the stereo Sam hesitated, wondering if he was doing the right thing. Then he listened to the bellowed words of the number on the machine, backed up by iron slabs of guitar chords. It was a song about killing your parents, about drinking their blood, then "taking the gas-pipe escape." Nice. Oh, very nice stuff. That decided him. He punched a button and cut off the CD in midplay.

Startled, Scott sat straight up in bed. "Hey!"

Sam took the CD out of the player, dropped it on the floor, and ground it under his heel.

"Hey, Christ, what the hell are you doing?"

Forty or fifty CDs, mostly black-metal albums, were stored in open-front cases on a shelf above the stereo. Sam swept them to the floor.

"Hey, come on," Scott said, "what're you, nuts?"

"Something I should've done long ago."

Noticing Tessa and Chrissie, who stood just outside the door, Scott said, "Who the hell are they?"

Sam said, "They the hell are friends."

Really working himself into a rage, all lathered up, the boy said, "What the fuck are they doing here, man?"

Sam laughed. He was feeling almost giddy. He wasn't sure why. Maybe because he was finally doing something about this situation, assuming responsibility for it. He said, "They the fuck are with me." And he laughed again.

He felt sorry that he had exposed Chrissie to this, but then he looked at her and saw that she was not only unshaken but giggling. He realized that all the angry and bad words in the world couldn't hurt her, not after what she had endured. In fact, after what they'd all seen in Moonlight Cove, Scott's teenage nihilism *was* funny and even sort of innocent, altogether ridiculous.

Sam stood on the bed and began to tear the posters off the wall, and Scott started screaming at him, opening up full volume, a real tantrum this time. Sam finished with those posters he could reach only from the bed, got down, and turned toward those on another wall.

Scott grabbed him.

Gently, Sam pushed the boy aside and clawed at the other posters.

Scott struck him.

Sam took the blow, then looked at him.

Scott's face was brilliant red, his nostrils dilated, his eyes bulging with hatred.

Smiling, Sam embraced him in a bear hug.

At first Scott clearly didn't understand what was happening. He thought his father was just making a grab for him, going to punish him, so he tried to pull away. But suddenly it dawned on him—Sam could *see* it dawn on him—he was being hugged, his old man was for God's sake embracing him, and in front of people—strangers. When that realization hit him, the boy *really* began to struggle, twisting and thrashing, pushing hard against Sam, desperate to escape, because this didn't fit into his belief in a loveless world, especially if he started to respond.

That was it, yes, damn, Sam understood now. That was the reason behind Scott's alienation. A fear that he'd respond to love, respond and be spurned . . . or find the responsibility of commitment too much to bear.

In fact, for a moment, the boy met his father's love with love of his own, hugged him tight. It was as if the real Scott, the kid hidden under the layers of hipness and cynicism, had peeked through and smiled.

Something good remained in him, good and pure, something that could be salvaged.

But then the boy began to curse Sam in more explicit and colorful terms than he had used previously. Sam only hugged him harder, closer, and now Sam began to tell him that he loved him, desperately loved him, told him not the way that he had told him he loved him on the telephone when he had called him from Moonlight Cove on Monday night, not with any degree of reservation occasioned by his own sense of hopelessness, because he *had* no sense of hopelessness any more. This time, when he told Scott that he loved him, he spoke in a voice cracking with emotion, told him again and again, demanded that his love be heard.

Scott was crying now, and Sam was not surprised to find that he was crying, too, but he didn't think they were crying for the same reason yet, because the boy was still struggling to get away, his energy depleted, but still struggling. So Sam held on to him and talked to him: "Listen, kid, you're going to care about me, one way or the other, sooner or later. Oh, yes. You're going to know that I care about you, and then you're going to care about me, and not just me, no, you're going to care about yourself, too, and it's not going to stop there, either, hell, no, you're going to find out you can care about a lot of people, that it feels good to care. You're going to care about that woman standing there in the doorway, and you're going to care about that little girl, you're going to care about her like you'd care about a sister, you're going to *learn*, you're going to get the damn machine out of you and learn to be loved and to love. There's a guy going to come visit us, a guy who's got one good hand and no good legs, and *he* believes life is worth living. Maybe he's going to stay a while, see how he likes it, see how he feels about it, 'cause maybe he can show you what I was too slow to show you—that it's good, life's good. And this guy's got a dog, what a dog, you're going to love that dog, probably the dog first." Sam laughed and held fast to Scott. "You can't say 'Get outta my face' to a dog and expect him to listen or care, he won't get out of your face, so you'll have to love him first. But then you'll get around to loving me, because that's what I'm going to be—a dog, just a smiling old dog, padding around the place, hanging on, impervious to insult, an old dog."

Scott had stopped struggling. He was probably just exhausted. Sam was sure that he had not really gotten through the boy's rage. Hadn't more than scratched the surface. Sam had let an evil into their lives, the evil of self-indulgent despair, which he transmitted to the boy, and now rooting it out would be a hard job. They had a long way to go, months of struggle, maybe even years, lots of hugging, lots of holding on tight and not letting go.

Looking over Scott's shoulder, he saw that Tessa and Chrissie had stepped into the room. They were crying too. In their eyes he saw an awareness that matched his, a recognition that the battle for Scott had only begun.

But it *had* begun. That was the wonderful thing. It *had* begun.

AFTERWORD
BY DEAN KOONTZ

After *Midnight* became the first of my novels to reach number one on the national bestseller lists, a critic in a prominent publication wrote that I was an overnight success and had been sold with "a massive and slick ad campaign" to a gullible public whose "lips move as they read his tedious novels about vampires in modern dress." *Midnight* isn't a vampire novel. Vampires do not appear in *any* of my novels. I have never written about a vampire in either modern or antique dress, nor in pajamas, for that matter. The vague and yet error-riddled details in the review made it clear that this man had not even skim-read the book. I killed him.

Finding his home address proved easy. He had once written glowingly about the town in which he lived. His number was listed in the phone book. With the number came a street address. When he answered the door, I said, "You don't know what 'tedious' is until you spend eternity in Hell re-reading the reviews you've written," and I shot him twenty times with a pair of ten-round 9-mm pistols.

In another version of this fantasy, I showed up at his door with a trained crocodile named Chloe. After savaging him at her leisure, Chloe ate him alive. Then she and I watched television together, capered in the dead critic's swimming pool, drank his vintage Scotch, and waited until she had passed his remains, whereupon I gathered him in a series of blue-plastic doo-doo bags, conveyed the bags to ground zero at the Nevada Nuclear Test Site, and from a safe distance of forty miles, I watched his remaining physical mass be vaporized into a gigantic radioactive fart.

In yet *another* version of this fantasy . . . Well, if I were to share with you every version, this volume would require an additional three hundred pages.

Midnight was not a vampire novel, and I was not an overnight success riding the crest of a tsunami of advertising money. Prior to *Midnight*'s ascent to the number-one spot on the list, I had been writing full-time for twenty years. I had never done a national book tour (still haven't), had never appeared on TV or been interviewed on radio to promote my work, and had been the subject of only one national magazine article (a nice piece in *People* related to the publication of *Watchers*, two years earlier). Consumer advertising for each of my hardcovers consisted of a full-page ad in the *New York Times Book Review* and three much smaller ads in the daily edition of the *Times*, which equalled approximately one-fifteenth of the average ad budget for other number-one bestselling authors.

I owed my success not to a generously funded marketing blitz, not to the machinations of a wily publicity maven, not to the fact that I had sold my soul to Satan (which I had not, in part because Satan wanted not just my soul but also my favorite Hawaiian shirt), but to a loyal readership that grew slowly book by book until it reached critical mass. In the years since *Midnight* made the list, I've several times seen it reported in print that I built a writing career "the old-fashioned way, through hard work and word of mouth." I don't think of this as the Old-Fashioned Way so much as the Frustrating Way or the Stupid Way, but for me it was the only way.

Eight years before *Midnight* was published, twelve years after I became a full-time writer, I had achieved paperback-bestseller status with *Whispers*. Although having a paperback bestseller is gratifying, the prestige and the greatest financial rewards are associated with best-selling *hardcovers*. I assumed that my success on the paperback charts would be a platform from which I could launch an assault on the more desirable hardcover list.

With curious vigor, my hardcover publisher and my literary agent (at that time) hastened to assure me that I was a "born paperback writer" with a fine future in a softcover format but that my books were not the kind of thing to succeed on hardcover lists, in part (this mystified me) because they were "too complex in structure, too demanding in their themes, and far too quirky." This made me sound like an avant garde, stuffy, intellectual shoe fetishist. As I've detailed in previous afterwords in this series, I nevertheless set out to gain hardcover success, and after being frequently chastised for my temerity and after being advised 1,236 times that I was investing too much hope in dreams that could never come true, I saw *Strangers* become a hardcover bestseller, then *Watchers* and *Lightning*, each a bigger success than the one before it. Then came *Midnight*.

When my publisher phoned to share the news that *Midnight* would be number one on the list, her excitement was not accompanied by a sanguine expectation of future triumphs. Immediately after sharing the good news, before I had time to work up a whoop of delight, she said,

"Enjoy, celebrate, but I don't want you to think that this will ever happen again. This is a fluke. You don't write novels that can regularly be number one." This assessment of the future prospects of my complex-demanding-quirky-shoe-fetishist fiction took some of the shine off the apple; however, I had not yet invented Chloe the crocodile and therefore could not indulge in fantasies of my publisher suffering a fate similar to that of Captain Hook.

I called my agent to report this conversation. She bemoaned the publisher's untimely candor and lack of finesse—but then agreed that this was likely to be the only book of mine ever to rise to the top of the charts. In addition to the aforementioned curses of complexity and quirkiness, I now heard that my imagination was "too ripe" for the larger mainstream reading public. Apparently the mainstream reading public prefers writers to have imaginations as hard and green as early-growth apples. Personally, I had always thought of my imagination not in terms of apples or *any* fruit, but as a chile: more flavorful than a poblano, hotter than a jalapeño, but not as hot as a Scotch bonnet pepper. My wife had always thought of my imagination strictly in terms of salty snack foods: the crispness of a potato chip, the twistiness of a Cheese Doodle.

My agent said, "Honey, just be grateful you'll get rich from all this before it's over." I said that I had already made more money from writing than I'd ever dreamed of earning, and tried to explain that I wanted a larger audience because communication mattered to me, because I wanted to touch hearts in the way that mine had been touched—and changed—by novelists when I was a lonely child growing up in the threatening shadow of a violent alcoholic father. She said, "That's very sweet," but there was an unmistakable note of impatience in her voice.

Critics all but unanimously liked *Midnight*, as the review excerpts in the front of this paperback should confirm, but as I worked on the novel that would follow it, I sniffed the computer screen for the noxious scent of a too-ripe imagination. As I write this afterword, *Midnight* has sold more than seven million copies in thirty-two languages, and to the best of my knowledge, not one reader has perished from the hideous effects of consuming the product of an overripe imagination, though a strange young man in Waterloo, Iowa, *was* hospitalized with severe paper cuts to the tongue when he became inexplicably involved erotically with the book.

In addition to several number-one paperbacks, the aforementioned publisher and I enjoyed four additional number-one hardcovers, after *Midnight*, and each time that she brought me the advance news she seasoned it with the admonition that this, too, was a fluke, and that I must not expect to repeat this achievement ever again. Each time, my agent concurred: fluke.

A friend suggested to me that I was like the woman whose first job in a company is as a secretary but who rises to be president: All those in the company who knew her as a secretary will never entirely respect her when she takes the top job. Perhaps these key people in my professional life were unable to forget my origins in the slums of paperback originals. Eventually, although I had considerable respect for my publisher and for her myriad successes, I moved on to a new publishing house. I also changed agents.

In the ten years since then (as I write this), I have seen eleven of my hardcovers rise into the top numbers of the bestseller lists, and five of those have made number one. In that same time, twenty of my paperback editions have appeared on the list, several at number one. I took some satisfaction in proving that it was not a fluke, after all.

Nevertheless, I've often wished that I could have slipped a magic potion into my publisher's lunch, one that would have stolen from her only the memory that I had begun as a secretary, so then no parting of the ways would have been necessary. There is something ineffably sad about having such success with someone you respect and then inevitably coming to a parting point, for the parting forever abrades some of the glimmer from even the brightest of memories.

I am fortunate that the folks at Berkley Books, past and present, have always been ardent supporters of my work and have never thought of me as having arisen from questionable origins, since they, too, spring from the wonderful world of paperback books. It was their idea to repackage these novels with handsome new covers and to let me spout off however I wished in afterwords like this one. Over the years, I have had every reason to be grateful for the enthusiasm of Rena Wolner, Roger Cooper, David Shanks, Mel Parker, Susan Allison, Susan Peterson, and Leslie Gelbman. In return, I have been determined never to embarrass them by behaving like a writer in their company.

I have been fortunate to write, for the most part, the books that I wanted to write, without regard for the market, and doubly fortunate that the market has always proved to be there for whatever kind of novel I've written. From the start, Berkley Books pushed my work with confidence, and everyone in their offices will be forever safe from Chloe, my crocodile. Chloe will not go hungry, however, for I will always be able to point her toward enough film-studio executives, film producers, and film directors to satisfy her appetite.

Ready to find
your next great read?

Let us help.

Visit prh.com/nextread